this is how it starts

REGIONRAT

A SIX GALLERY PRESS ORIGINAL
FIRST EDITION 2003
SECOND EDITION 2006

Copyright © 2006, 2003 Richard Laskowski

Library of Congress Cataloging-in-Publication Data
Laskowski, Richard A.

REGIONRAT, a novel / Richard Laskowski
p.   cm.- (Six Gallery Press)
ISBN 0-9726301-7-1

Manufactured in the United States of America.

WELCOME TO

REGIONRAT

Notes On The Text

About Exclamation Points: I hate them. Exclamation points seem wacky to me. I'm not wacky. Sometimes I'm not even sure when to use them or not. If I had it my way I'd remove all Exclamation Points from this text, but considering I have to turn in this revised edition in just a few days I've left all of them in place, because it would take way too long to get rid of them all.

About the consumerist use of the word *Because*: I have a love/hate relationship with *Because*. *Because* always makes my sentences look stupid, or like I don't know what I'm talking about. I'm about to give you a heavy dose of *Because*. While reading this story you'll notice I write the word *Because* way too much.

About *Italics*: I hate *Italics*. *Italics* seems silly to me. As with Exclamation Points, sometimes I'm not even sure when to use *Italics*. I've used *Italics*, dozens of times, for no apparent reason whatsoever.

About any markings from the Dash (—) family: I'm quite liberal with dashes—not sure what they do, but they look cool. I like to use the long ones to break up my sentence fragments for when I get high and can't complete a thought. And I'll use the small ones to separate compound words, *Because* compound words are unclean. They look like a pair of toddlers joined at the head. Nobody wants to see that kinda shit. Dashes are great for this kinda stuff. They look sharp. Sometimes I'll even toss a dash in there for when I don't feel like using a period. Dashes pretty much poke holes everywhere.

Sentence Structure: Sometimes it's there and sometimes it's not. I'm not a real writer.

"She lies and says she still loves him, can't find a betterman."

-Pearl Jam

this right here is

based on a true story

Dedicated to the REAL James Chapman

I used to sit on the shores of West Beach, making sure to keep far away from the rotting mixed-fishes, so I could chill-out and watch the sun set behind the everlasting city of Chicago. The northwest Indiana sun, a brutal and smoldering thing you can't even look at during the day, has burned my back so many times I got spots on my shoulders.

In the early evening the sun switches faces quicker than a single mother with a bipolar disorder. Just when you think you can't handle anymore if its abuse, it falls back into this warm, soft light. All of the sudden it's this harmless orange ring of pollution. And the Lake Michigan, so big if you didn't know what you were looking at you would think it was an ocean.

Behind where I sat was the most magnificent sight of them all: "The Steel Mills" is what we call it, but there's more to it. It happens to be the largest industrial complex in North America. Gary Works has fifty-seven production units on a four-thousand acre site. The facility engulfs six miles of Lake Michigan shoreline. You'll see the smokestacks jutting from the beaches they're built on, some with flames shooting from the peaks, others are already dead. There are factories of all kinds, each expelling their own earthtone smokes.

In the middle of this industrial world is the most famous of them all, the Eighty–Four Hotstrip. It's the mile long path a steel slab travels as it's burned, melted, flattened, shaped and then wound into those huge steel coils you'll see on the backs of semi-trucks when driving through The Region. This is our finished product.

When I'd stay too long it would get dark outside. The campfires start burning in the distance all along the beach. The older people who were there at sunset seem to be systematically replaced by young people ready to party.

I would stay longer to listen to the waves crashing on the beach, which strand drifting international trash onto the wet sand as they arrive, then they pull away.

Sooner or later the Gary cops will come out on four-wheelers to arrest people. They patrol the beach with wide beams of light as they scream into megaphones commanding the young people to return home now or face charges. It doesn't always end peacefully like that though. Sometimes the cops end up chasing people down in the sand, roughing them up, and then hauling their asses to the can. Where I grew up, hardly anything comes without confrontation.

The authorities have good reason to show signs of stress and to use force though, because the town behind the "Steel Mills" is the greatest evil of all. The once proud city of Gary, now a Gangsta Disciple shithole, it bubbles with crime and mayhem on just about every street corner. It's become a never ending flow of embarrassments to the good folks in northwest Indiana and most people have given up expecting Gary to get better and have accepted the city's dangerous dysfunctions. Nobody messes with Gary, Indiana. Gary is like a big ignorant bully, a drunken psychotic, belt–wielding stepfather of a city. And he hasn't shaved in weeks.

There's a name for this place. It's a name we say when talking about northern parts of both Lake and Porter County. They call this place "The Region" and all of its people are known as Regionrats, because we feed on just about anything to survive, and we are hard to kill.

1

It was the middle of winter outside and in northwest Indiana it was hovering in subzero temperatures. I was listening to some Nirvana on my stereo when Gabe called me that night.

"Wassup," he screamed with excitement.

"Hey, buddy," I greeted as I held the telephone at arms length. "You're yelling at me!"

"Oh, sorry," he said, quietly this time, and I placed the phone back on my shoulder and wedged it against my ear. "So you still want me to cruise by in the morning to get you?"

"Yeah. Actually I do, if it's *still* cool with you."

Two days before I had just gotten off of an airplane that flew in from Seattle where I'd attempted to runaway to. I couldn't quite make it financially, so I had to come back to home sweet home like Montley Crue. It was humiliating and sad, but something I could learn to deal with. The next morning I had to go back to the old school, Granite High School, and I was doing my best to look at the positive side of things. At least in regards to Seattle I lasted a little over six months, which is about five months longer than anybody thought I would.

"Killer, Ray. Look I'll see you in the morning. I'm supposed to call this babe back before nine."

"Sure, sure, whatever," I said sarcastically. "Later," and I hung up.

I only lived a block from school, but I wanted the lift because his car had heat and I knew we could smoke a bowl before classes started. It was too cold to walk and sobriety was something that just didn't mix well with life in The Region. We usually used cars to get high in so our parents wouldn't be onto us. We'd drive around the neighborhood streets and hit the pipe whenever there were no cars or pedestrians around.

For the most part, Granite High School and I parted on bad terms. Ever since I grew my hair long and pierced my ears there had been some minor frictions between the hillbillies and I, but that morning I was actually excited a little, because after spending six starving months in rainy Seattle I was honestly a little homesick.

The next morning it was snowing and flakes were floating down and blowing in the frosty gusts. I put on my coolest blue jeans. They were bell-bottoms from The Gap, new Timberline boots, and my favorite black DKNY sweater with the V–neck. I wanted to look good, but not so good that everybody would know I had dressed up on purpose. You can only dress up on purpose at a private school like Andrean. Andrean was the Catholic school I had gotten expelled from for some type of book stealing scam. That's something I don't like to talk about. At the public schools it was way more important to look tough than to look good. Besides, I had developed an image of not caring about school or my appearance there so I didn't wanna seem too much like a hypocrite. I had a very delicate reputation to uphold.

As I was waiting for Gabe I sat on the couch and watched the news and drank day-old Folgers. Gabe never needed to honk when he picked me up because he had no muffler on his car and I could hear the wheezing and coughing of his car's exhaust system within three blocks of my dad's apartment.

The news guy was plastic and he was talking about the NCAA Men's Basketball Tournament, The Road to the Final Four. They were showing Purdue highlights. I got to see some clips of Gerardo Thomas jamming on fool's grills. The Associated Press had named Gerardo the Player of the Year. Gerardo was from Gary and I got a chance to see him play in high school when I went to Andrean. He really was a killer on the court. He used to dunk on our whole team and then he'd give our fans the middle finger as he ran back down the court. With such charm, who wouldn't have guessed he'd turn out to be the national role model he is today? Now he's playing for the Milwaukee Bucks and shooting bogus commercials for the United Way.

I kept a keen ear so that I could hear the muffler coming down the street. I hadn't smoked any weed in three days and I was really starting to jones. I had some pot in the apartment, but I was trying to keep myself from smoking too much. Every now and then I'd give my system a brief vacation from the toxins, but three days was about all that I could stand without it. By then I would start talking too much and taking too many showers.

I heard a horn honking in the parking lot and I looked out the window anyway even though it wasn't Gabe's car. There was gray Chevy Celebrity with some typical teenager stickers in the back window, a psychedelic mushroom and a string of dancing Grateful Dead teddy bears. A slender girl with curly blonde hair got outta the car. She had on a nice stereotypical schoolgirl flannel skirt, light blue stockings or panty hose or whatever the hell they call them, and a black leather jacket. She had gray mittens on her hands, a matching gray scarf, and she was smoking a cigarette. It hung from her lips like she was Andrew Dice Clay's little sister. The smoke didn't hide what she really was, though: she was a Prep all the way. I figured she was picking up the girl who lived in the building across from mine. This other girl, my neighbor, was a Prep also, and since they travel in packs and laugh at each other's corny jokes like they do at those pyramid marketing meetings I almost ignored her and sat back in my chair. Everything was gray.

I was surprised when Gabe popped outta the passenger side of this Chevy Celebrity. He seemed catapulted by his own hyperactivity. He was not up to date in the fashion department, but lucky for him he lived in Granite where tight-rolled jeans and shaved heads with tails were in. He had on one of those brown bomber jackets with the furry collars—you know, the fake sheep's fur. Underneath a Hawaiian shirt sprang from his chest in an array of blunt colors, and his jeans were tight–rolled at the cuffs, standard issue. He looked up at me and both him and the girl motioned for me to come down, so I did. My ride had arrived.

I walked down the steps and up to the car and Gabe and I shook hands brother-style by locking fists like we were arm wrestling. I glanced at the girl. I thought she was really pretty. I didn't look her over enough to really be sure. It very well could have been a distance call, but at first glance she was beautiful. Lots of girls tend to be nice looking at first sight, and then when you keep looking at them they seem to deteriorate right before your eyes as if they are an ice sculpture set out for a wedding on July 4th. Gabe told me that her name was Erin, and I shook hands with her and Gabe told her my name was Ray.

"Thanks for the introduction," she smiled and said. "Hi,

Raymond. It's nice to meet you."

"Yeah, you too," I said. "May I add that you make me wanna put on my tap dancing shoes?"

Gabe starting laughing because he knew what I was talking about.

"Don't call me Raymond though, Ray is fine," I said loosening my grip, but she held on for a few more seconds, making the whole introduction really awkward.

She squinted at me and just had to ask, "*Tap dancing shoes*, I don't get it."

Gabe chimed in with the punchline, "You know," he laughed. "So he can tap, tap, tap dat ass!"

"That's totally foul, dude," she hissed.

"Hey, be cool," I begged. "I was just kidding."

"No it's fine," Erin insisted. "I'm cool with the comment I mean, I *do* have a sense of humor."

We piled into the car. I got in the back seat and I cupped my hands together and blew into my palms trying to warm them up.

"Man," I said. "I ain't used to this cold weather anymore. I'm freezing to death."

Erin started the car and put her cigarette out in the ashtray. There was a red lipstick stain on the snuffed filter. She pulled the Chevy outta the parking spot and Gabe immediately got out his bag of weed and started packing a bowl. It put a smile on my face like when you meet an old friend at the airport.

Where've you been all this time, you think to yourself.

Gabe turned to me and said, "Here's the deal, Ray. We're picking up some chick, yo. She don't smoke so we gotta cash it before she gets in the car." He passed me the pipe. "Here, bro, you can hit it first."

"Sounds good to me," I said and I struck a flame on my lighter and I politely lit the corner of the firmly packed bowl.

"Raymond, are you from Seattle," Erin asked me.

"No," I said, "I just went there to get away for a while. You know, I knew a kid out there and shit."

"Where are you from then, here?"

"Um," I hit the pipe again, and this time I held in the smoke longer and let it out in a pleasant cloud. "I'm from here in The Region unfortunately. East Chicago, Ogden Dunes and Valpo, to be specific. I've lived all over it."

"Dude, I know how that goes," she smiled.

After a few minutes of sparse conversation the bowl was cashed and we were all stoned. We pulled up in front of a small one level blue house and Erin honked the horn three times. I was way too baked and was drifting off into my own little world.

That's when I snapped out of my trance.

"I'm telling you the truth," Gabe said to Erin. "My uncle was the freakin sheriff of Lake County. He tells me everything that happens over there."

I was so blunted I missed the entire beginning of whatever it was that they were talking about.

"You're such a liar, Gabe," she laughed.

"Believe whatever you want to. I don't give a shit. In fact, I could care *less*."

I looked up at the house and the front door opened.

"Ok," Erin said. "Raymond, she doesn't smoke so don't say anything about weed. Gabe, hurry up and roll down your window so it doesn't smell too bad in here."

"Yeah like that's gonna freakin help. Cracking the window? Just tell her already. She won't care."

"Gabe, she *will* care," Erin insisted.

This good-looking girl stepped outside from the house.

So this is she, I thought in correct English, *the girl who will care*.

She wore black leather boots, black jeans, a white turtleneck sweater that looked like a shaggy carpet, and a big white and fluffy goose feather winter jacket. I got the chance to look her over from the car. She was thin, but I couldn't check out what her body was like because of all the winter garments. She had a sucked in, attractive looking face with sharp features, long brown hair, and she was wearing earmuffs, which I thought was kinda strange since I didn't know anyone who would be caught dead wearing earmuffs.

The girl walked in the front of the car and waved at Gabe and Erin. She smiled really widely and I thought she looked cute and I was thinking, *hell yeah*. She got into the back and sat next to me, but only because it was the only place that she could plant her ass down.

"Oh *yeah*," the girl said. "like it doesn't smell like *pot* in here or anything."

I laughed and said, "I'm not supposed to say anything about it."

"Oh *really*," the girl squinted at me.

"Yeah, and Gabe here has the window cracked so there's a good chance you wouldn't smell anything even if we had," I joked.

Gabe and Erin started cracking up.

"Milada," Gabe shouted. "Don't trip! Seriously, you wanna know what we're smoking?

"What?"

"Jack-shit, that's what! We weren't smoking anything. I think you're just paranoid."

Erin put the car into gear and drove off toward school.

"Milada," Erin said to the girl next to me. "This is my friend Raymond."

"Ray," I corrected Erin. "It's a pleasure," I said and shook Milada's hand.

It was my right hand and her left hand, which made it seem like we were holding hands, like, a couple. It made both of us feel a little strange.

"Same here," she smiled coldly and it made me think she might possibly hate me, and then she rolled her eyes and looked away and I became positive. She did hate me. She let go of my hand and pulled a strand of hair and flipped it over her shoulder.

"So are you really stoned?"

"No, not me," I said. "Besides, even if I were I wouldn't tell you."

"Milada, please leave Raymond alone," Erin called back to her. "He's new and you're making him feel unwelcome."

"She's not making me feel unwelcome. *I'm* fine."

"*Dude*," Gabe said to Erin. "He ain't new. He's just been on vacation."

"Yeah," Milada butt in. "I've seen him before at school."

"When," Erin asked.

"Last year," I answered. "I think I've seen you too."

Milada rolled her eyes again like I annoyed her.

"Raymond, you went to Granite last year—"

"Wait a fucking second," I held up my hand to Erin. Then I turned to Milada. "Did you just roll your fucking eyes at me?"

"*What*," Milada was pissed. She started hissing at me, "*What* did you just say to me!"

"You heard me, tons-a-fun," I said and I looked away.

"*Whoa*, dudes," Erin cut in. "Let's all be grown-ups for a minute here, ok? Raymond, I asked you did you go to Granite last year?"

"Didn't we just *cover* that," Gabe asked her.

"Yes," I called up to her. "But it was huge mistake on my part."

"What do you mean by that," Gabe asked.

"I mean I didn't know what it was really like before I enrolled."

"Yeah, like you're *so cool*," Milada said to me sarcastically. "What a joke."

"Only by comparison, churchy."

I smiled at her like an asshole.

"*Milada*," Erin shouted back.

"*Jesus Christ*," I sighed. "What is this, a fucking Jerry Springer episode?"

"I'm a Christian," Milada scolded me. "And I'm not embarassed to be one. I'm getting fed up with your language and swearing and crap. Please don't swear around me ever again!"

"Well, *shit*. I'm sorry," I pleaded.

"There you go again," Gabe corrected me.

"*Fuck*," I blurted in mocking anguish.

"That's *very* intelligent," Milada mocked me.

"Dudes! Please chill in my car," Erin shouted. "This is supposed to be a peaceful vehicle. Respect the Grateful Dead stickers."

The rest of the way to school the car was filled with tension. Gabe was the only one who was saying anything and nobody was listening to him anyway. He was hyperactive and he couldn't sit still so he was always talking and playing with things, fidgeting I guess you could say.

My thesis was I thought Erin was cool and Milada was a stuck up little bitch. I didn't know what the hell her problem was. I hardly said two words to her and she's already attacking me.

I had Art Appreciation during first period and I got to sleep most of the way through. I had General Math second period and there were no smart kids in the class (that's why it was call General Math). Mr. Maybin taught the class and he let us screw around for most of the period. My friend Jacob Drake was in the class with me, and so was his girlfriend Gisela. They were always fighting in class and Jacob would always get pissed and started calling her all these vulgar, yet poetic, names. It was funny to me.

That morning Mr. Maybin sent him out into the hall to cool off. I wanted to go cool off with Jacob also, but I couldn't. Instead I just got out my notebook and started writing a short story. It was about a concentration camp for senior citizens—it was either a short story or an original business plan.

On the way to third period I saw Milada kissing her boyfriend in the hallway. He looked sorta cool, but again only by comparison. He was dressed like a skateboarder and he even had a board that was leaning up against his locker, but in Indiana, just because you look like something, and you smell like something, doesn't mean you are one. He had a buddy with him who was wearing black jeans and a ratty plain white T-shirt. He had long blonde hair and he nodded at me like he knew me. I nodded back.

Around the corner I saw Erin and I said, "Hello," and I tried to play it cool and walk by, but she stopped me.

"So how's it going," she asked me and handed me a folded up piece of paper with my name on it. She looked around as if she didn't want anyone to see her handing it to me.

"What's this," I asked her.

"It's a letter."

"From who?"

"From me, stupid. Now don't let anyone see it, ok? I gotta go."

She left me standing there with this letter (or note, as the girls called it) in my hand. I couldn't wait to see what it said so I hustled to third period, which was Journalism class. It was my second year in a row taking the class due to my consistant failure. I was five minutes early so I sat down in the back and unfolded the letter.

Raymond,

I wanted to apologize to you for the way that Milada was acting in the car this morning. She and I have been fighting about something for weeks and I want you to know that her outburst this morning had nothing to do with you. Don't hate her and I hope that she didn't hurt your feelings. I thought that it was really funny the way that you were talking with her. I can tell that you are different, I mean in a smart way. It's not often that I meet a guy with brains at this school. Also, I wanted to know if you wanted to do something with me this weekend. I'm supposed to hang around with my friend Jolene and I figured that maybe me and her and you and Gabe could do something. Let me know a.s.a.p. I'm a person who likes to make plans. Call me tonight if you want, my number is 555–5682. Oh yeah, please don't tell anyone that you are going to hang around with me. I'm serious! It's really important and I'll explain when you call me, if you do. You better Raymond!

Secret Love,

Erin Watkins

Secret Love? I folded up the letter and stuck it into my shirt pocket. I just sat back and smiled and watched the other kids mingle and wander into class like the public education prisoners that we were. Love.

I was really starting to like this girl. I wished that I could run and talk to her right then. I wanted to be next to her all of the sudden. I wanted to talk to her for hours. I wanted to know everything about her. I wanted to know why I had to keep this a secret.

Did she have a boyfriend?

I doubted it. I couldn't wait until Friday.

Journalism class was taking forever. Mrs. Anderson made us watch a terrible movie called *The Absence of Malice.*

I took out my notebook when the lights were off and started writing Erin a letter, but then I stopped because it was cheesy to write back so soon and I didn't want her to know I liked her. Besides, she told me to call her so I decided that was what I was gonna do. I had to choose the right time to call. I wanted to do it right when I got home at 4:00, but that would be too soon and the last thing I wanted her to think was that I was anxious. And what if she wasn't home right after school and she never ended up getting the message? I didn't wanna call too late because she might be planning on going somewhere tonight. And I couldn't exactly call in the early evening because God forbid that she's, like, eating dinner with her family or something when I call. That would be horrible. Then I decided the best thing for me to do would be to have Gabe call for me. She did mention him in the letter and this way he could do all of the talking for me and if it turned out that she had a boyfriend or didn't like me, then it saved me some embarrassment, but I wasn't supposed to tell anyone so maybe Gabe calling was a bad idea. By the time class was over the negotiations I was having with myself remained at a standstill. It was lunchtime.

One of the only cool things about going to Granite had to do with lunchtime. It was the last campus in Indiana that still had an open lunch, which means we got to leave school grounds for a half-hour. For me and my friends, it was just another opportunity to get high. I never even saw the cafeteria at Granite the whole time I went there.

I met Gabe in the crowded hallway and he was standing next to Jacob Drake from my math class. Jacob was really huge and mean looking by the way. He might have been in his early twenties for all I know. Luckily he had gotten a chance to cool off in the hall earlier.

"Hey, bitches," I greeted them.

"What up, Ray," Jacob said.

"We're waiting for The Brain," Gabe said. "He's got a bigger car."

I knew who The Brain was, but I had never really talked to him before. His real name is Victor. Everybody sarcastically called him "The Brain" because he was a very reactionary person and was always saying the wrong thing at the wrong time. He was generally considered to be kinda dumb and his shitty manners were about as embarassing as they come. I had American History with him the year before

The Brain walked up behind Gabe and jabbed his middle finger and his pointer finger into his back like he had a gun and he said, "Spread'em Sally," and he laughed.

He had a shaved head and his hair was blonde with the standard issued tail hanging down from the back of his cranium, which was about as corny as you can get, white-trash to the maximum. He wore super old blue jeans, Wranglers fresh from Salvation Army, and a red San Francisco 49ers sweatshirt. He was also trying very hard to grow a goatee.

Gabe turned and said, "Jesus, Victor. When you said *spread'em* I thought we were talking about your mom for a second."

"Hey now," Jacob said. "Get off of moms, Gabe."

"Yeah. I know. You just got off of mine *right?*"

"How'd you know? That slut wasn't supposed to tell!"

"You fucking dirty bastards," I sneered.

Gabe introduced The Brain to me, "Ray, this is Victor, AKA The Brain. Victor, this is Ray. He's cool."

"What's up, hoss," he said to me.

"Nothing much, man."

"Didn't we have a class together last year?"

"Yeah," I confirmed. "American History."

"Cool watch," he looked down at my wrist..

"Oh," I said. "Thanks. It's an antique. Or at least it's really old. I found the watch in my grandfather's basement a few years ago and it's an old Timex that has a black leather band with little chains on it."

It was a tough looking watch. I still have it.

We all walked out to The Brain's car. It was an old black Mercury Cougar with some front-end damage. Gabe and I got in the back and Jacob got in the front. There was a crack in the dashboard with a rod of incense sticking out of it. The Brain took outta silver Zippo and lit it, sending the fragrant grayish smoke up in wavy streams. He turned on the engine and put in a Smashing Pumpkins tape, *Gish* in fact. We pulled into the lunchtime traffic jam and made our way up Elm Street. Gabe pulled outta joint from his shirt pocket.

"This is the only one I got," he warned us. He was lying. I saw his huge bag of weed with my own eyes that morning. Most pot smokers in Indiana are really into *equal contribution*, which can cause problems. Basically you have to give a little to get a little. People on drugs don't usually find themselves to be charitable very often, and this causes people to lie about how much they have, and so they're really big on matching each other.

Like, I might say to a friend, "I only have a bowl of weed left. Can you match me one?"

And he might say, "I don't have anything, but my buddy can match you."

This usually amounts to too many people and not enough pot to go around because this guy's friend might say he doesn't have any, but "his" friend does and before you know it, you've got two bowls of weed and six people huddling around it. Now you're a little pissed because you could've just gone and smoked your own bowl by yourself, all you wanted was a little company, but kids are so afraid to smoke by themselves because it's a sure sign you have a problem. I always used to smoke by myself because I was well aware of this phenomenon and I didn't believe smoking alone made you a junky. Besides, this way I was always able to conserve the pot I had, and it would allow me to share the wealth at all the *right* times. When I went to parties I would always pass around joints and I could usually feed about ten pot fiends at any time. It made me feel really cool to be able to do that.

"Victor, can you match me?"

"Ain't got none, Gabe," he said. "Sorry. I'll get you next time though."

"What about you, Ray?"

"No dice, jack."

I had an ounce stashed under my bed at home.

"Well fuck," Gabe cursed. "None of us are gonna get high off of this!"

"Chill," Jacob said. "I know a dude where we can cop some good weed at. Take me to Black Oak. I'll tell you where to go when we get there."

We smoked Gabe's joint and each of us got about three hits, which wasn't enough to get you stoned on Mexican weed (it was next to impossible to land any kind skunk buds in The Region so all we had to smoke was this brown brick weed from Mexico or Texas or Texico). Our differences between good and bad buds were just a variation of the Mexi-weed. Whatever the quality was, when it came time to do some weigh-outs, seeds and stems were included, which is pretty much bogus. When you packed a bowl you had to make sure you cleaned it out from the stems and seeds. The seeds were especially nasty to smoke. They smelled like shit and tasted horrible. If you passed around a bowl of weed with a seed it would usually piss people off. It was considered offensive and rude, and you would have to be an idiot or white-trash like The Brain or twelve-years old to not care about smoking seeds.

Black Oak was the only white neighborhood left in the Gary city limits. There was a serious concentration of Hilljacks in Black Oak (a Hilljack is a cross between a Jackass and a hillbilly if you can imagine that). The Hilljacks who resided in Black Oak were also generally referred to as "Oakers," or moreover, KKK members.

"Yo," The Brain said to me. "I live in Black Oak."

As we drove into Black Oak I got a little nervous because it's a really bad neighborhood. There was garbage everywhere. No one ever cut the grass on their lawns and every other mobile home had some kinda racecar with a number hand painted on it as it sat up on blocks in the driveway. There were even packs of wild dogs that ran around looking for food.

Jacob had The Brain park the Mercury on the side of the street in front of an old abandoned church.

"This it," I asked looking at the old church.

"Fuck no," Jacob said. "This ain't it. It's a little ways down the street. I just don't want him to know I brang a bunch of guys with me looking like the DEA and shit. I'll be right back, but first things first, cough up the cash, dicks. How 'bout we all put in five and I'll grab a twenty-sack?"

We all gave him the money and he got outta the car and jogged up the street and then darted into a yard and disappeared behind some bushes and trees. Ten minutes later he came back to the car and got in. We only had enough time to smoke while we drove back to school.

"Jackpot," Jacob shouted and packed a bowl. "All this guy sells is these dime bags so I figured we can smoke one bowl now and then divide up what's left into fourths. That cool?"

Nobody was really concerned about that, we just wanted to get stoned. We all had weed in secret.

"Dudes," I suddenly proclaimed, shocked by the barbaric presentation of the weed. "Why's it look like that?"

"You won't believe this, Ray," Jacob told me as he quickly rolled a joint. "This old man, he puts all his shit in a blender, stems and seeds and all. And then he stuffs it in these little baggies."

"*Seeds*," The Brain complained. "That's fucking sick! Only niggers smoke seeds and stems. I ain't no nigger I'll tell you that right now."

"Hey, dog. You're an idiot, Victor. Every bowl you pack has a seed inside it. Why do you think nobody ever comes over to your house," Jacob asked. "You don't gotta smoke any if you don't wanna. There. How's that for a tight little joint?"

"*Nah*," The Brain explained. "I'll be ok. Just pass that fucker around. And nobody nigger-lip it!"

I was high as hell when we got back to school and we all had our own little piece of weed left over for later that afternoon. I was way too high to go back to class so I decided I'd just skip the rest of the day. The Brain parked the car and we all got out.

"So let's meet here after school," Gabe suggested. "For round two."

"Cool," Jacob said. "What about you two dick-suckers? You in or what?"

"I think I'm gonna skip," I said.

"Yeah, me too," The Brain said.

Him and I looked at each other and nodded affirmatively.

"Suit yourself. See ya, dudes. I'm fucking late," Jacob said and he trotted back to school.

"I'll call you two cats when I get home," Gabe said and he left also.

"So what are you gonna do," I asked The Brain.

"Not sure, hoss. What about you?"

"I got NHL 95 for Sega, you down?"

"Shit yeah. I'm the fucking champ, hoss! Where do you live?"

"Just right down the street," I said and we got into the Mercury and went to my dad's apartment.

Nobody was home when we got there, which is what I figured. We bundled up and chilled out on my balcony and smoked a few cigarettes first.

"So do you mind if I ask you about something," he asked awkwardly.

"Shoot."

"Erin Watkins," he simply stated.

"What about her?"

"She's trouble, that's what about her."

"*So.*"

"*So*, I saw that she gave you a ride today."

"Yeah, but I didn't ask her to, she was with Gabe."

"Did she tell you that she liked you?"

"No. *Why* the fuck would you ask that?"

"*Serious*," he asked me.

"Yeah, dead serious, *why?*"

"She likes the new guys."

"I'm not new, man. I went here last year too."

"You're new to her. Listen," he said. "You're a cool guy, Ray, so I'm gonna let you in on something before you get fucked over."

"What's that?"

"Erin goes out with Jeremy Otsap," he told me like it was the big answer. I didn't get it.

"Who's that?"

"I know what you're thinking man. So what, right? Well, this guy Jeremy is a cool dude and not only that, but he's also the toughest motherfucker in town. He beats the shit outta niggers all the time. He plays linebacker at Wisconsin."

"Yeah, what else?"

"Do you *need* a what else? She's a scammer for one thing. She's been going out with Jeremy for two years and just last month she played my friend Derrick like a fiddle. He was new to her too and he ended up getting his face kicked in. It was a mess, the worst ass kicking of the year. He never even knew nothing about Jeremy."

"Just a victim of circumstance, eh?"

"You got it, hoss. Just like you'll become. A victim."

"Thanks for the info, man. I'll be careful. I swear to God I will. Here, let me show you something, but let's go inside first. I'm freezing do death."

"Don't be careful," he said as we got up. "Just stay the fuck away from her, that's all. Plus I heard she fucked a nigger once."

We went inside and I put in the NHL 95 cartridge and fired up the Sega. I went to the fridge and got out two beers and I reached into my pocket and let him read the letter that Erin wrote to me. He unfolded it, read it, and started laughing out loud as he opened the can of Old Style that I gave him.

"Dude, don't fucking call that whore," he said after he finished reading the note.

"Yeah well," I said.

"Listen to me, I don't care how tough you are, her boyfriend will bury you if he finds out you're talking to her. Trust me on this one."

"Just look at her," I pleaded my case. "She's fine. What would you do if you were in my shoes?"

"I've been in your shoes. Me and her fucked sophomore year."

"What about this guy Jeremy?"

"He wasn't with her then."

"This is all getting very interesting," I said. "Women are rather fucked up."

"Don't I know it."

As The Brain and I played NHL 95 for the next hour or so, I kept losing because my head just wasn't into it. My mind and heart were doing battle over whether or not I should call this girl or if it would be smart just to blow her off. I knew that blowing her off would be the safe thing to do. I knew the facts about Erin, or at least the evidence that I had learned from The Brain. There were quite a few things playing against her. First was that she had a boyfriend (a huge psychotic boyfriend). Second, she had a history of playing guys.

And then there was the kicker, that The Brain and her had fucked in the past and he really struck me as being pretty sleazy and racist and dumb.

Then there were the things I wanted to be true about her. One was that she liked me. She was different too. She was cool and she seemed smart. She was beautiful, I had to give her that one. She had her own car and that was a plus. She didn't mind me smoking pot either, an added bonus. She was my dream girl.

The Brain left my apartment around four and again he told me to heed his warnings. I told him I would and that I'd get a hold of him if anything further had developed with Erin, but that was bullshit. If anything was gonna happen it would be strictly between Erin and I.

5:00 rolled around and I still hadn't mustered up the guts to call her. I was waiting for a sign, something to point me in the right direction. I couldn't hold out for long and I knew I'd give in and call her sooner or later.

What's a phone call, I thought. *It's just a phone call between two friends. Why would I get my ass kicked for that? It would be totally innocent.*

What I needed was a reason to call, besides her telling me to. Just in case her big gorilla boyfriend ever got the chance to wrap his hands around my throat, then at least I'd have a good excuse. I didn't have any classes with the girl, so the homework method was out of the question. I needed no phone numbers that only she would have. I was stumped. I could ask her if she could get me some weed. No, too personal. Ah-ha! Maybe I left something in her car like a textbook or money or something like that.

That wasn't a bad idea, I thought.

I figured I'd go with that plan, but instead of the textbook ploy I'd use my wallet. I never did any homework and no one would ever believe that I gave two shits about losing a schoolbook.

I heard voices. They were part my voice and part The Brain's and as I picked up the phone and started to dial they were shouting things at me and I had to stop and listen.

"No, he'll kill you if he finds out!"

"Listen to The Brain, stupid!"

"What if she's not home, then the wallet excuse is useless!"
And then my voices were faded out by The Brain's voice.

"She's trouble."

"She likes new guys."

"She's a scammer. She played my friend Derrick like a fiddle."

"Don't fucking call that whore!"

"I don't care how tough you are, this guy will bury you."

"Me and her fucked sophomore year."

"I heard she fucked a nigger once."

I hung the phone up and I started to buy into The Brain's wisdom some more. There was only one thing to do that would get this girl outta my mind. I had to call another girl instead, and possibly have sex with that girl, but who in the hell would I call? I hadn't been in town for months. One thing was for sure. I had gotten around before moving to Seattle. I don't mean sexually, but I had lived in just about every town in The Region. I had dated a girl or two in each place I'd lived.

I fished out my phonebook and scanned the names, I passed right by the No-Way-In-Hells and then I stopped briefly at the Maybes, but then I came to a few names that I thought might work. There were a few girls in Valparaiso I was on fairly good terms with, and some would even be open to hanging out with me on short notice. They might be caught off guard by the sudden surprise phone call from a guy that hasn't called in over a year, but there were ways around that. Like I'd have to think of a good reason to call them as well. Valparaiso was forty-five minutes away though, and when you don't have a working car it seems even farther than that. So I removed any Valparaiso girls as options. I put the phone book away and said, "Fuck it," to myself because I just didn't have the heart to make lonely phone calls to random girls.

What I really needed was to hang around some guy friends, then we could all be lonely together. I called my friend Lewis Marshall.

"Hello."

"Lew the Jew! It's Ray. What's up?"

"Nothin, dude. Look here, I got Christine on the other line. I'm trying to get her to come over because my mom's at school tonight.

I got the place to myself."

"Hey, call me when you get off the phone. I'm at my old man's."

"Alright, peace." And he hung up.

Well so much for that, he had plans of his own with his girl and I didn't want to mess with that. I called Patrick.

"Is Patrick there?"

His older brother Alan answered. "No, who's this?"

"It's Ray. Do you know were he is?"

"My dad kicked his ass and he ran out the door awhile ago. How's your brother? What's he up to?"

"He's got his own place close by in Miller."

"Does he like it out there?"

"I think so."

"Tell him to call if you talk to him will'ya?"

"Yeah sure."

"All right. Later, Ray."

"See ya, Alan."

And I hung up.

Patrick was probably hanging out at Ricky's so I called over there.

"Ricky!"

"Yo wuzzup, guy?"

"What's up over there? I'm looking for some action."

"Oh, we got action, Kozlowski."

"What kind?"

"Patrick's here'n we got three roadies comin by fer some hot tub action. N'dey are *fucking hot!* Yo, you should cruise over soon."

"Patrick's there? Lemme talk to him all right?"

"Sure, jus'a sec."

"What's up, Ray," Patrick said when he picked up the phone.

"Hey, is that roadie mission for real? Do you think I should stop by?"

"Ray, we haven't hardly hung out since you went to shitty Seattle. Roadies or not you should come over and hang out with us."

"Ok well, I gotta wait for my old man to get home, then I'll borrow his car and head out there. My car ain't working."

"When's he getting home, cause we're jumping in the hot tub as soon as those whores get here."

"He should be back anytime now. Can you give me an hour or so to get there?"

"Yeah, an hour's fine."

"Ok, I'll head out there soon."

"Later."

"Peace."

I hung up.

2

When my dad got home from the bar it had almost been an hour since I had called Ricky's house. I drove the Bonneville like hell to the Lakes of the Four Seasons where he lived and I smoked a big old joint by myself on the way there. The Lakes of the Four Seasons is a white upper-middle class neighborhood. Primarily doctors, lawyers, entrepreneurs, and other successful business types own the homes. Ricky's dad was a stockbroker and his mom was a pediatrician.

There's only one road that leads into the neighborhood and all visitors have to check in at the security station and leave their name and license plate number. Despite the cold weather I had rolled down the windows to air out the car so I wouldn't be suspected of any funny marijuana business by emitting funky smells while checking in at the gate. I also stopped at the gas station before going through the checkpoint and dropped some Visine into my eyes to get the red out.

When I pulled up at the gate a heavy guy in a police costume took my information.

"Name please."

"Peters."

I had to give a false name because I was banned from the Lakes of the Four Seasons for an alleged boat theft. I am innocent. So is Patrick.

"First name please."

"Franco."

"*Franco Peters*," he questioned thinking that it was a strange name.

"Yes'ir."

"Who are you gonna visit this evening, Mr. Peters?"

"I'm paying a visit to the Collins Family this evening, sir."

If I said I was visiting a crook like Ricky they'd run my plates through for sure. I used to go to school with Carrie Collins who also lived in the Lakes of the Four Seasons. By using her family as a contact I was leading the guards to pass me off as a harmless nerd.

"You know the Collins family?"

"I know the daughter," and I gave him a wink.

He smiled passively, yawned, and checked a box on the page attached to his clipboard and waved me forward.

"Thank you, Mr. Peters. Please pull forward so I can take down your license plate number and then I'll wave you through."

I pulled forward and the cop held out his pen and shook it to get the ink flowing properly. He wrote down the number on a clipboard and then he gave me a wave and I drove on. First of all, when you are driving through the Lakes of the Four Seasons, especially if you commit fraud as you are checking in at the gate, you have to be careful not to speed because the place is always crawling with patrol cars. Since I had lied about my destination, I had to pretend that I was actually heading to the Collins' residence as I had originally stated. If I had taken a wrong turn towards Ricky's instead of the Collins' house then they would have grown suspicious of me in a hurry. I actually went so far as to pull into the Collins' driveway to make sure I wasn't being followed. I wasn't, so I proceeded with my mission to Ricky's house.

When I got to Ricky's I parked the Bonneville in a well-hidden place where you couldn't drive by and notice it as the car that was just at the gate and was supposed to be at the Collins' house. Ricky's bedroom light was off and his mom's car was parked neatly in the driveway, so I went around to the back of the house and went in through the sliding-glass door that opened up into the bottom level, which was used for recreational purposes. It was a complete living area with a large bedroom, full bathroom, full kitchen, and a huge living room with a hot tub, workout area, and a pool table.

Patrick and Ricky were inside and they were both wearing new clothes that looked as if they had never been worn before. Patrick was pacing back and forth talking on the phone and he nodded to me and waved at me to come inside. Ricky was practicing on the pool table and he came over to shake hands. He had on a black pair of Doc Martins and a baggy pair of white Eddie Bauer cords, and a black button down shirt that I had noticed in the window at the Gap a few weeks before. Most people thought Ricky was an African American at first because he had obvious physical traits that led you to believe this. He's got tight black curly hair, brown eyes and brown skin. But his facial features were more Spanish looking, possibly Jamaican, than they were African. He was a good-looking kid and he didn't have too much trouble getting girls back then. Ricky seemed to enjoy leading people to believe that he was some sort of a tough-talking thug. He even went so far as to pattern his speech in support of this image that he wanted to uphold, but in reality he was actually a well–spoken educated book-smart young man. When talking to him he sometimes switched back and forth with his speech, going from very basic Ebonics one minute and polished verbiage to the next. With one exception, when he would get fucked up the Ebonics dominated. And he was almost always fucked up in those days.

"Kozlowski!"

"Hey, Ricky," I smiled. "How've you been since the other night?" Ricky and me and Matt had all dropped Acid two nights before when they picked me up from the airport. He didn't remember ever seeing me.

"Excellent, jus' excellent, guy. We've mist you around here. How'd that *Seattle* action go for you?"

"It was great at first," I said and looked at all of the steam floating up from the hot tub. "But then when I ran outta cash it got bogus in a hurry."

I shrugged my shoulders because I didn't know what else to say. The truth is I couldn't take care of myself.

"Yeah," he answered loudly. "Wuz there lot'a fine bitches over there?"

"Tons. Especially the Asian ones."

"*Nice!* That sounz like some good *Asian* action. I'll have'ta make a Seattle mission some time in the future so I can get *me* some of that shit."

I took of my leather coat and had a seat on the couch.

Ricky walked towards the kitchen and said, "Wanna beer, guy?"

"Sure," I said.

He came back into the room with two red plastic cups filled with foamy lager.

"You got a keg or something," I asked.

He laughed and said, "It's exactly a keg, Kozlowski. I slammed six'a these beers since you called. I'm startin to get *real* fucked."

"Sweet."

"So mah parents are'n Mexico fer three more weeks. Patrick got two kegs'a beer. One fer personal use throughout the week, and one fer the party on Friday."

"You having a party on Friday?"

"Exactly, holmes."

"I saw your old lady's car out front, thought she was still home or something."

"Mah moms left'er car her fer security purposes."

"So back to the party," I brought up again. "That sounds tight. I'll have to check that out."

"Wait a sec. Wait a sec. You gotta bring some girls though, guy," he cautioned me. "Everybody knows you always got bitches, Kozlowski. I don't want the party turnin int'a sausage fest."

We called parties with too many guys and too few girls a sausage festival.

"Have you got in touch wit any fine Granite honeys or what, guy?"

"Yeah. As a matter of fact I have. What happened to the roadies that were coming over, though?"

"Patrick's givin them a piece of his mind. They on the phone wit him now an shit."

Patrick hung up and cursed up a storm on his way to the kitchen.

"What's up, Patrick," I called out to him.

"They fucking chickened out," he shouted. "Fucking bunch of complete idiots. They actually asked their parents if they could come over here! So stupid. Ricky's pure dirt. No parent in their right mind would ever let their daughter come over here."

"Fuckin bunk, strictly," Ricky said.

"They can't even sneak outta the house tonight," Patrick shouted again as he came back into the room with a cup of beer.

He was wearing a cool pair of blue jeans from Urban Outfitters that flared out at the bottoms and a thin sharp looking gray sweater.

"Why do they have to sneak out anyway," I asked.

"Leeder and her friends are only seventeen," Patrick said.

He always called girls by their last names.

"Isn't that *illegal*," I asked just kidding. I was mocking a square.

"Not for Ricky."

"Whateva, *Patrick Fuckowski*, you da one who wanna screw Janice Leeder."

"Shut the fuck up you fake-ass nigger! Who the hell asked you anyway? This ain't the fucking emancipation proclamation so sit your black ass down and be quiet."

"Yo, quit wit the nigga shit, Patrick, alright!"

"Yeah, Patrick, that's nasty," I said.

"You shut up too, Ray. Ricky, you little toy poodle," Patrick continued. "I've banged Leeder, like, five-hundred times already. Why would I wanna screw her again? I've worn that bitch out."

"What's one more time? Five-hundred and one, eh," I suggested.

"How've you done her, like, five-hundred times if she's only seventeen," Ricky asked.

"Ricky, you're the abortion that shouldn't have lived. I've been doing her since she was fucking thirteen and I was fifteen. You can get in a lot of action in four years."

"Don't you get tired of her," I asked.

"Yeah, but I ain't finished yet. I still got to get her up the pooper like your mom likes it, Ricky."

"Oh, Patrick," I scolded playfully in mocking offense as I laughed. "That's the worst action ever."

"Patrick! You're burnin me hardcore," Ricky yelled at him.

Each of us kept quiet for a few seconds while we sipped our beers.

"We got all this beer and pot and I even got a smidgen a'coke and there's no girls coming over," Patrick said, disgusted.

"Kozlowski's gotta lead."

"I do?"

"Yeah, guy. You do. Don't start holdin out on us. What about them Granite roadies you wuz jus tellin me about?"

"I don't know," I played it off and looked at my watch.

It was almost nine-thirty.

"I don't have any phone numbers and it's getting kinda late. It's a goddamn school night."

"Com'n, Ray. Stop being such a fucking pussy," Patrick bullied me. "Pick up the phone and give it a shot."

"Yeah, shit yo, we're feedin you our nice beer, guy. It's the least you could do. Givita try."

"Hold up. Lemme call Gabe and see what I can do."

I got up to get the phone.

"Where'd you leave the phone, Patrick? It ain't on the charger."

"It's on the pool table, retard. About six-inches from your masturbation hand. Are you fucking blind? It's right in front of you. Who's Gabe?"

"Gabe Reynolds," I belched from the beer and didn't excuse myself. "He goes to Granite with me."

"He cool," Ricky asked.

"Yeah. He's cool," I validated him and held up my hand. "Now shut the fuck up you guys. These people got parents who screen their calls. I got work to do."

I dialed Gabe's number and went into the kitchen to talk in private.

"Hello," he answered on the first ring.

"Dude."

"Dude who?"

"It's Ray."

"Hey. I just got off the phone with Erin."

"What a fucking coincedence," I hastened. "Listen. I need a little favor from you. I'm at my friend's house in the Lakes of the Four Seasons."

"*Yeah?*"

"Do you feel like hanging?"

"Depends."

"I got a wee bit a'coke over here."

"I'm there. Give me directions and then I'll shit, shower, and shave and I'll jump in the Tempo and then I'll jet."

"Not so fast, buddy. You must go *slow and low* in the Tempo like the Beastie Boys. First I need a favor. Here's the favor. We need girls."

"How many and which ones?"

"How about Erin and three of her friends. Cute ones. No dogs, Gabe! Don't hold out on me. I've seen you send out ugly ones so you can save the good ones. Don't do that. I don't care which ones as long as they ain't dogs. Bring an assortment."

"They ain't donuts, but I'll do my best. What's the number over there?"

"555-1112."

"Ray, I'll call ya back in ten minutes."

And we hung up.

I went back into the living room and Ricky had gotten the three-foot glass water-bong out and he was ripping tubes.

"Come hit dis, Kozlowski," he said and started coughing up smoke.

"Don't mind if I do."

"What's up with the ladies?" Patrick asked.

I inhaled a tube and then exhaled my hit.

"Looks like a go. Dude's gonna call back here in a coupla minutes."

"You guys smoke too much of that fucking reefer," Patrick was disgusted. "It's making you guys so dumb you can't even tell how stupid you act now."

"Yo, yo, yo. You snort too much *coke-cain,*" Ricky said cocaine in two distinct syllables as he pumped out more jive-turkey talk.

"Yeah? Well, you suck too much gang-banger penis when you pick up your OZ's up in Stoney Island from Jerome, you cracked out little black bitch."

"Yo, yo, yo. Your moms sucks too much dick, guy. And if I want the crack she's da first bitch I'd hit up," Ricky said.

He shouldn't have said that. I would never have said anything about Patrick's mom. It's what makes him the most angry, fittingly enough.

Patrick charged at Ricky and took him down. They started wrestling and cursing at each other. I just kept taking hits off of the bong and watching them roll around on the floor together. Then the phone started ringing and they stopped both stood up. Ricky was looking pissed as he was straightening his clothes and checking them for tears. The phone only rang once and then stopped as if somebody had changed their mind about calling.

Matt Morris came in just then and he brushed some snow off of his head and said, "Patrick, Ricky! You guys are pure dirt. What's up, Ray," he said to me. "Long time no see. Remember the other night with the **Acid**?"

"Yeah I remember."

"You stole my car!"

"I know, dude. You got it back though. Didn't you?"

"I'm just giving you a hard time. How was that *Seattle* action? Did you tell all the bitches 'in order to get ahead you gotta give a little head?'"

"All the time. Whores. All over the place, Matt. Seattle's fair. Hey, take a look at these two fucks rolling around on the floor. I'm just watching a fine example of primitive man here," I said and I shook his hand. "Cro-Magnon meets Neanderthal Man. It's a lot like one of them corny reenactments on the Discovery Channel."

"It's like the Moors invading Sicily," Matt said. "Except Ricky isn't a real nigger and Patrick is an Irish-Pollack."

"A frightening combination, indeed," I agreed.

Patrick's face was red from the wrestling match. He looked happy and excited and his hair was all messed up. "Kicked your ass that time didn't I? You look like a broke-ass Young M.C."

The phone rang again and I was completely baked.

"Ya ripped mah shirt, ass-fucker," Ricky said. "What's happenin, Morris? I was just working over Patrick like I do on the soccer field."

"Fuck Ricky. You stink, dude. That armpit smell could steamclean a diesel engine."

"Very funny, guy. I just took a shower."

"Phone's ringing, Ricky," I said and he slowly walked over and answered.

"What up," Ricky answered breathing heavy. "Cool. What about'chew," then he paused and listened. "Yeah, jus'a sec," and he tossed me the phone.

I knew it was Gabe because no one else knew I was there.

"Gabe."

"We're gold."

"No shit?"

"Gimmie directions."

"Did you talk to her?"

"Who do you think you're talking to? Of course I fucking talked to her."

"Awesome! Thanks, Gabe."

"Don't mention it, big boy. Gimmie directions."

"Ok, hold on. I'm gonna give the phone to Ricky so he can tell you."

"Cool," he said and I tossed the phone back to Ricky and he told him how to get to his house.

At ten-thirty, Matt, Patrick, Ricky and I were playing pool when we heard some arguing going on outside the glass door and then there was a soft knock.

"The ladies are here," I smiled.

Ricky slid the door open and I heard Gabe ask if I was here and I heard some girls giggling.

"Mr. Raymond is among us," Ricky confirmed.

He had mysteriously and suddenly reverted to speaking correctly.

"Right this way please."

Gabe came in and introduced himself, and then I greeted Gabe and introduced him to Patrick and Matt Morris. I put down my pool stick and walked over to the girls.

Erin walked in first and she hugged me and whispered into my ear, "You forgot to call."

She quickly let go of me and moved on to the other guys because they were new to her. And then to my surprise, Milada walks in of all people. Damn, she was so hot. And she hated me. It made me like her all the better.

"*Ahlaidya*," I nodded. "How delightful. So glad to see you. Did I say your name right?"

"Hi, Raymond. *Not* very nice to see you again," she said coldly, and quickly walked by me.

"Speak for yourself," I said to her as she walked by.

That girl Jolene was with them also. She was two years older than the other two girls and Ricky, a year older then Matt and I, and the same age as Patrick. That's some Polish algebra. In other words she was nineteen.

Jolene had brought another friend of hers named Lisa Diamond. I had the impression Lisa was her best friend because everywhere I'd seen Jolene around, school or otherwise, Lisa'd been there too. I thought Lisa was a little overweight, but she had a beautiful face and her total package resembled Betty Boop in a little strange sorta way, but I guess that might sound ugly to some people. Beauty is all a matter of opinion. In my opinion she was sorta cute. She had big brown eyes and brown hair and she had on brandless jeans and an orange wool sweater that looked like something a relative had handmade for her. Between her and Jolene, I had a hard time making positive identification of the brand names of their attire.

The reason that I could usually recognize these things is because Patrick, Ricky, Matt, and I were mall-bandits in our spare time, experienced shoplifters who hit one mall and then made returns at another mall with the same stores so we could collect the refunds. We were the sad truth about the stores that trust their customers without a receipt. With four of us working over a store, or five, we could walk away with a hundred bucks a piece at the end of the day.

I knew Jolene from Geometry class the year before when she was a senior and I was a junior.

"So which one of you jerks is Ray," she asked.

"Jolene," I spoke up, excited to be sought after. "You're looking at him."

"You know me from somewhere? I heard somebody say I knew you."

"Geometry."

"Come again?"

"*Uh*," I looked at Erin and she was lifting the cover of the hot tub.

"Whoa, dude," Erin yelled. "You gotta hot tub in your house!"

"*Um*," I continued. "We had Geometry class together last year."

"I don't remember you."

"Uh, I had long hair then," I said. "It was only for a few weeks. Then I moved out to Seattle. Now I'm back."

Something about her was making me nervous. I felt like she could see right through me.

"Remember, *uh*, I sat behind your boyfriend James Chapman. At least, I think he was your boyfriend."

"Sorry, but I don't remember you," she said, and she walked by me and started talking to Patrick.

Jesus that was weird, I thought.

I must've had that African Monkey AIDS they kept talking about on CNN every day back then.

"Hi. I'm Lisa," Jolene's friend jumped in front of me with a shy smile.

She wasn't as dominating as Jolene seemed to be, not even close.

"Ray," I reacted and we shook hands.

"May I get a foamy lager for any of you fine women," Ricky asked. "Some dangerous elicit narcotics perhaps," he said under his breath.

The girls didn't hear that last part, but I did, and it was funny to me.

"I'll take one, Ricky. Dude," Erin said.

She was always saying *dude* and that was one thing that really annoyed me about her. Soon there would be plenty of other things that bothered me more, but at first the *dude* shit was it. My friends and I said certain words too much also, but at least we invented them.

"I'll have a little one," Milada said sweetly.

"Bring me two," Jolene said laughing, but in a way she was serious.

"Ok," Lisa said timidly.

"Nice! You ladies are all very fine," Ricky said and he went to the keg.

Patrick turned the stereo up and after everyone had gotten a few beers in themselves we all felt a little looser. It wasn't a very exciting night and I was a little agitated that Erin seemed to be more interested in talking to Patrick instead of me. By eleven o'clock those two had disappeared to another part of the house. I didn't know what they were doing, but as a child I ate a lotta junk food and watched too much TV so I naturally always assumed the worst. I figured, knowing Patrick, they were off screwing around. I guessed that The Brain was right after all. I wished I would have listened to him sooner, at least I could be at home playing video games and drinking beer and smoking weed in the comforts of my own home.

Gabe, the girls, and I started putting on our coats because we wanted to smoke. Smoking cigarettes inside somebody's house is different from smoking weed because cigarette smoke hangs around and sticks to clothes and furniture.

Ricky came back from taking a piss and stopped us, "Whoa! Hold up. Where you guys goin? Nobody's skippin back to da crib, right?"

He had reverted back to ghetto talk.

"We're gonna smoke. Wanna come," I asked.

"Kozlowski. *Biatches.* Mr. Gabe. No need da go out into that harsh-ass weather just so you can smoke. Yo, yo, yo. We can totally go into the smokin lounge upstairs where there's plenty'a room fer everyone to have a comfortable seat, even if Milada's forced to sit on my lap."

"*Whatever,*" she vally-girled back at him.

"Oh, Milada," Ricky laughed out loud. "It'd be spin-city and you know it."

We all went into the lounge and it was a typical looking den, leather swivel chairs, a fireplace, lotsa books and dusty artifacts on the shelves, and even a stuffed moose head.

We took off our coats and had a seat. Ricky threw some logs into the fireplace and started a fire. He offered actual Cuban cigars, but only Gabe wanted one and he just put it in his pocket and saved it for later.

"Saving that for your next Jock party," Matt asked him.

Jolene changed her mind about the cigar and took one afterall and she bit the end off, lit it on fire and started puffing on it like she was a sports reporter. She could even blow perfect smoke rings. She reminded me of a blackjack dealer at a roadside casino in some reservation in Washington.

"So, Ray," Jolene said, smiling like she was gonna embarrass me.

"Yes?"

"Do you like Erin?"

"Erin who," I asked, playing along.

"Don't bullshit us," she cut me off.

"Oh no, guy. Sounz like she on yer ass," Ricky mocked.

"Chill out, Tony Montana," Jolene burned him, "I'm just messing with Ray."

Me and Matt laughed at the Tony Montana comment, since that's what we always called Ricky.

"Yeah, Ricky," Matt added. "You're such a dirt-bag-Ricardo-type thing. Plus your cologne is pure-butt smelling."

"No," I said. "I *don't* like her. Repeat. Do not. Satisfied?"

"No."

"Why not?"

"Because you're lying," Milada ganged up on me.

"I'm not lying. Besides, how in the *hell* would you know?"

"Why don't you like her," Lisa asked me.

"You're asking me if I like a girl who is off doing God knows what with Patrick 'Dick-em' Bukowski."

"Why do you say that," Jolene asked. "Is that his real nickname?"

"No," I said, "I was just saying it."

"Because we know Patrick," Ricky answered for me.

"But you don't know Erin," Lisa fired back.

"I know enough, *biatch*," I insulted her.

"What's that supposed to mean," Milada asked.

"No comment."

"No tell us, Ray. What did you hear, and from whom did you hear it," Jolene interrogated.

"Guys," Gabe jumped in to save me. "Leave him alone. Face it. Everybody knows about Erin."

The conversation went on in this fashion for the rest of the night, except the topic shifted from Erin to random people at Granite that Ricky, Matt Morris and I didn't know anything about. Gabe and the girls kept gossiping about people and telling old stories about them. Gabe would get up and do impressions of them and the girls would laugh every time.

By midnight I was getting really tired and announced that I was heading out. Everybody said good-bye to me.

Jolene and Lisa gave me a polite, "Nice to meet you."

"Raymond," Milada asked me shyly, taking me aside so the other people wouldn't listen. "Will you please give me a ride home?"

She looked nervous.

"The other girls are going out to another party and I have to be home at midnight."

"*Uh*, yeah. I guess so."

"Are you sure?"

"Yeah. I'm sure. Why wouldn't I be?"

"Well, because you know, about what happened in the car, in Erin's car."

"Don't worry about it. I'll give you a ride."

"Thanks," she sighed in relief.

"Grab your coat and so we can take off."

3

Milada and I hardly spoke as we were driving home. I had to cruise really slowly because there was tons of snow blowing about and the plows wouldn't be out to clear the roads until morning. I imagined what it would be like to be stranded in a blizzard with this pretty high maintenance girl. She would probably complain to me about the cold all night as if it was my fault. She'd scold me about Christianity for sure, because if we got stuck in a snowdrift then I'd have to curse Jesus and his gang as much as possible for making the whole world cold.

"Do you mind if we listen to some music," she asked.

"*Uh*, no, *um*," and I turned on the radio. "Just press the channel buttons to go through the different stations. I'm not sure what my dad has programmed in there. Probably some gay jazzy shit."

She rummaged through my dad's jazz and blues stations. She went right through the talk radio and stopped at an alternative rock station and they were playing a song by Green Day.

"Cool," she said and turned up the volume a little.

I sighed and rolled my eyes. I wasn't fond of Green Day's music.

"You don't like Green Day?"

I looked over to her and she was smiling at me waiting for me to say something clever, but I didn't. I just looked at her and she let me. I really thought she was a pretty girl and I was sorry I had to watch the road instead.

"Were you in Seattle when that guy from Nirvana killed himself?"

"You mean *Kurt Cobain*," I laughed, because she had to be the only teenager alive who didn't know his name by heart. "Yeah, I was in Seattle. They had a big candlelight vigil downtown that my friend Jon and I went to. There was, like, ten-thousand people there and they played his music and all the girls were crying and everybody was getting high. Courtney Love read his suicide letter or something, or maybe it was her letter to him. She called him an asshole."

"Did you get high?"

"I don't remember," I reactively played dumb. "*Why*? What's the big deal?"

"I'm trying to figure out if you're a pothead or not."

"Why does it matter?"

"I'm just curious. Erin's a pothead."

"Lemme give you a clue, Milada. I'm the George Washington of potheads."

"Erin's a stoner too."

"So what. What's that got to do with me?"

"You like her right?"

"I said *no* before didn't I? God, why do you people keep asking me that?"

"Because she says you do. She thinks you're cute."

"I don't know what gave her the impression that I liked her."

"Erin has a boyfriend anyway."

"So I've heard. *Uh*, that Otsap guy. Jeremy."

"Yeah. Where'd you hear that, Ray? I know *she* didn't tell you."

"No, *she* didn't tell me."

"How'd you find out then," she asked suspiciously.

"Fuck, *Milada*. You know it's really none of your business. I don't mean to be rude, but I'm tired of being asked about her."

"I don't really mind you swearing anymore. I was just annoyed at you because I thought you liked Erin."

"And that would *bother* you?"

"No, it wouldn't *bother* me. It's just that only a certain kinda guy go for Erin, mostly boys that only wanna have sex with her."

"I hate to break it to you, Milada, but that's the only reason any guy likes a girl. I thought you and Erin were friends."

"We *are* friends. She just has a bad reputation about sleeping with a lotta boys. Maybe I'm just looking out for her."

"Is it true," I asked and looked at her face again briefly. "About all the sex with a bunch of guys and shit."

"She says it's not."

"People are just making things up?"

"Sometimes I wonder."

We drove on the rest of the way and didn't say anything at all, which can be a sign that either you're comfortable with someone or you're very uncomfortable. After I dropped Milada off at her house I felt a lot better than I did earlier in the day when I was thinking about calling Erin. I was glad I learned the truth about her before she got the chance to burn me. I guessed I was wrong about Milada too. At first I thought she was a huge self-centered bitch, but it turns out she was actually really sweet. She was fucking hot as hell too. Her boyfriend was a lucky guy for having a girl with such good morals. They were few and far between in The Region. I wished I had a girl like that. I hadn't had a real girlfriend since before I left for Seattle and I was really starting to get lonely. Most of the chicks you meet in The Region are Catholic, and it's only my speculative opinion, but I suspect the Catholicism is the reason most Regionrat girls are jealous, possessive, and they always think they can screw guys over and then just apologize later. A nice girl was something to look forward to and treasure there. I hoped somebody like that would come along for me soon. I didn't wanna have to start beating my meat or anything.

When I pulled into my parking lot it was just about 1:00 in the morning and *High and Dry* by Radiohead was on the stereo, so I sat in the car for a few more minutes and had one last cigarette before going up to crash. It was really a shame Erin turned out to be so shady. I really thought, for some reason, she was different. Different from what, I had no idea. I just thought she was the one I've been waiting for all this time. Knowing what I know now, she was just the same as everybody else. Only God knows what she was doing with Patrick all that time.

4

The next day was Friday and when I woke up to go to school I found a note from my dad. He would be in Florida for the next two weeks since his second-wife lived out there, so when he would go to see her once every month or so he would take the shuttle bus to the airport and leave me his car in case I needed it. This was purely good action.

I immediately canceled any assumed plans of attending classes that day and I decided to go shopping instead. I didn't have much cash at all, but I still had one of the old tag-poppers from our mall-raiding days.

I took a half-hour shower, got high, ate breakfast at McDonalds, and I drove old lady-style over to South Lake Mall.

I went to the Gap and acquired a pair of jeans and then I paid for a cookie at Mrs. Fields and then I chilled out and watched a fashion show they were putting on in the middle of the mall. After I had watched these high schooler wannabe models walk the runway for a half-hour I walked back to the car and got high again because I felt faded and I still wanted to do some more shopping. I had the whole day to kill. I didn't have any more Visine so instead I just put on my glasses, which I never wore unless I was desperate to hide my red eyes. The only reason that I have them is because I have an astigmatism.

I went to American Eagle and was looking at shoes when she tapped me on the shoulder. I turned around and it was Ari Lopez. She was a year older than me and she had already graduated from Granite the year before. I hadn't seen her in almost a year and I almost forgot that she existed until I saw her again. I had asked Ari to go out on a date a while back, things got delayed, and the day before we actually hooked up she was planning on moving to Boston.

We went to a movie, *Goodfellas* I think, because that's the only movie people in the midwest will watch, and then I took her out to eat at Stones Bones. Nothing heavy developed though, to my demise, just a meaningless (to me) flirty friendship.

During our date she was nervous and stressed because she hadn't finished packing yet and I was just plain nervous and stressed because I knew she was moving and I felt like our date was a big time waste of my time and money.

Things went sour from there. This was disappointing to me at the time because I had a huge crush on her. I managed to end the night in decent shape and she promised to at least write from Boston.

And write she did. She wrote me perfumed letters once a month and they got increasingly romantic. I wrote steamy letters back to her. It got boring for me though. Being a teenaged guy, I wasn't all up into that hurry up and wait shit. I lived in the Midwest, land of half-off satisfaction and other lazy cheap thrills. It wasn't Hollywood.

I needed companionship right now, so I had started going out with some girl and this new girl made me stop writing letters back to Boston and when my ink stopped flowing it pissed Ari off even though we had no realistic relationship. Her later letters freaked me out because they were getting to be like hate mail.

And then there she was after all that time. After being bunked by Erin and having to talk in a lonely car with depressing Milada the night before, Ari was certainly somebody who peaked my interest. She was even more attractive than I remembered. Her hair was longer and she looked like she had gained a little weight in the right places, which are everywhere except the thights and waist, neck and arms. I remembered her as a girl and at some point while she was away she turned into a woman.

"Raymond, what are you doing here? I thought you were in Seattle!"

"Ari," I said and we hugged. "I just got back a coupla days ago. I thought you were in Boston."

"Oh, I've been back for a while," as if she was surprised I didn't know.

"Why? I mean, I thought you loved Boston. You always said so in your letters."

"Something kinda messed up happened to me and I came home."

"No shit. What happened to you," I asked.

"*Um*, well. Nothing that I care to talk about right now, at least nothing worth ever mentioning again."

She didn't want to tell me.

"I'm going on my break now, Raymond. Do you wanna join me for lunch?"

"Sure. I guess. You work here?"

"Yeah I do. I'm the Assistant Manager," she smiled proudly. She was bragging about it. It's funny that management is something Midwesterners tend to strive for in their lives. The pinnacle is US Steel Middle Management.

"Sure, Ari. Yeah. I'd like that. Let's go get some lunch."

We went to the Red Robin right there inside the mall and they sat us in a corner booth by the window. The host was an old man who looked as if he'd been forced into early retirement.

"The special today is the Four Cheese Alfredo on angel hair noodles and Jessie Baker will be your waitress today."

"Thanks," I said to him as he set our table and poured the water. I felt that my eyes had cleared up so I took off my glasses and hung them on my shirt. A stoning from Mexi-weed only lasts for about a half-hour, maybe an hour at best. It was snowing outside again and I shivered.

"You cold," she asked and took a sip of her water.

"I'm cool."

"Excuse me," she called to the host. "Can we get some coffee please ... coffee?"

"Coffee sounds good," I agreed.

"So I heard that you like Erin Watkins."

She smiled and shook her head at me as if I was a fool.

I was taking a drink and when I heard this some water went down my windpipe and I started coughing uncontrollably. I turned red in the face and Ari started laughing at me and she turned to look and saw other people looking over. They were wondering if I was choking.

"Oh, he's ok," she said to the people. "He's just embarrassed. Tell them you're ok, Raymond. Com'n, you're embarassing me."

I couldn't talk yet so I just held up my left hand and nodded that I was fine. After a few more minutes I was able to calm down and catch my breath. She was just sitting back and smirking at me the whole time.

"It's cute when you laugh," she pitched.

"Jesus, where did you hear that?"

"That you were cute?"

"No," I sipped my water again. "That Erin shit."

"You don't wanna know," she assured me.

"I do. I really wanna know because it ain't true and everybody keeps asking me about it. It's really fucking weird."

"You *really* wanna know?"

"Does a bear shit in the woods?"

"I'll take that as a yes," she said and rolled her eyes. "Her boyfriend is my older brother's friend.."

I put my hands over my face because I was suddenly worried. "Does he know?"

"*Jeremy Otsap*," she asked.

"No, Pee-Wee Herman. Of course I'm talking about Jeremy."

"Yeah, he knows. I heard that he's pretty pissed, but you're lucky for now. He's still in Wisconsin at college and he won't be back until March. And also I don't think that he knows who you are, but I'm sure he's anxious to find out."

"I'm not planning that he will," I promised her.

She stared out the window and laughed about something.

"What's so funny?"

"Oh, I was just thinking about something some guy from Boston told me about the city when I first got there."

"What?"

"He said Boston has good news and bad news. The bad news is there's nothing to eat but horseshit, but the good news is that there's plenty of it. And when he told me that it made me think that Boston isn't much different than this place."

I smiled politely.

"That's the dumbest saying I've ever heard."

She took a sip outta her glass and looked over the top of it and just watched me.

"Ari, you have to believe me on this one. I don't know why everybody is saying this. You've gotta help me clear this up. I'm gonna get killed by that psycho and for once in my life I'm innocent."

"For once, huh. That's a good one. What in the hell do you

expect me to do about it?"

"Can't you tell your brother something? Tell him I already have a girlfriend and I'm madly in love with this other girl?"

Her eyes sunk and her face shifted to this solemn expression.

"You mean another girl that isn't me? Why would I benefit from this?"

I noticed the level of psychotics increasing in her eyes and it was pissing me off.

"You're gonna have to do something for *me*, don't you think, Raymond?"

"Jesus Ari, what kinda fucking extortion question is that? I thought we were friends. Friends do each other favors, don't they?"

The waitress came over to the table and poured our coffee and then took our order. Ari got the fish and chips and I got a cheeseburger and a Coke. The waitress, I guess her name was Jessie Baker, pranced back to the kitchen. She looked sexy. I mean, wow. What an ass.

"What if I need a favor from you," she asked me.

"That depends on if you can help me or not."

"I can."

"How can I believe you? I just feel weird trusting you after all those hate letters you sent."

"They weren't hate letters. They were ... *emotional* letters. Besides, you just have to trust me."

"Fuck."

"What do you say, will you hear me out," she asked.

"Shoot."

"Well, there's this guy."

"And?"

"Well, he likes me."

"Yeah, so what's the problem?"

"He has a girlfriend."

"No way, Ari. I'm not fucking with somebody's girlfriend."

"You don't have to," she swore. "Besides, sometimes you act like you can mess with any girl that you choose."

"How do you know he likes you then?"

"Because I slept with him."

"You mean you had sex? I got news for you, that don't mean he likes you. Shit, it don't even mean he knows your last name."

"I'm pregnant."

"Christ, you think so or you know so, which is it?"

"I know so, I saw our family doctor at yesterday morning before work."

"Are you sure it's his?"

"Yes. I'm fucking sure!"

"I'm sorry," I said. "I didn't mean it like that. Who's this guy?"

"His name is Tim Miller."

"Never heard of him."

"He's older and he's from Ohio."

"Fuck. That's heavy shit, Ari. So, what do you want me to do?"

"Well, there's more I have to tell you first," she said and she looked out the window in silence.

Her eyes started to water and she looked like she was about to cry. I took her hand.

"More than you're pregnant?"

"Oh, this is hard," she trembled.

"Look, you don't have tell me anything."

"No, it's fine. It's just a matter of time before everybody knows about this anyway. You know how this place is."

"Yeah, it blows."

"Well," she whispered.

I waited for another word.

"I am," she stopped again.

I waited.

"I am H ... I ... V *positive*."

My jaw hung down like some Amazon titties. What do you say to that? Don't worry? Everything's going to be ok? I can't imagine how scary it would be to find out you're HIV positive. What was scary to me was how I fit into this. God. All those times I thought about making love to this girl. I'm so lucky it was just a fantasy.

"What about the baby," I asked and for once I was really concerned about something.

"I'm having an abortion."

"I don't know what to say, Ari."

"Well, when you figure it out, save it for Tim Miller."

"*Huh*, you don't mean—"

"I, *uh*," she hesitated. "I want you to tell him."

"Bullshit! I don't even know him and you want me to tell him that he might have AIDS, and so might his girlfriend? Oh, and by the way, congratulations on becoming a daddy! Are you *outta* your fucking mind? Fuck that!"

"Ray, he won't talk to me at all," she begged. "I want him to know before everybody finds out. I love him."

She started crying.

"Goddamn it," I kept my voice down. "Get serious. You love every guy you're with."

"Raymond, please," she pleaded between sobs. "I need your help. I promise I can get Jeremy Otsap off your back."

"God. How can I even think about that guy now? Do you know how you got it?"

"The doctor thinks I got it during a blood transfusion when I was thirteen, but I'll never know for sure where it came from."

"Oh my God."

The waitress brought our food to the table and was about to ask if we would like anything else when she noticed Ari crying. She looked at me like I was abusing the poor girl and she quietly scurried her sex-appeal back to the kitchen. I had completely lost my appetite, but I ate my cheeseburger anyway because I had to pay for it. Ari didn't touch her food at all and she had it wrapped up before we left.

I put my arm around her as we walked back to her work.

"Ray, I'm so scared."

"I know."

"My poor baby," she complained and held her belly.

"Look, how do you want me to tell this guy?"

"However you want. I can tell you how to find him. I just want you to tell him in person. I don't think anyone would wanna hear that kinda news over the phone or in a letter, do you?"

"No I don't think so."

"When do you think you can tell him?"

"Sooner the better, I guess. Where can I find him?"

"There's this guy named Anthony Falco who's having a *really* huge party tonight. Everyone will be there. That's were you'll be able to find him."

We stopped out in front of American Eagle and I hugged her tightly. I already felt like I was hugging a corpse.

"Will you be there tonight," I asked as I fought back tears.

I felt like if I kept talking to her I'd start crying. When I think of people being inflicted with AIDS and HIV I think of tribes in Africa and propaganda that it's only homosexuals who get it, not about cute teenage girls that I wanna date.

"No, I won't be there. I don't feel much like partying these days. What's to celebrate?"

"You know if I tell him tonight, he might tell everyone."

"That's fine, I'm leaving town for good in three days."

"Where are you gonna go?"

"My grandfather has a farm in Alabama and there's this special AIDS clinic in Birmingham where I can get some treatment. I figure I can live out the rest of my life down there. I might try to write a book."

"Shit, I could never write a book. If you write one I'll read it."

"Thanks."

A tear dripped from my eye and I tried to wipe it away without her seeing it, but she did and she smiled at me.

"You're really sweet, Raymond. I was stupid for not getting together with you sooner than that date we went on last year. Maybe I should've stayed with you instead of going away."

I couldn't respond to her because I was glad we didn't, and I sure as hell couldn't tell her how I really felt, *nervous*. I tried really hard not to let it out.

"But, I guess you're happy we never got together though, huh," she asked looking up at me with her big saddened browns.

I zeroed in on the skin around her eyes and I could see all the tiny wrinkles above her eyelids, which were washed in purple eyeshadow. Then I let my imagination run off and my vision dove into her body and I could see into her head. There were parasites everywhere, and they were eating her alive. Still I didn't say anything. All I could do was stare at her.

"Don't worry. You can't get it by kissing someone."

"I know," I said defensively. "I'm not worried about that."

But I was. I was scared to death. If this girl could get AIDS then anyone could.

"It's just so sad. You're such a nice person. I mean, I could have loved you, Ari."

She reached around my head and kissed me on the mouth and I just froze. I spent the whole time in Seattle thinking about what it would have been like to kiss this girl. Never, in my wildest dreams, would I have imagined it like this with her practically dead and my life just beginning. She stepped away from me and she had this defeated look of dread.

"I'm sorry," she said.

"Don't be."

It was probably the last time she ever kissed anyone in a romantic way for the rest of her life. On my way home I got stuck in traffic and I cried my eyes out for that poor girl. She was so nice, so beautiful, so young and she was dying. God. It was one of the saddest things I had ever experienced in my entire life. I've never felt the same as I did before that day. That's when I started to change for good. When I cried in the car for that girl I was moved with compassion for a human life, an emotion I never knew I had. When I got home I went into my bedroom and shut the door. I got down on my knees and said a prayer for her and I asked God to give me the strength to change into a better person. I wanted to become a respectable man, whatever that encompassed.

It had been years since I had really cried hard. I had been angry, had bottled up feelings, and had this don't-give-a-fuck attitude for such a long time that when I finally let everything out the tears came in floods and my nose became a snot river. Afterwards I took a really hot shower and felt a lot better. It was 3:00 and school was just letting out. I took a few bong rips and then lay down on the couch.

5

I was asleep on the couch, snoring (or so I would venture to guess), when the telephone rang and scared me awake. I didn't know how long it had been ringing and had no clue what time it was. It was nearly dark outside.

"*Ahhem,*" I cleared my throat. "Hello?"

"*Raymond,*" a girl asked.

I didn't know who it was at first, but I made sure the tone in my voice suggested I clearly recognized the mystery caller.

"Yeah. Hey," I said with familiarity.

"Why'd you go home so early last night? I wanted to talk to you, and you weren't even at school today."

It was Erin.

"Oh, Erin, *um* ... I was getting a little sick last night and I didn't feel too great this morning so I just slept. I'm not off to a good start at school, am I? Two days of school and I've only been there for, what, half a day? So what's up? It's really nice to talk to you again by the way. After last night I wasn't too sure you would call again."

"What do you mean by that, dude," she asked.

"Well, you seemed like you really liked Patrick. And then you went off with him somewhere and you two were gone for a long time, you know?"

"*What?* My God, dude! I don't like, fucking, Patrick!"

"Sorry. It's no big deal. I mean, I don't care if you do or not."

"Well I don't," she said like she was getting pissed off.

"I said sorry. Jesus." I was starting to realize just how nuts this girl really was, and I knew that any future conversations would have to be handled with newborn caution.

"It just pisses me off that you would think that because everybody is always accusing me off liking people when I, fucking, don't.

And now you are too."

I knew she was lying to me. Patrick always scored. Always. Always. He was the master when it came to hooking up with girls. Everything I ever learned about playing females, I learned from him.

"Look. Just forget it, ok?"

Then there was a long pause.

We were both searching for words.

"So what are you doing tonight," she asked.

"Well, I heard there was a big party tonight. Anthony Falco. I was thinking about cruising by there for a little bit."

"Yeah, dude. It's at Anthony Falco's house. I don't think I'm gonna go though, but maybe I was thinking we could get together afterwards, like, around midnight."

"That's highly probable. What are you gonna do instead?"

"Oh, dude. It's so awesome! Lisa Diamond and I are gonna get tattoos!"

"Really? Where at?"

"Long John's! Do you know where that is?"

"Yeah. I know Long John from when I was a kid. He knows my old man. He doesn't give tattoos anymore. He's just a really rich guy who owns a shitload of tattoo parlors now."

"Is that his real name, *Long John*," she asked.

"No," I laughed. "His real name is John Menesini."

"That's cool that your dad knows him."

"*Whatever*. People know lotsa people. Don't you have to be eighteen to get a tattoo?"

"Lisa has a friend who's an artist there. She says she can get me in no problem."

"Do you know what in the hell you're gonna get?"

"Yeah, dude. I'm gonna get a picture of an evergreen tree with the sun behind it."

"That's cool," I said. "Why the hell are you getting that?"

"It has something to do with my dad. Maybe once I get to know you better, I'll explain why."

"Well at least you have a reason. I hate when people get tattoos and have no reason to do so. Where are you planning on planting your fresh-inked evergreen tree?"

"*Um*," she laughed. "I'm getting it on my breast. Over my heart."

"Jesus. You're seventeen and you're have a greasy tattoo artist feel you up and put ink on your tits?"

"Whatever, Raymond! It's not like that!"

"Chill-out, Erin. I'm just fucking with you."

Our conversation went on in this fashion for an hour with her trying to impress me with the things that she's done, and in return I'd challenge the intelligence of her actions, and then she'd get mad. I never got around to ask her what exactly she was doing with Patrick all that time. I partly didn't care, partly it was none of my business, and partly I just assumed the worst.

After hanging up with Erin I called Ari to see if our plan was still on, but she wasn't home from work yet, so I called The Brain to see what he thinks of this whole mess.

"Victor. What's up? It's Ray."

"What's up with you, hoss? Good thing you weren't at school today."

"Why's that?"

"Everybody knows you're after that bitch, that's the bad news."

"Great, what's the good news?"

"Nobody knows who the fuck you are," The Brain laughed.

"So it's just a matter of time before I'm dead, right?"

"I wouldn't say that. There are ways that you can counter a disaster like this. I'll be your public relations guy. Damage control is my specialty."

"Then why do you have such a shitty reputation?"

"You're funny."

"How does everybody know? *You* didn't tell anyone did you?"

"Of course I didn't fucking tell anybody! Do I look like a sally to you?"

"No. What do you think happened then?"

"My guess is the bitch is telling people, talking like she always does."

"Fuck!"

"Tell me about it."

"What in the hell would you do if you were me," I asked.

"*Um*, well, if it were me, I wouldn't be talking shit to her in the first place. And if Jeremy ever came at me I'd shoot the bastard. If I were you I'd start packing some heat. I'd try to get to the bottom of who's saying shit. I'd also make it public knowledge that instead of liking that whore, let everybody know how much you hate the stupid bitch."

"You're very wise, Victor."

"I know, hoss. That's why I'm The Brain. If you want, I can help with the 'Hate The Bitch' campaign. I'll get it rolling for you. I'm an expert when it comes to this shit because I hate everybody."

"*Um*, let's hold off on that plan for now. At this point I'm not that concerned about what happens to me. If I have to I'll kick that Jeremy Otsap guy in the nuts and I'll run like hell."

"Yeah. Right. I'd like to see that one."

"I don't thinkit would ever get to that point. I'm just saying if it comes down to it."

"Let's hope it doesn't."

"So anyways, last night I'm at my friend Ricky's house, right?"

"Yeah?"

"Well, he wanted to have some girls over so I told him about Erin and he begged me to make the call, but I didn't wanna call her directly for personal health reasons, so I called that wannabe pimp Gabe and asked him to rustle up some pussy."

"Why didn't you call me? Gabe ain't the man, I'm the man!"

"Dude, I was in the Lakes of the Four Seasons and I didn't have your number."

"Oh."

"So he shows up with the bitch Erin and some of her friends, like, around 10:00 or so."

"Like who?"

"Well, that girl Milada for one."

"Milada, hah!"

"Yeah, and that girl Jolene and her friend who looks like Betty Boop."

"Lisa Diamond?"

"Yeah. Her."

"She's fine ain't she?"

"If you say so. Sorta. I guess. She's just ok for me."

"Com'n, Ray. That bitch is good to go!"

"What," I joked. "Like a bucket of hotwings?"

"Exactly," The Brain said.

"All right, so they come over and Erin disappears with my friend Patrick for a *really* long time, at least an hour, and I'm thinking, ok, just diss me after I invite your *slutty* ass to a party."

"Hah, what a whore! I ain't surprised I'll tell you that right now."

"Yeah. So I end up leaving at midnight without even talking to her, and to top it off I had to give that Milada a lift all the way back to G-town."

"Uh oh," The Brain said. "Now you're really playing. Milada's boyfriend is pretty much a pussy though, hoss. If you can't take him you should just shoot yourself in the head right now."

"No, I'm not playing her though. I just gave her a ride. That's all."

"Go on."

"Right. So I'm giving her a ride and she say's how much she likes Green Day, and I can't stand them, but that's beside the point. She starts grilling me about everything."

"Like what?"

"Like smoking weed, and then she says Erin says I like her, and only certain guys like Erin."

"Hah! What kinda guy?"

"Ones that, quote, wanna have sex with her, unquote."

"Fuck, that would just about include any guy who likes any girl."

"Tell me about it. I have never had any other reason for liking a girl that's for sure. So that's what I told her, but anyways she tried to get me to admit that I liked Erin. And I was starting to think someone put her up to it, like the whole, *give me a ride home thing*, was some kinda plan. It was just really weird. These Granite people are a lot more complex than I originally thought."

"That's strange," The Brain agreed. "Her and Erin are best friends, so I wouldn't be surprised if she ran back to Erin and reported everything you said to her. So did you ever find out if Erin ever did anything with your friend?"

"No I haven't found out yet. Erin denied anything went on, but I won't know until I ask Patrick. He'll tell me, and when he does I'll fill you in."

"So what are you doing tonight?"

"I'm going to that party. What about you?"

"Same. Need a lift?"

"Yeah, that would be really cool. Oh, and you know I just talked to Erin too."

"You did?"

"Yeah and, like I just said, she says nothing happened with her and Patrick, and she said everybody is always accusing her of liking people, and I'm like, well if you get wasted and run off with some dude what am I supposed to think?"

"You said that to her," he asked.

"No, but I was thinking it. I just told her to chill."

"Is she going to this party, because if she is you better stay away from her if people are watching."

"No she's gonna get tattoos with that girl Lisa Diamond."

"*What*, don't you have to be eighteen to get a tattoo?"

"She claims to know someone."

"She probably knows more dudes than you think," The Brain said and we both laughed.

"You know," I said. "That Jolene is a really cool girl."

"Hell yeah. She's cool as hell. She's the first person I hung out with when I moved here from Hammond."

"What's her boyfriend like?"

"James Chapman? He's ok. They've been going out for, like, four fucking years."

"Get the hell outta here. That's a long time for kids."

"I ain't lying."

"Hey listen: I'm heading to Kentucky Fried Chicken to get some hot-wings," I said. "What time you picking me up tonight?"

"9:30, 10:00 at the latest."

"Cool. See ya then. Just buzz the door."

And we hung up.

I grabbed five bucks from my safe and I went down to the Bonneville. I brought a Pearl Jam tape into the car with me and I listened to *Betterman* while warming up the engine. On the way to KFC I got pulled over for going 40mph in a 30mph zone. It was a bullshit ticket, but bullshit or not it cost me a hundred and twenty-five bucks that I didn't have. It was a good thing I wasn't smoking a joint because then I would have spent the rest of the weekend in the slammer. Ari would hate me for not following through on my end of the deal. And as soon as I got out Erin's gorilla boyfriend would pound me into something that resembles a pile of somebody who just jumped from the Empire State Building.

Once I got to KFC I pulled around to the drive-through.

"Welcome to Kentucky Fried Chicken. May I help you?"

"*Uh*, yeah, *um*," I said. "Lemme get a, *uh*, twenty piece hot-wings and, *um*, a large Coke or Pepsi. Huge. Or whatever the hell you guys have. And that's it."

"So that's a twenty piece hot-wings and a large Coke. Will that be everything for you today, sir?"

"Yes, *ma'am*."

"Your total is four-ninety-five. Please pull around to the second window."

"Thank you," I said and I pulled up to the second window and read the speeding ticket while I was waiting. Boy that really fucking sucked! I didn't even have a job. Where was I gonna get that kinda cash? I lit a cigarette and folded up the ticket and put it in my wallet. Then I heard the sliding glass window open.

The girl said, "Four-ninety-five please. *Ahhhh*," she screeched. "Raymond, what are you doing here?"

I was startled and I looked up and it was Milada. Another girl walked over to see. She was ok looking and she had long blonde hair.

"Oh, I've seen you," the other girl said. "You go to our school."

"Yeah, I do. I guess. Depending on what school you go to."

"Raymond, this is my friend Mindy. Her uncle *owns* this place."

"Yeah, my uncle owns this place," Mindy said.

"Yeah, that's what I hear."

"Gosh, I'm so embarrassed you saw me here, Raymond," Milada said and her cheeks turned red in a way like my car window starts to fog up.

"Jesus, Milada there's nothing wrong with working here. I don't even *have* a job."

"You don't?"

"No, but I'm gonna have to get one real quick. I just got a huge speeding ticket and I need money to pay for it."

Mindy walked away and came back with my Coke and she handed it to me.

"Thanks," I said.

"You're welcome," Mindy said. "Do you like Milada? Because she likes you."

"Say what," I grunted. "What a retarded thing to say to somebody."

"*Mindy*," Milada yelled. "God! What's the matter with you?"

"Sorry," Mindy said. "It was a joke," and she walked away.

"I don't know why she would say that. I don't like you. She is sooo not funny. She was joking about how everyone says you like Erin."

"Thanks."

"You know what I mean. I mean, I like you, but as a friend. I have a boyfriend," she smiled uncomfortably.

"So I've heard."

"From your secret informant again," she asked, trying to joke.

"Yeah, exactly."

"I'm jealous," she said. "Because you have a secret informant and I don't."

"Yeah. Well, I must be pretty lucky. Look, this conversation is gripping, really, but I've gotta jet. Is that chicken almost ready? And what are you doing tonight," I asked.

"What are *you* doing," Milada asked me back.

"I'm going to this party," I said.

"Anthony Falco's party?"

"Yeah, I think that's his name, you going?"

"I'm going. I'm going with Mindy and our friend Susa Beverly."

"Who's Susa Beverly? I don't think I've met her."

"You might have seen her at school," Milada said. "She's got straight brown hair down to here, *um*, she's really skinny, and really cute."

"Does *she* have a boyfriend?"

"Yes, *she* has a boyfriend," Milada said in a snotty way.

"Does he go to Granite also?"

"No, he goes to Lake Central."

"Oh, that's fucking great," I was disgusted.

"You have a problem with people from Lake Central, Raymond?"

"Oh, we go way back, babe. A bunch of those fuckers jumped me once and kicked me in the head a bunch of times."

"You probably deserved it," Milada suggested.

Just then Mindy came back with my paper bag full of chicken.

"Here you go, home-wrecker," Mindy said.

"That's funny to me."

I gave her my game face as I handed her a five and she went to get my change.

"So I guess I'll see you tonight," I said to Milada.

"Yeah," she smiled.

"Will your boyfriend be there, what's his name again?"

"Jason. No he won't be there."

"Why not? I've been looking forward to meeting him."

"Me and him have been fighting lately, so he's gonna see a band play in Hammond with his friend Mike."

"Oh well."

Mindy brought my change and I said "goodbye" to Milada and I drove off to eat my food. I was starving so I tore open that box of chicken and I starting chowing down on those little spicy legs and tossing the bones out the window. Back at home I devoured the rest of the hot-wings and I sank into the couch right next to my gut. I fired up a big phat joint and sucked down the rest of my Coke in—

between hits. After dinner I was baked beyond belief and I could hardly think. My heart was beating really fast, and every time I heard a car I kept peeking out of the window to see if anyone was pulling up into the parking lot. I was glad to be alone because I was feeling so paranoid. I went to the kitchen and drank a tall glass of water and then I went to the bathroom and dropped some Visine into my eyes. It didn't seem to help much, but at least I had the feeling that my eyes were clear and the high was decreasing instead of increasing.

I went and bolted the front door and then went into my room, put on my headphones, and put a Radiohead CD in my Sony Discman. Feeling exhausted, I fell down into my bed and closed my eyes and let the music carry me off to dreamland.

I had been home for almost week and still nothing good had happened and all of the sudden I was gripped with fear and slapped in the face by a blunt reality: *I made a big mistake by leaving Seattle.*

I shouldn't have come home and now I would be stuck in Granite, Indiana for the rest of my life. In twenty years I would be married to a woman that I wasn't attracted to and didn't love. I'd be smoking, drinking, and abusing my kids and the highlight of my week would be bowling on Saturday night. Oh God, it was a dreadful thought, but it was a realistic thought if I didn't start getting my act together. I had been back for almost week and already I needed to escape again. I was trapped. I was a fool. I tried to pass out.

I must have dozed off for at least an hour because when I woke up the music had stopped playing already and I was sweating. I sat up in bed and felt my heart pounding through my chest and I was taking one deep breath after another.

"I gotta quit smoking weed," I said to myself. "Shit's making me crazy."

It was almost 9:00 so I went to the bathroom and splashed water on my face and brushed my hair. I shaved and put on my nicest pair of boxer shorts (because you never know). Then I put on my new jeans and a black Champion hooded sweatshirt that made me look tougher. Granite parties were different from Andrean parties. At Andrean the idea was to look as sharp as possible while socializing. The guy who looked most like a girl got all the pussy. It was bizarro. And at Granite parties the purpose was to look as tough as possible. That's why the sweatshirt was a good bet, as well as anything black. I took out my earrings because I didn't wanna seem girlish. Even though it was freezing out I decided to go without a coat because the one that I had was a really expensive leather coat and I didn't wanna risk leaving it laying around at a strange house.

At about 9:45 the buzzer went off and I answered it quickly because I was expecting The Brain to pick me up any minute. It was him.

"Yo, let me in," he said.

"Just'a sec," and I buzzed the front door.

I heard multiple footsteps tromping up the stairs and I left the door open a crack and I went searching for my keys real quick. The Brain came inside with Jolene and two guys that I hadn't seen before.

"Yo," The Brain said.

"Hey," I said and I nodded to Jolene and the other two guys.

"You know Jolene," The Brain said. "And this is Billy Price," he put his hand on one guy's shoulder. "And this is Che Elias."

Billy Price was dressed normal in blue jeans and a T-shirt, but he had a really nice black leather jacket and lots of jewelry. Bling-Bling. He wore a gold chain around his neck with a gold cross hanging from the chain, typical of the Chicago area. He had gold rings on his fingers, and gold hoop earrings, and he had long brown hair that was tied in a braid and tucked into his jacket.

Che Elias had a shaved head, acne, and he wore black jeans that were tight-rolled, and a purple button-down shirt so ugly that it had to be from T.J. Max.

"What's up, guys," I said. "Have a seat."

They all took their coats off and sat down.

"You stay here by yourself," Billy Price asked.

"What kinda music you got," Jolene asked.

"*Um*, yes I'm by myself, and the CD's are there next to the stereo, Jolene."

"How do you pay the rent," Che Elias asked me.

"I don't. I'm just here for the time being. It's a condo. My old man owns the place, and he's in Florida."

"Oh that's a phatty deal," Jolene said as she slid a CD from the case and put it into the disc drive.

"What're you playing, sweet tits," The Brain asked.

"Mozart," she answered as *Le Nozze di Figaro* began blasting from the speakers. "I love classical music!"

"You get high," Billy Price asked me and pulled out a phat joint from his coat pocket.

"I invented getting high! Anybody wanna beer," I shouted.

"Everybody wants a beer, Ray," The Brain yelled. "Everybody."

I went to the stereo and turned down the volume.

"I'm sorry, Jolene. I'm tired of yelling. If this wasn't classical music I'd be evicted by now."

I went into the kitchen and opened the refrigerator and started filling my arms with five bottles of Old Style. I was thinking about the paranoid feeling that I experienced just a few hours before from smoking that weed. It worried me a little because until that day I had never felt any ill feelings from getting high. All of my pot escapades had been pleasant to say the least. I had also noticed lately that I had been getting these dull aches in my head. I felt them deep in my brain and they were soft pains, like a bruise that's almost healed. And the really strange thing about the aches was I only felt them when I shook my head really hard. I knew what it was all from. I had been smoking marijuana heavily for about five years by then, and I was eighteen years old during this time. And when I say heavily, I mean it. I was a heavy hitter. On average I smoked anywhere from two to five joints a day, and that's based on my own smoke intake, not what I shared with others, just me.

This was how my summer days went: Wake up and smoke, eat breakfast around ten and then smoke, eat lunch and then smoke, eat dinner and then smoke, recreational smoke later in the evening, right before falling asleep I'd smoke.

Doing the math I figure that I spent about 18,000 dollars on weed from the time that I was thirteen to the time I was eighteen. 18,000 dollars! Where did I get the money? Beats me, but I got it didn't I? I never had a job for very long and when I did I didn't earn much money. Most of the money was just what I got for birthdays or holidays from family. I bet at least eighty percent of that money went to buying dope bags; the other twenty percent probably went to fast food.

Sure I wanted to quit, but for some reason I couldn't. I didn't feel addicted and I didn't suffer any sickness from not smoking. If anything I felt better, mentally and physically. If I had to pick the roadblock of my quitting I'd say it fell on depression and the lack of a better thing to do for recreation. Besides, how can you quit when it's everywhere and everybody is doing it? How can you say no when someone offers it for free? How could I say no when Billy Price pulled out that thick-ass joint and started passing it around my living room?

I hit the joint and said with the smoke still in my lungs, "Ey Victor, how many peeble you thinks gonna be dere?"

I passed the joint to Jolene and The Brain said, "Fuck man, I don't know, fifty, sixty, a hundred, a lot of fucking people that's for sure. Everybody and their mother knows about this party."

"Do you guys think Clinton will be re-elected," Che asked us.

"Who fucking cares," The Brain said. "Who are you, Larry King? The election is like two fucking years away. All those bastards in Washington is all the same."

"That's not necessarily true," Jolene said. "No one is the same no matter where they are. Besides if you had read up on anything about Clinton's presidency, you'd know that unemployment is down, the economy is up, number of people on welfare is down, violent crime is down, and college enrollment among women is up."

"Yeah. Well, I ain't on welfare and I'm no college woman," The Brain let us know.

I said, "Hunter Thompson says Bill Clinton is a white trash hillbilly. No offense, Victor."

"Here, here," Che said and raised his beer in the air as a toast to The my comment. And then he goes, "Shit, violent crime ain't down around here."

"Yeah," Billy Price agreed. "If violent crime is down, they didn't include Gary in that statistic, because murders and rapes is way fucking high here and I never seen any president, governor, congressmen, mayor, or anybody ever do anything about this place. It just keeps getting worse and worse and worse."

I said, "What the hell are we gonna do for a living after high school?"

"Drive a truck," Che said.

"Pimp," Billy Price said.

"We can either work in them fucking mills or deal drugs. The choice is yours," The Brain gripped and he got up to take a leak. "Ain't America beautiful," he shouted while going to the bathroom with the door open.

"Speaking of politics. I guess we have an open door urinary policy," I shouted at The Brain.

When The Brain came back into the room Jolene said, "Why don't you guys shed the lazy shit and go to college if you want some opportunities? I'm doing it. I'm gonna be a doctor. One thing's for sure, I sure as hell ain't gonna sit around Granite, Indiana for the rest of my life feeling sorry for myself because I didn't get enough hand outs."

"Yeah, fuck that shit," I joked. "I'm gonna start lifting so I can get a football scholarship."

"They don't give free rides to water boys," The Brain had to tell me.

"I wanna do school sometime soon, maybe become a lawyer," Billy Price said.

He was Jolene's age and already outta high school.

"I just think that my life is too crazy right now to focus on school. I mean, I gotta freaked out mom with no job. I gotta dish out weed bags to pay her house payment, I got two warrants out for me and a third on the way, and I'm only twenty years old. I may not show it guys, but I'm fucking stressed out, like, all the time."

"You know what, Billy," The Brain spoke up. "You need to kick that old bag of bones outta your house."

"Who, his mom," Che asked. "Dude, your mom is old enough to take care of herself, don't you think, man?"

"Yeah, but she's my mom and I love her. That's all that counts for me."

"I'm gonna go to school," I said. "But first I'm gonna get the hell outta here."

"Dude," Brain said. "You just got back here. If you want out why in the hell did you come back?"

"That's a good question," I said. "For starters I had no money and I was living at my sisters, which basically sucked. I went to high school with nothing but Asians, which sucked. If I stayed I wouldn't have graduated on time, which would mean an extra year of this shit."

"You mean *that* shit," The Brain corrected me. "Over there in Seattle. *This* shit is right here."

"That would suck," Jolene laughed. "*Seriously.*"

"Tell me about it," I said. "And not only that, and you guys might think I'm nuts for saying this, but I had this weird feeling telling me I should come back home."

"Like a calling," Jolene asked.

"Yeah, definitely," I said. "Just like a calling."

"What did it say," Billy Price asked. "Was it, like, a fucking voice or something?"

"Maybe. If it was it was my own voice. I can't say what it said, I guess I don't know, but all I know is I had this powerful feeling I had something to take care of here, like, unfinished business."

"You're so high," Che laughed at me.

"Maybe so," I said. "But I'm an animal first, and a human second. If I'm a human in the woods and I come across a grizzly bear, my brain says maybe he ain't all that bad, maybe I should make friends with the bear. My animal instinct says to run up a tree like a fucking bastard on fire."

"Whatever that means," Jolene said. "Bears can climb trees."

"My point is I had an instinct to come home, to face up to

something, and I listened to that instinct, so here I am sitting around with you fucks getting high."

"I think your instinct is fucked up," Billy Price joked and he tapped me on the shoulder. "Enough with this voodoo talk, you guys ready to jet?"

"Word," I agreed and they got their coats on and drove over to the party in Billy Price's car.

6

It took us about ten minutes to get to the party and I had to sit in the back of Billy Price's car, wedged between Che and The Brain. The Brain smelled like Claiborne for Men and Che smelled like he took a shower in Drakar Noir. Between the two of them I thought I was in a crowded strip-joint.

The house was on a quiet neighborhood street at the end of a cul-de-sac. The whole street was filled with parked junker cars on both sides and there were stray trunk kids wandering about looking drunk and confused.

We all walked in through the front door of Anthony Falco's house in a single file line, Jolene was first and I was last. There was some kinda odd sounding instrumental Techno music coming from the stereo that created a dangerous and mysterious mood for the party. We all squeezed our way between the people and climbed up the stairs to the main floor.

I felt like people were watching me. In the living room all of the furniture had been cleared out and there were tons of people dancing. A fake-ass hippie kid was kneeling in the middle of the dance floor and he was slapping his palms in a rhythm on a pair of those gay-ass Congo drums, so trendy and boring. All of the lights were off except for the strobe light flickering rapidly, making everything seem like it was in slow motion. I suspected that somebody had passed around some **Acid**. Whoever it was, I wanted to locate the **Acid** distributor immediately so I could establish some kinda common ground with this fiend.

It was so crowded that after five minutes I was totally separated from the people I drove over with and as I looked around for them, I didn't see anyone that looked familiar, so I just stood against the wall and watched everyone trip out. If anybody wanted to know, I'd tell them I was just waiting for somebody. In a way I was. I was waiting for that Tim Miller guy that Ari wanted me to talk to. The only problem was I didn't know what he looked like. The place was so packed I didn't think I could find him even if I knew him. I thought I'd look for somebody who looked like they had a scorching case of AIDS.

That shit should be easy to spot, I honestly thought.

Another brok-ass hippie walked up to me and yelled into my ear, "Got weed, got **Acid**."

I shook my head *yes* and I gave him a five-dollar bill for a square. He went into the bathroom and then came out a minute later and he slipped me a little piece of folded up aluminum foil. You had to put it in foil because the **Acid** would absorb into most things, especially paper. It would even seep into your skin if you touched it, so when you cut a square from the sheet you had to use tweezers and a tiny pair of scissors. I put the **Acid** in my pocket because I didn't want to drop it until after I talked to the man of the hour about his surprise disease, not to mention his sprouting little fetus.

People started passing around joints and I managed to get two hits before they disappeared. Somebody grabbed my shoulders from behind and I couldn't see who it was at first. It was Milada, and she said something I couldn't hear. I nodded in a *hello* sorta way and she pulled on my arm and we went downstairs to the TV room where there was a different crowd of people, but it was quiet enough to hear what people were saying to each other. There were mostly a bunch of Prep and Jock-type dudes down there watching the Bulls game on the big screen. This wasn't the place for me, so I told myself I'd listen to what Milada had to say and I'd go back to where I felt more at home, with the dumb-ass hippies and the stoners. Milada still held my arm and pulled me through the people. She was looking around for something. She seemed frantic. Then we spotted Gabe there playing pool with a bunch of guys.

"Yo," Gabe yelled. "I knew you two would hit it off eventually!"

"Gabe, I *have* to talk to you about something," she said in a panicky sorta way.

"Ok, well I'll just call you later about that, now go on and have a good time with my buddy there," and he winked at me.

I smiled.

"*Now*," she yelled and grabbed his arm and led us down the hall to the bathroom. We went inside and she shut the door and locked it.

"*Milada*," Gabe said in a sly way. "I never would've guessed," he joked, suggesting a threesome.

One thing about Gabe is that he always had something perverted to say when chicks were around.

"Save it, Gabe!" Gabe disgusted her. "Save it for your *beat off session.*"

"*Ohhhhh*," I moaned like she threw a Mike Tyson punch. "*Beat off session.*"

"Jeez, what the hell is with you, girl," he probed.

"I heard some guys were looking for Raymond."

"*Huh*," I sighed.

"So what! Those guys ain't gonna do shit to Ray. They're not gonna do shit to you, Ray," he said to me and then turned back to Milada. "You know he's safe here, why the hell you trying to freak the kid out? Jesus H. Christ you're lucky he hasn't dropped any," and then he stopped himself cold with a thought. "*Whoa*, Ray! You didn't drop any of that **Acid** that's going around did you?"

"Not yet."

"Shit," Gabe soothed himself. "You almost had me freaked out there a second."

Milada took a deep breath and turned to me. "Jeremy Otsap wants a bunch of his friends to jump you tonight."

"*Jump me*," I questioned.

"Raymond, they wanna kick your ass. I think you should leave," she told me.

"Wow, that's heavy. I bet it's the guys down here watching TV, no doubt," I said. "Jocks always hated me for some reason. I don't know why, and what really confuses me about it is, I used to be a Jock myself. I can't figure out why they would single me out like this. I look enough like them to fit in, don't I?"

"Right on, Raymond. Sure if that's what you wanna hear then you look like a Jock, ok? Now please go home so nothing happens," she pleaded.

"Milada," Gabe said. "Will you just chill for a second? There's no need for anyone to be running home. Those guys like Mitchell and Rodriguez, all they do is talk trash and they never do anything about it. Why should Ray's case be different? Besides, when all of you girls start talking like, *oh that Raymond is so cute*, and then you start abusing your boyfriends in the next breath, of course they're gonna wanna kick his ass. So if anyone should go home, it's all you rumor starting girls."

"Bullshit, Gabe. You know I don't do that with my boyfriend!"

"You never said Ray was good looking in front of Jason?"

"Gabe, *shut up*," she bitched. "Not now!" She turned to me. "Raymond, don't listen to Gabe. He's drunk and he doesn't know what he's saying."

"Yes I do!"

"No, Gabe. You don't! Raymond will you *please* leave?"

"I would, but I can't"

"Why?"

"Why," they both asked at the same time.

"Because I need to talk to somebody first."

"*Who*," Milada asked.

"Tim Miller, you guys know him?"

Gabe laughed and said, "Yeah we know him, and apparently he knows you already too. He's the leader of all the redneck posse in Granite and he's Otsap's best friend. He's not exactly harmless either."

"Gabe, will you just shut up," Milada said. "Raymond, you can't talk to Tim. He's one of the guys who wants to kick your ass."

"Seriously?"

"Yes, Raymond."

"She's right, Ray," Gabe said. "But it ain't no big deal. Seriously. If you wanna talk to him, I say let's go talk to him. Right now in fact. I got your back, man. Trust me, nothing is gonna happen."

"Gabe, you're wrong," Milada said.

"No, Milada," I said. "I hear what you're saying, but I think Gabe is right. I've had lots of guys wanna kick my ass and it hardly ever actually happens. Besides, last summer I got stomped by thirty some odd Lake Central guys and I came out all right. It doesn't get any worse than that, so what's the worst that could happen by me talking to this guy?"

"Raymond! *Please,*" she pleaded. "You have to listen."

"Milada, I did listen and I see your point. I really do. The thing is though; I can't always run away from my problems, especially when I haven't even done anything wrong, you know? Besides, I've spent the last four years of my life living in an East Chicago where dudes get shot at on the street corner. Shit like that makes you tough, Milada. These guys out there, they're from Candyland. As far as I'm concerned they're harmless. I wonder if they really know what they're getting into by fucking with me. I'm not saying I'm a bad-ass and I can kick anyone's ass whenever I wanna or anything, but what I'm saying is: I just don't fuck around when it comes to issues like this. What I have to talk to that Tim Miller kid about has nothing to do with Erin, or me, or you guys. I'm gonna go out there and that's exactly what me and him are gonna do. *Talk.* We're just gonna talk about something. Peacefully. And if he wants to prove something to his friends afterwards by kicking my ass, well, then he can sure as hell give it his best shot, because I ain't about to lie down and take a beating from those fucks out there. I'll take a few of them out with me before I go down. That's a promise."

"*Fucking awesome,*" Gabe shouted. "Let's go!"

"You're with me, Gabe," I was excited.

"Fuck yeah!"

We went for the door and Milada stood in front of us, "Raymond, Gabe," she said. "Just promise me that you won't do anything stupid. Promise!"

"We promise," we said simultaneously.

Once outside the bathroom, we discovered that most of the Jocks had gone elsewhere. The TV was turned off and the pool table, the balls freshly broken, looked as if it had been stopped in mid-game.

"Hey," Gabe yelled to a kid who was passing out on the couch. "Hey!"

"*Huh*, yeah, *uh* ..." the kid moaned and looked around the room.

"Dude," Gabe said. "Where'd everybody go, man?"

"They were psyched about something, Gabe. I think they're outside or whatever. There's gonna be a fight and shit."

"Ok, this is it," Gabe said to me.

Milada was standing right behind me looking worried.

Gabe kept talking, "I'll go talk to Tim Miller and ask him to meet with you in private somewhere. He'll probably take it as a challenge so I'll try to keep him calm. What are you gonna talk to him about anyway?"

"I think he might have AIDS."

"*Ok*," Gave laughed. "Well, *that's* the funniest thing I've heard all day that's for sure. I'm sure you'll fill me in later, eh?"

"For sure," I said.

"All right then," Gabe said. "Milada, here's my car keys. I want you to pull my car around to the front of the house and leave the engine running just in case. You're gonna be the get-away driver, got it," Gabe asked her as he handed over the keys.

"Fudge, Gabe. You guys are giving me the biggest headache," she said.

When somebody says the word fudge in front of me I want to vomit. That's a born-again Christian hillbilly expression.

"Raymond, why can't you just leave?"

"It's way too late for that, Milada," Gabe said.

"Yeah," I said. "It is way too late. And please, I hate it when people say *fudge*. It's the worst."

We all went outside through the front door and Milada went off to fetch Gabe's car. The Brain, Billy Price, Che, and Jacob Drake were all outside smoking cigarettes when Milada hurried off looking scared.

"Hey, guys," The Brain said looking worried. "What the hell is going on? I need to talk to Ray a second, Gabe."

"Victor," Gabe said. "We are *fucking* aware of the crisis here, and Ray is fully prepared to settle this in the front yard."

"I am," I said. "I'm prepared."

"*Bullshit*," The Brain said. "There's *forty* of them fucking guys back here! Just go home, Ray. Don't listen to Gabe, he's fucking nuts. Everybody knows about him, just go!"

"Victor," I said. "There's something else going on that I have to talk to that Tim Miller kid about."

"Like what," The Brain asked. "Like him fucking that bitch Ari behind his girl's back? Everybody knows about that shit too. Just go home, man. There ain't nothing for you to prove here. Billy Price and me will give you a ride. Right, Billy?"

"Yeah, Ray Man. We'll give you a lift home."

"There's more to it then that, Victor," I said.

"Like what, man? What's so important that you need to get the shit kicked outta you?"

"Tim Miller has the AIDS virus and only Ray knows about it," Gabe blurted out.

"Now that's funny," The Brain laughed. "God. Why is that funny? Is there something wrong with me?"

Billy Price and Jacob Drake started laughing also and so did Gabe and I because it did sound funny.

"Get the fuck outta here," The Brain said in disbelief. "AIDS?"

"It's true, man," I said.

"Then I guess you better tell him what's up," Jacob Drake said. "We'll follow you guys to make sure no monkey business goes down."

"Dudes," I said to them as Milada pulled the car around and parked right at the end of the driveway. "I'm gonna wait here. Send the guy out front and just be ready when you do, because if any of those guys tries anything sneaky I'm hitting first, so send him alone if possible. This is serious shit I have to tell him."

Jacob Drake said, "AIDS is serious, bitches." And everybody started laughing again and the guys walked around to the back yard and I walked over to Gabe's car and Milada rolled the window down to talk to me.

"Raymond, this is so bad. I've never seen anyone fight before, and the last person I want to see fighting is you."

"That's sweet," I said sarcastically. "I'm touched. Really I am."

"No, it's not sweet. I'm freaking serious, Raymond. I hate violence!"

"Well, I'm not planning on fighting anybody so don't worry. I don't think this guy will be in the mood for fighting after he hears what I'm about to tell him."

"God, I just don't want anyone to do anything dumb. Oh Lord," she said and rubbed her forehead. "Do you have a cigarette?"

I took out my pack and gave her one. I held out my lighter and lit it while she clutched the smoke between her full lips. They were painted dark red. She squinted her eyes and sucked in to get the fire started.

"Somebody's here," she said as smoke leaked from her nose and mouth. "I think it's him."

I turned around and sure enough, it was *him*, Tim Miller. Alone. At least I figured it was him because I didn't know what in the hell he looked like. At first I froze as our eyes locked. He looked pissed off and I wanted to say something, but I was tongue-tied. He didn't look like he was carrying a case of AIDS at all. He looked fully capable of anything. A song sprang out in my imagination. It was the basic instrumental chords from *Three Days* by Jane's Addiction and hearing this, the situation felt just like a showdown.

"You by yourself," Tim Miller shouted to me.

He looked a lot different than I imagined. I pictured him to be tall, brown hair, nice looking, something like that, a big hillbilly-type of Jock. He wasn't like that though. He was rough looking. He had short blonde hair and was already going bald and he had on scruffy jeans and a rock-n-roll black shirt that was showing underneath a black jean jacket. He reminded me of someone that would become a Hell's Angel someday. He had the look of a maniac.

"I'm alone, man," I managed to say. My voice squeaked from fear.

"What's *she* doing here?"

I turned and looked at Milada in the car. "Get the fuck outta here, Milada," I shouted over my shoulder.

"But—"

"Get outta here!"

She quietly rolled up the window and drove off down the street. I hoped I didn't hurt her feelings, but I felt a ruthless shout was necessary at such a tense moment. I'd apologize later.

"*There*," I said.

He took outta cigarette and lit it with a match and then walked over to me. I was ready for him to knock my block off. I had seen it done before: a guy lights a cigarette to distract the opponent, makes him think he's not a threat at the moment, and then *POW*! But Tim Miller had no reason to do this. From the looks of him; he could easily destroy me at any moment. He didn't need any tricks up his sleeve.

"Gabe says you wanted to tell me something," he said to me as I noticed a bunch of people starring at us from the shadows, waiting to see the action.

I took outta cigarette myself and put it into my mouth.

"Got a light?" I asked him.

He took outta match and lit it. I was scared shitless and I smoked to make him think that I wasn't afraid of him. As he lit my cigarette I looked at the people in the shadows again and said, "Can we go for a walk?"

"Sure," he said and we strolled down the street and started to talk.

"Look," I said. "I know that you wanna kick my ass, but there's something that I've gotta say to you that will probably make you wanna kick my ass even more." I took a deep breath and continued, "But it's something I have to do because I made a really serious promise to somebody, and it's something I can't break, no matter what the circumstances are. So can I just say it, and then we can get on with the other issues?"

"Go for it," he laughed softly.

I sensed that I was amusing him.

"Ok," I said. "Well, promise that you won't do anything until

I'm finished saying it, because it ain't an easy thing to tell somebody, so I'm not sure where to start, so there's a good chance I might say something stupid."

"I promise," he said.

His promise sounded empty and meaningless.

"It's about Ari," I started.

"You sleeping with her?"

"No, I'm not. Fuck no. I swear to God."

"I wouldn't care if you were, but don't lie to me. She ain't my girl so she can do whatever she wants to, just don't lie to me."

"I ain't. I ain't lying, I swear.

I always tell the truth like Tony Montana on Scarface. Even when I lie.

"What is it then," he said as he flicked his cigarette butt into a flowerbed.

We saw Milada driving really slowly up the street.

"What the hell is she doing," he asked me.

"She's just worried about me. She's harmless."

"All right."

"Well, today I saw Ari at the mall."

"She works during the daytime. Weren't you at school?"

"I ditched."

"Right."

"Well, she started warning me about Erin Watkins, and I told her nothing was going on, and there ain't nothing going on with me and Erin. I swear to fucking God."

"And?"

"And we went and grabbed some lunch and I asked her if she could get Jeremy Otsap off my back for me, since you guys are friends with her brother. I don't mind getting my ass kicked because it's happened plenty of times, but I don't like getting beat up for no reason. That really sucks."

"I wouldn't know," he openly admitted to me.

"Anyway, she said she would try, but then she wanted me to do something for her."

"Hah," he chuckled. "That sounds like her, always wanting something in return. You know, last year she was the teacher's aide in my Black History class. *Black History*," he said sounding amazed. "Why the hell are they teaching black history in Granite? We hate black people and they hate us. You believe they teach that shit nowadays?"

"No, that's crazy," I agreed.

"Anyway, stupid class or not, I needed to pass the final in order to graduate. She got me a copy of the test and showed me the answers. I passed and then three weeks later she wanted me to sleep with her for it. *Fucking whore*, I thought. She told me this crap about how she loved me, and didn't give a shit about my girl. She's hot though so I ended up sleeping with her, which was a big mistake, because after I tried to break it off she freaked out and started telling me all of these lies. I think she has mental problems. She's told me twice that she was pregnant. Both times I made her take a test in front of me and both times it came up negative. The last time was just a couple of days ago. You know why she's fucked up don't you?"

"No, I don't," I said.

"For one thing I think her dad used to fuck around with her a little bit. Creepy shit, dude. Creepy. And then she went to Boston, rumor has it that she was raped by some guy at a college party. She dropped outta school and came home. She's been acting weird ever since."

"You're kidding," I said. "I'm starting to feel really stupid right now, I think what she wanted me to tell you is probably a bunch of bullshit. Maybe we should just forget about it."

"No, I wanna hear it," he insisted.

"Really?"

"Absolutely. Even if it's just for the comedy."

I took a very deep breath, and then I spit it out.

"She told me that she had AIDS, and was worried that you might too. She wanted me to break the news to you tonight."

"That's funny," he smiled. "AIDS?"

"Maybe it's funny now, but it sure as hell wasn't very funny when she was telling me. I feel like a fucking idiot now."

"Don't sweat it," he said. "It took a lotta guts for you to say something like this to me. Most guys are afraid to say anything to me."

"Aren't you pissed or afraid that what she said is true?"

"Nah," he sighed. "She's a really messed up person and what she needs is some psychological help. I seriously hope she gets it."

"That totally pisses me off that she put me up to this. Fuck, I got fifty guys just waiting to kick my ass back at the party."

"Yeah, but that's because of Erin Watkins. It ain't got nothing to do with Ari Lopez. This is all about Erin. Her boy Jeremy Otsap is pretty pissed at you. I would try to go on vacation next time he's in town if I were you."

"Hold up, listen to me for a second," I pleaded. "I've never done nothing with Erin Watkins. All I did was get a lift to school from her and then all these rumors started flying around town. I don't know if it's her who's starting the rumors or not. I really don't know what's going on."

"Yeah, I believe you, but unfortunately Jeremy is a hothead and just getting a lift to school is enough for him. See the thing is, he's madly in love with that girl, but he can't trust her. It drives him fucking crazy sometimes."

"What should I do?"

"For starters, stay away from her. She's got a boyfriend, man. And maybe if you're lucky everything will blow over. Look, I'll tell Jeremy that nothing is going on and maybe he'll chill out after that."

"Jesus, thanks man. I would really appreciate that."

"But, if I find out that you're lying to me, and you really are messing around with Erin Watkins, I'll personally come find you and kill you for making me look stupid."

"All right, it's a deal," I said and I extended my hand to shake.

He didn't reach back and left me hanging. He just looked at me and then he started to say something and I knew that something was up. My eyes grew as wide as Tom and Jerry saucers as my body filled with a dark alley fear.

"Oh, there's just one more thing," he said.

We stopped under a streetlight and looked at each other. He

smiled at me and then he punched me in the face. I went black and felt my body land hard onto the sidewalk. I was out cold.

7

When I opened my eyes, Tim Miller was kneeling down over me and holding my face with his huge beefcake hands—hands specially created to be natural meat tenderizers, like my head was globe that lost it's axel. My cheek stung really badly where he had hit me, but considering I had just gotten laid out on the sidewalk I felt decent enough. At least I still had all of my teeth and no part of my face was spewing blood all over the concrete.

"I'm sorry, man," he apoligized to me as if it was an accident. "Are you ok? I barely even hit you. I didn't wanna, but I had to."

"I didn't see anybody with a gun to your head, Tim," I moaned and sat up. "Fuck, man. That hurts real bad."

"I had to hit you. It was for your own good, Ray. This way people will still think they can't fuck with me, and Jeremy Otsap will be satisfied and he won't come looking for you when he gets back. It's a win-win situation for both of us. It is. I swear to God. You understand? You ok, man?"

"Yeah. Yeah. Totally. I'm fine," I said as he helped me to my feet.

I touched my face and mouth and looked at my fingertips for bloodstains.

"Better one punch from me than ten to twenty from Jeremy. I'll tell you that shit right now. You'll thank me later."

"No, I don't think that I will," I laughed. "But I do see your point."

"Com'n, man. Don't make me feel bad. You're not bleeding. I didn't hit you *that* hard. You got a little shiner starting, but that's about it."

"I guess you're right, man," I said. "I just wasn't expecting it. That's all."

"Yeah. Well, I think you should go home for now. It'll look weird if we both go and hang out at the same place after we fought."

"You call that a fight," I laughed again.

"Don't worry. I'll tell all the other guys you put up a good fight."

"Thanks," I was sincere. "Catch you later I guess."

I started walking down the street in a daze towards my dad's apartment. I wondered where Milada was with the car, because I was starting to really feel the cold. Too bad I left my jacket at home. If it hadn't been for mass amounts of adrenaline rushing through my veins from being hit, I'd freeze to death.

"*Hey*," Tim shouted to me from about forty feet away.

I turned and looked at him.

I was shivering.

"Call me if you wanna get some beers sometime or something. We'll keep it on the *down-low*. The Brain knows my number."

"Ok," I hollered back and I walked on into the frigid Indiana winter night.

I never did see Milada and by the time I walked all the way home, my feet were frozen and so were my ears. My damn ears were stinging so bad I thought they were gonna crack up and fall off my head. My fingers were so numb and the air was so cold that it was starting to hurt to breathe. To top it off my cigarettes were gone. Tim had probably taken them while I was knocked out.

"What," I was talking to myself. "That nigger went and ran off with my smokes. Either that, or they fell outta the pocket of my sweatshirt."

It was a good thing that I wasn't carrying any cash. I didn't have enough to be carrying around. All I had left was the remnants of what I had scrounged together to make the trip back home. It was the meager three hundred-dollar profit I received as payment from unloading my seventy-five Volkswagen Bus onto some dirty hippie from Bellingham, Washington. This made me think of the speeding ticket that I had gotten earlier and I promised to myself, as I trotted up the stairs to my apartment, I'd get a job tomorrow, or the next day, or maybe a few days after that.

Once I got inside I started a fire in the fireplace and I went to the stereo and put on some Ice Cube, the *Lethal Injection* album. I didn't turn the volume up very high though. I just wanted some background music so that I wouldn't have to listen to myself think. I looked at the clock and it was only eleven-thirty. Erin was supposed to stop by around midnight. I touched my sore cheek and thought I had a lot to talk to her about. The Brain was right. She sure was trouble. She was lots and lots of trouble, and I had only known her for a week. I wondered why I kept letting her get her foot in the door. I figured every guy goes through this stage with women, where they tend to be attracted to psycho bitches from hell. I love crazy ladies. I'm like a lion-tamer.

I went to my room to check out my face in the mirror. It wasn't looking nearly as bad as it felt. It hurt like hell just to touch under my eye, but all that was there was a small red lump and a tiny little cut that hardly bled at all. I went to the medicine cabinet in the bathroom and washed the wound and put some anti-infection cream all around the abrasion. Luckily there was still one Band-Aid left in the box and I put it right over the cut and under my eye. It looked kinda cool, like I was a boxer in some movie. Raging Bull or some shit. The phone started ringing and I ran into the kitchen and answered it.

"Hello?"

"Ray!"

"Hey, Gabe."

"Dude, what in the hell happened out there? Tim Miller said you guys had a scrap and then you took off!"

"Yeah. The guy basically kicked my ass right there on the sidewalk."

"Because of what you had to tell him?"

"No. Because of that bitch Erin. Her boyfriend put a bounty on my head."

"Did you tell him about the other thing that we talked about in the bathroom? You know, the *syndrome*," And then Gabe started laughing.

"No. Actually I didn't tell him. The situation tumbled outta control."

"I heard if you use some Preperation H before anal sex it stops you from getting AIDS. I heard somebody say so during detention last year."

"Maybe you should find out."

"So you didn't tell him about his AIDS?"

"No."

"Why not?"

"I'm starting to think that the AIDS thing I was supposed to talk to him about isn't true, so I dropped it. You guys didn't tell anybody did you?"

"No, we didn't. As a matter of fact The Brain, Billy Price, me and Jacob, we all swore that we wouldn't tell anybody because none of us wanna be next on that guy's hit list, but you can't expect it to be a secret for long, especially in this town."

"Yeah right, Gabe. You guys think it's fucking hilarious. Everytime I bring it up you guys laugh about it. I even think it's kinda funny and I just got beat up for it. How could you *not* tell everyone?"

"Ok so I told a few people. It's funny, man! What am I supposed to do. Don't worry though, Ray. Nothing will happen. Nobody believes that shit. If anything it makes Ari look stupid for making shit up. It'll totally fly under the radar with the rumors and shit."

"Let's hope it does because he hits really hard. He knocked me out cold."

"Dude," Gabe said with a sudden burst of energy. "You don't know the half of it. When we were freshman, Tim Miller and some other kids were mowing a lawn, they had a, *uh*, like, this cracker-jack lawn care business one summer, and Tim's friend accidentally cut off Tim's freaking toe!"

"Which one?"

"The big toe!"

"Serious? He ain't got no big toe?"

"No. Yeah. Sorta. He's still got one, but they had to put it back on as best they could," he explained. "And when he got back from the hospital, after having his toe sewn back on and all, he went after this guy who cut off his toe and hit him in the head with a bat. I think he spent time in prison for it."

"A baseball bat?"

"Or a shovel."

"Jesus Christ."

"Maybe it was his belt or a rake or a wooden spoon. Whatever. I sure as hell wouldn't wanna be hit by that guy with anything. You're probably a legend now, Ray. I bet you're the first guy ever to be clobbered by him and lived. Ray Kozlowski! Death-Defying!"

Then I heard a girls voice whispering in the background and I asked him, "Who's that?"

"Milada."

"What's up with her?"

"She's all freaked out because she drove by and saw you laying on the sidewalk and Tim was over you looking through your pockets. She was too scared to stop, so she drove around and went back by there ten minutes later and you were gone. She thinks you're dead, so I'm gonna let you talk to her in a second here just as soon as we're finished. Where did he hit you?"

"He hit me in the face. What do you think, man? They only hit you in the gut in old black and white movies."

"And at Valparaiso High School parties," Gabe laughed.

"At Valparaiso parties they finish with trying to apply the head-lock."

"No, no," Gabe shouted into the phone. "Even better. At Valparaiso parties they fold up a piece of paper into one of them triangle-thingies and do that lame field goal kicking game like we do in summer school!"

"Ok."

"Tim said that you put up a good fight before he got you. He told everyone he was impressed, but we didn't know if he was joking or not."

"Yeah. I just blocked a few punches before he got me. I didn't hit him at all though."

"That's good, because he probably would've gotten pissed if you had."

"Where are you," I asked. "Are you still at the party?"

"Yeah. I'm still here. Do you mind if Milada and I stop by?"

"No, I don't care. I could use a little company I guess."

"Ok, I'll see you in a few. Hold on I'm gonna put freak girl on the phone."

"Sure," I said.

And I waited. I could hear myself breathing into the phone. So I started breathing really heavy like a pervert would, just to see what it sounds like.

"Raymond?"

"Hey, Milada."

"Oh my God, did you hear that? It sounded like breathing or something. Is somebody else on the line? Hello? *Hello?*"

"Nobody's on the line. I didn't hear anything. I swear."

"Are you all right? I saw you lying on the sidewalk."

"I'm fine. He just got me with a good one, but I'm ok."

"I'm so glad I didn't see it, and you sound ok. You are *sooo* brave, Raymond."

"Thanks. There was no reason to worry. I told you nothing really bad would happen."

"Raymond, what happened *was* really bad. I'm so freaked out by it. Can we come over and see you?"

"Yeah. I already told Gabe that you could. Who's all coming though, because I don't wanna have a big mob of people over here. I'm not holding a post-fight press conference tonight."

"Just me and Gabe."

"That's cool. When are you guys coming by?"

"Soon. We're leaving real soon."

"Ok, I'll see you then. Can I talk to The Brain? Is he around?"

"I don't know were he is, but I'll tell him to call if I see him."

"Ok."

"Ok. Bye, Raymond."

"Bye," I said and I hung up.

Right after I hung up with Milada, the door buzzer went off.

Somebody's here, I thought. *Shit, it must be her.*

I looked at the clock just as it struck midnight.

Erin, I thought. *Shit.*

I went out onto the porch to look down, because I didn't wanna let just anyone into my house at this time of night. Sure enough, there was Erin standing by the front door shivering in the cold. She was by herself and I was glad for that.

"Hey," I shouted down at her.

"Hey, Raymond! Lemme in. It's really cold."

"Ok, just a sec," I said.

I went to the front door and buzzed her in, and then I opened the door and waited for her to come upstairs. I wondered if she would notice my eye right away and if so, would I tell her the truth about what happened, and *why* it happened? Whatever I did, I sure as hell planned on confronting her on all these outrageous rumors going around about her and me. She really pissed me off, but as soon as I saw her coming upstairs, and I saw how pretty she looked in the dreary hallway, all of those angry feelings vanished like money in my pocket and I started to feel warmth towards this girl instead of hate. I didn't care about whether or not she had a boyfriend, or about me being beaten by any thugs anymore. I just wanted to be with her. Sure. She was definitely trouble, but at that moment she was worth it. She was a problem I'd like to have.

"Hi, Raymond," she smiled and approached me with her arms held out towards me. She had snowflakes melting in her hair and when they liquefied they turned into something like glitter in the light.

"Hey, Erin," I said and we hugged really tightly in a different way than how friends and relatives hug each other.

"Did you get your tattoo," I asked her as we released each other and went inside.

"Yeah. Do you wanna see it," she asked excitedly. "Well, you can't, because there's a *huge* bandage covering it."

"No biggie, but hold on a second. I wanna run downstairs and put a note on the front door for my uncle. I'll be back in a minute," I said and then went and found some paper and a pen and started writing.

"What do you have to tell him?"

"*Um*," I said. "My dad left him some money for me and I told him that I wouldn't be staying here, because my dad thinks I'm gonna have wild parties. I just wanna tell him I'll stop by his place to pick up the money in the morning."

"Why don't you just call him," she asked as she wandered around the living room and looked at the pictures on the wall.

"*Er*, because," I started to say as I was trying to think of something to tell her. "I can't remember his number. Besides he lives in the building so he'll see it."

I finished writing and read the note real quickly before running down stairs.

Gabe and Milada,

Sorry, but I had to run somewhere unexpectedly.
I'll call tomorrow. I'm fine and don't worry.

Ray

"Where did you park," I asked right before I ran downstairs.

She looked up at me and smiled, "Lisa Diamond dropped me off."

"Why didn't she come up?"

"Why? Do you like her too," she asked and stared at me.

"Nice try," I said and ran down the steps.

I pinned the note to the front door and then ran as fast as I could back upstairs. If Erin and I were gonna continue to hang out, no one could know about it. Not Milada, not Gabe, not anybody. Except for maybe The Brain because I had to confide in somebody. Patrick and Matt and Ricky, I'd have to tell them. They won't tell anybody. Jon would have to hear a story about this. But that's it. That's all the people I would tell. Secrets kept too long can drive a guy nuts. I really didn't feel like getting killed over this, but on the other hand, I couldn't help but have this girl in my life.

I almost freaked when I got back upstairs, because Erin was right on my balcony in plain view of any visitors to my apartment, and Milada and Gabe were about to show up any minute. I ran to the sliding glass door and opened it.

"Erin!"

"Jesus," she yelled and turned towards me looking startled. "You scared the *shit* outta me."

"Hey, I'm sorry. I was just gonna tell you you can't smoke out here because, *um*, well, you just don't have to. You can smoke inside. It's nice and warm in here."

"I don't mind the cold right now, Raymond. Stop acting weird and come and join me. I have a cigarette here for you."

"Look. I can't stand the cold. Can't you just come inside? There's something that I *really* need to talk to you about."

She smiled, "You sure I can smoke inside?"

"Positive. It's cool. Hurry along now."

"Raymond, what's the matter with you," she asked and walked inside.

I slid the door shut behind her and closed the blinds. Then I even peeked outside and watched for a few seconds.

She sat down and picked up a magazine and started flipping through it. "Expecting the police?"

"Not exactly. Just chill a second."

"Look who's talking," she said as I turned to her and we looked at each other in the light. "Raymond! What happened? Did somebody hit you," she stood up and touched my face. "You're eye is getting all swollen. I didn't even see it at first. It's so dark in here."

"You finally noticed, huh?"

"What happened?"

"Tim Miller kicked the shit outta me at that party."

"Tim Miller did this?"

She had a cold look to her all of the sudden as if what I had just told her was somewhat shocking. The sentence I had just said to her obviously carried a deep, secretive meaning to her.

All she could say was, "Why?"

She didn't say it in a concerned, sympathetic way. It was more like an emotionless say-it-ain't-so kinda way. I almost was gonna laugh as I watched her squirm.

"Why," I asked her back. "Because of your boyfriend."

"You must think I'm the biggest bitch," she said sadly.

I shrugged my shoulders.

"Look, I'm sorry ok!"

She burst into a rage and was yelling in my face.

"I tried to tell him it was over and he wouldn't listen! I tried to tell him the truth, Ray," she was crying now and acting really crazy.

I grabbed her arms and held her to chill her out, "Calm down, Erin!"

She started sobbing and she buried her head into my chest and just cried while I held her. I have to admit, she had me feeling really sorry for her. Even if this was an Academy Award performance, I just wanted to take care of her. I wanted to protect her forever.

We both sat down on the couch and she continued to cry. I got her some Kleenex and she blew her nose a coupla times.

"I told him I didn't love him anymore, and he asked why. He got so pissed off."

"What did you tell him? Why don't you love him?"

"Because there's someone else. That's what I told him."

"What did he say then?"

"He wanted to know who it was, and I was afraid to tell him because I didn't want him to get all violent again."

"But you did tell him, didn't you?"

"I told him that it was you, Raymond," she started sobbing again.

"But we haven't even done anything yet. We've only talked a coupla times!"

"I can't explain how I feel about you, Raymond. I just know, and I can't deny it, especially to Jeremy. I didn't wanna lead him on.

"Well, for some reason it didn't work out that way, and you led him right into my face."

"I'm so sorry, Raymond. I never wanted you to get hurt."

"I know. I know. It's ok."

"No, it's not ok. You got beat up because of me, because of my ex-boyfriend."

"He's really your ex?"

She stopped crying and looked up at me, "Yes. We're so fucking finished it's not even funny."

"I'm just saying, because I got my ass kicked, according to Tim Miller, because you and Jeremy are still going out."

"We broke up yesterday, over the phone."

"You know, I had to promise Tim Miller I wouldn't see you anymore. And he said if I did, he'd come after me again. And I have a feeling next time I won't get off so easily."

"Raymond, they can't keep us from seeing each other."

"That's easy for you to say."

"Raymond, don't worry. We can still see each other in secret, without anyone knowing about us. And maybe everything will blow over in a few months."

"How come you never told me you had a boyfriend?"

She paused before answering, "Because," she sniffled. And then she got this mean look in her eyes and she told me. "Because. We've only talked a few times. Why should I have mentioned it already? Even if I had, you don't like me anyway."

"Well, I do like you. I really do, Erin. So maybe your strategy worked."

"Really? You really do like me," and she looked up at me and I sank under the weight of her beauty.

"Really," I said. I moved a strand of hair from the front of her face and tucked it behind her ear. "I wanna ask you something."

"What is it?"

"Well, I wanna, or, well, would you mind, like, if I kissed you?"

I received a warm and welcoming smile, and we both leaned closer, slowly, closer, until we kissed. After that kiss, I was hooked good and she knew it. From then on all better judgment was tossed out the window and I was whole-heartedly in love with her, or so I thought. I must have gotten slapped with a gentleman spell, because I didn't try to push the envelope with Erin after that first kiss. I knew most teenaged guys like me would have immediately gone for that breast grab. Instead I just held her there on the couch and listened to her breathe in and out. I felt her heart beat against my chest and I was convinced, that, outside of actual lovemaking, humankind knew no better love experience. Wood from the fire crackled and the clock on the wall ticked and ticked. The fan inside the refrigerator clicked on and began to hum itself to a cooler temperature. And behind it all on the stereo, a young and racist Ice Cube rapped about bitches, money, killing cops, and oppression by equally racist whites. It was like poetry, happening.

8

I had just dropped Erin off at her house and there were hardly any other cars on the road on that harsh, gloomy, Indiana winter night. It was almost 3:00 in the morning and my eyes were sticky and heavy from the two hour conversation I had with Erin in front of the gas fireplace. It seemed like we talked about everything in the world and in the end we both decided that we would be together forever, no matter what. While we talked I played good music and we smoked a whole pack of Camel Wides between the two of us. My dad's CD player had a six disc drive and I filled it with my favorite CDs: Smashing Pumpkins' *Gish*, Pearl Jam's *Ten*, *The Anthology of Bread*, The Doors' *Greatest Hits*, James Brown's *Greatest Hits*, and Credence Clearwater Revival's *Greatest Hits*. It was the best night of conversation I had experienced in a long time. Maybe weeks.

I ended up crashing around 4:00 or 5:00 in the morning and didn't wake up until just before noon. I walked to the sliding glass door and pulled apart the blinds to let in some daylight. There was a fresh six inches of snow on the ground and it was still coming down thick.

"Gotta get a job," I told myself. "Today's the day to find work."

The economy was about as depressed as could be in The Region, mainly because Gary had become such a crime infested shithole, and the steel mills had destroyed the natural resources that were once abundant twenty years before. This made finding a decent job kinda difficult, especially when you're eighteen, have no reliable car, and no skills whatsoever. My options were basically hard labor, retail, or food service. I had to get a job that was close to home, just in case I had to walk to work sometimes. There was a fancy Italian

Restaurant called Jack's Mama's Place down the street, a Jewel super market on the corner, a Shell gas station with a carwash, and various fast food joints like McDonalds, KFC, Subway, Wendy's, White Castle, and Popeye's Chicken. I would rather become a male prostitute than to work at one of the fast food places, so I was hoping to God I could land a job at Jack's Mama's Place even if I had to wash dishes.

Of course, the first thing to do that day would be to get high, and then try to sell the other half ounce of weed I had stashed away. I could get eighty bucks for it and that would tide me over until I received some kinda paycheck from whatever future earnings lay in wait. I called Gabe.

"Hello?"

"Hey, Gabe," I said. "It's me."

"Yo! You're famous now. Congratulations!"

"What do you mean?"

"Oh, oh, oh! Just about the fight with Tim Miller. No one ever stood up to him before so everybody thinks you're crazy. Where in the hell did you go last night? Milada was bummed when you weren't home. We got there fifteen minutes after she got off the phone with you."

"I went to Kyle Shepherd's because he had somebody who wanted this half OZ and I needed the cash real bad, but it didn't work out so I ended up going there for nothing. Speaking of which, I was wondering if you knew were I could bounce this thing today or tomorrow."

"I'm sure I can. Totally. I'm sure of it. What's the finders fee?"

"Dude I'm not moving a pound. I was just asking as a favor."

"Surly you can spare something, Ray. I mean, whether it's a pound or half an ounce I'm still taking the same risk."

"How about half an eighth? It's all that I got handy, and you can pinch the bag I'm trying to sell also. It's bomb weed too, dude. I got it from that dude that I know in Gary."

"I'm gonna have to network a little first and I can't talk about this shit when my mom is in the house, so how about I stop by after I make a few calls and then I'll shit, shower, and shave, and then we can take care of *bidness*," he accented like a jive turkey.

"Sounds good, man. What are you doing tonight?"

"A whole lotta nothing," Gabe said.

"I think Ricky's having another party. This time it's supposed to be a *real* party. Are you down for some of that *cocaine* action?"

"Whoa, Ray. Chill with the cocaine talk on the phone."

"Gabe, you ain't even a drug dealer. Nobody's tapping your phone. So do you wanna go to the party or not?"

"Possibly. I'll know more later, ya know?"

"Sure, sure, sure, man. I'll call over to Ricky's and see what's happening. So stop by soon so we can get this shit rolling because I'm totally broke. Hey by the way, do you know were I can get a job?"

"I can get you a job where I work at Burger King."

"I don't know about that place."

"It ain't that bad. You can get high in the walk-in."

"How about something non-food related?"

"Couldn't tell ya."

"Ok. I'll talk to you when you get here," I said and we hung up with each other.

I called Ricky and he wasn't home so I left him a message to call me. Ricky had this kinda answering machine that you could change the greeting from an outside phone using these touch-tone instructions. Patrick had given me the code, which was pound - seven - two after the recording picked up. For a while Patrick and I would always change his greeting to something funny. I called back and put in the code. I changed the greeting making my voice sound as close to Ricky's as possible. I've always been good at impressions. The new greeting went something like this:

"Hey dudes. This is Ricky! I'm the cracked-out nigger-pimp rock-daddy! I can't get to the phone right now. I'm out pimpin Chinese bitches and smoking crack rocks. If you really wanna get a hold of me you can beep me, but my pager's always blowing up, guy! Reckahnize! I'm out!"

Beeeeeep.

We were always fucking with Ricky like that. With Patrick and I, it was one of our greatest forms of entertainment. The best was when his mom would call his line trying to get a hold of him and then she'd hear that shit on his machine. I do a pretty damn good Ricky voice too, so sometimes you can't really tell if it's him on the recording or not.

At my apartment Gabe called this girl over named Leslie Hipp. According to Gabe she would be our featured buyer for the day. I had a problem with her right off the bat for two reasons. The first reason was simply because she was a girl and you can't trust most woman with drug situations. And second, I didn't even know her. In a place like The Region where the law is steel-fisted and cops are looking to bust people for any reason or even no reason, it just wasn't smart to sell semi-hefty amounts of marijuana to people who you didn't know. But I needed the money badly so I was willing, just this once, to play along.

We all sat in my living room, Gabe and Leslie on the couch, me in a chair across the coffee table from them. Leslie was a skinny little stringy girl who was sorta pretty in a white trash sorta way, like in a trailer park they'd think she was good looking. Better yet, she'd be hot only during visiting hours at the penitentiary. Her hair was dyed blonde and ropey and flat on her skull, no real chest to speak of, and she had no neck. It was like somebody took a sledgehammer and dropped a swing down on her head and jammed her neck into her torso. This amazed me and I wondered how in the hell she kept turning her head so easily.

I wasn't saying much of anything. I didn't have to because Gabe was doing all the talking. Besides, if this Leslie girl was a cop (which she obviously wasn't) or even worse, a pigeon for the cops (damn well could be), I wasn't gonna give her anything worth recording for a future court of law. I wasn't being paranoid either. The police in The Region were viciously oppressive to the all of Indiana's occupants, excluding far right wing Republicans, the richies. The cops where I grew up would stop at nothing to bust people for anything at all, looking in the wrong mailbox, riding your bike and not stopping at a stop sign, walking with a large group of people, smoking cigarettes if you're under eighteen, and making too much noise. You name it—if you had any business at all the cops were all up into it. And if they weren't, they wanted to be and would do anything at all so they could pinch you. They could even, for instance, pay a high school girl to buy some weed from some punk like me and then report back to them with names, phone numbers, and addresses. I would be an easy bust too. I was small, I didn't have any money to bail myself out of jail, and I was already on probation for an old assault charge so they were probably tracking me anyway, and most importantly I was a good link in their food chain. If a cop were to bust in on me trying to sell a sack of ganja, his whole purpose in doing this would to get me to squeal on the dude who I bought it from. If I snitched—and I wouldn't—but if I did, they'd go to that dude and pressure him to talk about his man, and so on and so forth.

"So Gabe," Leslie said. "I thought you brought me here for a reason. I've gotta be at work in an hour."

"Where do you work," I asked quickly trying to divert her because I didn't like her haste on making a deal and then expecting to just split right away. What the hell was that? When a person comes over to buy weed they better stay at least a half hour. It's common.

"Oh, I work at Tru–green/Chemlawn, right up the street."

"What is that," Gabe asked. "Some kinda fucking biosphere?"

"Are you the pooper scooper for the scientist," I asked sarcastically.

I laughed. She didn't.

"Oh, kinda," she said in a snotty way. "I'm a telemarketer. It's a lawn care service."

"It's a crazy time of year to be selling lawn care. How much to you make doing that?"

"Seven dollars an hour plus commission."

"Commission," I asked. "On what?"

"See, I call people on the phone and I ask them if they wanna free bid."

"What's a bid," Gabe asked.

"You don't know what a *bid* is," I asked him.

"Gabe," Leslie said. "A bid is when a person comes to do a job, but first they tell the customer how much it will cost. That's a bid."

"Then what do you have to do," I asked. "How do you get the commission?"

"Well, if they accept to have a bid done and they actually decide to have the service then I get an extra ten bucks."

"How much does it cost for lawn care," Gabe asked her.

"I don't know, maybe a coupla hundred, maybe more maybe less."

"Honey, they're ripping you off," I informed her. "That's, like, a one percent commission."

"Yeah. Well, it's better than no commission," she admitted.

"So Leslie," I said changing the subject to business. "What is it, exactly, you're looking for?"

"Weed."

I rolled my eyes and said, "Yeah, but how much?"

"Half an eighth."

I looked crossly at Gabe.

"What do you mean by half an eighth? They don't come in half an eighth. Eighths, quarters, half ounces, ounces, twenty, forty, eighty, and one-sixty. That's how it works. That's how the game's played. Now, how much do you really want?"

"All I have is ten bucks."

"All you have is ten bucks? Look, Leslie. If I sell you half an eighth," I said and held out my palms doing the this hand and the other hand gesture. "Then I have to find some other guy who's gonna buy half an eighth. It won't happen. People don't by half an eighth."

"*Hmmm*," she sighed and sat back in the couch and started thinking.

I knew that she was in no way a law enforcement official because if she were an informant she would've asked me for a pound, and she would have said cliché slang words like, marijuana, the good stuff, grass, or pot. Different words for the situation are used in different places of the country. In Indiana we said words or phrases like: a dub sack, ganja, reefer, dank buds, or Mexi. We also had words for a joint like: a spliff, a blunt, a stick, or a scud missile, which is when you roll up some crack rocks with the weed. It's guaranteed to knock anybody on his or her ass.

"How about you Gabe," she said without taking her eyes off of me. "You want in on this, a split?"

"Oh," I mocked. "A *big business* transaction, a Hollywood drug deal."

"I only got eight dollars," he said taking out a crumpled wad of bills. And he only offered because he felt stupid about her lack of funds.

"What about an eighth for eighteen bucks and Gabe owes you two," Leslie suggested.

"Jesus Christ, you're serious," I asked, becoming frustrated with the lack of progress.

I thought about it for a second or two.

"I'll be right back," and I went back into my room, unlocked the safe, and got out the half-ounce of dank, the digital scale, and my rolling tray.

I eyeballed what I thought was the right amount and put it onto the tray, picking up one bud at a time until the weight was right. An Indiana eighth can weigh anywhere between 3.5 grams and 4 grams. For eighteen bucks I made it weigh right around 3.0 grams. I knew damn well I'd never see the two dollars unless I stole it from the change dish in Gabe's car. I rolled the plastic baggy up nicely and licked it to make it sealed. Back in the living room I handed her the sack.

"Here you go. Four grams. That's a phat sack."

"Thanks, Ray," she said and put it in her purse.

I couldn't believe it. She was trying to pull a Fast Eddie on Gabe.

"Well I've got to get to work guys."

"What," Gabe said astonished. "You ain't gonna smoke any? You can at least give me my half."

She smiled and took out the bag and stuck her fingers inside. She took out half and just put it right on the table. You could really tell how much I skimped on the weight of the bag when it was divided like that.

"Gotta go," she said. "Bye, Ray. Bye, Gabe," and she went for the door.

"Whatever, Leslie," Gabe said. "Thanks for nothing."

"Later," I said. "Hey are you guys hiring at your organization?"

"My *organization?*"

"The lawn care place. I need a job."

"I can get you a job. No problem. Just come down and apply."

"Thanks," I said and she closed the door behind her.

I shook my head at Gabe.

"How was I supposed to know," he asked me. "Just forget it. Let's smoke a bowl, captain!"

"Now I'm fucked, Gabe, because instead of selling a half-ounce to one person, I have to sell a quarter, an eighth, and to two different people. This sucks, but I forgive you. You couldn't have known what her intentions were. It's not like you can get into specifics over the phone."

"Yeah," he said. "I had to, like, hint around and shit, and it took her a while to catch my drift."

"I hear you. You know anybody else who needs a bag?"

9

"This is what you get," Gabe told me as we drove through a carwash-type onslaught of snow and ice. We were headed back out to Ricky's house in the Lakes of the Four Seasons. There would be no imposter mission at the front gate this time, because we were riding in Gabe's car and they only check on the car's plates for information.

"Gabe, all this just happened to me," I said after I thought about whether or not I was deserving of all this instant drama in my life.

One thing I was sure of: nobody could know that I still talk to

Erin.

"Erin victimized me. I swear she's like an infectious disease. She's an airborne germ, like, like, Ebola and shit. I went too close to her and I ended up getting punched in the face by a wild gorilla who, for some reason, dates teenaged girls in our town. You should've warned me or something, gave me a heads up."

"*What*," he shouted and blew smoke in my face as he did it.

I didn't mind though. A funny thing about The Region, it's not considered rude to blow smoke in somebody's face because it's so polluted there. The regular air is so stinky. So when it comes to fresh air people are just like, "Fuck it." Everybody smokes lots of cigarettes and eats deep fried red meat. None of us give a crap if you blow smoke in our faces. Blow a fart in my face and you're gonna die, but I never care if somebody accidentally blows smoke in my face. There were four things that shocked me when I moved to Seattle that you'd never see in The Region: Homosexuals, vegetarians, people who don't smoke cigarettes, and guys who don't like sports. Seattle's a crazy flip-flopped inside-out world unlike any I had known.

"I didn't see this Erin shit coming, Ray. How could I warn you about an isolated incident?"

"Dude, you at least knew who she was, and knew about her past, and you knew she had a boyfriend, and you didn't say, 'hey Ray, watch out for her.' I found out the hard way. 'She'll make you famous around school, but she'll also get you killed.'"

"That's excessive. You act like I knew she was a serial killer. I got news for you. She doesn't clue me in on her crimes before she commits them," he smiled at me and blew smoke in my face again. "Sorry, Ray. Is that what you wanna fucking hear? She called me outta the blue and asked me if I wanted a ride to school with her and Milada. Then I go, 'Sure,' and then I tell her that, 'I'm supposed to pick Ray's Polish ass up' and she goes, 'Oh really. Is that the boy you used to hang around with last year, the one with the long hair?' I go, 'Yeah, but he don't got the hair like a bitch anymore. Well, at least not as long as it was. He's tough looking now.' She goes, 'He's really cute.' And I go, 'So is your boyfriend.' Then she tells me, 'Shut up and mind your own business.' So that's as far as I got with the inside information, Ray. If I knew that you were gonna get beat up for riding to school in her car then I would have told you. I swear to God. Besides, you didn't see me getting my ass kicked and I rode in the same goddamn car. So maybe there was other shit going on that you're not telling me about. We're friends, Ray. Don't you remember?"

Then he tossed his cigarette butt out the window.

"Friends don't let friends tangle with scandalous women," I said.

"Not where I come form," he let me know. "Around here that's the only kind they sell."

He pulled out another cigarette, put it between his teeth and pushed in the car lighter and he waited for about thirty seconds for it to pop back out. He was the biggest chain smoker I ever saw in my life. And compounding his habit was the fact that he was an all-state wrestler who was always jogging around town. Now that's mysterious.

My friend Lewis Marshall was the same way. He smoked joints and Newport cigarettes, and he placed among the top three in the state at running the mile two years in a row. I smoked and I couldn't run three blocks without coughing up a lung.

After he lit his smoke he continued talking and blowing smoke around the car and sometimes in my face.

"Besides," he said. "Why can't you find a nice girl like Susa or Tracy Fillipo?"

"Tracy Fillipo," I was cracking up. "Are you serious? She's gotta fucking butt in the front! Besides, even she's gotta boyfriend."

"Sure. They both have boyfriends too, but least they don't date cocaine-sniffing linemen. One guy's a hippie or something resembling a dude who thinks it's cool to wear hemp and the other is just a skinny runt of a *farkin* runt, some dude who writes for the school paper."

"I really don't know either of those two girls, Gabe. I just know who they are. Besides, from now on, I don't think that I'll be doing any specific relations with Granite girls anyway, or any girl who even talks to another guy for that matter. They seem to be hazardous to my health."

"There's some nice girls at our school, Ray. Don't worry, I'll hook you up tonight at the *par-tee*."

"*Whoa*," I became alarmed. "The only girls you can hook up with are from Granite. Why would there be any Granite girls at Ricky's house?"

"Because."

"Because why?"

"Nigger called me up and told me to bring girls."

"Who?"

"Ricky."

"How does he know your number?"

"We exchanged last time we were out here. He really wants me to get him some pills."

"And girls, right?"

"And girls," he confirmed. "I invited the whole Pantherette squad, plus I invited Milada, Jolene, you name it. If they're a bitch, I invited them."

I smiled and said, "Well, if it ain't Snoop D.O. Double G. You got us some bitches tonight, that's great."

"They're all bitches, Ray. All of them are bitches," he laughed and shouted. "Try this one on for size! *Beeiiaattcchh*!"

"Erin's not going is she?"

He said nothing.

"Dude. Gabe. If she's there I'm dead. I can't even be in the same country as her."

"You're Catholic aren't you?"

If you've ever read Catcher in the Rye by J.D. Salinger, what he says about Catholics is true. Gabe was always trying to find out of other people were Catholic like him just to see if he and the other person could feel comfortable being liars and scumbags together. I grew up Catholic and even I do it sometimes.

"Yeah," I said annoyed. "I'm Catholic, so what?"

"So pray. I didn't invite her. It's a free country. If you don't want her to show up at the only party going on anywhere at all, a party that all of her friends are gonna be at, you should definitely pray for a miracle."

"Whatever." .

When we drove up to Ricky's there was no place to park because the party was so packed. Gabe actually had to run over some bushes to get the car legally parked.

"This is as good a place to park as any, Gabe."

We got outta the car and slammed our doors shut. A pack of inebriated girls walked by us as they were heading to their cars. They got drunk too quick and were leaving early. One of them puked on her shoes and Gabe and I couldn't stop laughing at the thought of it being frozen on the driveway until spring.

Gabe pounced on the vulnerability.

"Hey girls, anyone need a lift home? My friend here likes girls with puke breath. It boosts his self-esteem."

They didn't answer because Gabe kinda looked like one of them hillbilly serial killers. We went our usual route inside, through the backyard and into the basement. There were kids all over the place, in the driveway, on the front steps, under the trees smoking and it was twenty frigid degrees outside.

Even when we got inside I still hadn't seen anyone I knew, but Gabe was talking to people left and right. He even knew the first names of most of the kids there.

He turned to me once we were inside and he shouted over the music. "These are all Granite people. I created a monster, but Ricky put me up to it!" He waved his pointer finger up at me as he said this.

"I think he got what he bargained for," I yelled back.

That's when Leslie Hipp popped outta the crowd wearing a boy's white T–shirt and some blue jeans. She had no socks or shoes on and her hair was wild and her eyes were spinning around like cute shapes inside a slot-machine. She was drunker then a hound dog trapped in the cellar.

"If only the trailer park dudes could see you now," I said and smiled to her.

She recognized me. She said something I couldn't understand

and she put her arm around me. She was holding a bottle of Bud Light and she screeched something about me being her friend to random people standing near us. She pulled me by the arm and started to tug me upstairs where it was quieter. Gabe shook his big head and walked away laughing at me. She made me sit on the top step with her as people squeezed by to get through.

"Ray-Man," she slurred. "Oh my God! I'm *soooo drunk* you don't even know."

That's the thing about your name being Ray, is everybody is always calling you Ray-Man, and this is a mystery to all Rays. It's similar to when people know some dude named Richard and they get cute and call him Richie Rich or Dick.

"I know you're drunk, Leslie. I really do."

"No, Ray-Man. You don't. Who's this guy having the party? He doesn't go to my school."

"He's a friend of mine," I told her. "Who in Christ's name did you here come with?"

"Why? Do you wanna take me into the bedroom," she asked and laughed her ass off and fell into my lap.

I propped her back up.

"No. No offense, but I don't."

I smiled and looked around. I was embarrassed that people were listening to this primitive conversation.

"I was just wondering. Was it Jolene? Whoever it was you came here with, I think they should think about taking you home. You're gonna end up getting hurt."

"It wasn't Jolene," she said while still laughing. "I came," she continued almost out of breath. "I came with your girlfriend."

"*Huh?* Leslie, I don't have a girlfriend. What the hell are you talking about?"

"Oh, to hell with it all. Fuck it all," she said and she got to her feet. "I have to pee. By the way, you look cute with your eye like that. Did you fall into a door-knob or something?"

She scuffed away with her intoxicated stumble and blended in with all the people.

Matt Morris came up the stairs and I hadn't seen him since the other night. I did get to see him briefly on the night that I got back into town because he and Ricky were the ones who picked me up from the airport. As soon as I was in the car Ricky was cutting up squares into doses and **Acid** was being passed around like a Lake Station whore. The big mistake I made was that I dropped when I didn't feel like it. You can't go taking Acid when you're not totally into it. It is, as I would imagine, like agreeing to butt-sex or some shit. When we got back to my dad's apartment I said goodbye to Ricky and Matt and they said they were going to chill in the parking lot and smoke a couple of J's before heading back to Ricky's house. I felt in control until I started walking up a staircase that I hadn't walked up in over 6 months and they busy pattern on the carpet wasn't helping much either. The zig-zags and circles and geometric shapes and shit were sending my thoughts around and around garbage-disposal-style. I was tripping extremely hard and I didn't have a key to the apartment so I had to knock on the door and my dad's wife answered with every bit of animated body language she usually has in real life times a thousand because of the **Acid** running amock on my insides. I tried to act cool. Man, I tried to act cool. Normal. I sat on the couch and didn't look anybody in the eye and I didn't take off my coat and I was almost oblivious to the pepper-spray of questions that my dad and his wife were asking me about Seattle and how it felt to be home and what's new with this person or that person. I was getting bits and pieces. I started to panic. I went to the bathroom and tried to take a piss but nothing would come out. I ran the water in the sink and I looked at myself in the mirror, which is the very last thing you should ever, ever, ever do when you're tripping on **Acid**. The person you see in the mirror won't be the person you've been looking at all these years. This was not my reflection. This was a dude staring back at me who wasn't me.

I heard my dad and his wife go into another room and I made my break for it. I grabbed my coat and I ran out the front door and down the stairs and when I got back outside Matt and Ricky were just about to pull away and I jumped into the back seat and told them to drive. I told them that we gotta get the fuck outta here. And since they're tripping on the same shit I was tripping on they took my order seriously and Matt put his car into drive and peeled out and we tore off down the street.

I felt a little better laying in the back seat and watching the night from the window, but something wasn't right. First the right nostral got clogged. Then the left shut down. Snot was building up. Then came the sore throat. Then came the icky feeling. It was probably jet-lag, but right then I didn't realize that. I didn't understand what was happening. All I knew was that everything I saw was moving around in ways that things just don't move around and I also knew that slowly I was losing my bodily functions. Back at Ricky's house his parents weren't home and I found myself alone. I didn't know where Matt and Ricky had gone and my throat started closing up. That's when the worst thought you could ever think while tripping on Acid crept into my mind. I was dying. I freaked out. I ran upstairs and found Matt's keys and then I ran outside and got in his car and started driving away. I couldn't see. I couldn't breathe. I couldn't think. I drove towards Granite. And I drove. And I drove. I went down streets I had never seen before. One minute I was lost and the next I knew exactly where I was and then the next I'd be lost again. I started getting scared about dying. I started to cry. On the radio there was nothing on but the shrill of commercials. I saw one of those signs with the letter "H" on them with an arrow. There was a hospital close by. I tried to find it. I wanted to make the tripping stop. I wanted them to shut my mind off. I drove around and around looking for the hospital and then out of nowhere I was back in the parking lot of my dad's apartment. Relieved, I went upstairs and checked the front door. It was unlocked. Nobody was home. I called Matt on the phone and told him I stole his car and that I was sorry. He and Ricky were tripping hard and they thought I was kidding and that I must be calling from another room in Ricky's house. I hung up on them and watched cartoons for the rest of the night.

Matt Morris had on a three-quarter-length black leather jacket from Wilson that we snatched in one of our mall missions a year before. Patrick had gotten a hold the famous tag popper. It was used to take the thing off the coat that beeps or explodes with ink if you try to tamper with it. With the popper, we could walk in, pop the alarm sensor or the exploding ink button off, and stuff the coat or whatever in a shopping bag, and just walk out. It was the most useful tool we had ever gotten our hands on. We must have stolen thousands of dollars worth of expensive merchandise while we had the popper. It got to be so easy that we knew that it had to end somehow, somewhere. And one day at South Lake Mall, it was over. We were in The Gap. We split up like always as if we weren't with each other. Ricky stood as the look out for security guards, my job was to distract the help with a bunch of stupid questions and I would try on thing after thing while Patrick and Morris stuffed their bags full of loot. I don't know how it happened, but all of the sudden three guards came in and pointed at old Patrick. One of the clerks must have seen him swiping some shirts and triggered an alarm. Ricky put his fingers in his mouth and did the high–pitched whistle and we all bolted from the store. We all got away except for Ricky. He tripped over one of the displays and knocked it over. The guards tackled him and hauled him away for prosecution. They tried to get him to rat on us but he wouldn't talk because he thought it was funny. They couldn't charge him with anything but resisting arrest, because he didn't have anything. And the worst part was that Patrick accidentally dropped the popper. Anyway, they confiscated the popper and Ricky got three days in the juvenile hall (suspended sentence) and one year probation. The day after the Gap incident, Patrick got nabbed at Foot Locker wearing some new shoes out the door. He got charged with a misdemeanor for shoplifting, didn't do anytime, but he also got a year probation. I almost resurrected our careers when I snatched a new popper from when I worked at J. Crew, but our karma had taken a turn for the worst so we retired from the mall missions for almost two years after that. I still used the new popper for small jobs.

"Ray," Matt greeted. "You fucking nigger! You haven't kicked it with me since the other night when you stole my car!"

I stood up and did the arm wrestling handshake with him,

"What's up, chief? No I saw you a day or so ago didn't I?"

"Maybe. Nothing much is up with me. Same old shit, bigger pile. How'd that dose work out for you that night at the airport anyway? I forgot to ask."

"I tripped my balls off. Thanks for that, man. I tripped so hard I stole your car. Sorry about that."

You could drive a person to suicide if you told them you had a bad trip because of the shit that they gave you, so I let him think I had a good time.

"Don't sweat it. Have you seen Patrick or Ricky Ricardo?"

"No, I just got here."

"Where are all these bitches from," he asked me.

"Granite," I said.

"You brought all these broads?"

"Not all of them," I said jokingly.

"Nice action, Kozlowski. We need more guys like you in this world. Com'n," he said to me. "Let's go find those bastards. I've got something special in my coat pocket."

Then I spotted a hot girl I had never seen and I said, "I got something special in my pants for that bitch right there!"

"Who," Matt asked. "Her?" And he pointed at the girl I was talking about. "Fuck that bitch. She's got AIDS."

"Really," I laughed. "That's funny."

I smiled at the hot girl with AIDS and followed him down the hall to Ricky's room. There were some guys Matt knew and I didn't in Ricky's room. Matt asked them if they knew where Patrick or Ricky were at, but they didn't, so Matt and I went into the bathroom and locked the door.

"Check out this action," he said as he took out a little wooden box. "You're gonna love this." He opened the box and showed me what was inside.

"*Mother fuck*," I said with my eyes popping out. "You better be careful carrying all that shit around. Don't get me wrong, I'm glad you brang it here."

I stuck my finger inside the box and moved around everything so I could take a mental inventory. There were a coupla grams of coke, three joints, some pills that I didn't recognize and, "Holy shit you got some hash," I said and I took out the stick and looked at it in the light.

"I got a little ball of opium too, and some heroin."

"Heroin? I never done it before."

The music started pumping from Ricky's room. It was the *Humpty Dance* by Digital Underground and the beats made thuds against the walls.

"I've been saving up this crap for years. I was gonna save it for a special occasion."

"What's so special about tonight?"

He looked at me very sincerely and said, "You're back, man. This shit here in this box, this is to us. Friends."

"Wow, dude. Thanks. But I can't do all of it. Why did you bring you're whole stash?"

"Nothing much. I got suspended today for smoking weed in the parking lot and I was afraid my parents would search my room while I was gone. If they found this shit they'd lock me up forever."

"So you guys are doing heroin now," I asked.

"We smoke it. At least Ricky and me do. Patrick is anti-drug now. It's stupid to shoot that shit. Me and Ricky put it in a joint and smoke it, like this joint right here," he said and held up a sleek little pinner. "You wanna try it?"

"Sure. What the hell," I said. "Let's fire it up."

He put the box down and held the joint to his lips and lit it, puffing and sucking the smoke out of it to get it going.

"There's really heroin in that," I asked him as he passed the joint to me.

"Quarter of a fucking gram there is," he said.

I didn't know if that was a lot or a little. I took a deep drag off of it and I noticed a slight soapy taste.

"Tastes a little like opium," I said. "Does it mess you up big time when it's smoked? I mean like it does when you shoot it?"

"I don't know, like I said I never shot the shit before, but I hear it ain't as powerful if it's smoked. You'll be fine, man, if that's what you're asking."

He hit it and passed it back.

"How many hits do I need?"

"No more than two," he said. "You should be feeling pretty chill right after this one."

He was right, because right after I passed him the joint, and as he was putting it out with some dripping water from the sink, I was struck with a dope high like I'd never had before. I felt warm and smooth, like I was *The Man*. I swear I saw a flash of lightning strike in the room. I leaned on the counter for support and tried to gather my thoughts to a respectable level.

"Are you cool," Matt asked me. "You all right?"

"Yeah," I said. "I'm cool, man. Really, I'm fine. I just needed to kick it on this counter real quick."

When I recovered my equilibrium, Matt and I went back downstairs to the recreation room where I first came inside. *Ghetto Child* by Curtis Mayfield was playing on the CD player. The room was even more crowded than before, some of the Jocks from Andrean had arrived: Napoleon Cole, Nick Kowolkowski, and Manny Bagnalio. They were all standing side by side in their Andrean letterman jackets. They were watching the show. The Pantherettes had arrived fresh from a performance in their uniforms and they had spread out through the room and were screaming and running around with beer.

"Looks like Ricky fed them some coke," Matt yelled into my ear.

Some of the smart nerds were there watching the Pantherette Show also: Mike Hayes (chemistry expert), Noel Simpson (math wizard), and Bruce Thompson (Highest G.P.A). You know, the NERDS. The rest of the guys from our Andrean gang were at the card table playing Texas Hold'em and hitting Craig Faruke's Grafix water-bong.

"Yo, what's happening Kozlowski, Morris," Craig said and nodded to us as he raised the bong and toasted us.

Joe Musso was dealing the cards, "Hey bitches," he called to us.

Joe Musso was as close to a hippie as any of us were. He had long brown hair, was heavy into LSD, he was peaceful, and back when he was still at Andrean he was popular with the girls as a ladies man. But now Ricky, Musso, and Matt were getting involved with a lotta hard drugs. Musso had lost the shine in his eyes, he wasn't half as sharp witted as he used to be, and certainly he was much less aggressive. He was still a good guy though, and I'd always liked him and thought that he was a cool person.

Benny Ramirez was there too.

"Ray-Man, Morris, come and hit this thing," he said.

Benny was one of those pretty-boy Mexicans. He was our answer to a straight local version of Ricky Martin and he was always friendly and everything, but there was something deep down inside me that wanted to kick the shit out of him. But with respect for my friends, who were also friends with Benny Ramirez, I never attacked him.

Paul Long was at the table next to Craig.

"Look at who's here! *Waz'up* fuckin fucks," he called to us.

Paul was always drunk and mean, but he was so scrawny and intoxicated all the time that no one ever kicked the shit out of him except for Michael Begnal. Paul spit in his face and Begnal knocked him out and started spitting all over him while he was on the ground crying. It was beautiful, and I remember it like it was yesterday.

"Fuck off, Paul," I told him like usual.

That's all I ever said to him. The other guys told me to chill and Paul kept drinking out of the whiskey bottle. I hated Paul, but for the same reasons as with Benny, I had yet to attack him.

And then Mike Begnal walked in with Karl Miles. The funny thing about Karl Miles was he grew up with Begnal and Patrick, then he moved away to where I was growing up in Ogden Dunes. Miles and I became best friends around age twelve. I met Patrick and Begnal when I was fifteen and became good friends with them too. But it wasn't until I was seventeen that I made the connection that Karl Miles knew these guys. They had been reunited in a way and now we all hung out together. It's a touching story, I know.

Begnal was the rare dark-haired Irish looking kid, a tan, rough face, and a taste for danger. He was one of those people who were just waiting to die. Everyone knew that he would be the first to die out of all of us. Both of his parents were already dead from cancer, and he had life saving heart surgery when he was eight. When he took his shirt off there was a big scar going from just below his neck all the way down to his gut. He had to be careful about his cardiac activity so he wouldn't croak from a heart attack. He couldn't play sports and he couldn't drink nor do any drugs. It was too risky. And whenever he did try anything dangerous he would always end up breaking his arm or something. Just last year he shattered his shoulder riding a bicycle. All that he could do was kick Paul Long's ass after school. He was probably the only genuinely nice guy out of all of us.

"Man," Begnal said as he came in. "I could hear you dicks all the way from my house."

Karl Miles was a strange guy. All of the girls liked him, but the guys knew that he was a way out there. His head was in the clouds. He used to tease animals when we were younger. And everyday when we were thirteen we would smoke his stepmother's hash. Then we'd go to the beach and toss Alka-Seltzer tablets up to seagulls. It would cause the bird's stomachs to bubble up with fizz and they'd die and fall out of the sky like rocks. We called it duck hunting. Karl Miles and I always got a big kick out of it. He was really fat when we were kids, and now he had grown taller and skinnier. Ethnically he was Croatian and he had a Slavic looking face with brown eyes. Karl Miles was into mountain climbing and other extreme type sports. He was Begnal's dream human. That's why they always chummed around together. He was a very strong kid, probably the strongest outta everybody, but he didn't look it. He looked thin and lanky. Miles didn't say anything, he just stared at people, and he didn't even smile or anything. He's mean. He'd kick anybody's ass.

By now I had become entirely whacked out by that funny joint that Matt and I had smoked. Matt had a bottle of beer and he kept trying to take slugs from it even though the cap was still on it. Craig was talking to me and I couldn't understand what he was saying. His voice was deep and slow sounding like a Walkman running outta batteries. All I could do was walk away. I had to find a nice place to just chill out where nobody could bother me.

No such luck though. When I turned around it was like a scene out of one of those cheerleader horror movies because Erin, Milada, and Jolene and some Panterettes were in my face. They were all really drunk and excited and I couldn't understand what they were telling me. I knew what words they were saying and I could make out the sentences, but I was only getting bits and pieces of the meaning.

They were talking too fast and I just couldn't keep up so I just smiled and said, "Yeah, yeah, yeah."

Erin grabbed one of the Pantherettes that was close to us and she seemed to be introducing me to this round girl in a Pantherette uniform.

Now she's got guts, I thought, *being so round and wearing such a revealing outfit.*

The girl was called Sydney and she looked very scared and uncomfortable around me. Anyone with half a brain could look into my eyes right then and see how berserk I had gotten off of that funny joint.

I just shook my head at Sydney and said, "Yes, yes, yes," like my favorite character Dean from *On the Road* by Jack Kerouac. I needed help, and then Jolene, Milada, and Sydney went away and left Erin standing there.

I needed guidance so I said to her, "Erin, I'm really messed up. Matt fed me something in the bathroom."

"*Ok,*" she said in a tone like she wanted me to tell her more.

"I'm not gonna pass out or anything, and I'm not dying. I just need to not be around so many people. My environment is critical to whether or not I go mad right now. Are you picking up what I'm throwing down?"

The slow mind-bending beats of *Red Rain* by Peter Gabriel began pulsating from the stereo.

"Is anybody else listening to this? You aren't recording this are you?"

"I can help you," she said. "Follow me."

"I can't," I said and she took my hand and led me upstairs to the third floor where not many people had ventured to yet.

That's another thing about Indiana people is that they're always grabbing your arm and pulling you around against your will. We walked down a dark hallway and I could still hear *Red Rain* playing even though we were too far from the actual music, but it was still playing clearly in my head, in my imagination. We stopped just outside the guestroom room and some kids were in there and they were playing *Check Yourself* by Ice Cube on the stereo. She leaned me up against the wall and I felt my face melting away, my worries dripping from my finger-tips and for once in my life I was at complete peace. Heroin was the shit man. I loved it.

Kids: do heroin. Just one time. It totally rocks the house.

Erin went into the room and was talking to some people and motioning to me. Soon a group of guys that I knew very well, but didn't completely recognize, came out and walked past me, some of them nodding at me, some patting me on the shoulder, and some going right by with tunnel vision. The next thing that I knew Erin was pulling me into the room and she shut and locked the door behind us.

I knew the room. I had been there plenty of times in the past and banged drunk teenage girls in there. It was the guestroom, or that's what Ricky called it. It was a lot like what you would find in a presidential suite at a luxury hotel. It was one huge room, about 1000 square feet, and it had the king-sized waterbed, a master bathroom, fireplace, deck, and even a small kitchenette, and a pimpy chandelier.

I asked Erin to turn on all of the lights, including the TV and the bathroom light. Anything that gave light, I wanted to see it. I needed light. She turned on every light she could find and she poured me a glass of ice water and sat me down on the sofa, but I wanted to sit on the floor instead so I did.

"Oh, Raymond," she said. "Didn't your mother ever explain peer pressure to you?"

"My mom is a robot. Besides. It's ok. I wanted to do it."

"You said that Matt fed you something. What was it?"

"Heroin," I said.

"You shot fucking *heroin*," she scolded me.

"No," I rolled my eyes. "No, we smoked it, didn't shoot it, no needles involved. It was the best. Matt did me a huge favor."

I sighed and I leaned my head back and I laid down on my back to rest. I shut my eyes and she knelt down next to me and stroked her fingers through my hair. I got a feeling from her hands like the one that I used to get from my mother, who was usually a very mean woman, would do when I was really little and feeling really hurt mentally or physically. Back then when I was three or four years old I remember thinking, as my mom would rub my head, *so this is what mothers are for.*

Then some nauseous bomb exploded inside my stomach and I felt the barf shooting up to my mouth like water from a fire hose. I leapt to my feet and ran to the bathroom toilet. Erin took off right after me. A few feet from the pot and I'd already thrown up in my mouth, and it puffed my cheeks like I was holding my breath. I shoved my head inside the toilet and let it all come out. First the load that was in my mouth, then the tacos that I had eaten about an hour ago at Taco Bell with Gabe before we made the journey, and a few minutes later some clear disgusting liquid.

She helped me to my feet, got me a glass of water and did her best to get my cleaned up by wiping my mouth with a warm, wet hand towel. I backed into the wall, slid down to my ass and I passed out, into blackness, no sound, no lights, and only the smell of fresh flowers and Pine-Sol.

Then I woke up. This was some time later, maybe an hour, maybe less. Maybe more ...

Erin started humming a song. I didn't know if she was humming a tune to keep herself company or as an attempt to comfort me in my delirium.

"Erin," I asked from somewhere that felt at least ten miles away from her. "What is that song that you are humming, what's it called?"

"I'm sorry, is it bothering you? I was just—"

"It's fine, I liked it," I said. "What's it called, what's the words sound like?"

I opened my eyes and looked up at her. Her face hung over mine looking down like the Goodyear blimp, only she was much more pleasant to look at. She was chewing gum.

"It's Reggae music. I'm sure that you've never heard of it."

"Reggae music," I said. "But what is the song called?"

"Well, the song is called *Give My Love.*"

"Ha'ya," I laughed. "That's a hell of a song to be singing right now."

She smiled and said, "It's a song my older brother used to play all the time, and I heard him hum it to my grandmother while he was keeping company at the hospital. She died of cancer."

"Everybody around here dies of cancer."

Ever since then I've always thought about her humming that song whenever I'm really sad and depressed. It always makes me feel better, that is until I remember all the messed up shit that happened next. Then I feel sick.

10

Kevin Mishlevich, Lewis Marshall, Chris Roebuck, and Kim Donnelley pulled up to Ricky's out of control party around eleven-thirty. Even from the street you could see that things were crazy and fucked up. There were drunk-dry beer bottles and various forms of cardboard and plastic litter everywhere and there were even cars parked on the lawn.

Kevin is my cousin, and everyone's parents loved him because he was a nice kid and he was respectful, smart, and extremely polite. He loved his grandmother, was every girl's best friend, and had a big blond curly mop on his head. It looked a little like a clown wig. Poor Kevin, just like me, was one of the poverty stricken kids at Andrean; he didn't have his own car, so he had to share his mom's Chevy Cavalier. Kevin was always trying to keep me out of trouble. As far as he was concerned, all of my friends were the worst losers. He got along with them well enough, but he still thought they were losers and he usually wasted no time reminding me and my friends of our confusions.

Kim was the second real girlfriend that I ever had, the second girl that I had ever slept with, and the first that I had ever almost loved. I think that she loved me for real while we dated, and it's possible that she still did at the time of the party. When her and I actually went out it only lasted three months or so, because my dick personality took over and I got greedy and cheated on her with my third real girlfriend that I actually almost loved, her best friend at the time. Fittingly enough, Kim's old best friend became Kim's sworn enemy.

Lewis, Kevin, and Chris were all runners on the track and cross-country teams at Andrean. Kevin was a good student. No drugs. And he was honest. Lewis was an average student, half African-American and half white, a heavy smoker of weed and Newport cigarettes, and ranked third in the state in the mile. I told you a little about him earlier when we were in the car with that "Smoke Blower" Gabe.

Chris Roebuck was two years younger than us, also a gifted athlete, maybe more so than even Lewis Marshall, but he was extremely heavy into drugs and alcohol and also a shitty student. The three of them would always try to get me to join the cross-country team because my older sister was an All-American 800-meter runner at Andrean and it was supposed to be in my blood. They tried to make me think that it's cool to be on the cross-country team. I knew better. A guy on the chess club has more cool than a cross-country runner. And even if I wanted to join, talent isn't enough. You actually have to be in shape to go running. What they didn't realize was that it just wasn't in my lungs. At that time I couldn't run three blocks without being seized with suffocating exhaustion. Besides, I was too busy getting fucked up and trying to steal and get laid to take any sport or activity seriously.

"Oh shit, *dog*," Lewis said and took out a Newport from his pack and lit it. "Roebuck, I thought you said Ricky was just having people over."

"I did," Roebuck said. "What to you call this, money?"

Kim spoke with a worried look on her face, "Maybe Ray doesn't want me here. Maybe I should go. Should we leave?"

They remained parked for a minute and watched the house with interest.

"Fuck it," Roebuck said. "Let's get in there and throw down. Let's party, guys."

"I heard that," Lewis said. "Word. I'm about to get me some girl's numbers. That's all I know."

"I don't know," Kim shook her head. "It looks like it might get busted."

"Word nothing," Kevin scolded Lewis. "We got a fucking meet tomorrow and I'll be damned if you guys are gonna spend the night in jail."

"Chill out, Kevin," Roebuck said. "It's cool. We'll just hang out for a few, scoop up Ray, and then we can book."

"No way in hell, Chris," Kevin snapped. "Don't bullshit me cause I ain't having it."

"I think we should leave," Kim asked. "What about Ray? Are we just gonna leave him here? Maybe we should. He can take care of himself."

"I don't know, guys," Kevin said. "If Ray gets arrested again, he might be serving time after that fight last summer with those Lake Central guys."

"Yeah," Kim said. "That's true. The last thing Ray needs is more trouble."

"What thing last summer," Chris Roebuck asked excitedly. "What thing!"

"Ray kicked the shit outta some jerk," Kevin explained. "So bad the guy landed in the hospital for three weeks with emergency surgery. Kim was there, ask her about it."

"Can't we talk about something else," she sighed. "I hate fighting. I hate talking about fighting."

"Then he stole a boat or something," Lewis added.

"Oh man," Kevin moaned. "Kim, you have to just go get him! You're the only one he'll listen to."

"I'm not going in there by myself," she refused. "What if Patrick is in there? I hate his guts and he hates mine. If I go in there and he sees me he'll start teasing me in front of everybody."

"Lewis and me can go in," Chris Roebuck suggested.

"Yeah. Fuck that," Kevin said. "And leave me and Kim out here for six hours while you two idiots smoke bowls outta gravity bongs and chase girls."

"Dog, we'll only be about ten minutes," Lewis said seriously.

"No way, Lewis," Kevin said. "Nothing ever takes just ten minutes with you. I know you better than that."

Sure Lewis could run pretty fast, but when it came to any other form of movement like getting dressed or taking a shower or eating, he was the slowest motherfucker on the face of the Earth. He had never been on time to anything a day in his life. He doesn't even know what time is all about or how it works.

"How about we all just go together," Kim said. "But what if he won't leave?"

"Maybe we could break up this party with a shotgun blast," Roebuck joked. "Gary Shotgun Killer in da house!"

"He'd do it too," Lewis laughed.

"Shut up you two," Kevin bitched. "This is serious. We either gotta get Raymond outta here ourselves or figure outta way to end this party before the cops show up. Anybody got any bright ideas?"

"Just the shotgun idea," Chris Roebuck said.

"Maybe we could start a fire in the bushes," Lewis said, chuckling a bit. "Have our own little burn down session. I gotta blunt in my coat pocket."

"I know what to do," Kim excitedly said as she leaned forward towards the front seat. "We can make every one think that the cops are already coming. Then every one will leave. Ray and Ricky and Patrick and Matt won't be scared off so easily so once most other people run away it'll just be us and Ray and his friends."

The guys looked at each other after she made the suggestion.

"That's not a bad idea," Kevin said. "But how are we gonna do that? And who's gonna do it? It sure as hell isn't gonna be me."

"Somebody can just go in there shouting that the cops are coming," Roebuck said. "Act all scared and shit. It's simple. It really is."

"Ok, so who's gonna do it, Chris," Lewis asked.

"Not me," Chris Roebuck said. "Only an asshole does something like that while people are having a good time. We need somebody who's used to ruining a good time. Sounds like a job for you, Kevin. Besides, Kevin, why don't you just leave old Ray alone, huh?"

"Because he's stupid and he's always fucking his life up," Kevin said. "Now who is gonna go in there and start shouting? Lewis? How about you?"

"Yeah right. I ain't doing that shit. Can't we do paper, scissors, rock or something," Lewis asked everyone.

That idea sounded fair enough to everyone and they all put their fists in a circle and counted off. They all chanted at the same time: "One, two, three, *shoot*!"

11

Leslie Hipp just sat back in the chair and quietly listened to Jolene and Lisa Diamond go on and on about all the cool things they'd been doing with Erin Watkins. All of Ray's idiot-ass friends were there still playing cards and smoking pot and sniffing anything that had a texture softer than sand.

That Ricky guy is so trashy the way he keeps putting his arm around Lisa Diamond like that. And that Patrick! Oh my God, what a complete asshole, she thought. *Any time a person says anything serious or meaningful, he rips into them. He has a way with words like no one I've ever met in my entire life. It's a shame he uses his talent for evil purposes only. And how about that Paul Long? He got so excited when all of the slutty Pantherettes showed up and now look at him, passed out on the floor sipping on his own drool. The kid Craig was the one with all of the pot. He keeps taking more and more weed outta his little purple Crown Royal pouch. That boy Joe Musso is kinda cute; too bad he's fried on drugs though.*

Milada, sat next to Leslie and looked all freaky and innocent, and laughed at every story Jolene told about her and Erin, adding to the details by chirping shit like, "Oh yeah, we did that too!"

Leslie knew damn well if Milada ever got the chance to stab

Erin in the back she would do so in a second.

That's exactly why she's going after Ray, Leslie thought, *because she knows Erin likes him. Me and Jolene have been really close friends ever since I was in third grade and Jolene was assigned to be my Fourth Grade Buddy, and now we hardly ever hang out together at all.*

It seems like Jolene is moving on without me, but why? Neither of us has changed much over the years, with the exception of growing up. Things were really going great. And then came Erin Watkins of all people. Freshman year she was a big nerd and nobody knew who the hell she was. Sophomore year, she was the biggest prep and got in with that crowd. And now junior year she's suddenly turned into some kinda hippie Dead Head, and Jolene's new best friend.

"Yeah, yeah, yeah, where is that catching-mitt anyway," Ricky asked about Erin. "Somebody go get her and bring her to me. She's got sucking to do over here!"

And then Ricky grabbed Craig's water-bong and held it up in the air. All the other guys laughed. They always laughed at everything Ricky said because it was funny how he'd say anything around anybody. Patrick was the same way. Even the victims of Patrick's evaluations laughed at his jokes because they were all secretly afraid of him turning his insults up a notch on them. When Patrick is criticizing somebody it can always get worse, even if his opening line actually makes you cry. There's always more where that came from. Always remember that.

"*Dahhhhhh*, Ricky," Craig hissed. "You're too crazy, man. I'd like to see this Erin broad that everybody keeps talking about though. Where the hell is she? Does she exist? Is she inflatable?"

Leslie knew were she was, but wasn't about to tell on her, not yet anyway.

Then she shook her head and thought: *Ah, what the hell!*

"I know where she is," Leslie said and she looked right at Milada because she was pretty damn sure that Milada had a crush on Ray.

And then she looked at Jolene, because if Jolene knew what Erin was doing behind her boyfriend's back, she'd be so pissed. If there was one thing Jolene hated it was sluts giving other girls a bad name.

Leslie paused and then said, "Check up in that big bedroom

upstairs."

And then all the dudes started rolling with laughter and sleezy comments. Jolene's was totally annoyed. Milada blushed and smiled and all the guys went on with their little, "*Oohs,*" and, "*ahhhs.*"

"Oh yeah," Joe Musso cracked up. "Who's she up there with? Who's stinking up Ricky's sheets with her, huh?"

"Raymond, that's who," Leslie stated.

Craig piped in a comment. "Ricky's sheets couldn't get any stinkier than they already are."

'Ray's with Erin," Patrick blew up with laughter. "That little fucker's been home just a little bit and he's already moving in on my bitches again. I taught him everything he knows! He owes me lotsa commission! When you guys find them, ask Ray how my dick tastes."

"Kozlowski's burnin me in my guest bedroom," Ricky realized. "Fucking bogus action! Strictly bunk."

"Are you sure she's up there with Ray," Jolene whispered to Leslie.

"I saw them go in there about an hour ago, I swear. Her and Jeremy are broken up though, right," Leslie asked even though she knew that they weren't. She just wanted some kinda excuse for spilling the beans.

"Not that I know of," Jolene said. "Who told you that?"

Patrick looked at Milada and licked his lips, "How about you, candy-cane? Since Erin's been contaminated by Ray I'm gonna need a replacement. I expect you to start immediately. No bullshit."

Milada looked stunned and didn't know what to say. All of the guys started laughing again. She shot Patrick the dirtiest look she could come up with, which wasn't dirty enough.

Patrick laughed it off and he told her, "You can't hurt me. No matter how hard you try. I gots no feelings. Stick with me and your Christian-ass is headed straight to hell, baby! Together we'll commit every sin. Every single sin."

"Fuck you," she screamed and jumped outta her seat. Her chin wrinkled and her maple syrup eyes filled with tears. She covered her face and ran away down the hall.

"Wow," Ricky was surprised. "What the hell was all that about? That's some bunk-ass behavior. Totally bogus! Get that bitch a bottle of Zanex."

Jolene shook her head at Ricky and then she turned to Patrick as he still stood there with a smirk on his face.

"What the hell did you do that for," Jolene asked Patrick. She didn't expect an answer. She just wanted him to know that she meant business.

"What," Patrick said to her. "Eat shit, Rosie O'Donnell. I didn't do anything. You're friends are fucking nutjob whores. Blame Milada's Christ-loving parents who make her go to that church every Sunday. Giving her a low self-esteem and shit. Gotta have Jesus to wipe your ass. That's who should get the blame. Blame the followers of Jesus for teaching her that illogical way of life. Don't step to me with that shit."

"I better go see if she's ok," Jolene said and she got up from the table and went down the hall.

Leslie got up and left and so did Lisa Diamond. They left all of the guys hanging and the tension was so thick it caused them all to errupt in laughter.

12

Milada ran straight to the bathroom and slammed the door and locked it. She leaned back into the door and slid down onto her butt and started crying for real. She was afraid of so many things. She was scared of having to leave the house after Senior year, scared of breaking up with her boyfriend. She wondered if she was gonna go nuts because it seemed like she would break into these crying fits almost everyday now.

I know I'm depressed, she thought. *But I don't know why. I mean, I really have no explanation whatsoever. My parents are still married and they love each other. They have always done a good job taking care of me and my younger brothers. They never abused me in any way. I never went hungry and I have all the clothes that a girl could want. I have a cute boyfriend who loves me and, for whatever reason, I don't love him back anymore. I go to church every Sunday and I even sing in the choir. I get good grades in school, and I'm pretty. I'm very pretty, in fact, and I don't feel conceited saying so because everybody tells me that. They tell me I'm maybe one of the prettiest girls in the whole school, but I still feel so low, so worthless. I'm lost.*

She continued to cry. Images of Erin and her as little girls flashed through the darkness of her mind.

Her and Erin were the best of friends, absolutely inseparable, but it isn't that way anymore. Milada and Erin haven't been too close since well into the year before. Milada just couldn't figure out what went wrong with their friendship.

Was it me who changed, she thought. *Was it Erin?*

It was both of them changing in different ways. It's just sad because Milada honestly didn't trust Erin anymore—with boys, with money, and not even with her old clothes. Erin would always lie to adults when they were kids, but even in spite of that Milada was always confident she never lied to her about things, but she didn't think that at all anymore. Now she feels like Erin lies to her all the time, about everything. For instance, she was in some bedroom right now doing God knows what with Raymond. Erin told her nothing was going on with her and Raymond. She swore on their friendship about it. She actually put her hand on the Bible when Milada didn't believe her. Then when she finally did end up believing her about not liking Raymond, Milada stupidly went and confessed to Erin that she liked Raymond very much and that she was thinking about dumping her boyfriend Jason for him. Then Erin actually gave me her blessing to go after Raymond, as if he was her property in the first place, and again she swore that she didn't like him. She is so going to hell. Milada gotta tissue and blew the snot outta her nose.

How could I be so stupid that I believed her whoreish lies?

Milada actually felt sorry for Raymond. If Erin was really lying to her, then Milada knew for a fact that she's lying to Raymond about her boyfriend.

He probably doesn't know a thing about it, she thought. *I bet he thinks she's in love with him. I bet he thinks he loves her. He's just gonna get hurt. Erin always sets guys up and then hurts them in some way, either by cheating on them or having them get beat up because of her pack of lies. I mean Jesus! Raymond has already gotten his ass kicked because of her, and here he is up in the bedroom with Erin. How stupid could he be? What's next for him? Death? And here's me, locking myself into some stranger's bathroom as I cry and talk to myself like a dirty homeless person. I'm so screwed up.*

There was a knock on the door.

"Milada? It's Jolene. Are you ok in there?"

"I'm fine," Milada sniffled up her snot and tore a foot and a half of toiletpaper from the spool. "I'll be out in a second."

"Can I come in? Is it ok if I come in?"

Milada gathered herself and wiped the tears from her eyes one last time and then got up and opened the door and let Jolene slip in and then she shut the door again and locked it. Jolene pulled a tissue from her purse and wiped the running mascara from Milada's cheeks.

"Milada, don't cry over what that guy out there says. He's just another player. He just wants attention from people."

"It's not him."

Milada sighed and sat back down on the cold bathroom floor.

"Do you wanna talk about it," Jolene asked and she sat on the toilet. "You know you're always in for a serious talk when you're sitting on the toilet to get comfortable."

"Jolene, did you ever like a guy you knew would never like you back, because there was someone else, like, another girl who was cooler and more prettier?"

"I've been with James over four years now. I haven't had much chance for pursuing various relationships, but," Jolene smiled in a way that only girls can do when there are no guys around. It's the bad girl smile that can make a boyfriend go schizophrenic with jealousy. "I don't know."

"But what," Milada smiled back with the same sly smile, only hers was less menacing.

"Well, like, there was this one time. It was before I ever started going out with James. I was in seventh grade."

Milada's eyes widened with much interest and she gave Jolene her full attention the same way any woman would do when there was juicy gossip floating around the room.

"There was this older boy," Jolene continued. "And he lived a few streets over from me."

"How old was he," Milada asked. "Just curious. Because there's old. And then there's creepy old."

"He was almost eighteen. He was just older. He was still in high school when we met. His name was Mark Nestorovich and my mom hired him to cut our grass every Saturday because that summer my older brother had broken his leg during baseball practice. Mark was a cutie. They called him Nessy. Oh, Milada, I had the biggest crush on this guy. I used to watch him cut the grass."

"That sounds boring."

"With his shirt off."

Both girls laughed quietly.

"He had the best tan I've ever seen in my life. And he was still basically young, but his muscles were like a man's. He was such a hunk and I would stare at him through my blinds the whole time he was out in our yard pushing the mower around. When he'd have to push it really hard the muscles in his arms would bulge out and I would just get so faint whenever I saw it happen."

"Oh my gosh," Milada hushed. "I gotta hear the end of this."

"When he'd leave I'd lay back on my bed and daydream about what it would be like to be married to him."

"*Really?*"

"And to make love to him."

"You thought about making love in *seventh* grade," Milada was so surprised. "I'm such a geek. Here's me still playing with Barbies when I was that old. I hadn't even thought about kissing a boy until, like, three years ago. I've only done, like, *it*, once in my whole life ... make love I mean."

"Well, that's a good thing. I watched a lotta TV while I was growing up. It's where I got all of my sex education. Besides Milada, I was just thinking about it, but there were lots of girls my age that were actually doing it, like on a regular basis."

"Tell me about it."

"Yeah."

"So what else happened with the lawn boy?"

"Well, mostly I just watched him the whole summer and I wished and prayed that I could be with him, but I knew I never could because he was so much older and more experienced than me. We didn't have anything in common at all. The thought of me never being able to be with him just killed me. I even thought about committing suicide. Can you believe it! I was in such a mess over this guy. I mean, I actually thought that he was my one and only true love and that I'd never in my life get another chance with a guy like that."

"How did you get over him?"

"Well, it wasn't that easy. Finally towards the end of the summer I got up the nerve to talk to him, but I would only go outside when nobody else was home because I didn't want my brother to tease me. Nessy and I would just sit there in the lawn and talk for hours until somebody came home, and then I would act like I never even knew him when my family was around. I had imagined up this whole big secret love affair. And then things started to go a little faster than what I was used to. He started telling me things, like, how smart and mature and pretty I was and, girl, lemme tell you, I believed every single word he told me. Every goddamn word of it. One night he even came and tapped on my bedroom window in the middle of the night and he kissed me and gave me a flower he had picked in the neighbor's yard. It was *sooo* sweet, Milada. I was so much in love with him. My heart just ached whenever we couldn't be together. After we kissed," Jolene took a deep breath. "Oh my God I'm such a dork, but I asked him if he was my boyfriend."

"What did he say?"

"He said he was, but I could never tell anyone because of our ages and all. So I agreed to keep it a secret. After only a few days he started pressuring me about it."

"About what?"

"About sex, what do you think? Anyway, I didn't wanna do *it* yet, mainly because I was scared of it hurting and I was sure I'd get pregnant."

"He pressured you? That's really creepy," Milada let her know.

"I know, but it gets worse. One Saturday my mom and my

brother were gonna be gone all day. They went shopping for some new clothes or something. Then Nessy came over and I let him into my bedroom. This was, like, a really huge deal because I had never let a boy into my room before when no one was home. We both sat on my bed and we started kissing heavier than I'd ever kissed before. I didn't even know what the hell I was doing so I just kept trying to block his tongue with my tongue. I thought it was some kinda contest or something, a joust. And then he started acting really cool, ya know? Like he just came over to hang out with me. He kept telling me how pretty I was. Then he opened up his backpack and pulled out this bottle of red wine. He asked me if I wanted to drink some and I told him I had never even touched a drop before. He said it was easy going down and that wine doesn't really mess you up like other stuff does.

"*Yeah right*," Milada hissed.

"He took the bottle and chugged some of it and then he was, like, 'see nothing happened.' I still wasn't sure and then he told me that his five-year-old little brother drinks wine all the time and that his parents let him do it because wine was ok to drink."

"You believed that horseshit?"

"Every word. I was in love, Milada! So I tried some and I really liked it. It wasn't that bad at all. He kept passing the bottle back to me and he wasn't even drinking any. Before I knew it, I was *sooo* drunk and I felt *sooo* good. He started kissing me again and he had my clothes off really fast, but I liked it because I was drunk and was sure this was the guy I was gonna marry. He told me I was too young to get pregnant. God I was so stupid, Milada! We had sex right there on my bed with the door wide-open and he didn't wear protection or anything. That's how I lost my virginity. I told Lisa Diamond about it and then she told everybody and when Nessy found out people were talking about us he lied and said it wasn't true. And then he never talked to me ever again. I was so devastated."

"That's *such* a sad story," Milada felt bad for her.

"Yeah, and one time about a year later I saw him while I was riding my bike. It was, like, he was stopped at a stop sign in some convertible with some slut in a motorcycle jacket. I was wearing sweats. I felt so ugly. I said 'Hi' to him and he acted, like, he never even knew me. It was so rude."

"What an asshole."

"So the point is sometimes a girl feels a certain way about a guy they really know nothing about. So just make sure you really get to know this guy, whoever he is, before you really throw your heart into a commitment."

"I guess you're right," Milada agreed. "I feel so much better. Thanks."

"Hey, it's getting late. What do you say we go have fun while this party is still hopping?"

All of the sudden: BANG, BANG, BANG!

There was a vicious knock on the bathroom door. It scared Jolene and Milada off of their asses and onto their feet. The two girls stared at each other in guilty horror. It was an unmistakable knock. It was a cop knock.

13

Chris Roebuck burst through the front door like a suspiciously jealous husband, his eyes cold and silent like John Wayne. For a second or two he just stood there as his green eyes shifted back and forth scanning the room. There were people everywhere and all around there was mad juvenile drunkenness.

Well, he thought, *here goes nothing!*

"*Coooooooops,*" he screamed so loud his mouth went in full circle.

No one listened. A few people looked over to see who the psycho was in the doorway. The Pantherettes still danced. The Jocks still horsed around and the music played on.

He took a deep breath and then tried again, "*Coooooooops!*"

Lotsa kids froze and didn't know what to do. A few cunning fellows were already making the slip out the back door, but still a large amount of people paid Chris Roebuck no attention. Frustrated, he ran into the living room and headed right for the stereo. A drunken kid from Granite got in his way and Roebuck lifted his knee right into the nuts of the drunken kid and dropped him into his own shadow. Now kids were shocked and everybody stopped messing around. Chris Roebuck ripped the stereo's power cord from the wall and music left with a quick booming thud, all bass: Zzzzzoop!

"*Fucking cops are coming*," he screamed again.

It sent everyone scurrying for every exit like a bunch of Japanese shoppers in a Godzilla film. Everyone was freaked out and confused. No one knew how much time they had left before the Gestapo arrived.

First thing you have to do in a situation like that is to grab your coat. That's another thing about people from Indiana, they could have a thousand dollars in late bills, mouths to feed, and toilet paper to buy, and with their last three hundred bucks they go buy a black leather coat.

And then, if you aren't driving the night the cops come and bust the party, and you were counting on a ride home from someone, it is imperative you find that person at once, with absolutely no fucking around whatsoever.

Chris Roebuck just stood back and smiled his scumbag grin and watched what he had created. That's when Kevin socked him in the shoulder.

"*Chris*," Kevin was extremely frustrated with the current status of the Break Up the Party Mission.

"What the *fuck* did you do that for, asshole," Roebuck shouted at him and rubbed his upper arm. "I should drag your ass outside right now!"

"Dickhead, you were supposed to find Ray before you opened up the can of worms!"

"You never covered that in the mission briefing!"

"I didn't think I had to! Com'n let's go find him," Kevin said and pulled Roebuck with him. They ran as fast as they could considering it was a madhouse with hoards of people bumping into each other as they tried to escape.

Kim ran right into them and almost knocked Chris Roebuck

over.

"What do we do," she hysterically asked. "What if he runs away?"

"Stay here in the living room," Kevin ordered. "If you see him, grab him and tell him to wait for us!"

Kim had a look like she was busy processing information and then she ran away. Kevin and Roebuck were confused about where to look first. They were standing by the stairs that led down to the front door.

Lewis was there holding the door open and he was saying goodbye to everyone like, "Goodnight, thank you, come again please," and so on.

It took about ten minutes for most everyone to clear out and they still hadn't found me. However, Kevin did not give up hope that I was there, because there were still three rooms left to check that they didn't try. One was the Den, one was the guestroom at the end of the hall, and one was the downstairs bathroom. Chris Roebuck and Kevin and Lewis were afraid they'd bust in on somebody having sex or something so they decided to check the downstairs bathroom for me and hope for the best.

"I'll go check it out," Chris Roebuck said and Kevin and Lewis followed him downstairs.

They stood in front of the door to the bathroom. The light was on and it sent out a beam that covered their shoes because the hallway was dark. Some kid had knocked over the lamp while running by. Chris Roebuck was about to knock when he looked over into the room by the card table, and there was that bum Paul Long, lying on the ground all passed out.

"Hold up a sec, guys," Roebuck said. "Look over there," and he pointed at Paul Long's poisoned and intoxicated passed-out body.

Roebuck walked over to him. Kevin followed closely behind and Lewis walked right over and kicked Paul Long as if he was a hunter testing a killed animal.

"*Shhhh*," Roebuck hissed and pointed down at Paul. "Don't kick him yet. This is a dream come true."

"I hate this guy," Kevin said. "Look at him, all that he does is suck on the bottle all day."

"We gotta fuck with him," Lewis begged.

Chris Roebuck knelt down and picked up Paul's arm and let it go limp and drop on the floor.

"He's out cold, money," he said and looked up and smiled. "Kevin, you don't have to stick around for this if you don't wanna. I don't wanna fuck around with your morals or anything like that."

"Well, I do hate that guy. Paul Long, what a loser. Fuck it," Kevin said in a rebellious way. "I'm staying. Let him have it."

Good gave way to evil and Kevin began to laugh wildly.

"All right," Roebuck said.

He was so excited that Kevin wanted to do something bad for once.

"Watch this," Roebuck said and he reached into Paul's back pocket and took out his wallet. He took all the cash out. Paul was rich so it was almost a hundred bucks. Then Kevin grabbed the wallet and went outside on the sidewalk, dropped the empty wallet onto the ground, unzipped his fly and pissed all over it. Lewis couldn't stop laughing and he was getting excited also and so he hauled off and kicked Paul in the stomach and it made the kid barf all over himself.

And he still didn't wake up.

"You think he's *dead*," Kevin asked.

"No. He ain't dead," Roebuck said. "He just puked. He's totally alive. What else should we do to him?"

"Let's pick him up," Kevin said. "And put him in the hot tub! Make sure you don't get any barf on yourself. Be careful, guys. And keep his clothes on when you put him in. I'll get the cover off." Kevin took the cover off and Roebuck and Lewis very carefully picked up Paul and sat him up in the hot tub and when they did the oily barf started drifting and blending in with the hot water. He still didn't wake up. They all started cracking up laughing.

"Here," Roebuck said. "Let's put this empty beer can in his hand, that sloppy-ass drunk."

"Kevin, you gotta take a picture," Lewis said.

Kevin was a photography nerd and he always had a camera around his neck. Then as a prop Lewis found an empty beer can and put it in Paul's hand. Kevin snapped a few pictures of Paul in the hot tub with barf all over his face and a can of Old Style in his hand.

"Ok, that's enough fun for me," Kevin said between laughing fits. "Let's take him out and put him in the bath tub so he doesn't drown. Christ, we don't want him to drown do we?"

Roebuck and Lewis failed to answer, suggesting that indeed they did want the prick to drown. Roebuck tried to think of an excuse keep Paul in the hot tub.

"But somebody's in the bathroom still, remember," Roebuck mentioned.

"Well, what the hell should we do with him then? Seriously," Lewis said. "We can't just leave him here in the tub, he's all fucking passed out and shit. Roebuck, this is your responsibility, dog."

"*Responsibility*," Roebuck questioned as if he'd never in his life heard of such a word. "I've never heard that word before, man. Are you speaking English? He's lucky that it's the middle of winter or else I'd just throw his ass in the lake. But hey, maybe that's not a bad idea. He'd get frozen. That'd be funny. You guys think we messed up the water by getting his puke in it? Don't these things come with water filters?"

"Look," Kevin said. "I'll get us into the bathroom, at least I'll knock and see who the hell is in there if you two knuckleheads carry his ass in there. I've gotta bad back and I'm not about to mess it up before the meet tomorrow."

"That sounds fair. Go for it," Lewis said.

"Yeah," Roebuck laughed. "We'll carry him all right. I hope we don't drop him though."

Kevin walked right up the door and took a deep breath and hesitated for a second because he was nervous about what he would find in there. If you've ever worked a restaurant that's in a trashy neighborhood you might be able to relate, because of what you sometimes find in the restroom after some weirdo's been in there for a while can be scary.

BANG, BANG, BANG!

Kevin knocked as hard as he could. He figured some drunken bastard had locked the door and passed out in there so he wanted to knock loud enough to wake whoever it was up. Anyway, he banged on the door as loud as possible like a cop would and for about thirty seconds or so he didn't hear anything at all. No one answered and he was about to knock again when a girl's voice called out as clear as a Washington view.

"Who is it?"

Kevin turned and smiled at the other guys and they were already standing there holding Paul's dripping wet body. Lewis had his legs and Roebuck held onto his torso.

They looked at Kevin like they were thinking, *why don't you say something? This guy's heavy.*

"You ready," Roebuck asked Lewis.

"Yeah," he answered. "One, two, three," and then they both let go of Paul at the same time and let him drop to the floor. Then they picked him up again.

"*Um,*" Kevin said in his polite voice. "We gotta kid out here who really needs to use the bathroom. Are you almost through or what?"

He heard a second girl's voice behind the door. They were whispering. Paul groaned and did a squeaky little hiccup.

"It's a good thing this kid is such a skinny pussy," Roebuck whispered. "I couldn't carry Patrick's fat-ass anywhere, but with old Paul here you just take his money and toss him wherever you wanna."

The doorknob turned slowly like it does in scary movies and then the door opened and the light flooded the dark hallway. Of course you know who comes out of the bathroom. It's Milada and Jolene and they are surprised as hell that the party has disappeared. And to top it off here's a tall goofy kid with a big nest of blonde curly hair and two bozos carrying around a sopping wet lifeless body.

"Hey ladies," Roebuck said. "I won't tell if you don't," and he raised his eyebrow as if they were up to something naughty in there. For some reason guys always get a kick outta when two girls go into the bathroom together. I guess it has to do with too much imagination and too little experience. It's a lesbian thing.

"Who's the dead kid," Jolene asked.

"He's not dead," Kevin explained. "He's just passed out drunk."

"Yeah," Roebuck piped in. "He's just a little tired is all."

"Why is he all wet," Milada asked.

Lewis and Roebuck carried Paul right by them and into the bathroom because they had been holding him for so long their arms were about to fall off. They laid him in the bathtub and closed the shower curtain.

"There," Roebuck said loudly. "Think he needs a shower?"

Lewis laughed, "He just had a bath so let's just leave him alone for right now, dog."

Jolene stood in the doorway and asked, "What the *hell* happened to him?"

"Yeah. Why won't he wake up," Milada also asked.

"Oh," Roebuck said. "Kevin here, he let out, like, the deadliest fart in the world and it just knocked old Paul out cold. Poor mother fucker. He never saw it coming."

"Very funny," Jolene smiled.

"What's your name," Kevin said to Jolene. "Who are you?"

He always interrupted and made an attempt to change the subject when Roebuck said something stupid and embarrassing.

"Jolene."

"Jolene, I'm Kevin and this is Lewis and Chris. This stupid kid in the bathtub drank too much whiskey and fell into the hot tub. And since he won't wake up we thought we'd put him in the bath tub so he don't get everything all wet, or drown."

"Oh," she said and she walked over to the tub, pulled the shower curtain aside and looked at Paul. "Oh yeah, I remember him. What an idiot."

"Where did everybody go," Milada asked as she walked over to a window and peeked through the blinds.

"The cops came by and scared everyone away," Lewis said. "Look, *uh*," he wanted to know Milada's name.

"Milada," she smiled.

"Milada," Lewis said it outloud to himself. "Girl, if you need a ride home I'd be more than happy to provide one for you. It'll be real smooth."

Chris laughed and said, "Dude. You don't even got a car."

Lewis was always something of a ladies man. He was thin, but muscular. He was half-white and half-black and his skin color was a dark olive color, like a Korean. And his hair was, like, loose silky black curls, and he had gray eyes. Aside from his looks he was an athlete. He played the guitar and he was a black belt in Aikido. And he was raised a Buddhist which is pretty interesting if you're from Indiana.

"Thanks, but I drove her here and I'm driving her home," Jolene said to him so Milada wouldn't have to answer.

"We gotta fast car," Roebuck said as a joke that was a cross between the Tracy Chapman song and a sarcastic slam to Kevin's driving situation with his mom's car.

"Nobody has a faster car than me," Jolene bragged. There was always such power in her voice. She never got nervous while talking to anybody about anything. It's not often that you meet someone with so much self-esteem and pride.

"What kinda car you got," Lewis asked as he took out another Newport and lit it.

"Can I get a cigarette," Milada asked him.

"It's menthol," Roebuck warned her.

"Oh, never mind," she said.

Chris razzed her. "No to the menthols. She hates niggers."

"I don't *hate* black people. I just don't like menthol. No offense."

"None taken," Lewis said. "What kinda car?"

"It's a Ford Mustang."

"Kevin has his mom's poopy family car," Roebuck said. "It's fresh. We always cruise for girls in it on Friday nights. We never find any though."

"That's great," Jolene said. "God, I can't believe this house is so empty. We were in the bathroom for only, like, twenty minutes and the place was packed when we went inside and now it's like this."

"Maybe somebody cut a finger and spilled some AIDS," Roebuck said.

He could never be serious, not even for a second.

"Maybe there's a sadistic murderer in the house," Lewis gave an idea. "And everyone escaped except for the very brave, but very stupid guys and the pretty cheerleader-type girls with the high pitched screams. Maybe only one of us will get away."

"Look," Jolene got sarcastic. "You guys are *sooo* funny, but it looks to me like the cops came or something and everybody just left. We've gotta find Erin and Lisa and Leslie," she said to Milada.

"All right," Roebuck said. "Kevin there's even hope for you with three more girls in the house."

"He'd have a better chance with a girl than you," Jolene said. "Lotsa girls go for smart guys that have something to offer other than corny jokes."

"Oh no," Lewis sighed.

"You're burning me," Roebuck said and laughed it off.

He thought it was funny when you insulted him. It got him fired up.

"Hey," Kevin said. "It's funny you're looking for someone because so are we. Maybe you know him?"

"What's their name," Milada asked.

"Ray," Lewis told them. "Ray Kozlowski."

The girls laughed and Jolene said, "You guys are Ray's friends? That's *sooo* funny. So you guys go to that school he used to go to right?"

"Yeah. We all go to Andrean," Chris Roebuck said. "They teach us to be numb-skulls."

"I believe you," Jolene said. "I've met the others."

"You should see what Ray does when he finds drunk people lying around. He's the meanest sonavabitch outta all of us," Roebuck said.

"I thought you just found him like that," Milada questioned him.

"We did. Sorta," Kevin explained. "Just so you girls know, I'm not an asshole like these guys. I just end up getting stuck driving them around all the time."

"Look. We haven't seen Ray in a really long time," Jolene said. "But last we heard he was upstairs somewhere. If you guys see anyone who's looking for me I'll be out by my car, ok? Lisa and Leslie always know to meet me at the car when shit like this happens.

I think they're probably there, but just in case you see them is what I mean."

"Ok, I'll keep my eyes peeled," Kevin said. "And if you see Ray tell him to come inside."

"Bye, boys," Milada said as Jolene and her went out through sliding glass door.

"Bye, blonde girl," Roebuck was talking to Jolene. "I'll call you!"

"Like hell," she said and they were gone into the blowing snow-storm.

14

The next thing I knew I was laying on the floor by the bed and the side of my face was planted deep into the carpet. Erin was sitting beside me. She was crying. I sat up not knowing what to say to her or what to say for myself after barfing my guts out and saying God knows what to her.

"I'm sorry," I said to her in the soberest voice I could come up with. I sounded like a little boy and that made me feel like I had just given an empty apology. I touched her hand and she pulled it away from me.

She spoke: "Raymond, I thought you were different. I never pictured you wanting to die by doing heroin. You scared the living fucking shit out of me. I didn't know what to do."

"Erin," I paused because I had nothing to say for myself, but I thought it would be even worse not to say anything at all. "God," I said. "I'm fine. I'm fine. I was never even close to dying. I didn't even feel sick. That shit was the best."

"You pucked your guts out."

"That was from being dizzy."

"I just want you to go and brush your teeth," she ordered me.

"You want me to what?"

She smiled and sniffled. "Brush your teeth. You should always brush your teeth after throwing up because the **Acid**s in your stom-ach can eat up your teeth."

"Trailer park," I chuckled.

"Just do it."

I was thinking mood swing, because I can always point them out when a girl has one. But then again who can't, they're so fucking obvious. I agreed and I went and brushed my teeth with a travel-size toothbrush that I opened brand new from it's plastic casing.

"The maids keep this place like a hotel," I called to her in the other room.

When I came back outta the bathroom she was sitting on the bed with her shoes off.

"Come and hold me, Raymond," she said with her arms reaching for me.

"Oh shit, bulls-eye with the mental instability. Now you're happy again," I teased her. "You're back and forth Great America thrill-ride-style except for I don't gotta wait in line for an hour for it to start happening."

"What?"

"Huh?"

She crossed her eyes, squinted at me.

"What did you just say?"

"Me?"

"Yeah."

"I didn't say anything," I played stupid.

"Yes you did. You called me a Great America ride or something. What the hell is that supposed to mean, dude?"

"What? You're crazy. I didn't say anything. I didn't."

I sat next to her and we embraced and we both leaned back into the mountain of throw-pillows with my head resting on her fully inflated breasts while she rubbed her hand up and down my back. She smelled like flowers or flower perfume and I could hear her heart thumping. I imagined the heartbeats to be telling me the story of her life. I was sure that it was the most wonderful heart on Earth. Never skipping a beat. Always pumping in new life. Never stopping. Never stopping.

"Raymond," she said. "I want you to promise never to do that again, as long as we're together. Do you promise?"

"I promise," I said. "Are we together?"

"Forever," she said with conviction.

"That shit was good though."

In my mind I thought, well, *what about him? How can we be together forever when she's together with Jeremy?*

I kept my doubts to myself and for some reason I trusted her like I've never trusted anyone in my entire life. To me, her word was it. The truth. Together we were real in the most phoney place in America. In The Region everything was artificial. Even the people.

"I love you," I said to her. I was nervous and wondered if I shouldn't have said that. She didn't say anything for a few moments and I just continued to listen to her heartbeat and I thought if I listened carefully I could hear the answer pumping through her chest.

"I love you too, Raymond," she said strongly. "I love you too."

We kissed for the second time right then on the bed, with me reaching my face up towards her to do so.

We stopped kissing and she asked me: "Do you believe in mental telepathy?"

"You mean like reading somebody's mind?"

"Yeah," she said.

"I don't know. Do you?"

"I believe it can happen when two people's emotions are really connected. Will you try it with me?"

"Can we do it naked?"

15

Ricky came staggering outta the den with his girlfriend Alexis. He was wearing his dad's aviator jacket, Oakley razor-blade sunglasses, flowered Ocean Pacific Bermuda shorts, and a Puma tennis cap that made his dreads flare out like a poop-stained feather duster.

Ricky and Alexis were tripping on **Acid**. That's why they had been cooped up in the den for hours. Ricky grabbed his dead grandfather's old cane and started swinging it in circles, a regular tap-dancing performer from the State Fair.

The livingroom was all clear of kids except for our heroes. Chris Roebuck, Kevin, Lewis and Kim were sitting on the sofa and appeared to have made themselves at home. There was something cool about Ricky's living room. It had this part of the floor in the middle of the room right in front of the fireplace that was about three feet lower than the rest of the floor. It was a big square about twelve feet wide and twelve feet long and inside the square were two leather couches and a glass coffee table. That's the Polish description. The English translation is it's a sunken living room.

"Wuz happenin, guys," Ricky called to them.

And then he started messing around. He was doing this tapdance with the cane still swinging around.

"I'm, like, Sammy Davis Jr..," He called to them with a thick slur..

Kim started laughing and couldn't stop.

"Dude," Lewis said. "You gotta stop making your woman look bad with all that shit."

Lewis hated Ricky because he knew Ricky was a phony and Ricky idolized Lewis because he was the real deal.

"What's your name again," Lewis said to Ricky's girl.

"Alexis."

"Girl, if you get tired of his fried-banana ass you can come and be with me, ok?"

"Yo, Ricky," Roebuck said. "You look like a dancing monkey at the Big Top."

Then he gave Lewis the rock in agreement.

"Ricky, stop fucking around," Kevin said. "We need to find Ray. Have you seen him?"

He stopped dancing and put his arm around Alexis and he started stroking his chin. He was trying to think.

"Kozlowski," he asked them. "He could be anywhere. That bastard could be anywhere. He's a transformer ya know?"

"Ricky, you're tripping," Roebuck said.

"I saw him earlier," Alexis whispered. "Over there in that room."

She pointed down the hall. Alexis hardly ever said anything, and when she did she always whispered like a little old woman might do. Roebuck stood up and cupped his ear with his hand so that he could hear better.

"Come again, sweetheart?"

She smiled bashfully and just pointed again, "Down there."

"He's in the guest room," Kevin asked. "I thought we checked in there. Who's he in there with?"

Everyone assumed I was in the room with a girl, they just didn't know who.

Kim frowned and looked hurt, "Maybe we should just let him be."

"I'm with her," Lewis said. "I wouldn't want you faggot-asses to come busting down my door if I was with a bitch."

"On da other hand, maybe we should git to da bottom'a this right away," Ricky said. "Transformers, they always be makin a mess. Am I right, or am I right? Yeah, yeah, yeah, guy. Yeah."

"Yo, I'll check it out," Roebuck said and he stood up and started walking down the hall.

"Ya know, Mr. Kevin," Ricky said. "I wuz gonna have a party tonight, but it looks like nobody showed up except fer you guys."

"Maybe the lizard scared people away," Alexis whispered.

"What lizard is that," Kevin laughed.

"Oh," Ricky explained. "We found a couch lizard in da den. It wuz very large and I had da feed it golf balls. Have ya ever seen one, guy?"

"Afraid not," Kevin said.

"Indeed," Ricky said. "Would anyone care fer a grilled-cheese sandwich?"

Then Patrick came inside from the porch. He was alone and he seemed to be freezing his ass off.

"Ricky, you cracked-out nigger fuck," he yelled. "Have you seen any damn police?"

"I think it was a false alarm," Kevin laughed and when he laughed he always shook his head around. It would send his blond curls dancing around like popping corn.

"*Wazzup*, Kevin. Chris, hey. Kim," Patrick nodded to them. "Kim,

I'll take you home in a second. You'll be the one tonight! And don't be late. Where's that bitch, Kozlowski? He owes me commission."

Roebuck laughed again, "He's in the love shack with some girl. We're waiting for him to come out."

"Hah," Patrick grunted.

"Hah-hah," Ricky mimicked with his sunglasses and that cane.

"Shut up, Jackson Five," Patrick said to him. "Kim, who do you think Ray's in that room with?"

"How should I know," She sighed, but she tried to pass it off like she didn't care.

"Well, it ain't you is it," he said most unsympathetically.

She didn't say anything. She just stared down at her shoes.

Ricky was standing in front of the stove now and all four burners were turned to **HIGH** and glowing red. He was only getting bits and pieces of the conversation again.

"I'm gonna go check the room out," Roebuck said and he went down the hall.

"You better cover your eyes, Kim," Patrick warned her.

He was deliberately trying to make her cry and it was working. Her chin quivered and her eyes watered. She really cared about me and every time she thought I would change, something like this would happen.

Someday, she thought, *I should just go with Patrick just to piss Raymond off. Then I'll be done with him once and for all. Stranger things have happened.*

This did happen eventually. And I didn't give a shit. So much for that plan.

16

Erin and I were sitting Indian-style on the floor. We were both in our underwear and facing each other and trying to guess what the other was thinking. We weren't guessing anything right.

That's when Chris Roebuck started pounding on the door. Erin and I got scared because it sounded just like a cop knock.

"Hurry up and get dressed. Go unlock the glass door to the

deck," I told her. *"Quickly!* I'll go check and see who it is. Get ready because you might have to run."

She got dressed and so did I. Then she went to the door and when she had it unlocked and opened a bit I answered the door, but it was only Chris Roebuck. Erin came back in and acted as if she wasn't planning on running anywhere, like she knew who it was and was just getting some fresh air.

"Hey, champ," he said.

"What's up there, Chris?"

"Is everything cool in here," he asked me and peeked in around my shoulder so he could get a look at who I was with.

"Yeah, man," I said. "This is Erin. We were just having sex is all."

"Right," he patronized me. "Listen. Kevin sent me in here. He's worried that you might be *getting into some trouble*, if you know what I mean." Roebuck chuckled and smiled at Erin. "Hi there," he said politely.

"You know what, Chris? Tell Kevin to eat shit," I said.

"I would, but old Kim is out there too. Kevin's got his panties in a bunch about you getting arrested all the time and Kim is paranoid that you don't love her, which, like, everybody knows you don't. And so, for the sake of my sanity, I was wondering if you wanted to maybe ditch *this* one in a nice way, so *that* one out there doesn't start crying and shit. I wouldn't ask, but quite frankly you don't have to ride home with the crazy bitch."

"Kim is here," I asked. "Shit."

"Yeah. She's hot on your trail," he smiled at Erin.

"Oh, Ray. So you gotta girlfriend. I should have guessed. Really I don't care. It's cool. I know you don't want her to see me," She smiled and put her hands on her hips. "I'll just climb down the deck here. It ain't that far down, plus I have to see where Jolene is, dude. We've been in here a long time and I bet she's looking for me by now. She told me if we got seperated that I should just meet her out at the car."

I turned to her and tried to explain, "Kim and I got nothing going on. Look, Erin—"

"It's cool, Raymond. Don't sweat it. It's no biggie, dude," She didn't even care. And then she disappeared into the dark. "Nice meeting you, Chris Roebuck!"

Then Chris and I could hear the boards of the balcony creaking and then we heard her lose her grip and then we heard the soft thud of Erin's body hitting the ground.

She said, "Fuck," really loud.

"*Hah*," Chris laughed. "She's nice, huh?"

"Yeah, she's cool," I agreed and I walked passed him. "Thanks for the warning, man."

"No sweat," he said.

I walked out into the living room and saw that everybody was gone.

"Where the fuck is everybody," I asked myself as I trotted down the stairs to see if everyone was really gone. I wondered if I still had a ride home. The only person who was down there was Erin. She had just come in from the outside.

"Hey. Funny seeing you here," I mentioned to her.

"Oh my God! Everybody's gone," she freaked. "How in the hell am I gonna get home, Raymond?"

"Are you sure Jolene left already?"

"Her car isn't even here. All of the cars are gone!"

"Oh shit," I said as Kevin, Kim, Lewis, and Patrick came stomping in from the outside.

"I think the cops came by," Patrick said. "This is your woman?" he asked me about Erin as he glanced back at Kim.

I didn't know what to say because I didn't want Erin to know too much about Kim and at the same time I didn't want Kim to know about Erin and Patrick knew this, yet for his own entertainment he forced the issue.

"I'm not anybody's *woman*, Patrick," Erin said to him. "Don't play like you don't know me."

That'll work, I thought to myself.

"She's not anybody's woman,"

"I've never seen this girl before in my entire life, Kim," Patrick said. "Who are you?"

"That's not how we rehearsed it, Patrick."

Erin was getting pissed at him.

"Yeah, that's what I wanna know," Kevin said. "Who's this nice girl?"

"Erin," she said and she reached out and shook Kevin's hand.

And then she introduced herself to everyone else in the same fashion.

I looked at Kim and she looked at me. She just stood there quietly, looking shy and pretty. She was always such a nice and loyal girl. No matter how many times I hurt her, she always found some way to forgive me. It happened so often that many times I found myself taking advantage of her. Like at this time for instance, she was under the impression that when I returned home from Seattle we were gonna get back together. I had to tell her something in order for her to loan me money for my plane ticket. And here I was with this pretty girl and everyone was acting shady.

Kim stepped outta the group and said, "Ray, I need to talk to you upstairs. Right now."

"*Nice*," Ricky shouted.

The other guys put in their two cents also.

"Hey, Kim," I said. "Let's chill a second."

"*Now*," she barked at me and she stormed upstairs.

I couldn't remember the last time she actually raised her voice to me. I turned to Erin because I wanted to explain.

"Don't even bother, dude," she told me and she went huffing and puffing outside. Kevin went after her.

What a nutty mood swing that was, I thought. *First she's, like, Ok I'll just jump off the deck, and now she flips out and takes it all personal.*

"*Ah*, Ray. She's crying," Patrick shouted. "They're both crying. Oh this is awesome! I love it when you do shit like that. It fucking kills me! I couldn't of done it better myself. Did you see that, guys? He made two cry at the exact same time. Absolutely brilliant! Seriously. That was fresh."

"Good action," Ricky agreed.

"It was fun while it lasted, huh," Chris Roebuck said to me.

"Thanks a lot, fellas," I said to them and I moseyed upstairs to talk to her.

I took my time so I could think of a good excuse to tell Kim. I wasn't really worried about Kim freaking out much more because we had this talk a thousand times and she always ended up forgiving me, but it was Erin I didn't know about. What was I gonna tell her? Then I was thinking, *why should I have to tell her anything at all? She's the one with the boyfriend.*

Kim was a lotta things, but she wasn't my girlfriend. It annoyed me that she was making such a big deal about this. Like I said before, we went out when I was a sophomore and she was a freshman. We were just casual, but at first things got outta hand. We went steady for three whole months and in those few months we got silly serious—like we talked about marriage and all that garbage, which is utterly ridiculous. Around the same time my mother kicked me outta the house and I had no place to go, so Kim's parents said I could stay there for a few weeks until my dad turned up because nobody knew where in the hell he was.

I had no job. I paid no rent. I ate their food and I never gave it a second thought. After a coupla weeks of living with Kim we were at each other's throats. She freaked out and told me she didn't love me anymore and that she wanted me to leave. That hurt my feelings so I told her I always thought she was piece of shit in bed. It was an ugly scene.

Upstairs I heard sniffling and crying coming from the den.

"*Kim,*" I called to her and I pushed open the door. She was sitting on the sofa and she had her knees pressed against her chest. She was hugging her legs and she wouldn't look at me.

"Could you please close the door," she asked. "I'm sick of our relationship being everyone else's business."

"What the fuck are you talking about," I said. "Nobody's ever in our business."

"Oh *right!* Ray, you tell your friends everything about what you do with girls."

"I do not!"

"Yes ... you do," she corrected me. "Your idiot friends, like, that *asshole* Patrick, think messing around with different girls is cool, so they encourage you to do it more."

"Look," I said. "Say whatever you wanna about me, but don't drag my friends into this."

I was hoping to swing the argument away from the subject of Erin if possible; maybe, I thought, she'd forget why we started arguing in the first place, but I had no such luck.

"So who was that *whore* that you were with in the bedroom?"

"Erin? I wasn't *with* her in the bedroom, Kim! Are you insane?"

It was my strategy to make her think that she was crazy. I knew she was insecure about herself, and she had a lotta emotional problems.

"Stop telling me I'm crazy! I fucking *hate* you sometimes!"

She jumped up and started slapping at me like Whitney Houston on Bobby Brown. I grabbed her arms and held them.

"Kim, *please* calm down! Calm down and let's talk about this. Every time we get into an arguement you have to turn it into some kinda cage-fight!"

She started crying hard and we held each other.

"Oh God," she cried. "Why can't you just love me," she just cried and cried.

"Kim," I said knowing that I'd regret it. "I do love you. It's just you freak out too much and I can't handle that shit. Why can't you just be cool?"

"Oh, Raymond. How can I be cool when my boyfriend is in the bedroom with another girl? How?"

"*Boyfriend?* Kim, didn't you see me come outta there by myself?"

"Ray, I thought you came home so we could be together. I was so excited and I told all of my friends. On the way over here I kept telling Chris Roebuck and Kevin and Lewis how much we loved each other," she sniffled. "And that you flew all the way home just to be with me. And then we get here and you're in the room with some girl. I'm so fucking embarrassed. I could just die."

I sensed she was starting to calm down so I just said, "I'm sorry, Kim. Things are gonna change. I mean it, starting right now."

"Do you swear to God?"

"Yes, I swear to God."

"My parents went to Illinois for the weekend to see my grandma," she hinted.

I knew what she was hinting about. She wanted me to spend the night at her house. She always wanted me to stay the night with her when the folks were away. Kim claimed that staying in a big empty house gave her the creeps, and she couldn't sleep if I didn't stay over, but it was really so she could sex me.

"Oh yeah," I said.

"So, do you wanna stay the night with me," she asked looking up at me.

Kim had a beautiful face. It was her best quality. She also, aside from the self-esteem freak-out incidents, had a great personality. I always felt comfortable enough around her that I could be myself. With a lotta girls you have to get into character whenever they're around, but I never had to act a certain way around Kim.

"Is Steven gonna be home," I asked.

Steven was her older brother and my older brother's best friend. I originally met Kim through him. I asked if he would be home because he was a mean son-of-a-bitch and he'd give me the beat down if he caught me spending the night.

"I'm not sure," she answered. "Does it matter if he's home or not?"

"Shit yeah it matters. He'll kill me if he catches me at your house."

"Ray," she sighed. "No, he won't be there. He wouldn't care anyway because he likes you. He really does. Besides, if you're my boyfriend why would he get pissed about that?"

She had made me her boyfriend again. She was always doing this.

"I don't know Kim. I just don't wanna take any chances on my life right now. I just got punched in the fact last week. Look. I love you. I really do love you. It's just I don't know if I'm ready to tell everyone we know yet. I don't think that sounds like I mean it to sound, but I'm being honest with what I'm telling you."

"Then come home with me if you love me. Steven won't even

be home until the sun comes up and it's not like he comes into my bedroom and checks up on me."

"Ok," I said. "I'll come with you."

"I love you, Raymond."

"I love you too, Kim. I already said that."

17

"**H**ey, Erin! Where the fuck are you going," Kevin shouted at her through the stinging winter wind, but the air was too cold for his voice to carry. The words froze to death a few feet from his mouth and vanished.

All he could see was her jogging body bobbing up and down and getting further away as she chased somebody's tail-lights. He pulled his coat up over his face and he ran after her. As he ran to the end of the driveway, towards where he lost sight of the girl, he heard a car door slam shut. He reached the road only to see the taillights of a car disappearing into the blizzard. Erin was nowhere to be found.

WATERBONG INTERMISSION

You just read 153 pages of a story with very little structure portrayed with unattractive characters who are supposed to be from northwest Indiana. This is beyond your wildest dreams.

REGIONRAT resumes very shortly, so now would be a good time to roll a joint and break out the Barely Legal Magazine, because there's a sex scene or two coming up. I swear to God.

18

When they reached the part of County Line Road that led through the snow-covered farmlands and headed back towards Granite, all of the girls in Jolene's car were excited about escaping the police. They felt kinda like fugitives all crammed together in the getaway car, but even to Jolene there was nothing more excruciatingly hard to listen to than four teenage girls ruthlessly yapping and screeching all at once, all of them fighting to be heard and nobody listening, sounding like Friday night at the dog pound. To some it's a nightmare.

"Oh my God, dude," Erin screamed over everybody.

"I didn't see the police," Milada confessed. "Did anyone see the police?"

"I think I saw a cop in the bushes," Lisa Diamond shouted. "I swear I saw one!"

Leslie Hipp was in the front seat. She rolled down the window and snow mixed with cold wind came gusting into the car and it made them scream even louder.

Leslie stuck her head outside the car window and yelled.

"The cops are chasing us! It's the middle of a blizzard and I'm fucking drunk still!"

Then she started barfing it all up in splats and it made everybody laugh, everyone except for Jolene. She was very protective about her new car. It's a fucking Ford Mustang for chrissakes. Jolene pulled over on the side of the road and screamed.

"Shut up! You guys are *fucking* up my car and you're all outta control!"

Leslie hung over the car door and Jolene grabbed her and pulled her back into the car. She held the little switch forward and rolled the window back up.

"Leslie, Goddamnit! If there's any throw-up on the side of my car you're washing it as soon as we get back!"

Jolene turned to the back-seat and Lisa, Erin, and Milada looked stunned. All three of them were smoking cigarettes.

"And how many goddamn times do I have to tell you there ain't no smoking in this car!"

She turned back around and gripped the steering wheel with both hands and was growling and breathing heavy. Leslie had just passed out, and the three girls quickly extinguished their smokes into the ashtray.

"Sorry, Jolene," Lisa Diamond whimpered.

"Jeez, dude," Erin said to Jolene. "You're freaking me out."

Milada didn't know what to say so she didn't say anything. Sometimes all you can do when you're around somebody volatile is wait and just see what happens. It's ok, you usually don't have to wait long when you're dealing with such a splendid psychotic like Jolene, the Mustang-driving, trash-talking Midwestern tomboy.

"Look," Jolene said trying to calm herself down. "I'm sorry. I guess I lost my cool. I'm having my period and I just don't know. I'm sorry I yelled at you guys."

Jolene started the car and drove on and everybody was quiet. And it was beautiful mood swing, one of the best of all times, and it was something a guy only could have hoped to study—from a distance that is. If I actually saw it I'd probably give it an 8.5 for originality for the period comment. I'd give a 9.0 for style, because she pulled the car over and I'd give a solid 10.5 for screaming and acting like Sam Kinnison, God rest his soul.

The real reason Jolene was upset had nothing to do with her car, or Leslie puking, or the smoking, or (forgive me for saying this) her menstrual cycle. It had to do with her boyfriend, James Chapman.

She wasn't sure if she loved him anymore.

Let me rephrase that, she thought. *I love him, but I'm not in love with him.*

Everybody knows that's a classic way of saying you just don't love someone anymore. They were supposed to go to see a movie that night. James had wanted to see a horror movie for weeks and Jolene promised she would go with him, but then she heard about the party at Raymond's friend's house. And if there was one thing that she was most tired of about having a steady boyfriend it was not having fun anymore.

No matter how close you are to that special somebody there is always something missing, she thought as she guided the car along the solid double yellows.

And that something missing is usually fun and freedom.

She felt, like, as long as she was with James she wouldn't be able to go out to bars when she got old enough. She wouldn't be able to go on road trips with her friends. She basically wouldn't be able to be herself. She would have to spend her entire college years living for somebody else, behaving in accordance with another person's preferences. It had to stop soon. So she ended up avoiding his phone calls all day because she didn't have the heart to tell him she wasn't going to the movie. As if not calling him and telling him she had other plans was better than letting him know the truth so he wouldn't be sitting around worried sick all night.

It was a horrible thing that she did to him and she knew it. The car was just too quiet and she couldn't stand to hear herself think about what a witch she was so she popped in her favorite mix-tape and turned the volume *way* up.

When they got back to Granite, Jolene decided to drop off Leslie first, just in case they had to carry her into the house. This way at least the other girls could help her. It's always very hard to lift a drunken person by yourself.

They pulled into Leslie's driveway. Her house was a white colonial style home and it had these fake-ass Flamingos in the front yard that were purely for decoration, tasteless and unoriginal. They gave the house a generically Floridian appearance.

Luckily Leslie's little nap on the way home refreshed her enough that she was at least coherent enough to stumble into her house on her own. They all sat in the car and waited until she got inside the house before they left because the Gary rapist was still on the loose, and the evening news had every woman too freaked out to go anywhere alone at night.

Lisa Diamond and Milada got dropped of with no problems after that and the last to go home, next to Jolene, was Erin. But before Erin got outta the car, they sat in her driveway and had a little chat about things. It was secret time.

"Dude," Erin started. "Are you pissed at me for being in the bedroom with Raymond? I didn't wanna talk about it around the other girls."

"No, I'm not mad. I'm a little shocked, but I ain't mad really."

"It's just hard."

"What?"

"The fact that Jeremy lives two hours away and I can only see him on holidays and vacations and random weekends. That isn't any way to have a relationship if you ask me. This is high school."

She took outta cigarette and offered one to Jolene.

"Smoke? Can I smoke in the car, just this once?"

"Sure, whatever," Jolene granted. "To tell you the truth, I sometimes will smoke in here. I try not to let other people smoke in here because they'll take advantage of the rule and start burning holes in all my seats. I'll take one too if you're gonna smoke."

She took the cigarette from Erin and lit it with a book of matches she had in her pocket. Then she popped her Rage Against the Machine tape in and turned the volume down real low so they could talk comfortably.

"Do you like Raymond a lot?"

"I think so," Erin whispered.

"What do you mean by that?"

"Well, he's just awesome you know. He's smart and cute and he's funny. It's just, I think he has a girlfriend and the fact that he's gotta girlfriend and I've gotta boyfriend makes it all kinda seem, like, it's not real. I kissed him twice already."

"*Really?*"

"Yep, and he's a really good kisser."

"Why do you think that he's with somebody else," Jolene asked.

"There was this girl at the party. She showed up after everybody was gone and was acting all jealous that he was in the room with me."

"Did she tell you something? Did Ray tell you who she was?"

"No, but like I said, she got all jealous when she saw me with him. And all of Ray's friends were cracking jokes about it, and Ray looked uncomfortable as hell. He probably thinks I hate him because when that girl came around I just left all pissed-off and didn't even say goodbye to him."

"So what are you gonna do now, now that you've kissed him and all? It's only a matter of time before everybody knows, you know how this shit works. The rumor-ripple ends up to be a tidal-wave. You might as well fuck him now since that's what they'll all think."

"I know. I guess I'll just wait and see what happens next. You know, Jolene, if I wasn't with Jeremy, and Raymond wasn't with that girl, I think we could really love each other. Have you ever felt that way about James, like I feel with Jeremy, hopelessly, I don't know, trapped?"

"All the damn time," Jolene admitted and they both laughed. "But mostly I know I love James and so I try to not let it get to me. Part of the reasons I feel trapped are probably because of problems I have within myself."

Jolene didn't wanna tell Erin about what really was going on with her and James. Because no matter who you tell something to, even if it's your best friend in the whole world, things have a way of becoming public knowledge. You say it and you think it's no big deal, but it always ends up stinging you in the end.

They both put their cigarettes out at exactly the same time and Erin yawned and said, "Jesus, dude. I'm really tired. I'm gonna go in and hit the sack."

"Ok, call me tomorrow?"

"Cool. I will."

19

That Night I forced Kevin to give me a lift all the way to my apartment so I could pick up The Poop, its engine had miraculously decided to start running again the day before, and so I wouldn't be stranded over at Kim's house in the morning.

Kim and I fooled around until about 2:00 in the morning, I told her the nice things that she wanted to hear. I started rubbing her ass and I casually pulled down her underwear and I turned her around and did her from behind and I talked a little shit to her. I lasted about two minutes and thirty-five seconds, and I was embarrassed as hell and I acted like it never happened before, but she knew I was lying and acted like it didn't matter. Mainly I just laid there all night and thought about things. The only reason I felt bad about sleeping with her was because I lied to her about loving her and all. It wasn't about her so much; it was really about me leading her on like a dick. Like I said before, Kim is a really great girl and any guy would be lucky to date her.

I left Kim's house really early in the morning, like, around 6:00 or some ungodly hour like that. It was sure as hell still dark outside, and if you think it's cold outside in general during winters in the Midwest, try waiting until just before the sun has come up and the night has had a decent chance to freeze over things for a few hours. Try going out at dawn in the middle of winter when there's two inches of ice on your windshield that you couldn't crack by letting Andre the Giant whack the car with a grave-digging spade.

I ended up cruising through the drive-through at McDonalds and got the usual: Sausage-Egg McMuffin, two hashed browns, and a large orange juice.

Once I got home I turned off the ringer on the phone and I smoked a joint that I had rolled in the car while I was driving on the freeway. Then I peacefully fell asleep and all morning I had dreams about Erin. She kept hitting herself and then blaming me for it. Then I closed things out with one of those dreams where I'm a kid again and I'm riding a bike down a steep hill and there's a cliff there and I fly right off of it unexpectedly and I'm falling. It's always scary because I think I'm gonna die in a second, and then right before I smack into the rocks below I wake up all freaked out and clutching my pillow.

When I woke up it was around 11:00 in the morning, which is pretty late for me. I'm not the type to really sleep in. There was a message from Jon on the machine saying he was back in town from Seattle and I should stop by his place around 4:00, and I should give him a call as soon as I got the message.

Jon was living out in Washington with me. We both moved out there right around the same time because his sister lived there and so did my sister. It was one hell of a coincidence. So we thought it would be cool if we both went to check it out. Eventually, not long after me, he fell onto hard times financially just like I did and he had to move back to Valparaiso where he came from. His mom was a truck driver so it was practically like he lived alone because she was on the road for three weeks outta every month. It was the best thing that ever happened to us. When you're a teenager and you've gotta spot all to yourself with no parents around it's worth more than ten kilo's of cocaine to a Cuban stranded in Miami's South Beach. I called him up as soon as the message was done playing.

"Daddio," I said when he answered the phone on the second ring.

"Hey," he said. "Ray."

He never said too much over the phone because all we ever talked about was drugs.

"So you're back already, from Seattle," I asked even though I knew that he had been back for a few days already, and that I just called him at his mom's house in Valparaiso.

"Yep," he said. "You should stop by. I got something you might like. I brang it back from Seattle."

"Oh yeah," I said. "You got some of them *nuggets?*"

In the state of Washington you can get some of the kindest bud in the country and once you've tried it, if you're a hardcore weed smoker, you can't live without it. You can also pick some of those funny mushrooms in the grass for free in Washington if you look hard enough in the right places, and in Indiana kids buy the same mushrooms for fifty bucks a quarter. Jon was hip to all these oportunites and he didn't waste much time cashing in.

"Just come over," he said. "I got green ones. I got DirecTV. I gotta pool table in the basement, and I got—just get over here, ok?"

"Sure thing, but hey. Do you mind if I bring by my friend Victor? He's cool."

"Whatever," Jon said. "I don't care."

"Cool, I'll see you around 4:00 or so."

"Late."

"Bye," I said and I hung up.

I decided to call The Brain and see if he wanted to come along with me to Jon's house. His phone rang about six or seven times before somebody answered.

"*Hahlow*," his mom said and then she cleared her throat. She smoked a lotta cigarettes.

"Can I speak to Victor please?"

"*Sleepin*," she said. She was a tough lady and she had one of them Kentucky accents. Sometimes I wonder why I'm so nice over the phone when I call there because she doesn't care if you're polite or not.

"Can you tell'em that Ray called please?"

"Yeah."

I was in the middle of thanking her for taking the message and she hung up on me. I had a feeling The Brain wouldn't get the message so I figured that I'd just drive over there around 2:00 and check him out.

It was Sunday in case you haven't taken the time to figure that out yet. I had been home exactly one week. And so far I had messed with three different girls and was working on a fourth. I had gotten a hefty speeding ticket, eaten nothing but fast food, and spent all my money except for my last five bucks. I smoked almost a half-ounce of weed, gotten drunk about fifty times, tried heroin for the first time, loved it, and briefly went insane. Then I skipped school three outta five days, kissed a girl who may or may not have had the AIDS virus. I fell in love again and I had even gotten punched in the face by a man-child/gorilla-apelike thing who dates girls in high school.

It's funny how it all seems so normal while it's happening and when you take five minutes to recollect it makes you dizzy. I guess that's life, just like when I was living it I felt that my life at that time couldn't have been more meaningless and normal and boring, but here I am today being moved enough by those distant experiences to write a book more or less about those very same things.

20

I pulled up to The Brain's house around 2:00. I said the minimal greeting of, "Hey," to his older brother who was outside tinkering underneath the hood of his car.

He ignored me.

The sun was out and the temperature had skyrocketed into the lower fifties. All of the ice was rapidly melting and every now and then these huge icicles that had been frozen to the edge of the houses for months would break off and come crashing sharply into the firmly packed snow.

It felt a lot warmer than it was because the day before there was a blizzard with below zero temperatures overnight. Everyone was driving around with their windows rolled down and there was a line about a mile long at the automatic car wash. Guys that were pure dirt with mullet haircuts and fake-ass gold chains were walking around with their shirts off. All the little kids were out in the streets playing basketball or making snowmen. If anyone had any kinda tape or CD with a song about summertime, be it Will Smith or Janice Joplin, they had it playing really loudly as they drove by as slow as possible so you could take them in all at once. That's the way they wanted things on a day like that.

Sometimes the weather is really freaky in The Region. The temperature can fluctuate drastically from day to day. It would be warm and sunny one day and freezing and snowy the next. And when we changed seasons it was never a gradual decrease or increase in temperature as the days and weeks past. Changing from fall to winter was like stepping off a cliff. One day in late September you'll be at the beach sweating your ass off, and the next day it's snowing out and you look all stupid because you accidentally wore shorts to school that day. Then it would stay cold for the rest of the winter until late April when you're sledding one day, and completely surprised to be back at the beach the next. I have no scientific explanation for these seasonal mood swings. All I can say is it's no secret to anyone that Mother Nature is a woman. My other guess is Lake Michigan and the high pollution from the mills does a lot to influence the weather. Even the climate has some kinda industrial engineering behind it, as do the towns, as do the people of those towns.

But anyway, when I knocked on The Brain's bedroom door he simply said, "Come in." So I did.

He was curling twenty-five pound dumbbells and he had a lit cigarette that he was smoking dangling from the corner of his mouth. He's the only person I know that smokes while they lift weights. I didn't notice until then how ripped this kid's arms were. It was like he had two baseballs where his biceps were supposed to be. The Brain was one of those guys who when he wears baggy jeans and a big red 49ers sweatshirt he looked like a scrawny pussy, but when he had his shirt off he actually had muscles all over the place.

"What's up, hoss train," he said to me as he continued his repetition without even hesitating.

"Hey, man," I said and I sat on his waterbed and I stuffed my hands into my coat pockets. It's kinda humbling when there's nowhere to sit but a waterbed, because you sink down and it's impossible to sit up straight. You have to slouch the whole time. Even the act of handing something to somebody while you're sitting on a waterbed is a huge pain in the ass.

He put down the weights and he let out a sigh of exhaustion. He immediately picked up his electric guitar and plugged it into the amplifier. He had a Pearl Jam guitar songbook that told you how to play all the songs from the Ten album and he started messing around. He looked nervous about something.

"I didn't know you played guitar," I mentioned to him.

I really didn't give a shit if he played the guitar or not, I just thought he would wanna tell me all about it. Guitar nerds are all alike. They all think they're gonna do it for a living someday. If I wanted to list all of my stoner friends who play the guitar I bet I could fill about ten thousand pages. In The Region practically every dude plays the guitar, and if they don't then they play the bass guitar. I know all these guys that are in bands that are always missing one member, usually a drummer. They're always asking me if I know anyone who plays the drums and I always say no because I always try to stay clear of musicians. They're psychotic. They're good to smoke pot with though. Plus they're fun to play video games with.

"I ain't that good, Ray," he said—and he sure wasn't. "I've only been playing for a few months. I got the guitar from Eben Foster. You don't know him. He's this kid who lives on the next street over. I fronted him a quarter and he never paid me so I took the guitar instead."

"He just let you?"

"Hell yeah he let me!"

The Brain's mom poked her head inside the room and said, "I'm goin da flea Market with Ruth!"

"Whatever," The Brain said in a really rough way.

"An turn dat goddamn thing *down!*"

"Ok!"

"Don't *ok* me. Your ass betta be gettin a job today, hear? I ain't kiddin!"

"Ok, dammit!"

A few minutes later the front door slammed shut and The Brain put down the guitar and he shut the door to his room.

"You'll never believe what happened to me last night. I think the cops might be after me."

"What do you mean," I asked as he cracked the window to his room and then he pulled out a joint, lit it, and passed it to me. I took a big old monster hit and started coughing.

"Last night," he began. "I was ridin in Billy Price's car. I was in the back seat. Billy Price and Che was up in front. We were all trippin on **Acid** and we were just cruising around town."

He hit the joint a coupla times and then passed it back to me.

"Then what," I asked and I took a hit.

"Then Billy Price and Che started playing lock-eyes. You ever heard of that?"

"No, what the hell is it?"

"It's like a staring contest. First person to take their eyes off loses."

"Sounds like *fun*," I said sarcastically.

"Not really," he said. "Billy Price and Che were doing it while they were driving down Beverly Avenue."

"*Yeah*," I happened to mention, obviously not that interested.

"Only neither of them fucks was takin their eyes off each other."

"Yeah?"

"I was trippin my nuts off and I didn't even see it coming."

"*What?*"

"The house at the end of the street when the road ends. We crashed into it."

"You *crashed* into a house?"

"Right through the fucking brick-wall and into the goddamn living room. Some old man was taking a nap on the couch and he slept right through it. There was empty booze bottles all over the livingroom. We freaked out and we all ran away. I ran all the way home and I don't know what happened to those two idiots."

"You guys left Billy Price's car wedged into the side of the *house?*"

"Fuckin eh, I don't even know if anyone else besides the old man was home or not. There was nothing in the paper this morning so maybe nobody else was home."

"Oh my God," I said. "That's fucking unbelievable!"

"Ain't it? Anyway, I was gonna ask, if it's cool with you, if I could lay low at your place for a coupla days, just until I know the cops ain't searching for me no more."

"Yeah. That's cool. I was actually gonna see if you wanna go outta town with me tonight. I'm headed over to my friend Jon's house in Valparaiso."

"Perfect," he said. "I think I need to get outta Granite for a little while. When are we leaving?"

"How's ten minutes? I already got my shit together so whenever you're ready to go is cool. Why do you think the cops are gonna come looking for you? I mean, it wasn't your car or anything. It's not like they can trace it back to you."

"Yeah, but it was Billy Price's and I was thinking when they grab him sometime today, or whenever they find him, he'll either rat on me or they might be able to get my fingerprints or something."

"Well, let's get the fuck outta here then," I said.

"Maybe we should see if I can get another bag of weed before we leave town," he suggested.

"Save your money, dude. You'll be able to spend it wisely where we're going."

"You sure," he asked as he quickly stuffed a few changes of clothes into a backpack.

"Positively."

It took about thirty-five minutes, two joints, and the front and back of a Tears For Fears tape to get to Jon's house in Valparaiso. When you first drive into his neighborhood you can see money everywhere. Not literally, but all of the homes are upscale and lotsa people have fancy cars and trendy landscaped lawns and shit.

"I went to grade school with the girl who lives there," I pointed to the largest house on the street, the one with the steel gate at the end of the driveway.

"Yeah," The Brain said. "Is she hot, is she good looking?"

"She's ok," I said. "I haven't seen her since fifth grade. That's when my parents got divorced and I moved to The Region."

"You should try to hook up with her again. Maybe you could get her to buy you some new clothes instead of wearing that preppy gay shit all the time."

He was joking about that one—at least I hoped he was.

"Yeah, look who's talking," I said. "You got a different 49ers sweatshirt for every day of the week."

"You're funny. Actually it's the same sweatshirt every day. That's my team, dude. You gotta represent!"

I took a right into the older part of the neighborhood, the part with the smaller, shabbier houses that all looked the same other than being painted and sided in different colors.

"What," he said to me like he was surprised, but not pleasantly. "You mean he don't live in one of them huge houses back there? I was getting excited for a second there, Ray."

"No, he's poor like we are. The Man has the neighborhood set up so you gotta drive past the things you'll never have every day on your way to whatever job people have when they grow up. They wanna keep the poor folks in check."

"Those were some big houses. There ain't no goddamn houses lookin like that in Granite or Hammond."

"That's because they spend all their money on crackrocks and eating out at Ponderosa."

"Kids eat for free there on Tuesday nights."

Jon, like everyone else in Indiana, had a basketball hoop in his driveway. When The Brain and I pulled up, Jon and some friends of his were playing a pick-up game. Jon's friends were kinda my friends too, but only because of Jon. I never would have met those guys if it weren't for him.

Ron Beck was there and he was really tall and could actually dunk a basketball, or so I've heard, because I had never seen him do it. He was a few years older than we were and he was kinda like an older, skinnier, more presentable version of Gabe. He dressed the same as Gabe did, and the best way I can describe it is that it was five to ten years behind the times and that's no understatement. We're talking Hyper-Color shirts, stonewashed jeans, and Chuck Taylor All-Stars. The only thing that really set Ron apart from Gabe was the fact that Ron drove a nice car, he was nice looking, and he didn't do any drugs. Gabe on the other hand would pump his system full of any kinda narcotic or hallucinogen that he could get his hands onto. And the effects of these poisons had turned Gabe into a sweaty and homicidal bastard who always got a little too excited around girls. It made you nervous to even bring your sister around Gabe. R o n wasn't that way. He was a nice kid with manners and he was charming around girls and not oppressive like Gabe.

Marty Mount was part of Jon's gang too and he was hip to the times way more than his friends were. His outfits always reflected what was currently being shown during music videos on MTV at and he was one of those guys who could get along with everyone. Even if Marty hated somebody's guts he would still get along with them. He didn't like to cause trouble with people and I think he was the only one of Jon's friends who you could have a serious and halfway intelligent conversation with.

Stan Franklin followed Marty everywhere and that's how he ended up being a part of Jon's gang. Stan always dressed however Marty was dressing and he used the same slang as Marty. Old Stanley had a sister who was my age and she was really popular amongst my peers, but for some reason I had no idea who she was and I knew a lot of freaking people in that town on account that I had lived there for seven years, ever since I was four-years old until I was eleven. When I asked Jon about the kid's sister, whose name was Brenda by the way, he always said that she was pretty hot.

There was one other kid there that day. His name was Red Nobles and he wasn't playing basketball because he was notoriously unco-ordinated. He was the skinniest asshole that I had ever seen. Now I was a skinny kid, but Red was ridiculous. He made me look like a cage-fighter. I would always look at him and try to guess how much he weighed and I often wondered if he had any shred of muscle on his entire body, or fat for that matter. He was nothing but bones, skin, bones, red hair and more bones. He had tons of red hair on his head. Tons. It was long and curly and it puffed out almost into an Afro. Red was actually his real name and the hair was just a coinci-dence. You could throw coins into his hair and they'd disappear. His hair was like a thick jungle and we all joked that if you threw a penny into Red's hair you could make a wish.

Stan and Red had nicknames that we called them. We never referred to them by their names because they were too strange to go by regular names. My cousin Kevin came with me to Jon's one time and he got such a kick out of Stan and Red that he invented nick-names for them. He'd crack up every time anyone said their nick-names. He called Red "Little Horse" and he called Stan "Mugwum."

When The Brain and I got outta the car they all had their shirts off because the weather was getting into the upper fifties. The Brain and I just watched them play for a few minutes. It was a two-on-two game and Jon was the best player by far. He faked a behind the back pass and then finished it with a reverse lay-up. Then he dribbled the ball between Mugwum's legs and he ran past him real quick as he picked up his dribble again and he sunk a little mid-range jumper.

Jon's talents lay in his hands. Anything that he does with his fingers or hands, he does it well. You should see him shoot rubberbands. I've never seen anyone who has better aim with shooting rubberbands in my entire life. I've seen him shoot flies on the wall from across the room, I'm not kidding. Like I said, anything that he does with his hands and fingers he does well. Whether it's spinning a basketball, rolling perfect joints, flicking coins, or throwing a hanging curveball. With his hands he can do everything so well that it gets to be kinda entertaining. He doesn't do anything productive with them though. As talented as he is he somehow managed never to accomplish anything.

After the game Ron Beck said that he had a date so he got into his pearl white rag-top Mustang 5.0 and drove off. He drove that car everywhere he went, even to Jon's house, even though Ron lived right on the next street.

We all went inside Jon's house and messed around for a while. He took The Brain and I into the kitchen and showed us how to make Drain-O bombs with some liquid Drain-O, aluminum foil, and an empty Coca-Cola two-liter. We made a few and tossed them out the window and we all laughed when they exploded. Jon told us to be really careful. He said the bombs had enough power to take your fingers off no problem. Those things are pretty fun to make, and if you've never done it I highly recommend building one some day and tossing it out into your back yard. Be careful though, because it freaks the neighbors out pretty easily. They might think somebody's shooting a shotgun or something.

After that, Jon rolled a joint about six inches long and as thick as the average penis, your's, not mine. The joint was flawless and smooth and it smoked easily and didn't run on us a single time.

Lame-O Lesson: When a joint runs it means the rolling-paper is burning a streak up the side. This sucks when it happens because it distorts the quality of the hits if the run is bad enough. It's kinda like cutting a hole in a drinking straw. When a joint ran it was a clear sign that the roller didn't know what they were doing and that they're just a novice. A good run in a joint is in the same ballpark with seeds in somebody's bowl. They both suck. They are uncalled for. Jon's joints never ran, and they were never too tight either. When a joint is rolled too tight it won't smoke. A joint that's rolled too tight is a lot like trying to suck up mashed potatoes with a straw. If you try to suck too hard you're libel to pull your sinuses right outta your face.

I put in a Helmet CD and we all crowded around the coffee table and smoked that huge joint until it was nothing but an oversized roach. It was rolled outta some dank buds from Seattle and we were all blitzed.

The phone rang and Jon got up and went into the other room with it. Little horse and Mugwum sat at the kitchen table and played cards. The Brain and Marty and I started zoning out on the TV because *Inside the NFL* was on tape, which is one of the best sports shows of all time. Jon had recorded it during football season. They covered every game of the past week and made the clips and highlights seem like a movie. Jimmy Johnson. Dan Marino. That one black dude ...

"Marty," I said. "What's going on around here tonight?"

"Usual, I guess," he said shrugging his shoulders. "Smoke some pot. Try to get some chicks. You know how it goes. Pretty boring stuff if you ask me. We should go out to Granite maybe. It's pretty lame around here."

"No way in hell are we going back to Granite, motherfucker," The Brain snapped at him.

The Brain can be really, really rude sometimes. He wasn't trying to be offensive to Marty, it was just the way he talked and I think Marty picked up on that and didn't give it too much thought. The Brain is just straight up white trash. There's no other way of saying it.

"Cops are looking for me over there, ok. So next dude who says he wants to go to Granite is gonna get his head kicked in."

"What did you do," Little Horse asked him from the kitchen table.

"Nothin, dude," The Brain snapped again. "Are you writing a

fucking book or something?"

"Reckless driving," I laughed. "Except it's an unusual case because he was the backseat driver."

"You must have been pretty reckless then," Marty said.

We all left The Brain alone about his troubles because we were making him nervous and he wasn't the type of kid who it was fun to agitate. He was too much like an animal. Lotsa the kids who grew up around Hammond or East Chicago and Gary were like that, at least way more so than the kids from Valparaiso.

Then I heard a sound like a spit wad being fired and then a little thud right above my head that sounded like a dart hitting the board, only Jon didn't have a dartboard. I was confused and then I saw Jon coming down the hall with a big-ass smile on his face. He had his little blowgun in his hand that blew darts and he was coming towards me very excitedly..

"Holy shit," he cried. "I got it," and he pointed right above my head.

"*Jesus,*" The Brain said. "I ain't never seen nothin like that in my fuckin life," and he laughed. "Look at that little mother fucker! It's still alive! It's moving!"

"I don't think you killed it," Marty said. "It's still moving!"

I turned and looked behind me and there was a big moth pinned to the wall by one of Jon's darts. It was struggling.

"That went right by my head you ass," I said to Jon as he took out his camera and snapped a Polaroid of the slain bug.

I thought it was disgusting because I think insects are the foulest things on the planet, especially moths and flies.

"If I wanted to hit you in the head I would have," Jon said. "You guys, you see how good my aim is now? I can fuck shit up with this little blowgun."

"*Dude,*" The Brain said. "Lemme try that thing. I wanna shoot something."

"Ok," Jon said. "Come over to my mom's room. We'll open the window and there's some sparrows that are always on this tree in the backyard. They're even there in the winter. I think they're too stupid to fly south. Let's take a few cracks at em, eh?"

"Sure," The Brain said and Jon handed him the blowgun.

"But take a few practice shots on the wall here first," Jon said and he sat down across from me like he wanted to tell me something.

"Guess what," he asked me.

"You're pregnant," I said.

"Very funny. Guess again."

"I don't like games, man," I said.

And it was true. I hated playing things like cards and board games, and especially guessing games, I hated them the most. Any game that isn't a sport wasn't deserving of any of my time.

"Brenda Franklin is coming over. She's coming to pick up Mugwum here. He's her little brother."

"That's what I hear," I said sarcastically, because I didn't know exactly know who in the hell she was and I wasn't sure if I was supposed to know her either because I couldn't tell what Jon was getting at. "Dude," I said to Mugwum, "I don't know your sister, I swear I don't."

"What do you mean you don't *know* her," Jon asked me. He was surprised.

"I don't know her. Why should I?"

"She knows *you*. I just talked to her on the phone and she said she knew you."

"From *where*?"

"You went out with her cousin, man. It was last year. I remember," Jon tried to refresh my memory.

"Who," I asked him. "I went out with a lotta girls last year."

"Janice, man."

"Janice *Brown*?"

"Exactly," Jon said.

I went out with Janice for only two weeks and as far as I was concerned she was nothing but a spec of a memory that I didn't ever even think of. I stopped seeing her mainly because her dad would never let her go anywhere and I lived forty-five minutes away so it just wasn't something worth pursuing.

Sure, I loved her at first. Like I said, I always fall in love real easily, but I am a one girl at a time guy. I really am. If I'm in love with a girl, I can't love another until I'm not in love with the old one anymore. That's just the way I was. Lucky for me, I fell outta love with Janice pretty easily also, especially once I got to really know the girl. So once I found out that Janice was a girl who suffered from severe mood swings, and had an oppressive father, I quickly did not love her anymore and I just stopped calling her. I didn't even tell her that I was breaking it off. Usually you would think if you're breaking up with a girl the least you could do was give her an explanation, but I'm a real coward sometimes and I'm frightened of confronting my problems. Luckily for me I was smoking dope heavily and it covered up any feelings of guilt that I might have had. In fact I never felt anything at all. I was never happy or sad, never mad or glad, I didn't want or need anything except weed, food, and something to drink because I was always high.

Chocolate Milk.

"Of course I remember Janice," I said to everyone. "But I never met anyone in her family, and I never met no cousin that's for sure."

"Well," Jon said. "The funny thing is: this girl Brenda, who happens to be Mugwum's sister, is terrified of you. She said you like to hurt women. In fact, she was scared to come over and pick up her brother because you were here."

"What the fuck are you talking about!"

I was surprised as hell because I couldn't think of any reason why a girl would be scared of me in a physical way—emotionally yeah, you could be scared of me, but this was a real surprise, it really was.

Then Mugwum spoke and he usually never said anything. We always talked about him like he wasn't in the room even though he would be sitting right next to us.

"My cousin said you used to hit her, and that's why she broke up with you," Mugwum said. "She says that about all the guys she goes out with. I swear all the females in my family are nuts."

"It ain't just your family, ok," The Brain said. "All of them are fucking whores if you ask me. They're all crazy, every last one of them. There's nothing but a pack of witches in this world. Lucky for us there's some slutty ones."

"Well," Mugwum said. "If Brenda is all freaked out I'll just go wait outside for her then."

"No, it's cool man," I said. "I ain't gonna mess with your sister. Besides, it's cold as hell out now that it's getting dark out."

"I got a better idea," Jon said and he grabbed the keys to his truck and tossed them on the table in front of Little Horse. "Little Horse, give the boy a lift home and we'll tell Brenda that you got a ride home when she gets here."

Little Horse and Mugwum did what they were told and they left after a few minutes. And when I heard the front door shut, a bright idea came to me. I was sulking about being labeled abusive by some girl who didn't even know me. It's not like I was heartbroken about having my reputation dragged through the dirt. I was pissed for logical reasons. For instance, let's say Janice gets another boyfriend who hears this lie about me, and he all the sudden decides to play John Wayne and him and all of his friends corner me in some dark alley and they kick the shit out of me? It was a real possibility too, believe me. Sure it could happen anyway for the things that I really had done, but I sure as hell didn't want to get my ass kicked or anything for something that I hadn't done. Lately I had been getting beat up on a regular basis, and to tell you the truth I was kinda getting tired of it and I didn't want it to happen anymore.

Oh well, I thought as I listened to Mugwum and Little Horse start the truck in the garage. *It's not like I can do anything to change things now. I might as well have fun with the situation.*

Brenda was on her way over to the house and I thought I might play a little joke on her, just for her being stupid.

"Hey, Jonny," The Brain said.

"Hey what, tuff guy" Jon said and he quickly shot a rubberband at a fly over on the window, but this time he missed and then he said some cuss words.

The Brain was amused my Jon's marksmanship, "How the hell do you have flies in your house in the middle of winter?"

"Flies just don't die when it gets cold out, dude," Jon bitched as he shot another rubberband and knocked over a candle on the table that a fly had landed on.

The fly squirmed in pain on the table, that is, if flies even feel pain.

"I never miss twice."

"Yeah," Marty said. "Especially when you've got rotting shit all over your kitchen. Flies love it here, man. It's like the Bahamas for insects here. It's a fucking paradise for bugs."

"But hey," I said to Jon. "You still have that old pellet gun, the one that looks like a real nine-millimeter handgun?"

"Yeah," he said. "I still got the goddamn thing, but it's broken. It doesn't shoot anymore. If you want something to shoot I got a real gun here you can use."

"It's cool. I don't wanna shoot it. Fuck. What do you think I am? I just wanna brandish it around the house a little bit, if you know what I mean."

"With Brenda on her way over," Jon questioned me while raising one of his eyebrows. "You wouldn't."

"Ha! I would," I said. "And I'd enjoy it. That's funny to me."

"The cops," The Brain said. "What about the cops, man? What if she calls the cops on you for pulling a damn gun on her?"

"I ain't gonna pull the gun on her. I won't point it at anybody. Nobody's gonna call the cops. Teenagers never ever call the cops, man," I said. "I can break it down into a science if you wanna. I ain't gonna shoot her or anything. I'm not that big of an asshole, even if it is just a pellet gun. I'm just gonna let her see it. It'll be great. We'll all get a big kick out of it. I swear we will. When she gets here I'll go hide in the Jon's room because he told her I wasn't here. Let her smoke some weed and then bring her back, like, you guys wanna show her something cool. And then I'll do the rest."

I spit my words out as fast as I could because I was so excited. I always loved messing with people. I still do, although today, now that I'm kinda grown-up, my antics are a little bit toned down, but the anxiousness is still there.

"She'll be here any minute so get me that gun, Jon, and I'll go to work. You don't have, like, a camcorder or anything do you? It would be awesome if we could tape the expression on her face as she runs outta the house."

"Sorry," Jon said. "No movie equipment here, but I'll get that gun."

He went to the hall closet and pulled down the pellet gun and handed it to me. It was shiny and black and other than the fact that the hole was too small to fire a real bullet it looked pretty real, just like a real gun.

"Sure you don't want the real one," Jon asked me while I pointed it at the mirror to see what I looked like with a gun in my hand.

"No, man," I said. "Are you crazy? This will do just fine. I'm going back there. So do you guys know what to do? Are we cool?"

"*Yeah*," Jon said annoyed with me. "Of course we know what the fuck to do. Jesus Christ. Do I look, like, a retard to you?"

He always got annoyed when you questioned his ability to do anything at all. He never wanted anybody's help with anything, even if you were just trying to be nice.

"Ok," I said looking at myself in the mirror. "Lemme hit that pipe real quick before I go and hide. I don't wanna be waiting long with nothing to smoke."

"Here," Jon said. "Just take it."

He took a bowl already packed with weed outta his shirt-pocket and handed it to me with a lighter and everything. It was a ceramic little job that was shaped like an oval. It was dark gray, almost black, and it had the symbol of an Ankh on it. It was Jon's favorite pipe and if it were ever lost or broken or even chipped in the slightest bit he'd have a cow. Years later some psycho bitch caught Jon cheating on her and she took the pipe and ran over it with her car and smashed it into a million pieces. Jon started crying.

"Thanks, buddy," I said and I snatched the pipe outta his hand.

"Dude, watch it! This thing isn't made of steel like your mother's cunt."

"Chill. I got it," taking an extended hit. " I don't got much time so here I go."

I went back into Jon's room and shut the door and waited. After a minute or two I got tired of waiting for her to show up and I began to worry that just letting her see the gun wasn't gonna be enough excitement, too theatrical, not enough impact, so I started to brainstorm for a few ideas.

What I really wanted to achieve was to exaggerate the impression that she had about me. Like, since she thought I was an egomaniac woman-beater then I wanted her to experience something much worse than that. I wanted her to think I was pure dirt.

As I was sitting around thinking I noticed an old Ouiji Board sitting on the shelf of Jon's closet just collecting dust. I didn't know what I would do with it, but it was a good first ingredient for my chaotic recipe. Then I glanced around the room and noticed he had a card table that wasn't being used. It was just folded up and sitting up against the wall. I also noticed, just as the doorbell rang and Brenda stood outside shivering, that there was an unusual amount of candles that littered Jon's room. Guys don't usually have a shitload of candles in their rooms. Jon's room looked like a Yankee Emporium display case.

I peeked outta the window and saw that Jon was answering the door and letting her in. I had to act fast because I knew if things didn't go well I wouldn't have much time to work with. So I hit the pipe again real quick a coupla times and I grabbed the card table and set it up in the middle of the room.

Then I got the Ouiji Board off the shelf and I set it up on top of the table. Then I got a chair and put it up up to the card table so I would have something to sit in. I stopped to listen to what was happening in the livingroom for just a second and I heard Brenda asking about her brother, and Jon telling her that her brother was already gone. Then he invited her to hang out for a coupla minutes and she accepted, which bought me a little more time so I could prepare to scare her properly.

Then I ran around the room and I grabbed every last candle that I saw and placed them all around the table in a in the form of a **666**. Then I had to light them all. There were a lotta goddamn candles so it took at least five minutes and I burnt my hand twice, but it was worth it.

I heard Brenda out in the living room saying something about her smelling smoke and I had to put a pillow up to my face so I wouldn't laugh out loud. I felt glorious and in just a minute or two I'd be a regular prince of darkness.

That reminded me of a joke I heard when I was a kid. I don't remember the joke all that well, at least not well enough to tell it, but I remember this one line from it. I figured this one line would be perfect for starting my little game without waiting any longer. So I sat at the table and tucked the gun into my pants and I was about to yell this line when I saw this naked little doll that Jon had in his room. So I picked it up and put it sitting up on the table very near to all the candles. Now everything was perfect.

I was sure of it and I yelled, "I'm king of the walls! Come suck my balls!"

They were just finishing off, yet, another joint when my voice carried down the hallway like a silent fart. It wasn't loud enough to where it was in your face, but if you were listening you could easily hear it.

"What the heck was *that*," Brenda asked Jon and The Brain in a very curious way.

The Brain tried not to laugh, but he did a little.

"I'm not sure," he said in a shady way. "Maybe we should go find out, *eh?*"

He couldn't be subtle if he tried. Stupid Hillbilly.

"I think somebody said something about somebody's *balls*," Brenda said.

"Maybe it was a ghost or something," Marty tried to bait her on.

"No kidding, *huh*," Jon said. "A ghost. Let's go check it out."

He squished the joint out into the ashtray until only a dying wisp of smoke slid a few inches into the air and then disappeared.

I heard them coming down the hall so I started doing this little chant in front of the sacrificial naked doll and the melting **666** candles. I sat there in front of the Ouiji Board and I chanted over and over.

"Jesus, you bastard. Leave this house at once. Jesus, you bastard. Leave this house at once. Jesus, you bastard. Leave this house at once!"

I knew it was a dreadful sin, but I'm Catholic so I figured I'd just go work it off in confession on Sunday like everybody else, except for I hadn't actually been to church in years. So when I figured on Sunday, I actually meant in a few years or so.

The door slowly opened and just for show I put my hands into the air and I started wiggling my fingers towards the ceiling. And then when I knew Brenda was watching with the word "Terrified" written all over her face, I faked like I was kinda having a seizure.

"Oh my *God*," She screamed. "Who is *that* Jon? What's the *matter* with him? What's he doing here?"

"Hey, bitch," The Brain said. "Just calm the fuck down. That's my buddy Ray, ok? He's harmless."

Jon and The Brain were laughing their asses off, but Brenda didn't think any of it was funny because she didn't know I was putting on an act. She thought I was a real Satan worshiper.

She was staring at me like she knew me from somewhere, but she couldn't really place me. Then it hit her.

"*Ray Kozlowski*," she asked like she knew I was the guy who her cousin had told her about, but she was still kinda in denial. "You mean that's the Ray I told you about? The one who abused Janice? Oh my God," she said as she took a few steps back.

She bumped into the wall and it scared the shit outta her. The Brain and Marty couldn't stop laughing. I was afraid they were gonna ruin the joke so I started increasing the madness so she wouldn't have a chance to use the little logic that she had.

"Smiling faces," I screamed. "Smiling faces sometimes! Slice them up into little sandwiches!"

This made her flip out. She ran into Jon's mom's room and slammed the door shut and locked it. We all laughed hysterically for at least five minutes. It was great action. It took us about twenty minutes of talking through a locked door to convince her that I was only putting on a show for her and finally she came outta the room and sat in shock on the couch.

Jon and Marty were in the living room trying to calm her down, but it was hard because The Brain kept referring to her as "Bitch" instead of "Brenda." She didn't like that.

Every time the other guys thought about what I did they started laughing. I was in the bedroom blowing out the candles when I felt the gun still in my belt and I thought to myself, *shit. I forgot to use the damn gun.*

Sure, I had done enough damage already, but I knew it would be perfect if I capped off the excitement with a great climax. So I tucked the gun back into my pants so the butt of the gun obviously hung out below my lower back.

I went out into the living room and did a little chit-chatting until Brenda was halfway convinced that maybe I wasn't such a huge lunatic. She even started using complete sentences and making small talk again and it appeared she was almost ready to drive home. She said she thought what happened was funny and that she was feeling better now. She lost her cool and she calmly blamed it on the fact that she was stoned outta her mind.

I decided that I'd apologize to her, just because I'm one hell of a nice guy sometimes, so I said to her, "Hey, Brenda. I'm sorry. I didn't mean anything by it. I swear that I didn't," and I extended my hand to her and we shook on it.

"It's ok," she said to me. "Maybe you're not such a bad guy after all."

"Oh that's funny to me. That's the exact same thing Janice said to me after I apologized for pile-driving her into her bedroom floor. Just kidding."

"Sure," she said.

"Yeah," I said. "You're right, Brenda. I ain't a bad guy at all. You just have to get to know me. Damn," I said. "My head sure itches all of the sudden," and I pulled the gun out and started scratching my head with the damn thing.

When Brenda saw me with a shiny black pistol she freaked so bad I thought her head was gonna pop off like a dandelion blossom. It was beautiful. It really was. She got up and ran down the hall, screaming all the way, and she locked herself in Jon's mom's room again. We couldn't stop laughing. It was the all time funniest thing I had ever done. I started crying because I was laughing so hard.

A half-hour went by and Jon still couldn't talk her outta the room. She kept saying she wouldn't come out until I was gone. I tried apologizing to her again, but she wasn't buying into it. She seriously wanted me gone. She wasn't coming out until I was very far away. I told the guys that I'd be a good boy and I'd at least go hide out in the garage until she left. I had enough fun for one day and I didn't want to cause the girl any permanent damage. So I told the guys to tell her that I was really gone and I tossed the pellet gun on the kitchen table and I went down to the garage to wait it out.

In the garage I climbed onto a workbench and put my ear as close to the vent as I could. I could kinda hear what they were saying. I couldn't understand them word for word, but I could at least tell how the situation was progressing. After about ten minutes she came outta the room and it sounded like she was grabbing her keys and putting on her coat so she could leave. She kept saying how crazy I was and it made me proud.

That's when something came over me. I opened the back door and walked around the side of the house. I wanted to ambush her one last time before she left, just for the hell of it. So I went and I got underneath her car and I waited for her to come outside.

The front door opened and she practically ran to the car, but right when she was fumbling for her keys I crawled out from the back of the car and I stood up all of the sudden, like, I was some kinda demon.

She turned pale white and I cried, "Where you going so fast? The party's just beginning!"

She let out a horrible shriek and she dropped her keys into the snow. And instead of picking them up and getting into the car for a quick getaway like a normal person would do, she ran like hell all the way back to the house and she slammed the door and locked me outside.

21

While The Brain and I were cruising out to Jon's house before I scared the shit outta Brenda that night, Milada was walking eight blocks to Main Street Park to meet her boyfriend Jason Neagu.

Yeah, I know it's a stupid name for a park. It's named after the street it's on. I guess it's better than no name at all, but then again maybe not. It's not like there's anyone important from Granite to name it after and people aren't known for being creative where I come from. They usually just name things the same names they always hear, like Central this, or South that.

Anyway, Jason told Milada earlier in morning that there was something important that he needed to tell her and that he couldn't talk about it over the phone. They decided to meet at the park to talk it over, because neither of them had a car and the park was a good place that was in-between where they both lived.

He really bugged the crap outta her.

The whole relationship was a joke, she thought while doing her lazy walk to the park on such an unusually warm winter day.

Just two months ago she was absolutely positively in love with him. There wasn't anybody else in the world she could've loved more. And now, for the past few weeks or so, she couldn't stand to even look at him. She wondered if the feeling was mutual.

Really though, most girls thought Jason was cute and so did Milada, a long time ago, but not anymore. Every morning he always had eye crust and it was disgusting! That's probably what bothered her the most. If it wasn't for that gross crust they would probably get along fine, she might even still be in love with him, but then again there's also the fact that he always cries when they argue. It happens, like, every single time. They could get into an argument about anything stupid, like, over which religion is the best, if there is a best one, and he'd spint it into an attack on his personality and make it seem like it was the end of the world. He always freaked out and accused Milada of not loving him anymore. And then he starts, like, pleading and crying almost right away for forgiveness, even if he didn't do anything wrong.

Milada absolutely hated it when he did that. It just made her turn into a bigger bitch than she probably already was. Who can love a guy who cries about everything and complains? He was always complaining about everything, from this town to the way she dressed. He had a problem with everything.

I'm sorry, she thought and smiled, *if it's ninety degrees outside I'll wear my bikini top wherever I wanna.*

He would always accuse her of wanting to pick up guys as the reason for the bikini. Isn't that stupid? What girl has to walk around trying to pick up guys? Guys will hit on you no matter where you are, what you're doing, and no matter what you're wearing. If anything, guys hit on a girl less when she'ss wearing kinda revealing clothes, and more when she's dressed up in something more conservative.

Sometimes, she thought again as she walked down the damp sidewalk carefully trying to avoid stepping on the cracks. *Sometimes I wonder if he's so jealous because he's cheating on me.*

Maybe he felt guilty about something and was desperately trying to find some guilt in her so it would even things out and he would feel better. It was something a therapist said on the *Montel Williams Show* last summer. It made perfect sense too, but maybe not with Jason. He was too sweet and timid to be cheating, and considering how much he talked about love and marriage, and even having kids, and what their names would be, he wouldn't ever do that.

22

Jason Neagu quietly whispered his words into the telephone so that his mom wouldn't be able to hear, "Yeah, I love you too. I do." And right before he hung up he answered the caller's question, "Yeah, I'm gonna go right now, baby. I'm gonna do it."

After he put the cordless back on the charger he grabbed his house keys and put on a sweater. He was gonna go without his winter jacket today since it looked so damn warm outside. It was like a goddamn summer day in the beginning of February. That made him think of Valentines Day, which made him sad. He felt sorry for Milada already.

"Was that Milada on the telephone, Jason," his mother asked

him.

"Say what," he stared at her in a questioning way like he heard her, but was still processing the information, she must have heard him on the phone. "Yeah, mom. That was her. Look. I'm gonna go out for a little while, ok? I'll be back for dinner."

"How is she doing? Does she still like the sweater you gave her for Christmas," she smiled at him like he was a ten-year old kid and it was his first girlfriend.

He stopped at the front door and stared at her.

"How the hell should I know if she likes the damn sweater, *huh*? Jesus ma, you act so *weird* sometimes. Christmas was a damn month and a half ago and you're bringing up that sweater."

"Oh, sweetie. I'm sorry if I made you mad. I'm only trying to say something nice, Jason. She's a nice girl and I wanted to say something nice because I think it's important you know your parents like your little girlfriend."

"Little goddamn girlfriend, ma? Gimme a break," he said and he opened the door and slammed it on his way out.

He couldn't wait to move outta that damn house. He was so sick and tired of living with that woman. She was always trying to get up in his business. Jason was already planning on skipping his Senior year to head out to California. He played the guitar and figured he could probably hook up with a good band once he got to Hollywood. Anything was better than living in Granite with all those steel-working, bowling-on-Saturday, God-fearing, small-town Catholics. It was enough to make you puke right there on the sidewalk.

So this was it, in another ten minutes or so he would be at Main Street Park telling Milada what he had to tell her, and he wasn't quite sure how she would react to the news, but he knew that it probably wouldn't be pretty. Things like this never are.

Maybe she knows already, he figured.

Not about this last time, but from before. If she did know something, she was keeping it a secret pretty easily, and that wasn't her style. She may seem sweet and all, and nice, but when she gets pissed she's the biggest bitch of them all, even to her own mother and father, who by the way are the nicest set of parents that any kid could want. Milada always treated them like garbage though.

She's just a stupid bitch, he thought. *She'll never have a serious relationship ever again because she can't open up to people without insulting them.*

He started rehearsing what he was gonna tell her. He practiced how he was gonna say it and what he would say to her when she freaked out.

Hell, maybe she'll be glad, he thought.

Maybe she die laughing since she was always treating him like a fucking asshole. It's not like he deserved to be treated that way either. He'd always been nothing but nice to her from the very first day they got together. He took her out every weekend, bought her dinner, rented the goddamn romantic comedies she wanted, even bought her hoochie mamma clothes.

This ain't just any small town girl here. Milada was high maintenance. Jason was willing to bet he had to spend about a hundred bucks on her every two weeks on average. That's a shit-load of cash to a sixteen year old kid. That's, like, half of what he made from his job. She kept half and he kept the other.

She would start acting like she loved him so much when they were ever around a bunch of clothing stores. Of course he'd buy her a shirt or a skirt or whatever it was she wanted that particular day. Sometimes it's a Sheryl Crow CD, sometimes a Sound of Music on DVD, sometimes it's a belt from Marshall Fields, or even a ring here and there from Zales Jewelers. He'd buy whatever she wanted for her and then she'd start acting all sexy, like, she wanted him, but it usually wore off in about ten minutes or whenever they got back from the store. Then she'd turn back into the cold bitch she really was.

Man, he felt sorry for the next sap who has to put up with her crap. What a bunch of garbage their relationship was. He was tired of it and he thanked God it would be ending today, in about five more minutes.

23

There was this tank from one of the World Wars that was permanently stalled in the Northeast corner of Main Street Park, and that's the exact spot where Milada and Jason were supposed to meet.

Jason Neagu walked up to the park at the furthest corner from the tank and he could see her standing there like a little miniature plastic doll. She was kinda leaning up against the tank with her long brown hair blowing around in the breeze. She was smoking. He couldn't see the cigarette from that far away, but he could see her putting her fingers to her mouth and then relaxing, and then all over again. She also kept pulling her hair behind her ears so it wouldn't get in her face. He knew she was beautiful and even from a great distance she obviously looked it.

He was starting to chicken-out the closer he got. He wanted to run away, because all of the confidence he previously had in telling her what he wanted to tell her had been quickly draining and had started to change into this wimpy laziness that came from a fear of confrontation. Pussing-out wasn't a choice he could make anymore though. This was something he had to do, even if it meant he had to make a fool outta himself, and her. He had to do this even if she broke down and cried, or even if he did, which wasn't that unusual.

When she saw him coming, she waved and even smiled and it melted his heart just like it did when he first saw that smile at the Lake County Fair the year before. At the fair he had seen her standing alone by the Tilt-O-Wheel. He approached her and casually asked her name. She told him and mentioned that she was just waiting for her friends. He ended up buying her a ticket to the ride and they rode it together to pass the time while she waited, and they had been together ever since.

From that moment he was sure they would be together forever, and he never in his wildest dreams thought things would come down to this, with an argument over cheating and lost love and lost youth while standing in front of the infamous Main Street Park tank.

Life sure is a bitch, he thought as he walked right up to her.

"Hey," he said shyly.

He felt so uncomfortable around her, like he couldn't be himself. And this was a feeling he'd had for some time now. Her mood swings were so severe sometimes usually he was afraid to talk at all.

"What did you bring me here for, Jason? I'm cold and tired of this shit."

That pissed him off right away, but he didn't lose his cool. Instead he bit his lip. He knew she wasn't cold, at least not literally, it was almost sixty degrees.

Tired of my shit, he thought. *Look who's talking, the queen of all moody bitches.*

He really wanted to say it now, but he was too chicken-shit. He was willing to bet his new guitar that he was way more tired of this shit than she was, and that's why he brought her there on that day, so he could dump her once and for all.

"Look," he slowly started. "Before you totally lose your cool, there's something I've gotta tell you about last night."

"Jason, I don't give a shit about last night. I don't even care if you went off and fucked some slut. I just wanna break up. I don't even wanna see you anymore."

She looked away from him. She couldn't even look him in the eyes.

What is she hiding, he thought.

"I've been trying to tell you about breaking up for a really long time, but you never listen to me. I'm sorry."

She didn't sound sorry. She said sorry the same way people tell homeless people when they beg for a little bitta change.

"You're breaking up with *me?*"

"I'm sorry."

"Well. I'm not sorry, Milada. I'm not sorry that I *cheated* on you last night!"

"What?"

"You heard me," Jason insisted.

"Yeah right. With *who?*"

"None of your goddamn business, that's *who?* God. Why are you such a bitch to me all the time? I couldn't take it anymore so I cheated on you!"

"Well, it's not my fault you can't keep you dick in your pants!"

"Shut your fucking mouth! It is your fault! All you ever are is a bitch to me! Everything I say pisses you off. We've been together for a year, Milada, and we've only slept together *once!*"

"So this is about sex, *huh?*"

"No, dammit! It's not about sex. It's about affection. You're always so cold to me. I can't stand it."

"Well, I'm sorry I can't put out enough for you, and I'm glad you found some whore, because I'd rather it be somebody else than me. I never loved you like I said I did, Jason."

"Oh, that's a fucking slap in the face. You never loved me, *huh!*"

Tears shot-gunned up into his eyes and he silently kept telling himself over and over, *don't cry now, not right now.*

"How can you fucking say that to me, after everything I've done for you?"

"You've never done *anything* for me, Jason."

"Never done *anything* for you?"

"*Never.*"

"Well, I'm glad, because you're a rotton fucking bitch! I came here to dump your ass today! I found someone else who actually respects me for who I am. So I don't need you anymore."

"Who is it," she asked as she started to cry. There was only so much nastiness she could dish out before she lost it. "Who?"

He hesitated for a second, because the other girl made him promise to tell Milada about the affair without giving away who it was, but the opportunity to hurt Milada was too great.

"Candice," he said like he was giving the winning answer in a game of trivia.

"What do you mean? Candice who?"

"You know who," he said.

Candice Lieberman was her next door neighbor. Milada was even friends with the girl, or at least she thought she was.

"You're a liar, Jason, a goddamn liar! I can't believe you would even drag Candice Lieberman into this!"

"I'm not lying."

"You have to be lying! How could you two do this to me? I

fucking hate you, Jason. I hate you!"

"I don't know what else to say to you," he admitted.

"Newsflash! I have someone else too, loverboy, as a matter of fact."

"*Bullshit.*"

"I do. I'm dead serious."

"*Who?*"

She scanned possible names in her head. Again she looked away and was afraid to look at him. She wanted the one name that would piss him off the most, the one name that would make him the most jealous.

"Ray," she said. "Raymond Kozlowski, the new boy."

24

Two weeks had gone by since the gun incident at Jon's house and surprisingly to me, I didn't miss one single day of school during that whole span of days. I couldn't ditch even if I wanted to though, because I had used up all of my sick days in the first two weeks when I first got home.

First thing on the Monday morning after The Brain and I went to Jon's I got called down to the principal's office and Mr. Cox informed me that if I had one more unexcused absence then I wouldn't be graduating that year.

"Do you understand what I'm saying to you, Raymond," Mr. Cox asked me all like he was an authority figure.

He was an old principal and he smelled like three day old cigarette butts, and he had the nerve to wear a brown tie with an orange flowered pattern outta the house.

"Sure," I said, hoping to tell him whatever he wanted to hear so I could go home. "I understand completely."

The jerk called me to his office to discuss my attendance problem ten minutes before school let out for the day, and he was the typea guy who always beat around the bush. It took him a half–cup of coffee, four stories about the old days, and three quotes from writers he admired just for him to tell me my attendance was lousy.

"I'm not so sure you really understand what I'm telling you, young man."

"Ok," I said. "Could you explain it to me frankly, sir? In a more clear way that I can understand."

I was trying to be a little bit of a smart-ass because I felt he was insulting my intelligence.

"Frankly, Raymond," he laughed and I caught a whiff of his unflossed toothy breath. It was like a gust of wind laced with stale Marlboros and nine cups of instant Folgers. "If you miss one more day of school, excused or unexcused, you will not graduate. *Period.* That means you will have to repeat senior year again. One more day, Raymond."

He held up his pinky finger to symbolize the number one.

I wanted to show him another number one with my middle finger, but I didn't.

"One more day and you are officially a member of the class of 1996. Are we clear?"

"Yeah, we're clear," I said. "I promise I won't miss any more school, sir."

It took me about twenty minutes to fully convince the bastard of my dedication and finally he opened the door and let me escape like a fish that just had the hook taken outta its mouth.

So here I was: two weeks later and I had been to school ten days in a row. And they were very painful days. Not ditching school to me was exactly like trying to kick a nasty drug habit by going cold turkey. To top things off, I had no more women in my life. Erin had stopped talking to me completely. She wouldn't even so much as say hi to me. I believed she was spooked by the Kim incident at Ricky's house. And much to my disbelief Kim had burned me and she started going out with some lumpy pansy who went to her school. She actually told me to stop calling her. Yes ladies and gentlemen, I had hit rock bottom, but at the very least I had no teenager-style gorillas hunting me down in the streets and hallways. I could walk the alleys freely and frequent any party I wanted to without any fear of a two-fisted Hilljack assault.

It was Friday afternoon and spring had finally arrived. The snow was gone, flowers were beginning to bloom, and kids everywhere rode their bikes in the streets, and Jon and I had even begun going to baseball practice again. We played for the American Legion League on a team called East Chicago Post 369. American Legion had a system of teams that spanned the entire country. The organization was intended to be a development league for potential college athletes, and Jon and I played against lots of kids who are in the Majors now.

Unfortunately for me, I didn't fit the mold of the rest of the kids in the league. I was arguably the worst player on any team by far. I wondered why they even gave me a uniform. I was a good athlete, and I had the skills, but I was so hooked on drugs and alcohol that my performance on the field was consistently below pathetic.

I wanted things in my life to change for the better. I really did. What I really wanted more than anything was to kick my drug habit. At that point in my life I was ingesting anything under the sun that I could get high off of. I was even huffing airbrush propellant from time to time, sometimes even while I was smoking pot, drinking, and tripping on **Acid**. Mainly I used drugs with Ricky, Jon, and Matt Morris, and sometimes Chris Roebuck. And we had a lotta good times that have given me pages and pages of good stories, but what I really wanted was to quit using.

I didn't know myself anymore. I used to be a little boy like Smashing Pumpkins, with dreams and aspirations, but now I was just existing and hoping things would just turnout ok. I had no idea who I really was anymore. Sure, I had a name and a face, but what made me go and do things was even a mystery to me. I was a stranger to myself.

The last time I had gotten stoned was that Friday morning on the way to school with Gabe. I had made the decision that I was gonna kick sometime during second period and I didn't meet up with the guys at lunchtime because I knew if I was around the weed I'd smoke it. So instead I took a walk to Main Street Park and just sat under a tree and closed my eyes. I prayed to God to give me the strength to quit and I also retraced my steps back to the first days that I started chasing a buzz. I wanted to know where it was that all of this came from. I wanted to know how I had lost myself so easily.

I'd been addicted to drugs of various kinds since I was fourteen-years old. This isn't easy to talk about, and even though I write about things of all topics, about myself or otherwise, this is the most difficult thing for me to discuss by far. Experts always say the first step to getting clean is to admit that you have a problem, and I say if that's the first step, then it must be one hell of a long road to travel, because by the time I was eighteen I could easily feel the addiction in my body and see it in my face whenever I looked in the mirror. Not only could I admit I was addicted, but I knew I always would be and it didn't bother me much. I think when you try to quit doing something that you know hurts you, something you like, something you honestly need, it feels a lot like trying to take over the world with a can of mace. It just doesn't seem possible. It's hard to imagine what life would be like without your vice.

Addicts will often lay in bed at night and say to themselves, "I can do this, I can, but what will I do instead?"

What would I do instead?

I first caught a buzz from a Virginia Slim I had stolen from my mother, but it was so insignificant of a feeling it passed in about ten-seconds and by the time I smoked my fifth cigarette the feeling was extinct. I was twelve when I first started smoking cigarettes habitually. I stole Virginia Slims from my mom and I walked across the street and into the woods and I smoked there, savoring every part, letting whatever it was that people enjoyed about smoking soak me. That ten second feeling, that buzz, was exactly, like, listening to a beautiful song, but the problem was, deep down, I knew this song wouldn't be good enough to listen to over and over again. Cigarettes weren't gonna make me high for long. Soon I could inhale whole packs in a day and not feel anything outta the ordinary except for a longing for the tobacco when I wasn't using it.

A few times I drank beer and got drunk because it's an obvious choice when you're looking for a fix to whatever your problem might be. Whether it's nervousness, stress, low self-esteem—which in my case I felt all of these feelings—alcohol can be a good friend to those of us who aren't as desperate as others.

It depends on how you look at it. Booze doesn't fuel me as well as it does most people. I like drinking fine, but when I drink too much I just wanna fall asleep, and this is a feeling I get even before I've had enough booze to make me act a fool. Still, a year after I smoked that first Virginia Slim, I thought about the feeling I got and I desperately wanted to duplicate it somehow, and for a longer period of time.

My older brother used to suck on chewing tobacco. He was three years older than I was so naturally I thought whatever he did was the coolest. With this in mind, and the longing I had for that first buzz, I lifted a chew outta my brother's stash and I went into the woods with it. It was disgusting and it tasted so horrible that it made me gag and wanna puke, but man I was messed up. I had a buzz like you wouldn't believe. It was twice as good as a cigarette buzz. Fuck that, it was ten times as good. And it only took a second for it to set in, which is what every drug addict strives for in a fix, convenience and a speedy process.

The next day I bought my own chew with some money I had saved up from cutting lawns around the neighborhood. Once a day I would go into the woods and have a chew. And sure enough I got the same buzz as the first time. Only it seemed like every time I did it, it would last maybe one-second or two less than before, until after a few weeks of consistent use I didn't ever feel it again no matter how much chew I sucked on. Again, all I felt was withdrawal symptoms when I wasn't using the stuff.

I found myself switching back and forth between cigarettes and chew for a year or so, always trying to duplicate that feeling somehow, but never even coming close. The only way I could come close to that buzz again was if I laid off everything for a month and then I would lean hard into the habit again. Then I could at least capture fractions of that buzz, but on again off again is no way for any addict to live. That's the main problem with addicts is that they know no real way to live, but are constantly searching in all the wrong places for a reason to keep breathing, eating, and sleeping.

When I got into high school I was so depressed that I hit the bottle as hard as I could every weekend. I had graduated from beer and moved with authority into hard alcohol like vodka and whiskey or anything cheap. It was cool for a little while and all my friends were doing the same thing as me. It also provided one important aspect of drug addiction that I chased after, and that was finding some real way to feel numb to my problems, but that was about all it did for me that I really enjoyed. Other than that, it just made me act like a dickhead all the time. And it made me throw up every night, which wasn't enjoyable at all. I never was much of a drinker and I guess I'm not too glad for that. I say this because drinking is obviously more socially acceptable than using drugs, and at least if I was an alcoholic I wouldn't have to go sneaking around all the time. I could just go to the bar and tie one on with hundreds of other people just like me. I swear, alcoholics have it easy compared to drug addicts.

So everything was pretty much downhill from there. I was using every drug obtainable to a teenager, flunking all of my classes year after year, and I had squelched any athletic ability that I had in exchange for literally nothing.

I sat under that tree in the park, feeling so miserable I started to cry. I wanted to smoke some weed so badly, but I was scared to death of the road I was headed down. It was one of those horrible cries where the reason is everything. I cried for my parents, my friends who were also hooked on drugs, the fact that I had to go to back to school, and for my inability to really fall in love. A heart of stone is just a cookie-cutter-Rolling-Stone figure of speech, but if it applied to anyone it was me. I didn't care about anything or anybody. I didn't even love my family. I didn't even wanna be alive anymore, but I was too chicken-shit to ever commit suicide. In an emotional sense I had no place to go. I was homeless at heart.

When I was walking home after escaping from the principal's office, a car full of girls from my class drove by and actually threw garbage at me. I recognized one of them, the driver, but didn't really know any of them personally, and I wasn't sure if they knew me, but it really hurt my feelings. I knew it was a sign from God that I had a hard road to follow to sobriety. I already started to have my doubts about whether I could actually come clean. Especially when there were random girls throwing garbage at me. And everyone that I hung around with was just as hooked as I was. The last thing addicts wanna see is somebody who is trying to quit. It's depressing. It happened all the time when kids would say that they were quitting and then the next day they were getting high again. It was, like, having a Christian trying to convert you at lunch and them seeing them at the bar talking to a hooker come sundown. It got to be a joke after a while when a kid said he's trying to quit.

People would say things like, "Yeah right, just hit this," or, "You quit smoking weed, eh? You'll be back tomorrow."

These statements aren't real encouraging and it wasn't something I was looking forward to. I wondered if my friends would even like me anymore if I quit using.

I recognized the driver of the car full of trash-throwers as a girl from my class. Her name was Sydney Stocker and she would make a habit of letting everyone know she was hot shit. Somehow she had managed to sneak her fat-ass onto the cheerleading squad, which went straight to her head. She would always brag that her parents were rich and she even drove a 1985 red convertible Monte Carlo Supersport. Everyday I had to walk by her locker during the break after third period and she was always talking to her friends about this guy and that guy. And the crazy thing was she must have weighed at least two-hundred pounds. She was like a walking side of beef that had escaped from the clutches of the meat-locker. Don't get me wrong, I don't hold grudges against people just because they have a weight problem—I'm not one of those assholes. In fact, I don't discriminate against people in any way. It's just when a person's personality is completely ugly it exaggerates all the bad things I see in them. To be fair, she was beautiful in the face. She had striking good looks for a girl her size. And I suppose if it weren't for the nasty attitude, and maybe the extra meat on her bones, she would probably be a very beautiful woman.

Man, I couldn't wait to slash her tires on Monday! I didn't even know if I could hold out that long. I figured I might have to find out where she lived and slash them that night. If she had a boyfriend that wasn't imaginary I'd slash his tires too. He'd be guilty by association. She was gonna pay.

When I got back to the apartment I checked the mail and there was a letter for me from Seattle. It was written by my ex-girlfriend Maggie. I wasn't expecting any letters from her because we were right in the middle of a semi-serious relationship when I just decided to up and move back home. I didn't even tell her until about three days before I was supposed to catch a plane. I was afraid to tell her and the only reason I did was because I didn't have any other ride to Sea-Tac. I hadn't heard from her since she drove me to the airport. I remember I just wanted her to drop me in front of the terminal, but she insisted on coming with me to the gate and she stayed with me until my flight arrived even though I was almost two hours early. It was a real drag for me, not because I didn't want her to be there, because in reality she was really a sweet girl and she was pretty smart too, and beautiful. It was just, one thing I hate more than anything is saying goodbye to people. I just wish people would go and come back without making such a big deal about it. I feel the same way about holidays and birthdays and I think lotsa people like me feel the same way. When you're addicted to drugs you don't like anything that has to do with showing emotions.

So I was really anxious to see what she had to say as I tore open the envelope and unfolded the letter. After getting bunked by two different girls I liked, and having garbage thrown at me, a love letter was just what I needed. I still have a copy of it, so I'll share it with you.

Raymond,

How are you? Are you happy to be home? I miss you a lot and I wonder everyday why you went back home after all of the horrible things you've told me about that place. You made it sound like a place I would never, ever want to visit. I hope you come back to Seattle someday and I hope you look me up if and when you do because I thought that you were a very interesting person. Lots of things have happened to me since you left. Victor is thinking of going back to Thailand after school is over, and my parents decided to get a divorce because my mother found out about my dad's girlfriend. Remember? She was the lady I told you about. Anyway, my dad ran off to Hawaii with her. She's almost twenty years younger than he is. It's disgusting!

Actually the things I've just told you is kind of the good news. The bad news is really bad so I'll just come out and say it. I have ovarian cancer. I just found out I have really big tumor down there and I'm afraid I might die. Writing this letter is making me start to cry because I'm starting to see how pathetic my life really is. I wish you were here because you are the only person I can really talk to. I also want to know what's going on with you. When you left you told me we could still be together and we could just have a long distance relationship. Although I knew it was impossible, I was happy that you still seemed interested in pursuing things. But now that everyone asks me how my boyfriend is doing I have to make things up because you haven't even so much as given me a phone call since you've been home. So I guess what I really want to know is, what's the deal with you? If you wanted to break things off you should've just told me instead of leading me on. I still would have given you a ride to the airport if that is what this is really all about. That really hurts my feelings, Ray. Am I stupid or do I just feel stupid? Anyway, I want you to write back just so I know you actually got this letter. If you don't want to be with me, just tell me. I won't be mad at you because I know deep down you're just a confused little boy, and I don't mean that as an insult. I'm just being honest. Anyway, write back soon and I'll then write you if I'm not dead from cancer by then.

Love,
Maggie

"*Jesus,*" I said to myself as I finished reading the letter and plopped down on the couch. "Why does she have to be so dramatic?"

So instead of simply feeling like shit, I now felt like total shit-on-a-stick after reading that.

Am I really that big of an asshole, I thought to myself. *Nah. I was just freaking out from all this sobriety garbage. I mean, who am I kidding anyway?*

I figured I should at least give Maggie a call and see how she's doing especially since she's got cancer and all. So I went to my room and dug her phone number outta my desk. I have an address book, but I never really use it. Instead I just write down numbers on random pieces of paper and I even forget to write the names of the people the numbers belong to. I just have stacks of scrap paper with a phone number or two scrawled in the corner with my crappy handwriting. I found Maggie's on the back of a Burger-King receipt that was stuffed inside my old wallet. So I picked up the phone and gave her a ring.

"*Hello,*" she said.

She answered on the third ring. To some people that matters. I can jump to all kinds of conclusions from whether people pick up on the first or second or third rings. Maybe I'm crazy. Maybe you are.

"Maggie! It's me."

"Who?"

"Ray, dammit. Who in the hell do you think?"

"Ray. I wasn't expecting you to call. Sorry, but you know I haven't heard from you in over a month."

She was lecturing me like she was my parol officer or something.

"Jesus, Maggie. I've called you four times already and you never call me back," I said, lying like a whore on Las Vegas Blvd.

"You haven't called me, Ray. When have you called? Name one time you've called."

"I don't leave messages. You know that."

"Since when? And how in the hell would I know to call you

back if you don't leave messages? That's stupid."

"Since always, because I hate to leave messages. I don't like the way my voice sounds when recorded."

"Besides, Ray, I actually do call you and you actually don't bother to call *me* back."

"You're full of shit."

"No, Ray. You're the one who's full of shit, not me."

"Ok. Just drop it all right? What's this crap about cancer?"

"It's not crap. I have it."

"How do you know," I cross-examined.

I knew it was a stupid question, but it's a question you just have to ask when somebody tells you they have cancer. There is no way around it, but the cancer victim never understands this. Silly cancer victims.

"Because the doctor told me, Raymond. *Duh*," she said like I was an idiot.

She always did that to me. She thought she was way smarter than I was.

"*Doctor shmocktor*," I said. "Did you get a second opinion?"

"Raymond you don't understand. I have *cancer*. Do you need me to spell it out for you? I–H–A–V–E–C—"

"Chill with the spelling-bee, ok? I do know how to spell. I catch your drift, but what does this all mean? Why do you think you're gonna die?"

"Raymond, do I really need to go into this? I have Ovarian Cancer. Do you know what that means?"

"I know what it means, ok? Why'd you write me a letter telling me that you are practically dead?"

"You got my letter?"

"*Duhhhh*," I said like she always said to me.

It felt good to get her back.

This was the kinda healthy relationship we had. I was glad I moved. She started to cry, but not in a full-blown sob. She was just getting choked up so her words were backfiring like an old Ford.

"I, I just. I'm just s, so scared, Ray. What am I gonna, gonna do?"

"Jesus, Maggie. You're not gonna fucking die. It's 1995 and the chances of people dying from cancer are, like, slim to none anymore. Isn't that the way it is now? Didn't your doctor tell you that?"

"No, no, no! That's not the way it is. As usual you don't know what the in the fuck you're talking about. This is a deadly disease. *Deadly*!"

"I heard you the first time."

"I'm sorry. I didn't mean to shout at you."

"It's ok."

"Look, Ray. I really need you here with me. I want you come back to Seattle. I'm getting my own apartment and we can live together."

I was silent for a second, because I still didn't have the guts to tell her I didn't have any feelings for her anymore, at least in a romantic way, but I was a closet chicken-shit. So I tried to make it seem like I really wanted to join her in Seattle, but I couldn't.

"Aren't you gonna say anything," she asked me.

"Maggie, I wanna come and be with you. I really do, but I just can't get up and leave on a whim."

I knew it was a stupid thing to say right after I had said it.

"Why not! You left me on a whim! The only reason you told me in the first place was because you wanted a fucking ride to the airport!"

"That's not true, Maggie," I tried to be very calm. "I wouldn't do that to you. Please don't say things like that to me. It's very insulting. It really is. Only an asshole would do something like that."

"Look Ray, I really need you here right now."

"Well, I've got no money."

"I'll put your fucking plane ticket on my American Express Card! Now pack your shit and get out here *now!* I've got *cancer* !"

"Whoa, hold up there," I said. "You're starting to scare me just a little bit now, ok? So just calm down or else I'm gonna have to hang up and I don't wanna do that to you, but—"

"But nothing! You're nothing but a fucking lying bastard—"

Click.

That's all she heard as I hung up on her.

"Boy," I said to myself as I tossed the phone across the room. I wanted to get it away from me. "My day just keeps getting better and better. What next, a visit from one of Erin's new boyfriends, an arrest warrant for brandishing a firearm at Brenda, or perhaps I'll just get sick and die tonight? That seems like a fitting ending to this fucking day!"

I was so pissed-off that I had to end my sobriety streak at just over seven hours. I went to my room and got out the three foot Grafix bong and pulled down four whole bowls on my own. I needed maximum relief and that's exactly what I got. It was a pure pleasure like an Enya song.

25

For the rest of February I had nothing but hellish and boring days.

I ended up working at that lawn care place that Leslie Hipp had told me about. I did telemarketing there for a few weeks and got two paychecks in a row, but none of the money went to my speeding ticket. I put the money to good use though, copping an ounce of weed and smoking most of it within ten days.

I got fired from my telemarketing job for being late three times in a row and actually the last time I was late I was so tardy I didn't even show up for work at all.

Shit at school was weird. Aside from The Brain and Gabe and Jacob Drake I didn't meet anybody new to hang out with and there had been no contact between me and any females for a while. For the first time in my life I was unpopular. I couldn't figure it out.

A month ago at that time I had a different girl calling me or knocking on the door practically every day and now I felt like I couldn't convince a crackhead hooker to come home with me even if I had a hundred bucks, a shower, and an eight-ball. That's the way the laws work though. Whenever I was with a girl I liked, all these other girls would show up and seem interested, but then I couldn't do anything because I already had a girlfriend. And just as soon as the girl I liked dumped me, none of the other girls would wanna talk to me anymore because girls like unavailable guys better than ones who are taking applications. I felt like building a machine that would just kick me in the ass all day so I wouldn't have to leave the house. And to top things off I had now been to school for twenty-two whole days in a row and I didn't know how much more I could take. I even did my homework.

I felt like the biggest idiot in the world for coming back home to a place that had nothing to offer to anybody. I was smoking more pot than I had ever smoked before. I got high just about every two hours on average, which worked out to about six to ten times a day, and that's no exaggeration. Even when I was at school I found ways to smoke. When I wasn't in class I could catch a hit or two in the bathroom, at lunch, before and after school, and during gym class when we went outside. I was a sneaky bastard. Any really experienced pot smoker can make the bowl fire just about anywhere, at anytime.

Then the first weekend of March came around. It was Friday night and I decided I would lay low at the apartment instead of going out because I was afraid that I was cursed. No good came outta me leaving the apartment anymore and I didn't feel like taking any chances outside in the cold world so that night I decided I would become a recluse. At 11:00 I even thought about going to bed early, and that's when the front door buzzer sounded off. I had a visitor.

"Hello," I mumbled hesitantly though the intercom.

"Yo, it's Gabe! Open the fucking door please."

"Hold up," I said and I buzzed him in.

I heard Gabe stomping his big clunky feet all the way up the three flights of stairs. I held the door open as he blew right by me and made himself at home. He threw his coat on the table, went to my fridge and helped himself to an Old Style, and then he went and sat down in my favorite chair, put his feet up on the coffee table, and he farted really loudly and laughed it off. Farts were funny to him. I wanted to tell him how disgusting I thought it was for him to let loose his digested Whopper farts into my favorite chair. I mean, if anyone is gonna fart in that chair it should be me. In Indiana (when people fart) you're not supposed to say anything unless you wanna complement them on the sound and power of the gas. I'm a bit more civilized than the average Regionrat, so instead I just kept quiet and let Gabe wallow in his own fumes

"So what are we doing," he asked me as he waved his hand in front of his crotch to ward off the stink.

I closed the door and locked the deadbolt. Gabe was acting extra-hyper and I knew I was in for a long night. The thought of staying up all night babysitting Gabe while he was jacked up on speed made me yawn, but I was also feeling really lonely and I kinda wanted some company. It's a desperate and sad feeling to be sitting at home on Friday night when you're in high school. It means something bad. It means you're a dork.

"We," I said as I sat down on the couch and turned on ESPN to watch Sportscenter. "Aren't doing anything because I have bad luck. I can't leave the house until my curse wears off."

"You haven't gone out in three weeks, dude. Who cursed you?"

"I think I cursed myself somehow."

"That's tuff, I curse myself all the time."

"You are a curse," I said as I pulled my rolling tray out from under the couch and I rolled a little joint with some shake that had collected around the indented edges of the tray.

"I talked to Erin today," he said as he crossed and re-crossed his legs. Then he crossed them again. He was very hyper, even more hyper than usual. I was pretty sure he had taken some speed, which for him wouldn't be too unusual. He was like a walking pharmacy. Gabe was the main pill connection around town. He was always getting his hands on uppers, downers, volume, speed, and especially ecstasy. He was one of those people who people who could hook up with all kinds of obsscure drugs, a regular Jack of all types of dope.

"Erin's a name I'd like to forget about," I groaned.

"Apparently," he said as I handed him the joint and a lighter. "She doesn't feel the same way. She keeps asking about you."

"That's *great*," I said sarcastically.

That's one thing about me: I can't stop being sarcastic. I'm especially sarcastic when something terrible happens. Even when some-body dies I have to crack some kinda sarcastic joke because it drives me crazy when things get too serious.

"I bet she's asking around for somebody to kick my ass. Do you think I have time to pack my things and get outta town this time, or is it too late? Are the thugs on their way over already?"

"Don't be silly," he said. "Her and Jeremy finally broke up for good. He's going out with somebody else now. I would guess that's the reason she was asking about you. I don't think she could ever not be with somebody. That's the type of chick she is."

"Well, as desperate as I may be right now, I'm not her man. Believe it or not, I'm trying to straighten my life out now, so the next girl I go out with is gonna be nice and honest. *Period*," I said.

When I said the word *period* I felt gross because it made me feel like Mr. Cox's little speech had rubbed off on me. And sure enough, even Gabe picked up on it.

"Period? You sound like Mr. Cox. He's always saying *period* this and *period* that. It drives me crazy. He sounds like a walking men-struation."

"I know it's disgusting. Please excuse my language. So what did you tell her?"

"*Who?*"

"*Erin*," I said, shaking my head.

He made me say her name outloud and I didn't wanna give her that much credit. When you start saying a girl's name a lot it's usually a sure sign you like her and that wasn't the direction I wanted to go.

"I told her I hadn't talked to you in a while, and I didn't know what was going on with you."

"Good man," I said to him. "You're watching my back."

"Then I told her if she wanted to know about you then she should just call you herself. I told her my name wasn't Cupid. Then she said she didn't have your number anymore, and that's the reason she hasn't called."

"Yeah? And?"

"And so I gave her your number."

"Fuck, Gabe!"

"What? What am I supposed to do?"

"Ok. I'll break it down for you," I said. "If a nice girl wants my number, then give it to her. If a skank like Erin wants it, then tell her you don't have it. It's that simple."

"I thought you liked her. That's why I gave her the number. If you want me to think you don't like her then don't go making out with her and feeling her up and all that garbage."

"I never felt her up! Where in the hell did you hear that?"

"Chill, Ray. It's just a figure of speech."

"You know, Gabe, if I could have just one wish, do you know what I'd wish for?"

"A pound of weed."

"Not even, and I wouldn't wish for money either, or fame for that matter. You know what I'd wish for? It would be that you never introduced me to that girl in the first place. The only thing I got outta knowing Erin was a black eye and a bad reputation. I should've listened to The Brain before any of this ever happened."

"Whoa! Hold on a second," Gabe said. "*The Brain?* What did *he* tell you?"

"Nothing. Forget I said anything."

"Fuck that. What did he tell you?"

"He just told me to be careful because she had a boyfriend."

"Let me tell you something about The Brain," Gabe said. "This is just between you and me. Don't go repeating this. And I heard this from Erin a while back so don't go talking to her about this either, ok?"

"Sure," I said.

"See, I heard The Brain likes Erin."

"What makes you say that? You mean he *likes* her or he *liked* her?"

"He *likes* her, and always has."

"Ok, I don't believe it, but if it's true what does that have to do with anything?"

"Dude, use your head. You told The Brain you liked Erin, you tell him you think she likes you, and all the while he likes her too. What do you think he's gonna tell you, to go for it? Hell no he's not!

He's gonna tell you whatever you will believe so he can convince you that you don't like her and that it would never work out. That way he can cockblock you and have her for himself. He's nothing but a fucking cockblocker, Ray. He's always been that way. It's because he's short. He's got small-man's syndrome. From what Erin tells me, her and The Brain messed around a coupla times about six months ago. Then she decides she don't like his ass anymore and tries to break it off, but he doesn't listen. See if there's one thing about The Brain, it's that he can't take no for an answer. Everybody knows that. He's creepy with bitches, Ray. He always brags about licking bitch's assholes. He's got serious problems so don't be going and taking relationship advice from that dude. This is the only guy in town using the Begging and Pleading Plan to get pussy. He calls constantly. He cries on the phone to girls. He begs, Ray. He's a begger. Don't take advice from that pussy."

"So what's the point?"

"The point is: he's been stalking her ever since and whatever he might have told you about Erin should not be taken seriously because the kid lies all the time, and not just to you about Erin, but to everyone about anything. I mean, I like the kid, but he's got *serious* problems. He licks assholes, Ray. Assholes."

Seeing Gabe talking about somebody else having serious problems with girls made me quiver. I mean, Gabe was a complete wigged-out maniac. I was constantly hearing stories about him stalking girls and now he's telling me all kinds of trash about The Brain. You know what they say, about it takes one to know one.

"Well, I'm not sure what to believe and I don't even know if I really care what's the truth," I said. "All I know is I got beat up for talking to her and he hasn't. That leads me to believe Erin is the one lying about shit and not The Brain. If he likes her and everybody is supposed to know about it, then why hasn't her gorilla boyfriend come after him then?"

"*Easy,*" Gabe said as he shifted his weight in the chair. His pupils were so dilated that a big black circle engulfed the blue color in his eyes. "Because nobody knows, but you, me, Erin and The Brain. She's kept it a secret because she didn't want to see The Brain get his ass kicked no matter how weird he was acting about the whole thing. She says he cries so much and begs for pussy that she feels sorry for him. The only reason her boyfriend found about about you was because Ari Lopez told Tim Miller, who then told Jeremy. Erin just wishes nothing had ever happened between her and The Brain. She says they were drunk every time and he'd always try to finger her asshole and when she'd stop him he'd confront her and be like, 'com'n. You can't sit there and tell me you don't like your asshole licked.'"

"Yeah well, *whatever*. I don't really care."

"The Brain's a mud-cutter, Ray! He tosses salad!"

"If she likes me so much then how come she fucking ignores me all the time. I mean, it's not like I'm chasing her or anything, she can't even say hi to me when I pass her in the hallway. That's just plain insulting, don't you think?"

"That's why I'm here, to explain," he said.

"You mean she *sent* you here?"

"*Exactly.*"

"That's sick."

"Hold on. Just let me explain."

I sighed and started rolling another joint, "Go for it. This should be real interesting. You know it's funny, no matter how much dope I smoke I still have to deal with more problems. It's not supposed to be that way."

"Erin isn't talking to you right now because she really cares about you."

"That makes me laugh. That's the funniest thing I've heard all day."

"I'm serious. See, she knows you and The Brain are friends and the last thing she wants to do is fuck with that. She feels like if she keeps talking to you, then it would drive a wedge between you and The Brain. Get it?"

"That's fucked up. If The Brain liked her he would've told me. It's as simple as that."

"*Bullshit,*" Gabe said. "Why? Why in the hell would he tell you anything? I mean, how long did you know him when you first told him about your situation with Erin, an hour, a day?"

"About an hour," I said feeling kinda stupid. "Maybe I see your point."

"Yeah, an hour. Now why in the hell would he tell you anything? He didn't know who in the hell you were, and if he told you about him liking her also he would risk the same fate that happened to you at Anthony Falco's party. It would've been him laid out on the sidewalk instead of you."

"Can I ask you something, Gabe?"

"Sure," he said, grinning at me like he was an all-knowing genius who just so happens to have taken a dozen caffeine pills.

"Ever since I've known you, you've always been in the middle of everybody's business. Why is that?"

"That's a good question. I guess, and this is just a guess, I enjoy being in everybody's business and people sense that, so they just tell me things. Plus I'm always listening for clues and when I hear one, I pry until I have all the juicy facts."

"You should be a journalist," I suggested.

"Screw that. I wanna be mayor."

The thought of Gabe being mayor was a sick one. As a matter of fact, though, he was our class president and that's no bullshit either.

It made me laugh again and I said, "If you get to be mayor someday, then I'll bang my dick on the heater."

"I'll remember that you know."

"I'm sure you will. So what are you trying to tell me here, that I should give Erin another chance, that I should just wait until she feels like talking to me, what?"

"Well, I've actually got specific instructions from her. She wrote something down for you."

He reached into his pocket and took out a folded up piece of paper and gave it to me.

"I ain't gonna read it to you," he said and he took the joint I had just rolled and he put it to his lips and lit it.

"What the fuck," I mumbled as I took the folded up letter. "A secret message? What is this a James Bond movie?"

I unfolded the paper and read it. It was short and sweet and it went something like this:

Raymond,

By now I hope that Gabe explained things to you. I'm sorry for not talking to you and I hope it's not too late to pick up where we left off. We need to talk tonight. Meet me at my house so I can explain things myself. I'm having people over tonight so don't let the cars freak you out. I broke up with my boyfriend so no one will want to beat you up. I promise.

Secret Love,

Erin Watkins

I put the paper on the table and I just let out a big breath of air. All this drama was driving me fucking crazy. I looked at Gabe and he had already smoked half the joint without even passing it back to me, but I didn't even care.

I shook my head and said, "She wants me to come over to her house."

"I know. I just came from her house. Plus I snooped and read the note on the way here. I was curious. Her parents are outta town for the weekend. They're visiting her older brother or something. I'll drive you over there. We can go together."

"Who's all over there," I asked him.

"Not too many people. Just Jacob Drake. Me. Jacob's girlfriend Gisela. Erin. Jolene ... and that's it."

26

We got into Gabe's car and drove over to Erin's house. I swear he didn't stop talking the whole way there. I don't know how he didn't come up for air. It's amazing.

The funny thing about Gabe's driving is when he stops the car he doesn't gradually slow down. He just comes to a complete stop right at the last second and it jolts you right outta your seat every time. He doesn't do it to show-off either. He just does it outta habit and it doesn't seem to bother him much, and he did a good one on the way to Erin's house.

There's a set of train tracks about five blocks from where she lived and as we approached them the gates were flashing and coming down. A big locomotive towing about a hundred cars full of steel-coils came down the tracks like an avalanche at about sixty miles per hour. Gabe didn't even seem like he was paying attention to the flashing red warning lights at the crossing. He just kept talking and looking at me while he drove. He didn't even look at the road one single time. As we got about twenty feet from the tracks the first few train cars went zipping by, pulling a garbaged scrap-papery wind in gusts. I slammed my foot on the imaginary brake and clutched the panic-handle on the door as hard as I could because Gabe didn't show any sign of slowing up. I was sure we were gonna plow right through the gate and get crushed by the train. And right when I was about to screech like a kindergartener during a horror movie for him to stop the car, which would have been embarrassing, he slammed on the brakes and came to a sudden stop about two feet from flashing red lights. I swear I about pissed my pants.

"So last week I got into an argument with my brother," Gabe said with his hair all messed up and sweat pouring down his face.

He didn't even care.

"About what," I asked as the train went rumbling into the darkness with a blur.

I straightened up in my seat and did my best to regain my composure.

"About when Andre the Giant died. I say a long time ago and he says it was right after Wrestlemania IV. He's so fucking stupid sometimes! My blinded-diabetic-grandmother knows more about professional wrestling than he does. What a fucking nerd he is sometimes. You know he never played any sports like me. He just did his goddamn homework all the time. He never even went out on the weekends. He's my mom's wet dream. He's everything my parents ever wanted in a son and I'm everything they never wanted," he laughed.

"You can say that again," I said. "He's at the University of Depauw now, right?"

"Yeah."

"What's he studying there?"

"Law. He wants to be a lawyer."

"Good," I said. "You're gonna need one plenty of times in your life."

"He wants to be a tax attorney. That's useless to me."

"Oh. I guess you're right."

"Wait a minute. I just remembered something," Gabe said as he hunched forward and reached his hand under the seat in search of something.

He felt around for several seconds or so. It didn't matter because you had plenty of time to do things while waiting for a train to pass in Granite. It's the railroad capitol of the United States and there are about fifty trains that thunder through each day, and each one lasts around five minutes.

"What're you looking for," I asked.

"Got it!"

He came back up and his face was as red as an apple and in his hand was a joint that was bent in all these weird angles, like it had been down there for weeks.

"If that joint were a little kid it would be riding the short bus to school. Are we really that desperate," I asked like an asshole, even though, deep down, I knew I would always accept smoke marijuana in any of it's Earthly forms.

"What the hell are you talking about? You don't wanna smoke this? It's totally fine. Look, dickhead. There's really nothing wrong with it at all. I dropped it the other day and I just remembered about it. Come on. Stop acting like a fag and light it!"

I took out a dollar bill and wrapped it around the joint and straightened it out as best as I could. I inhaled the largest hit I could fill my lungs with. It was a power hit. A power hit is when you pinch the end of the joint with your thumb and your pointer finger and you put your lips around the fingers and not the joint. Then you suck in just like you would on the joint, but the hit is inhaled with much more force than if you were just sucking on the joint itself. It's a good way to hitta joint because you get a larger hit with a minimized effort, and you don't get the tip all wet with spit. Pot-smokers *hate* when somebody wet-lips the joint more than they hate anything I've told you about already. Wet-lipping is the all time worst thing you could do. It's worse than a run in the joint and it's way worse than a seed in the bowl.

We were finished with the crooked joint by the time the train passed and as soon as the gates lifted Gabe ran every **STOP** sign on the way to Erin's house. Gabe pulled into the driveway without slowing down at all and came to a jolting stop just a few inches from the garage door. He made me stay in the car for a extra few minutes because a song was still playing on the radio and he seriously thought it was bad luck to turn a song off in it's midst.

I'd always ask quiz him on different scenarios.

"What if you're late for work or something, and you've gotta get outta the car right away?"

OR

"What you got pulled over by a jittery cop who ordered you to turn off the engine and step outta the vehicle immediately?"

OR

"What if you pull up to a stoplight and Susa Beaudette was in the next car over. She's drunk and wearing her Pantherette uniform. Before the light turns green she tells you her Parents are in Cancun and you should by and watch a movie with her. Then she drives off. You get home. You get all spiffed up."

"Shit, Shower and Shave!"

"Yeah. And then you jump into your car and drive over to her house. As you're pulling into her driveway you see her looking lazily into the dark night. She's only wearing her underwear. You park the car and some shitty song like *Right Here Right Now* by Jesus Jones is playing on the radio. That is not a good song, Gabe. Say it's just beginning and still has over 3 minutes left until it ends?"

He had the same answer for every question.

"You gotta finish out the song, Ray. There's really no other choice."

He had in his Counting Crows tape and that song called *Mr. Jones* was finishing up. Gabe loved Counting Crows with a passion. He thought they were (I'm not shitting you) the greatest band that ever lived. I think loving Counting Crows that much should be classified as its own mental illness.

When the song ended we went up to the sidewalk and outta nowhere and for no particular reason at all, Gabe jumped up and slapped a bird feeder right off its post. It sent birdseed and crap flying all over the place and he just laughed it off. Destruction of bird property was funny to him. I think he only did it because he thought I would think it was funny. I did.

I was really nervous about going inside. It could be an ambush. There entire football team could be in the basement and I wouldn't even know it. That might not even be Gabe.

I stood by the door and waited for Gabe to gather his thoughts so he could ring the doorbell or something. Instead he just ran right by me and barged right into the house and he left me standing there by myself in front of the open doorway.

Gabe disappeared down the hall and I could hear kids laughing and I could feel the warm heated air from the house pouring out into the night. There was a painting on the wall, a landscape, a place in the mountains that was covered with evergreen trees and there was a gushingly powerful river that cut through the forest. When I looked at it I pictured a bunch of American Indians stalking animals during daily hunts.

It was a real nice painting and I stepped inside and closed the door behind me and I looked at the painting up close. On the bank of the river there was a deer that had stopped for a quick drink. I touched the painting and felt that it was real paint and not a copy of a painting and I thought it was nice. I never did like prints of paintings. They just don't capture a scene like real painting does. I looked closely at the deer and imagined it looking up at me and becoming startled. It jolted back into the forest and it was gone. There was still a ripple in the pool of water where it had been drinking. Then I closed my eyes and opened them again and the deer was back drinking just as it was when I first noticed it.

"Raymond," a girl said. I knew Erin's voice without even looking at her.

"Hey, Erin," I said. "What's going down?"

"Nothing. What are you doing over here?"

"*Uh*, Gabe invited me," I explained.

I thought she didn't know I was coming over for some reason. I was embarrassed as hell.

"No, I mean, you're just standing here by yourself. I knew you were coming over. I sent Gabe to go get you? Didn't he explain things to you? Didn't he show you the note?"

"*Oh*," I laughed a little and smiled at her. "Yeah. Totally. Actually I was just looking at this painting on the wall here."

"Do you like it?"

"Yeah. It's real nice."

"I painted it myself."

"No kidding? You did this? It's really great. I didn't know you were a painter."

"That's because I never told you, and I never really thought of myself as a painter. It's just a hobby I've had since I was little."

"Wow that's really great," I said as I glanced back at the painting and I took off my black leather gloves and stuffed them into my coat pockets. Sure enough there was her a phrase that took my breath away above signature in the bottom corner if the painting,

Secret Love,
Erin Watkins.

She walked closer to me and asked, "Can I take your coat?"

"*Uh*, sure," I said.

A song started to play on the stereo. As soon as the beautiful guitar music and I heard the voice of a little boy saying, "Look mommy, there's an airplane up in the sky," and then I knew it was

Goodbye Blue Sky by Pink Floyd.

"But hey. Erin, *uh*. Could you put it somewhere that's really safe? This is my lucky leather jacket. I know it sounds corny, but this jacket really means a lot to me and I just wanna make sure nothing dirty happens to it. I usually don't even wear it outta the house anymore."

"Sure," she smiled. "Com'n. We'll put it upstairs in the hall closet."

I followed her up the stairs and it seemed like with every step there was a different framed picture of some little kid. There was something that looked familiar to me about her, but I couldn't really figure it out until we got into the light of her parents' room. Then I figured out she was wearing a shirt of mine, but I couldn't remember ever loaning it to her. It was a Tie-dye shirt with a picture of Bob Marley on the front. Under his face it just said "Bob."

"Hey, is that my shirt," I asked. I knew it was and that it was impossible for somebody else to have one just like it because my friend Lewis had made me that shirt for my birthday. His uncle had a T-shirt shop in Gary. This shirt was one-of-a-kind.

"Yeah, don't you remember," she asked and seemed embarassed that I didn't remember as she hung my coat up in the closet. "You lent it to me when I came over to your house that one night. Remember? After I had gotten my tattoo? I spilled beer all over the shirt I had on and you let me wear this one home."

"Oh Yeah. I just forgot, that's all."

"Do you want it back? Because I'll give it back"

"*Uh*, yeah I do, but you can hold on to it for a little while. I don't need it or anything. I just didn't remember how you got it."

The fucked up thing is I didn't remember how she got the shirt because this story about her spilling beer on herself never happened. We were drinking. We got drunk. She must've snuck into my room and stole that T-shirt. She was trying to tell me stories, playing off the assumption that since I got drunk then I must not trust myself to remember everything that happened that night.

"Good," she said. "I just *love* this shirt. It's my favorite shirt in the entire whole world. I just love Bob Marley."

She turned and faced me and embraced herself like she was trying to hug the shirt and she smiled at me.

"Yeah," I said. "I want it back, but you don't have to, like, give it to me right now or anything. I know where you live, right?"

"Yeah. You do."

"My friend Lewis gave that shirt to me a while back. Remember him? You met him at Ricky's house. He was that pale black kid that dresses real nice, the one who hates Ricky."

"I remember him. He seemed really nice."

"He is. He's really nice," I confirmed.

Then there was this weird minute when neither of us said anything. We just looked at each other and smiled, only I kept looking away because I was still high off of that crooked joint Gabe had fished out from underneath the seat in his car. I was afraid she'd notice I was baked so I tried really hard to think of something to say that wouldn't come off, like, I was just saying it to break the silence because I suspected that she suspected I was stoned, but I think she liked the silence.

"*So*," she started to say with a smile and then paused.

I swallowed and felt my Adam's-Apple shift up and down in my throat.

"So," she said again. "Smoke any heroin lately?"

"*No*," I laughed. "I wish. Not since that one night. What about you?"

"Whatever, Raymond. As if I would smoke some fucking heroin, dude."

"I know, I was just joking. Why the fuck would you ask me that anyway?"

"I was just joking."

"God."

"Look," she sighed. "Let's go downstairs. We wouldn't want people to start jumping to conclusions as to why we're upstairs so long do we?"

"No. We wouldn't," I said and smiled.

I'd never been so blatantly manipulated before.

Erin and I went back downstairs and into the livingroom, whatever you call it. And there was about ten people huddled around the room listening to music and drinking beer and chain-smoking Camel

Wides and Marlbroro Reds.

Erin gave me a semi-formal introduction.

"Everybody," she shouted over the music. "If you don't know him, this is Raymond. He's our new friend."

I just nodded at everyone. Most of the people I pretty much knew already, and they were Gabe and Jacob Drake, Jolene and Leslie Hipp, Lisa Diamond and some girl who I didn't know right next to Jacob Drake. Jolene was there with her boyfriend James who I had seen around once or twice, and Che Elias was there also. Then there was this one guy with some blonde chick who I didn't know.

The guy got up and shook my hand.

He was real friendly and he said, "Hi man, I'm Bobby Cluck. I heard all about your fight with Tim Miller, dude. That's awesome. Glad to meet you." And then he pulled up the blond girl by the arm and he made her stand up to meet me. "This is my girl Betty."

I shook his hand. Then I shook her hand. I always shake a hand like the person's hanging off a bridge and I'm trying to save their life. Bobby's handshake had about as much grip as a rotting corpse. "Betty this is that dude I was telling you about that almost kicked Tim Miller's ass a few weeks ago."

"Oh," she said.

"Hey. How're you doing," I said. "Bobby and Betty, eh."

I nodded to his girl and she sat back down and started gossiping again. Jacob Drake came over and shook my hand. He was looking like a crazy son-of-a-bitch. He looked more pale and his deep voice brought out the best of his spin-off New York accent. His hair had grown into more of an Afro that could rival anybody in the movie *Superfly*. He was dressed a lot like Gabe and he had the same look in his eyes that Gabe had that night and I imagined they were probably on the same shit since they always hung out together all day long.

"What's going down, Jacob?"

"Ray! You little, bitch," he laughed. "Did you know I'm Erin's next door neighbor and shit? Hell, we're practically fuckin related right, Erin," he shouted over to her, but she didn't say anything.

I don't think she heard him.

"Hows the wrestling team working out for you? Gabe says you're pretty good."

"Yeah, I'm the type-a-guy who fuckin pins Gabe's sorry ass all the time at practice," he shouted over to Gabe even though he was only a few feet away.

"My ass," Gabe yelled back. "You couldn't pin me if I had no arms and no legs and my name was Matt."

"Try me bitch," Jacob laughed.

"You wanna go outside right now, Jethro?"

Gabe got in Jacob's face, but you could tell they were just messing around.

"Jacob," a girl scolded him. It was that girl who I had never seen before. She seemed like she meant business.

"I'm taking away the rest of your beer, Jacob! You're done for the night!"

"Oh man, that's harsh," I said.

"*Ah*," Jacob said to me. "Don't waist your fuckin time listening this bitch. She's always talkin shit," he said as he formed his hands into a mouth shape and started chomping them like PAC-Man. "Nutten important ever fuckin comes outta her mouth. She amazes me sometimes how she can say so many useless things at once. I can't fucking believe her shit sometimes," he said at her. "Cuttin me off, Jesus Christ Almighty. I'm the man. You ain't the man!"

"Well, aren't you at least gonna introduce me, Jacob," the girl said. "Could you be any more rude? He has no manners," she said to me.

"Bitch, step back," he yelled at her. "I'll introduce you when I'm fuckin good and ready. Ray, This is my fucking curse. My fucking hex, Gisela."

"I'm his girlfriend," she said in a proper way as she stood up and shook my hand again.

"Nice to meet you," I said.

There were still two other girls there who I was just noticing and who didn't bother introducing themselves, and to my surprise I knew one of them. It was the fat girl, the one they call Sydney, the one who tossed garbage at me earlier in the afternoon.

What tremendous fucking luck, I thought.

I was happy to know I at least had a mission to accomplish there that night. I wanted to drive Sydney crazy by whatever means I could think of. There was no way in hell this girl was gonna get away with tossing trash at me. I left her alone right then because I didn't want her to know that I knew who she was. I wanted to attack with stealth. I didn't have a clue who the other girl talking to her was, for all I knew she was one of the girls in the car. One thing was for sure, whoever she was, she wasn't gonna get any mercy from me. I wasn't sure exactly what I would do to them, but I knew at the very least I wanted to talk to them alone somehow so I could say weird things to them with a straight face, just to see how they'd react.

I had a strong hunch they must've had some kinda reason for throwing trash at me because it wasn't like I was the school retard or anything, and it wasn't too common that a bunch of girls would wanna pelt an innocent bystander with Burger King trash just for fun. That's more, like, something my friends and I would do, but not a bunch of chicks. That was uncharacteristic.

Then Sydney got up and went over to the phone that was tucked away on a coffee table along the wall. It was about six feet away from me. Right before she grabbed the phone I walked over to Sydney and grabbed her wrist to keep her from picking up the phone. I whispered to her so no one else would hear what I had to say to her.

"Hey, girlie girl," I said. "You using the phone?"

She looked at me like I was a retarded drunk and just said, "*Uh,* yeah," in the snootiest way possible.

"Oh goodie. I love it when girls use the telephone. I'd dig it if I could just lick a little of your spit off the mouthpiece when you're through. You. Are. Precious."

She froze because I was already starting to freak her out, "What?" she asked. "Precious?"

"I could hold the cord for you or press the buttons or something. Wouldn't that be great?"

"Uh, that's ok," she said and she turned her back on me and dialed and put the phone up to her ear. I didn't wanna freak her out too much right away so I decided I'd go sit down in Sydney's chair and mess with her friend a little.

I sat down next to the girl and she turned her back to me right away.

"Hey there," and I picked up a magazine and put it in her lap. "You should read this," I said to her like there was something interesting for her to read inside it. I looked down and saw that it was the TV Guide.

"I'm sorry," she questioned me looking confused.

"What're you *talking* about?" I asked back, trying to confuse her. "Why should I read this?"

"Huh," I said and I gave her the weirdest look that I could. "I'm not Stanley, sorry. I don't know who that is. You got the wrong guy. My name's Ray."

"Oh my God," she whined. "You're *not* weird or anything."

She said it as sarcastically and as bitchy as she could and looked around the room for help, but everyone was too wrapped up in their conversations and Jacob was yelling too loud so nobody else was listening.

"I hope this seat isn't taken," I asked her.

"Uh, yeah. Actually it is so—"

"That's because I'm sitting in it, *biatch,"* I said quickly.

Already she was fed up from my bullshit so she quickly got to her feet and went outside to have a cigarette. It was a big mistake on her part though, because I didn't even have to be sneaky about messing with her outside. I waited a minute and acted normal in front of the others and then I said to Jacob that I was gonna go have a smoke so I got up and went for the door. And then Jacob said he was gonna have one too and he came with me, which pretty much nullified my harassment mission temporarily. That was fine with me though, because it would probably freak the girl out even more to hear me have a normal conversation with somebody.

I waited up for Jacob as he put on his cheesy Top Gun bomber jacket. It was one of the ugliest coats I had ever seen in my life. It wasn't fashion ugly either, like a lot of the styles around during those times. It was just plain ugly. It would look terrible no matter time or place, like it was donated to him while staying in a homeless shelter. It was made of some kinda animal skin, or imitation animal skin, and it just didn't look quite real. It was, like, Nazi suede. There was something about the texture of the coat that told me only some freak scientist could have developed it.

"It's a good thing you're coming," I said to him. "Because I just remembered I forgot my cigarettes."

"Don't worry, nigger," he yelled. "I gotcha covered like one a Ron Reagan's secret service guys."

"That's a good one," I said as I slid open the glass door.

Sydney's little trash throwing friend, my victim, was standing with her back to us blowing smoke up into the air. When she heard the door open she turned and looked at me. She got so startled by my appearence that she actually dropped her cigarette onto the grass. I felt like that poor kid that Eric Stoltz played in the movie *Mask*.

"Precious," I said to her. "There you are!"

"*Eh*, Kimble," Jacob said to her. "What up?"

"Nimble. That's a great name," I said.

"*Kimble*," she corrected me.

"Bimbo. I Got it down pat," I said.

"Are you a retard or something," she asked me very seriously.

"If that's what you're into," I suggested. "And from the looks of things, if I were you, I'd be into just about anything that would come close enough to cast a shadow on me."

"Excuse me?"

She put her hands on her hips and did the Jerry Springer-guest-neck-jibber-jabber.

Then I laughed and went, "Jerry! Jerry! Jerry! Jerry!" I couldn't keep my cool anymore and I started laughing real hard. "Look," I came clean with her. "I'm sorry. I was just messing with you because you bitches tossed trash at me this afternoon, remember?"

"Oh my God," she leaned close and took at good look at me. "That was *you*," she asked with her eyes getting all big like baseballs with bullet holes in them.

"What in the hell are you cocksuckers talking about," Jacob yelled.
"That wasn't me, man," she said to me. "I mean, I was in the
car, but it wasn't my idea and I didn't throw any trash at you. I'm
dead serious. I swear, man."

"What about the other girl," I asked her.

"Which one?"

"You know," I said smiling. "Your deluxe, more roomy verson
of a friend, the girl you were just hanging around with inside, the
one with the car, the driver, the beached whale—"

"I get the point. And it's not nice to make fun of people because of their weight."

"I fucking *hate* fat people," Jacob yelled. "They everywhere I
look nowadays. They always up in McDonald's ordering this, that,
and the other Super-Value Meal."

"Hold on," I said putting my hands up to Kimble and I formed
a T. "Time out. Jacob, *why* in the hell do you talk like that? You've
got some kinda weird-ass accent, like, I've never heard of before.
What is that, some kinda Mexican, Chinese farmer-type thing?"

"It's fuckin New York!"

"Dude, I know a New York accent," I said. "Your's is different.
It's like a New Yorker, but with a strange Beverly Hillbilly twist to it.
I'm not trying to be a dick," I insisted right away. "I'm just trying to
describe it as best as I can."

"Well, I ain't from New York City," Jacob began to clarify. "I'm
from upstate, from a small farm town around Buffalo and shit."

"Ok," I said. "That explains it. I was just wondering. Now back
to you, Precious," I pointed to Kimble. "Why did you and your
friends decide to throw trash at me? And don't fucking tell me it
was for no goddamn reason either. Girls just don't do shit like that
without a reason. I don't wanna hear that. I don't."

"You don't have to get all *hostile*," she let me know right away.

"Precious, if I was getting *hostile*, the whole fucking neighborhood would know, ok? So go ahead, spill the beans."

"Yeah. Spill the dang beans already, you guilty-ass bitch," Jacob
yelled. "Stop fuckin around already!"

"Ok," she said as she tossed her cigarette into the bushes. "I guess you deserve to know why, but you can't tell anyone I told you. Both you guys have to fucking *promise* me this conversation won't leave this backyard. I mean it. I'm dead serious."

"Look," I sighed. "If you tell me what's up then I'll never bother you again and I swear to God I'll never rat on you. Jacob here feels the same way. Don't you?"

"Yeah, Kimble," he yawned. "I won't tell a *mothah fugah.*"

"*Ugh,*" she quivered. "I hate when people use that expression."

"Jacob, your Ebonics is finally getting through to people. She just picked outta phrase she recognized," I laughed. Then I turned back to the girl and pressed the issue.

"Please tell me," I begged. "I can't take it anymore. I need to know."

"Ok, you guys both know a kid named Jason Neagu right?"

"No. I don't," I said.

"I know'em," Jacob said. He elbowed me in the ribs and said, "Milada's boyfriend, dog."

"Ex-boyfriend," Kimble corrected him.

"Oh *yeah,*" I said and raised an eyebrow. "I know who that is. They're all broke up and stuff now? I know who that kid is. But, *uh,* what in the hell does he have to do with you guys throwing garbage at me?"

"Well," she blushed. "He found out."

I just stared at her. I was waiting for her to finish her sentence.

"He found out," she said again.

I asked, "He found out about what?"

"About you and Milada. About you guys messing around."

"Me and *her,*" I asked just as surprised as ever. "Rewind a second. There is no *me* and *her,* and never was. I'm serious, if there was I'd admit it, believe me, because she's hot."

"Yeah, well that's your own business, not mine," she said. "But anyway, Sydney and him are friends and he thinks you were messing with Milada while they were still together. He would never confront you himself because he's a coward, so he's been telling people to do stuff to you if they ever see you. You didn't hear it from me though. Do either of you guys got another cigarette? I just ran out."

"Sure, Precious. Jacob, hand her a poop will you," I said and I motioned for Jacob to hand her a smoke.

"Ain't this about a bitch," Jacob yelled and took outta poop from his Marlboro pack.

"You said it, Jacob. That cliché was very appropriatly used," I agreed with him and then turned back to her. "Well, I guess thanks for telling me."

"No problem, but remember I never told you, ok?"

"It's a deal," I said. "Jacob here ain't gonna tell anyone either. Promise her, man," I said to him.

"I promise, Kimble. I won't tell a *mothah fugah*," he laughed.

"Oh whatever, Jacob!"

"Hey, can I ask you one more thing, Kimble?"

"Sure," she said to me. "Go ahead."

"Why the hell does this kid Jason, Milada's boyfriend, or ex-boyfriend, where'd he come up with this idea about me and Milada? Who told him this thing, the sexy stuff with his girl, how would he get that idea, or why does he think this was going on?"

"I'm not really sure, but I think Milada probably told him when they broke up."

"It couldn't have been her," I said. "Because nothing ever happened, so why in the hell would she just make something up? That would be pretty stupid."

"Well, it *is* Milada we're talking about," she said like a bitch.

She started to go inside so I said, "Ok, thanks. I'm serious. Thank you."

She tossed a hand over her shoulder and muttered a simple, "No problem."

Jacob and I just stood there for a second. He took outta poop and offered it to me, but I didn't feel like smoking so he lit it for himself. I wondered what Kimble meant by that thing she said about Milada telling her ex-boyfriend about me and her while they broke up. Was I missing something? I mean, I knew Milada wasn't all that smart, but this seemed different. No, this was defiantly a clue. Was Milada, like, some huge liar like Erin, a rat, or even worse—a conniving little bitch?

"Brother," I said to Jacob. "What do you know about that girl Milada, anything?"

"Lil' bit. She's been hanging around with my girlfriend Gisela lately, ever since she broke up with her boyfriend."

"She ever say anything about me around you?"

"Never ever, nigger."

"What about Gisela? Do you think Milada might have told her something?"

"I guess it's possible, but they would never tell me some shit like that. I can't keep a secret."

"What's with that name? *Gisela?* Is she half Asian or something, because she looks it. And I ain't no language expert or anything, but I thought a Gisela was, like, a Japanese prostitute. That's a fucked up thing to name your kid don't you think?"

"She's a gook alright, Ray," he said about his own girlfriend. "But look here, a *Geisha* is a prostitute. I dunno about what a Gisela might be, I never axed her what it mean. She sure as hell don't act like no prostitute I'll tell you that shit right now, been with her for over a month already and she still ain't been given up no *puntang.*"

"That's harsh, but I guess if you like a girl you don't want her to be the type that sleeps with you right away, because if she did that with you, then she might do it just as easily with somebody else."

Jacob took a deep drag off of his cigarette and blew the spent smoke out through his nostrils. I always thought it was really gross when somebody did that.

"Depends on the girl I think. So what's yer deal man," Jacob asked. "You new around here or something? Are you a new kid to this school?"

"Kinda, sorta," I answered. "I first went to Andrean for my Freshman and Sophomore year. And then right before school let out I got expelled for this school book operation, which I was able to defraud the school store outta hundreds and hundreds of bucks before somebody told on me. Then, since my dad lives in Granite, I came to this school for my entire junior year. The whole year I just really didn't hang out with anybody here at all. Most people didn't even know my name. Then for the first part of this year I had moved out to Seattle and I went to school the first half of the year there. I went broke, and now I'm back to finish out my senior year in Granite. It's terrible."

"Oh yeah, how was Seattle?"

"Rainy, and a lot like living in China, or some place where everybody drives really slow and they all pronounce every word when they talk. If you went there you would think they were speaking Croatian or some shit like that, but other than that it's one of the most beautiful places I've ever been in my entire life."

"Uh, huh. And what makes you think people in China drive slow and pronounce their words?"

"I'm not sure why I even said that."

"Seattle, huh? No shit! You see Kurt Cobain while you was out there or what?"

"No. I didn't see him. I didn't see anybody from Pearl Jam or Soundgarden around town either, but everybody would always talk about how you could see some of them dudes at the coffee shops in Queen Anne or Capitol Hill. I don't know. I never saw nobody."

"*Mothah fugah.* I'm gonna go back inside. You coming, Ray?"

"I'll be in there in a sec. I'm just gonna take a whiz around the side of the house here real quick."

Jacob went back inside and I walked around to the side of the house where I had a perfect view of the street. I stood by a bush and unzipped my pants, but I didn't go yet, because I kept looking at this car parked in the street. I pulled my pants back up and I walked closer to the car, trying to wonder why I kept looking at it. It was a Monte Carlo Supersport. That's why I kept staring at it, because it was Sydney's car! I reached into my pants pocket and felt my knife. I contemplated a real quick vandalism mission. I looked both ways down the street and didn't see anyone coming so I walked up to the car and tried the handle and to my surprise it was unlocked.

Good action, I thought.

So what I did was, I pissed inside the car, my stream hit right on the floor in front of the driver's seat first, then I spread it all over the inside of her car.

"Lovely," I said to myself and laughed quietly. "This is funny to me."

When I was finished I carefully put my guy away and zipped up my pants and tucked in my shirt and casually shut the door. I started to walk into the back yard again, but I had to stop real quick, because I got an idea for some finishing touches. I crept back to the urine-mobile and I stuck my knife into the front-left tire and listened to the air as it escaped in gusts.

It's funny how pissing on somebody else's property suddenly makes everything worth while.

Headlights that started out very dim and got increasingly brighter approached from the north, so I folded up my blade and I ran into the back yard and I went inside as if nothing had ever happened. Everyone was too busy socializing to even notice that I had been gone. And I did my best to keep my status incognito.

Gabe jumped up onto the table and asked Erin to dim the lights.

"I've gotta show you guys my new standup routine," he shouted to everyone.

Gabe wanted to become a comedian someday and he was always practicing. Sometimes he had some pretty good bits, but other times they weren't so hilarious. For starters, Gabe only did stolen material that he got from movies and stand up acts like Steve Martin, Eddie Murphy, or Chris Rock. Sometimes they were funny, because at least they would remind people of Murphy's *Delirious* or *Raw*, or that *King Tut* bit that Steve Martin used to do, or when Gabe quoted lines by Chevy Chase or Cousin Eddie from *National Lampoon's Vacation*. He'd do lines from the movies all day long, like *Airplane* and *Spaceballs*. So sure, people laughed at Gabe when he did these routines, but it wasn't all him. He just reminded people of how they laughed when they first saw these movies or acts, only it wasn't quite as funny when Gabe did them, but it was at least more entertaining than sitting in Erin's livingroom listening to all the kids try to top each other's "I'm cooler than you" stories.

So he was on the table doing a Pee Wee Herman thing that transformed into something like Ed Grimly's idiot dance. And then he jumped onto the floor and started doing that dance that Ed

Grimly actually did, with his forearm pressed against his forehead, hopping on one foot, and otherwise looking as strange as possible. We all gotta big kick out of it.

Everybody gave Gabe some applause when he was finished and Jacob had to give that token small town line, "My cousin does that act perfectly. It's funnier than hell every time he does it!"

People in big cities hate attention and small town people fight over it like a school of sunfish around a tossed out hotdog. I was getting real nervous because I was afraid Sydney would soon discover that her tire had been slashed and her automobile urinated in, and I was afraid somehow everybody would know it was me. Whatever was gonna happen with Sydney, I wanted to get outta there before it did. I was about to ask Gabe for a lift back to the apartment, and the words were so close that my mouth was open, my lips ready to form sounds, and breath was starting to tumble across my tongue, when I was interrupted.

"Raymond," Erin called to me. "Raymond, come here," she rotated her hand like a wheel in reverse as she stood by the front door with Jolene and Bobby Cluck.

Bobby was a Nine Inch Nails freak, always wearing the band's propaganda, and he was a nice clean-cut looking guy, and was kinda smart, other than the goofy look on his face all the time.

I walked over to them and said, "What's up?"

"Dude," Erin said. "We're gonna go outside to smoke a joint."

"Yeah," Bobby said and held up a joint. "I got this big phatty."

"Really," I said not too interested. "*Ah*, no thanks though. I don't really feel like getting high right now."

"Com'n dude," Erin said. "You can't just flake on us!"

"I thought this kid was the man," Bobby said to Erin. "Erin told me you smoked more weed than anybody and here you are saying no thanks. That's fucking hilarious!"

"You said that, Erin? See that's exactly why I shouldn't. I'm kinda trying to quit, or at least cut down a whole lot. I sure as hell don't wanna be known as the guy who smokes more weed than anybody. That's so fucking loser-style."

"Raymond, you have to. For me, ok," Erin asked. "Just this

once, because I never get to hang around you anymore."

"I just don't feel like smoking."

"Look," Jolene said to everybody. "If he doesn't feel like it we should just leave him alone."

It was nice of Jolene to stick up for me, but at the same time the way she said it made me feel like a loser or something. I felt like I was holding a sign that said:

I'M A PATHETIC, DRUG-ADDICTED LOSER

They agreed with Jolene, mainly because everyone seemed to listen to her. She was a leader. And they turned and started going outside when I stopped them and said, "Fuck it. I'm in," and I followed them out to the garage.

I gathered that Erin's old man was some kinda handyman or a carpenter or something like that because of the garage's appearance. He was a neat freak. The garage wasn't used for parking cars and storing old bicycles. Erin flipped a switch on the wall and the automatic door to the garage started to open up very slowly with a buzzing rumble sound that only an electric engine seems to make.

"I don't wanna stink up by dad's garage," Erin said to us. "But I don't want the whole neighborhood to see us either."

She turned off the garage door so it was only open a few feet.

"You can't stink up a garage," Bobby Cluck informed us. "Garages are already smelly, aren't they?"

There was a wall covered with tools that were hung by nails. These weren't rusty old tools either, like the kind you find in an old house that's had a history of different families over the years. These tools were new looking, shiny, and they were all hung in some kinda systematic order. The larger tools hung on the lower racks and the smaller one's were on top. Power tools, like, electronic screwdrivers and power-drills were hung on the next wall above three shelves, each of which had its own red toolbox. Along another wall there was a workbench with a clock made of wood that was in the process of being built. And above the workbench was a long shelf that held completed clocks of all different sizes, shapes and styles. In the corner there was a full-sized refrigerator and I opened the door to see what was inside. There was nothing but a few bottles of beer and worms stored in Styrofoam containers. I closed the door and noticed about five fishing poles that hung along the far wall like you would hang pool sticks around a table.

The most noticeable thing about the garage itself was how clean and spotless it was. I had never seen a garage that was kept this well. There was no dust, dirt, oil-stains or spider-webs in sight. It seemed just as well kept as the dining room inside the house. There was even a section by the door with a couch, chair, coffee table and a television that was hooked up to cable. It was obvious that Erin's old man spent a lot of his free time in here. It was his room. There was no doubt about it. It was easily one of the coolest, but most bizarre garages I had ever been in.

Everybody sat on the couch, but Jolene and Bobby Cluck were sketched out because the garage door was hanging open a little. So Erin closed it to a point where there was about three inches of open space between the floor and the door. Erin turned on the TV and turned the channel to MTV and we watched the last half of *The Real World*.

"Real World my *ass*," I said as we passed around the first joint. "They should make them get mugged and fired from their job in the same day or something before they call it that."

"How about *The Bogus World*," Bobby Cluck suggested.

"Dude, or how about *The Halfway Real World*, because it's only real if you film twenty-four hours a day," Erin added.

"How about turning on VH1," Jolene said. "This show is *sooo* stupid. Whatever happened to playing music videos on MTV?"

We passed around the joint and chatted about politics for about fifteen minutes. Everybody was pretty baked at this point except for me. Over the years I had developed a strong resistance to THC to where I wasn't getting very stoned anymore. Instead I just felt dull and sorry that I had smoked any in the first place. When I first started getting high as a youngster I always had this misconception when I got stoned that it made me sharper, keener and more in tune with my surroundings. It's not the way weed works in real life—or in *The Real World* for that matter.

That's when the driveway went from dark as a Cubans hair to being completely flooded with headlights and the sounds of scripted gossip from the television was laced with the squeaking of the metallic fibers from the brake-pads of some car that was pulling in. It didn't bother me at all until the others reacted in a way with shocked look on their faces and the frozen body language that led me to think the cops were in the driveway, or something just as serious. It gave me no reason to believe that Erin was expecting anymore company for the evening.

"Oh shit," Erin sighed.

"*What*," I asked, trying not to sound worried, but in a way like she better start explaining things before I freak the fuck out.

"Do you think it's really them," Erin asked Jolene.

"If it is that would suck majorly," Jolene assured. "I'll go outside and see what's going on."

"Raymond, you have to hide or get lost or something," Erin ordered me.

"What the fuck are you talking about," I asked, totally confused. I felt like a soldier who just got caught in an ambush.

Jolene ducked down and looked underneath the garage door and confirmed whatever Erin's fear was.

"It's them!"

"It's *who*," I asked. "The fucking cops?"

I wished someone would tell me what was happening, because if it was the cops I didn't really care too much. I hadn't been drinking and I didn't have any weed on me. I didn't bring any for exactly that reason. It was in the job description of the Granite police officers to prowl the night in search of nonviolent criminals to hassle.

Then it hit me. Why would I be the only one who would have to hide or get lost if it were the cops outside? I stood up quickly and zeroed in on the backdoor to the garage and then I looked back at the flood of light pouring in under the garage door.

"Hey, Ray," Jolene turned to me and said. "Jeremy Otsap is outside. Erin's ex? It's time to get lost, unless you want him and his friends to catch you here. Tim Miller's with him and they look as if they're here for a reason."

"Somebody must've told him I was having guys over," Erin said. She was worried sick.

"Wasn't me," Bobby said as he picked up his pack of cigarettes off of the table and put them back in his shirt pocket. "I'm just gonna stay outta the way if you guys don't mind. I sure as hell don't want those guys on my case."

"Ray, what are you waiting for," Erin said as she grabbed my arm. "You have to leave now!"

I looked at the backdoor and then I heard about ten different car doors slam shut. The only thing I could do was run out the back door and try to make it the two miles in the cold back to my apartment. Even still they'd probably hunt me down in the street and smear me into the concrete and then toss me like McDonald's burger wrappers into some wooded area. Knowing my luck, I'd probably land in some drainage ditch and drown to death. Plus I'd have to live with a pussy reputation for the rest of my existence in this town. Pretty soon every guy around would be trying to work me over just for practice. There was no way in hell I could go out like that, no matter who was outside. I didn't care if King Kong Bundy was out there. I couldn't live the rest of my life as a sissy.

"I'm staying," I said like Sylvester Stalone playing Rambo. "I can't keep running from these guys."

Erin laughed at me, but not in a funny way. She laughed in a way like I was freaking her the fuck out.

"Raymond, you can't be serious. Please. Just go. I promise I'll lie. I'll do whatever it takes to get Jeremy off your back. I swear to God I will, dude."

I heard the deep voices of men gathering in front of the garage. They were laughing and carrying on about beating the shit outta somebody. I could tell they were all pretty much drunk, which could be a good or a bad thing. It would be good if they were so drunk that they couldn't see straight and bad if they were just drunk enough to do something crazy like accidentally trying to kill somebody like in the movie *The Outsiders.*

"I'm not going anywhere," I said again. "I'm dead serious. I'm not scared of that guy, Erin. And I'm not just saying that, because I could care less if you're impressed by my bravery or not. All you do is lie to me anyway."

"*Excuse me*, dude," she asked to me as she raised her eyebrows to me like I was in big trouble.

"You heard me, bitch," I said and smiled to Jolene and Bobby. Bobby laughed and Jolene just rolled her eyes.

"Well, are you guys gonna stick around for the show or what?" Nobody answered me because they knew I had lost my cool. I walked over to the switch that Erin flipped to open the garage door and I turned it on again and watched the door slowly open. The talking and chattering outside went suddenly quiet as the inside of the garage was steadily exposed to them. I walked back over to the door and just stood there and waited. I saw a bunch of shoes at first, and then I saw the legs of about seven or eight guys and they all wore jeans that were tight-rolled at the cuffs. Then I saw a bunch of thick bodies with clinched fists on their sides. Finally the door was open all the way and Jeremy Otsap, Tim Miller, James Chapman and a bunch of other goons stood there staring at me like they wanted to punch every single tooth outta my mouth. These guys weren't like the Preps from the movie *The Outsiders*; these guys were pure dirt.

"*Howdy* to a bunch of urban cowboys," I said to them.

"Oh my God," I heard Erin mumble in the background.

"Holy shit," Bobby Cluck sighed. "I can't believe he just said that."

Jolene walked up and got in-between them and me and she said, "Look. What the hell are you guys doing here?"

She was practically yelling at them and I was kinda hoping she'd scare the bastards away because I was starting to get real scared. Everybody from inside the house found out something was going down so they all piled outta the house and into the front yard to watch. I saw Sydney walk right over to one of the goons and start whispering to them and then I remembered how she got up and used the telephone right away when I got to Erin's house. She must have called them and told them to come and get me.

"Jeremy," Jolene screamed and pushed him in the chest. "Go home!"

"Fuck that," he said. "I ain't going anywhere!"

I noticed a car parking at the end of the street and it took a few seconds for the headlights to shut off, which made me figure that whoever was in the car noticed the commotion up at the house. I really wanted the cops to show up right about now. I was all by myself.

"You just couldn't listen to me," Tim Miller said to me. "You're an idiot, man. Now you really fucked up, because when Jeremy's done with you, I'm gonna get my fill too."

I just kept my mouth shut and didn't say anything as Jeremy pushed Jolene outta the way and got right in my face. He was huge and I would have been looking up at him if I had the guts to look him in the eyes, but I didn't, so I just looked at his throat.

"You like my girl, asshole," he asked me. "You ain't so slick no more."

"So I heard you've gotta new girlfriend now."

"Who in the fuck told you that?"

I didn't say anything, but lemme get something straight for a second here about what was going through my head at that moment. It wasn't exactly how you might be thinking. I wasn't a big shot. There was no part of me that believed I had any chance at fighting my way outta this mess. I didn't feel tuff, nor did I want anyone to think I was a tuff-guy. Honestly, I was just tired. I was tired of the lies, tired of the rumors, tired of the running and avoiding, tired of the hiding. I just wanted to take my beating so I could just get it over with. This guy had wanted to crack my skull ever since I first got that notorious ride to school with Erin awhile back, and I had been kidding myself in thinking that somehow this moment would never happen. So I decided I was just gonna have to let this guy work me over in the driveway. There was no other way around it. I was hearing *Say it Ain't So* by Weezer in my head.

Oh yeah. Feels good. Inside.

So I just stood there thinking, and staring at Jeremy's neck, because I was scared to death. It was like a scene outta some old made for TV Western like *Rawhide* from when I was a kid.

The air was thick and steamy, even though technically it was still winter. My nerves were making everything seem exaggeratedly heated. I felt just like I was standing in front of a firing squad right before the triggers were pulled and the deadly bullet-like fists begin to riddle my body. I was, more or less, helpless, and I knew it. I stepped up like a real man, because it takes a real man to give himself up to take a beating. I was surrounded, frozen with anticipation, and scared shitless. My stomach began to churn and tumble and my hands went almost completely numb and they felt as if they had fallen asleep from lack of circulation. Jeremy shoved me in the chest and I stumbled a few steps backward.

"Jeremy, please," Erin screamed. "I'm calling the police!"

"Go ahead," he shouted at her. "This will just take a minute and I'll be long gone by the time they get here!"

"Oh God, Raymond," Erin cried.

She was starting to sob as if she really felt sorry for me. I couldn't tell if it was an act or not.

"I'm so sorry. I'm so sorry," she covered her face with her hands and started crying even harder.

"Shut the fuck up," Jeremy screamed at her. "What! Do you love this fucking guy or something?"

He took a step towards her and grabbed her arms and tried to pull her hands away from her face.

"*Huh!*"

She wouldn't answer. She just kept trying to turn away and cover her face again.

"Answer me, you fucking bitch!"

"I'm calling the fucking cops," Jolene yelled and she ran inside.

Jeremy shoved Erin and she fell onto the ground. I stepped towards him and Tim Miller put his hand on my chest and said to me, "No way."

"What the fuck are you crying for," Jeremy asked her again. "Two years I gave you and I still can't trust you! Now answer the fucking question! Do you love this little asshole? What are you, fucking him or something?"

She let out a few more deep sobs and then uncovered her face and looked up at him and then at me.

"Yes," she said as if she were never more sure about anything in her entire life. "I'm fucking him, Jeremy. Is that what you wanna hear?"

"God," I kinda laughed.

Jeremy was about to boil over. His hands started shaking and he kinda took a step towards me.

"Whoa, Erin," I pleaded. "Tell the truth, I mean we're not—"

And then Jeremy turned and swung his fist around and socked me right in the mouth. The punch destroyed me and I fell to my knees and then I crawled into the grass. I spit a big mouthful of blood onto the ground and then followed it up with another.

"*Oh shit*," I mumbled to myself.

And then I felt an instant pain in my chest as Jeremy hauled off and kicked me in the ribs like I was a soccer ball and it sent me tumbling into a thorny bush. My vision began to blur and I felt dizzy, like, I was about to faint from the pain. I knew my ribs might be broken. It hurt to even breathe and blood kept falling outta my mouth. The word 'stitches' floated across my imagination one letter at a time.

I heard arguing and looked up at everybody in the driveway as I tried to crawl away and hide. I thought maybe I could still get up and run away. I got to my feet and jogged a few steps before I collapsed from the pain in my chest. I fell to all fours again and watched the blood and saliva drip from my mouth. I took my tongue and felt my teeth and they were all still there, thank God. I thought maybe I should just play dead.

Fortunately for me I was starting to go into some form of shock and the more I dipped into this other world the more the pain faded and the more my anger started to take over. The anger transformed into rage and I began to feel like I had enough energy to run five miles.

I got onto one knee and faced the crowd. Jeremy started to come at me and Erin grabbed his arm and tried to hold him back from beating me anymore. He turned in a powerful motion and backhanded her across the face and sent her spinning outta control. Luckily before she fell to the ground Bobby Cluck caught her and tried to hold her up. Jeremy turned his back to me and ran over and started screaming at Erin as he hovered over her. Bobby laid her on the driveway and scurried away like a scared little bitch. Jeremy just waved his fist in the air and began calling Erin every name in the book. Jolene came running outta the house and begged him to leave her alone and warned him the cops were coming.

"You goddamn good for nothing whore," he screamed at Erin. "I should fucking kill you right now! You think somebody else is gonna love you like I do? Guess again, bitch!"

He stepped back again and started shaking his fist the same way he did right before he laid into me the first time.

I got to my feet and ran at his back like I was stealing home in a baseball game and right before he started to swing his fist down at Erin I thrust my boot between his legs and kicked him as hard as I could right in the nuts. I heard Jeremy's big body slumping to the ground and all the groans and sighs from all of the guys watching. I turned around quickly, shaking my fist, because I expected his friends to attack me, but Tim Miller held them at bay as if he didn't want anyone getting involved. I'm sure he wasn't protecting me necessarily. Most likely he was trying to spare Jeremy's reputation, which was suffering a bit after I had just struck him down in front of everybody. If his buddies jumped in and kicked my ass it would look like he needed to be protected from me, which wouldn't be good. His only hope was to deal with me himself. Jeremy started to get up again and I hauled off and clocked him in the mouth, dropping him like I meant to do it. Jeremy labored to get back to his feet. When he finally stood up he was swaying back and forth like a tall tree in a hurricane.

He stumbled towards me and said, "I'm ga'kish ya ash!"

In translation he wanted to kick my ass, but I had messed up his mouth pretty bad and the words weren't working so good anymore. He swung at me with an overhand-right that I saw coming no problem. His fist came barreling down towards my head and I threw my torso back and dodged it. He swung so hard the miss left him unprotected. He looked like he was all twisted in the end of a baseball swing. He knew he was screwed and his eyes widened as I drove a left-handed knuckle-sandwich into his nose. He back peddled like somebody does when they're playing tug-of-war and the other person lets go of the rope outta nowhere. Jeremy fell into a car and then fell flat onto his face and didn't even move at all. He was knocked out cold.

Tim Miller and the other goons had seen enough, so they started to close in on me. Right then everyone heard this explosion and since we were all from The Region we very quickly realized that someone had a gun.

I turned and saw The Brain standing there with a pistol pointed up in the sky. I didn't know what to do next, so I ran as fast as I could down the street. I didn't know where I was going other than just running away. I ducked across a coupla yards and jogged down another street that led towards my apartment. I was afraid the other guys might be following me, so I cut across a few more yards and down another street that ran parallel with the one I was just on. I ran another half-block until I got a cramp and couldn't breathe anymore. I walked up onto the sidewalk and stood bent over with my hands resting on my knees as I tried to suck in every last bit of fresh air I could. I was really outta shape. I was starting to get cold because I wasn't wearing my jacket.

And that realization just about horrified me.

I had left my lucky leather jacket hanging in Erin's hallway closet. There was no way in hell I could just leave it there, especially after I had mouthed off to Erin and called her a bitch and a liar in front of everybody. The only thing I could to was to turn back and somehow tip-toe into the house, grab my leather jacket and escape without being seen. It seemed like an impossible mission with the house full of goons. Most likely the cops were enroute with the brawl and the gunshot. Nightime temperatures were dipping fast and I had no jacket on. I had blood just falling outta my mouth.

27

"Hey! Jeremy, wake up," Tim Miller called down to him as he tried to shake the slain linebacker awake, "Can you hear me, Jeremy? Wake up! Now!"

"His face is, like, in a pile of blood," Gabe said. "Shouldn't we, like, move him away from it? He could drown. *Ah*, it's so gross!"

"Yeah, he's right," Jacob told Tim Miller. "We should probably turn him over or some shit. Give us a hand, assholes. He's a big fucker!"

It took three guys to turn Jeremy over onto his back and when they did his eyes opened. His pupils were rolled back into his head and he suddenly coughed up a bunch of blood that ran down his chin and neck. It freaked everybody out and they all jumped back a few steps and groaned as they stumbled over each other to get outta the way. They treated the moment as if a grenade had just gone off in his mouth and they were running for cover. Tim Miller bent down and picked up Jeremy's shoulders and helped him into a sitting position.

"He can't lay on his back or he'll choke on his blood!"

"Should we take him to the emergency room," Jolene asked. "Where's the fucking cops? I called them fifteen minutes ago!"

"Oh fuck," Bobby Cluck said. "This is really bad. He's gotta go to the hospital or something. We can't just leave him here. He'll die! Look at him!"

Jeremy coughed up another glob of blood.

Jacob yelled, "*Daaaaaamn!*"

Erin crept over to Jeremy and she reached down and touched his face.

She was still crying and she whimpered, "Oh my God, what happened? Oh God," she cried again. "What happened?"

She started to cry harder as she noticed blood on her hand and she wiped it off twice on her blue jeans. Gisela helped her to her feet and hugged her. Jeremy groaned and tried to say something. Tim Miller bent down closer to hear him better.

"*Whahappin*," he slobbered.

"The kid," Tim Miller gently said. "He hit you with a rock or a stick or something, man. It was a cheap shot. You never saw it coming."

"*Whoa*," Gabe interrupted right away. "It wasn't a fucking stick. He hit him with his fuckin—"

"Shut the fuck up," Tim Miller screamed and it hushed up the whole crowd of kids. There was dead silence. "I said what I said. It was a fucking stick or a rock!"

This was a lie like nobody's business, but as a friend Tim Miller was really trying whatever he could to salvage what was left of Jeremy Otsap's reputation. The most important thing to do was to lessen the embarrassment as much as possible.

Jeremy groaned again as if he wanted to say something. Everybody leaned in closer to listen.

"*Tag*," he breathed. "*Me da da hoshpidle.*"

And then he took a deep breath and hammered up another ball of blood that sent everybody into a frenzy.

"*Shit*," Tim Miller swore. "Somebody help me get him into the car! We gotta get him to the emergency room. Let's go!"

28

My walk back to the crime scene seemed a little like a scene from one of those 1960's war movies that are shown after midnight on basic cable. It was, like, one of those dramatic parts where a soldier escapes death on the battlefield only to find he has to return to the commotion to save a buddy. Or because he had forgotten something extremely important enough to risk everything for the second time, something, like, a lucky leather jacket. I even started to pretend my leg had been blown to shreds so I started dragging my foot like a zombie or, like, some retarded gimp. I was definitely losing my cool by resorting to playing childish games when I was facing such an enormous recovery mission for my lucky leather jacket. But that's just the kinda shit I do when I'm nervous. More stress for me usually results in more clowning around.

Up ahead headlights came into view. I could easily tell it was a police car, especially because of the slow cruising speed and the spotlight scanning the bushes. I turned and started jogging back in the other direction only to find another prowler approaching with high-beams in the distance. I froze there on the sidewalk as I debated whether or not I should just give myself up. I figured they would just come to my house and arrest me anyway. Maybe if I knew my jacket would be safe I would have gone back home. But I knew as long as that jacket was behind enemy lines I had to remain a free man and do whatever it took to get it back.

Outta the corner of my eye, from the other side of the street, a dark figure came sprinting across the street in my direction. It was a man and I was too confused by it to react. The cars were getting closer and closer and in about thirty seconds I'd be in their view. I knew if I got arrested I'd never see that jacket again because I had called Erin a lying bitch and then kicked her boyfriend in the dick. I figured she was probably stuffing the jacket into the fireplace as I stood there.

The mysterious man tackled me and sent me hurling into the bushes. He was strong as ten shots of Absolute Vodka and he started to drag me deep into the next yard in an obvious attempt to evade the spotlights.

"The Gary Rapist," I squelched. "He does butts!"

We had just ducked behind a shed when I looked and saw the man had a 49ers sweatshirt on and then I looked at the face and saw it was The Brain. The two patrol cars stopped in the street and seemed to be discussing a plan or something.

"Jesus Chri—"

"Shut the fuck up," he said hoarsely. "You trying to get us busted? Keep your mouth shut, hoss!"

The two police cars ended their conversation and continued on with the search. When they were outta sight I got up and dusted the dirt and grass from my jeans.

"Thanks, man," I said. "They almost had me. Jesus Christ, man. You shot a gun into the air! I didn't even know you had a gun!"

"You're fucking lucky. Why in the hell were you just standing there?"

"I don't know."

"Look," he said. "I got my car parked by Erin's house. I saw what you did to Jeremy—fucking awesome. Were you surprised when I blew my pistol into the air?"

"Yeah! I almost shit my pants. Thanks."

"Don't mention it, hoss. I'm gonna bring the car around. You stay here and hide out until I get back."

"I can't. I have to go back."

"What the fuck are you talking about? Are you outta your fucking mind?"

"I left my jacket. It's real special."

"Fuck that, Ray! Listen to me: those cops are looking for you. I saw the whole thing go down from across the street. They had to take Jeremy to the emergency room. Right before they took him to the hospital about five squad cars pulled in and all of Jeremy's friends fingered you. They told the cops you attacked him with a stick or a pipe. You can bet if those cops find you they're gonna wanna beat your ass and ask questions later."

"Are you serious?"

"Fuck yeah I'm serious," he scoffed. "What the hell do I look like, some kinda *sally*?"

"No, but I can't leave my jacket there no matter what. I can just sneak in and grab it and then I'll hide out in Valpo at Jon's house until everything blows over."

"That'll never work, man."

"I have to try. That coat means a lot to me and I'd be ruined if I ever lost it. I can't expect you to understand, but it's gotta be done. There's no other way around it."

"Ok. Hold on and let me think," The Brain said as he stared down at the grass and tried to work out the situation.

"How about I go back and get it for you. You can tell me where it is and I'll just go back and grab it. Nobody will suspect anything. And then I'll come back and scoop you up and I'll take you out to Jon's house and we can crash there. Then I'll make a few calls in the morning and see what you're up against."

"Wow," I said. "You'd do that for me? That'd be so rad of you, man. You have no idea how much it means to me."

"Obviously I do, otherwise I wouldn't be fucking doing it now would I?"

"Guess not."

"Ok," he said. "Here's a cigarette. Here's some matches. I'll be back here in twenty minutes to pick you up. If I ain't back in a half-hour then something's wrong and you're fucked. At that point you're on your own."

"I hear you," I acknowledged. "Good luck, man."

He disappeared into the night.

Another night gone by in a young stoner's life. One minute I'm getting high with a hot chick and some friends in the coolest garage in the country, the next I'm a wanted felon stuck outside in the cold behind a shed with no jacket, a cigarette, and some matches.

29

I was crouched behind an old rusted metal garbage can in the dark shadows of a fiberglass-spidery shed. I debated whether I should smoke the cigarette now or later. I wondered whether I should wait for The Brain like he said, or whether I should just set out on foot for home. Should I forget about the jacket for now and try to actually get a desperate wink of sleep that night? I struggled to make up my mind in a hurry because the air was getting colder and colder.

Meanwhile, while Jeremy Otsap was being scraped off Erin's driveway, while Erin tried to come to grips with her boyfriend being rushed away to the ER, while The Brain jogged in secret back to the scene of the crime in order to find my jacket and save me from trouble, I had almost made a decision. While Patrick, Ricky, and Matt Morris had gone to Chicago to hit the bars with their new fake

ID's, Ari Lopez sat in an AIDS treatment center in Birmingham and scribbled in her notebook about having HIV and about how no one from The Region believed her. She wrote stories about crushes and love-loss and lies. While all of these things were happening I finally decided to wait things out.

I took out the cigarette and tried to light it, but the matches The Brain had given me were wet for some reason. My lighter wasn't working either. It was outta fluid so I shook it up to see if I could get it to spark a quick flame. I bent over and cupped my hands over the fire mechanism made by a company called BIC. I tried to light it again and this time I was lucky and I got a tiny flicker that I was able to light the cigarette with.

While my father packed his clothes into a suitcase in Orlando to prepare for his trip home for a few weeks, my mother sat awake in the middle of the night and wondered how she would ever make her house payment without having to borrow money from my grandfather again. While Kim Donnelly drove home from a party she wondered why I was such an immature asshole. And she tried to understand why I always never failed to lie to her about my true feelings. And while the Earth continued to spin on its axis and revolve around the sun, Maggie from Seattle was at her desk trying to write a letter to me explaining forcefully that if I didn't come back to Seattle she'd find me and kill me. While Maggie poured her heart out onto a page, and while a tear fell from her face and ran the ink together in a single word that said "Trust," Mrs. Myrna Petrovic happened to glance outta her kitchen window as she awoke for a middle-of-the-night glass of water. And she saw what appeared to be a man hiding in her back yard behind her fiberglass-spidery shed. The realization of a creep hiding in the dark corner of her yard made her drop the glass she held in her hand and it shattered all over the floor. Her heart swelled and bolted into her throat, and it beat giant thuds of worry in rhythms into her head. Her husband Chase wasn't home. He was working a double shift at US Steel. Her grown son Chase Jr., an amature bare-knuckle brawler, had gone out for the evening. Normally one of the two would go out and protect their property in this situation, but she was alone now, and defenseless. She picked up the telephone and dialed 911, and she reported a suspicious man who looked like that sex creep the evening news calls "The Gary Rapist" and he was incubating himself in her backyard. Police where almost instantly dispatched to the Petrovic residence. The two officers that had been patrolling the neighborhood had a pretty good idea who the man was in Mrs. Petrovic's backyard at 4367 Idaho Street, and it wasn't the Gary Rapist.

Just moments before my arrest, and a few minutes after I had finished my cigarette, and about ten minutes after Mrs. Petrovic had called the cops on me, I suddenly heard an urgent voice inside that told me to run while I still could, but I ignored the message and decided to continue waiting for The Brain. Besides, I had to take a piss real bad.

I was pissing on the fence and in midstream when the high powered flashlight lit up the entire end of the yard where I had been hiding out in. It plastered my shadow against the fence and it made me seem twice as tall as I really was.

"Hold it right there," the cop ordered.

"What's that," I asked in a way like I didn't understand him.

I really had no choice but to stay put until I was finished relieving myself.

"I said *hold it right there!*"

"I am. I'm holding it, sir."

"Now do us all a favor and *slowly* put your hands against the fence and *DON'T MOVE!*"

I squeezed the last few drops out, because that's what guys always gotta do. No matter how much you jump around and dance, the last few drops always go into the pants. The pipe isn't as efficient as you ladies might imagine. Tell you something you don't know.

So I started zipping up my pants while I looked over my shoulder at the cop. He thought I was going for a weapon or something and he flipped out and started screaming at me as he drew his pistol and aimed it at my head.

"I said DON'T FUCKING MOVE! You understand English! Now do as I say and put your hands on the fence!"

"You don't have to yell, I was just—"

He suddenly slammed the butt of his gun into the back of my head and it sent me ramming into the fence. I tried to grab my head because it hurt like hell and he grabbed my arm and twisted it behind my back and slapped the cuffs around my wrist and then he efficiently twisted my other arm down and locked them together behind my back. Then he shoved my face into the wood and started kicking my legs apart.

"Yeah, you're real fucking smart ain't ya, big guy! How's bout trying that tuff big guy stuff on me, *huh?*"

"*Wha*—"

"Didn't I tell you to keep your mouth shut? What do ya not speak any goddamn English?"

He started patting me down and he found my knife and pulled it out and said, "Here we go. what's this, *huh*, for picking your teeth? Ok. Ok. Let's not take all night sorting this out. Sooner you do as I say the sooner you go home. Where's the drugs?"

"I don't have any," I smiled and said.

"Don't lie to me, big guy!"

"I'm not."

"What are ya doing out here, *huh*? You trying to peek in on old ladies? You a sicko?"

"*Please*," I disgustingly said.

"You're the kid from the party, right? The big sucker-punching guy we heard about?"

"Yep. Call the FBI and take me off their list," I said to him like a smart-ass.

He jabbed me in the kidney with his fist. "Yeah. Yeah. Yeah. well, I don't think you're so tuff. I think you're a little pussy if you wanna know."

"*Aghh*," I moaned in pain. I was pretty sure he had split my head open. "I don't got shit!"

He turned me around and started walking me back to the

prowler that was parked in the street.

"You have the right to remain silent," he said. "Anything you say can and will be used against you in a court'alaw."

"Spare me the Miranda warning would ya," I asked him. "I think we both know that I don't got rights."

"Shut up."

"Look at me. I'm a teenager. I got a stoner's look. I live in The Region. Don't talk to me about having rights."

He slapped me in the back of the head and started to drag me to the car as if I was resisting arrest.

"You ain't so fucking smart, big guy," he shouted at me.

He slammed my face down onto the hood of the prowler and he pulled out his CB and radioed for backup from the second cop who was looking for me.

"The kid's getting funny with me," that's really what he said to the other cop.

But he was wrong about one thing. I was smart to a point. I was smart enough to keep my mouth shut from then on. I knew I was completely at this guy's mercy. He had the authority to do whatever he pleased with me. Not even the laws of the Bible applied to me anymore. I started getting dizzy and cold and I almost started to cry, and I would have, but I knew this cop would kick the shit outta me if I started acting like a sissy. I pegged him for a wife-beater and the last thing I wanted him to think of me as was a little bitch. Guys from The Region certainly have no right to cry. So I turned to stone and held back the tears.

He stood in front of the car and continued his radio jargon. My eyes watered and I turned my head away from him and looked into the front of the prowler. There was another cop sitting in the passenger seat. For some reason I hadn't noticed him yet. Our eyes met for a few seconds and then he pressed his index finger, pointed up against his mouth and nose in a gesture for me to be quiet.

"*Shhhhh*," he hissed.

Then he smiled, but not in a condescending-copper way, but more like in a genuine way, like, he was giving me some honest advice about my situation. I swallowed a rumbling of snot and sniffled and nodded affirmatively.

The cop left me lying there on the hood in the freezing cold until the other squad car showed up. It drove up alongside with its lights flashing. The two cops chatted about what happened at the party and talked about getting a witness to positively identify me, meaning they wanted somebody to finger me as the one who had ruthlessly attacked Jeremy Otsap. They wanted to charge me with Trespassing, Resisting Arrest, Possession of an Illegal Weapon and Aggravated Assault. I was pretty much fucked, to put it very basically. Meanwhile, the cop inside the car, the one who told me to be quiet and pointed at the roof, had fallen asleep. He was actually napping.

The cop who had just arrived said he had a witness in his prowler. I looked over at the other prowler, but the windows were tinted and I couldn't see who it was. I was sure it was probably Jeremy Otsap because I didn't really believe at this time I had actually hurt him bad enough to go to the hospital. I thought I had just knocked him down or something and The Brain was just exaggerating. That's why I ran away, because I was sure he was about to get up and kick my ass.

The other cop walked back to his car and opened the back door to talk to the witness.

Then he closed the door and shouted, "That's our guy! Let's take him to the station and book him."

"Let's go, sweetheart. What do ya say now," he asked me as he picked me up and stuffed me into the back of his prowler by putting his hand on my face and kicking my feet until I was all the way inside. "Now I don't wanna put up with anymore fucked up shit from you. You're in enough trouble already so use your brains and keep still back here. I gotta few more details to clear up and then I'll take you to the station for check-in."

He slammed the door shut.

"Shit," I said to the other cop in the front seat. I thought he was asleep, but I talked to him outta anger. "Your friend is very charming. You did see him beat the shit out of me, didn't you?"

"*Ah*, it's such a lovely night," the cop answered.

I guess he was awake.

Then he goes, "You see how the leaves swirl about in the gusts of wind, always keeping busy? Even while they're dead they still manage to dance, which is the way with all things on the Earth. Everything reaches peak value after it's gone. This is true. These skies may look black and deserted to the average eye, but to me they are a vast world full of beings and places that we could never even begin to understand or imagine, up there past the stars, up in space."

"*Uh*, yeah," I said as I tried to judge how much of a lunatic this cop was, like, on a scale from one to ten. "Do you mind if I smoke in here? I think I can actually bring my hands close enough to mouth to manage a few puffs."

"You have free will. I think you've demonstrated that to everyone tonight. Smoke up."

"But do you think Tackleberry out there will get pissed-off if I do, or is it a common thing when somebody gets tossed into the back of a squad car that they light up a smoke? That's how it always goes down in the movies."

"*Tackleberry*, that's a good one. I love the Police Academy movies. Those are good comedies. I would imagine he'd get a little upset if he caught you smoking in here, but at this point, what do you gotta lose, *eh?*"

"Exactly. Do you think I can bum one off of you? Plus, if you could light it for me and put the thing into my mouth that would be totally rad," I said as I leaned up closer to him.

"Hold on, let me decode this one," he said as he shut his eyes tightly and rubbed his forehead. "Bum is either what I am, meaning a hobo or some sort, or my rear end. The only problem is the word was used as verb. Totally *Rad?*"

"I meant, like, can I borrow one from you, a cigarette?"

"I don't smoke," he said quickly. "It's really bad for you."

"Yeah," I said as I leaned back into the seat. "Me neither I guess. I was just a little nervous is all."

"You should be a little nervous, but not about jail."

"What should I be nervous about then?"

"Well, for starters, you should be nervous about the direction your life is heading, Mr. Kozlowski. And second, your heart has been petrified. You are somehow spiritually retarded in a way. No man can go through life thinking and acting out in the ways you do."

"How'd you know my name?"

"I read it in your book."

"Ha," I laughed. "That's a good one. You borrowed a book from me?"

"Your life is your book, son. It doesn't matter whether or not you've written it down. Your story is still open and has most likely been read cover-to-cover by millions of souls."

"What the hell are you talking about," I asked. "Did you guys get a new interrogation memo today or something? Stop playing. You must have heard my name over the radio or something, right?"

Right then the other cop got back into the car and started the engine.

"Comfortable," he asked me as he worked the engine a little.

"Not at all," I said to him.

"Good. Good."

"Thanks for asking though."

"Don't be a smart-ass," he mumbled under his breath as he put the prowler into drive and we drove off.

Over the next few minutes I tried to predict my near future. If everything went good for me, I'd probably get released from jail in an hour or two. I was eighteen now, but still a child at heart, so I doubted they would be interested in throwing me into county jail. When you're seventeen the cops never wanna bother with the Juvenile Detention Center because having to deal with legal gaurdians is a pain in the ass. I had been arrested my share of times before I turned eighteen and they usually tried to scare me a little by threatening to lock me up forever and then they'd call one of my parents and turn me over to them. I was hoping for more of the same that night, more so than I ever did before. The only problem was my dad wasn't gonna be back until the next day, and my mom wouldn't even think of answering the phone this late at night—and besides, she had no money and lived an hour away. There was no way in hell she'd come and get me even if she did answer the phone.

A funny thing happened on my way to the police station, and

no, this isn't Bob Hope talking. It's still your fearless hero who happens to be fueled by Budweiser right now. A call came over the radio and the dispatcher said some code numbers and mentioned a serious situation, some gang activity at Cline Avenue and Ridge Road.

The cop who arrested me said, "*Ah*, Jesus to hell," (whatever that means) and he turned on his siren and pulled a vicious U-turn and headed to the disturbance.

"What's up?"

I leaned forward. I suddenly felt like a deputy. If this was the movies and the cops were outnumbered, they'd give me a pistol and deputize me on the spot.

"Just remember to keep quiet," the driving cop said to me.

The other cop, the eccentric one, answered me. "There's shots fired and an officer is down, possible hostage situation. And they're calling every available officer to assist. It sounds like a big deal."

"No fucking shit, *huh*," I said. "In *Granite*?"

"Who in the fuck are you talking to," the driving cop asked me as he ran a stop sign. "You need a drug test or something?"

"No, sir. I don't do any drugs."

I'm not sure if it's a standard thing to take a prisoner into a war-zone, but it was happening. And I knew enough about Regionrat law to know things don't always go according to the official rules. Part of me was already planning my lawsuit against the city for jeopardizing my life and the other part of me was excited about getting the chance to eyewitness this kinda situation.

"Is this glass in this car bullet-proof or what," I asked.

"Keep quiet, big guy," the driving cop said to me again. "You ain't got nothing to worry about!"

"It doesn't matter," the eccentric cop said to me over his shoulder. "If it's your time to die, you'll die, bullet-proof glass or not. And I can tell you, from experience, is your work isn't done here, so to speak. You've got nothing to worry about until you're at least forty-one or forty-two. Shit goes down hill from there."

"Have you been drinking," I asked him.

He didn't answer as we closed in on the shooting scene.

"I know you aren't talking to me that way," the driving cop said.

"I'll deal with you proper when we get back to the station, believe that!"

We arrived at the scene. The driving officer, the one who I figured held in a great deal of sexual tension, pulled the prowler over a safe distance away from where he believed the commotion was coming from. Up at the end of the street there were lotsa flashing cop lights. It was kinda, like, a seedy part of town.

The sexually oppressed officer turned to me and said, "Stay here until I get back."

I pulled my handcuffed wrists out from behind my back to show him how stuck I was and I rolled my eyes and said, "I don't know, there's a Taco Bell around the corner. I might get hungry."

"Little dickhead," he growled and he got out and started jogging over to all of the flashing lights around the corner.

I saw him pull his gun out again and put it by his side.

The other cop sat in the car with me and I figured he was guarding me or something.

"So, what's your name," I asked him.

"Officer Paul Jessup," he introduced himself.

"Nice to meet you."

"Likewise."

"How come the other cop never talks to you?"

"Because he can't see me."

I laughed and said, "Right. That's what I thought."

"You don't believe me, do you?"

"You're not very funny, sir."

This crazy cop was the last thing I needed to be dealing with. He either had a stale sense of humor or he was off his rocker with a gun in his holster. It was a scary thought.

"I'm not trying to be funny."

"So what," I asked. "You some kinda ghost?"

"Kinda, do you ever read The Bible?"

"*Uh*, sometimes, but not really. Why?"

"Here, let me show you something," he said.

He got outta the car and walked around the front and started looking around. Then a group of black kids started walking in our direction. They were about my age, but it's hard to tell because black guys are usually lots younger than they look. There were four of them and when they got close Officer Jessup walked in front of them and started to scream Bible quotations and waving his hands around like a lunatic.

He said things like, "And I saw another wild beast ascending outta the earth, and it had two horns like a lamb, but it began speaking like a dragon," which is from the book of Revelation.

The kids just kept on walking and bullshitting with each other.

"If anyone has an ear," Officer Jessup screamed. "Let him hear!"

And then one of the kids put his arm across the group and stopped and said, "Hold up. Yo, hold up!"

"What's up, B," another kid asked. "What'chew trippen on, kid?"

"Y'all hear dat?"

"Yo," another kid said. "Da only noise I kin hear is dat fat burger fryin up at the White Castle, yo!"

"*Word*," another kid said.

"Dude, stop bullshitten so weez kin get to da WC before it close!"

"Yeah," the first kid said again. "Shit yo. I jus thought I heard somethin. Leez go."

And they started walking past Officer Jessup as he stood there. As they walked away from him they were passing the car I was locked up in and Officer Jessup started screaming again.

"If anyone is meant for captivity, he goes away in captivity! If anyone will kill with the sword, he must be killed with the sword! Here is where it means the endurance and faith of the holy ones!"

And he pointed right at me.

Then the first kid stopped the group again as he looked right at me. That's when I recognized him. It was Sammy Baker from my baseball team, East Chicago Post 369.

"Hold up," he said to the group, "I think I know dis *mothah fugah*." He walked over to me and knocked on the glass. "Bitch, is dat you?" Lot's of the ghetto kids from East Chicago Post 369 called me bitch because I had really long hair for a while.

"What's up there, Sammy. It's me, man. I gotta hair-cut. You dig it? Are you dudes out keepin it real or what?"

"Still look kinda long to me. Kid, what dey got ya in here fo? Yo, ya need some help?"

"I need a lotta help right about now, Sammy," I said and I tried to show him my cuffs.

"Yo, leez drive his ass up outta here, y'all," he said to his friends. "We gonna drive dis here car down the alley and shoot dat chain off of you, ok," he confirmed with me and he held up his shirt so I could see the handle of his gun.

"Sounds like a plan," I said. "You can see ok right?"

Sammy went for the door handle of the driver's seat and it was actually unlocked. He opened the door and started to get in. Officer Jessup pointed to the car and Sammy lost his balance and fell outta the way while the door slammed shut and the power locks activated sealing me in the car. Sammy tried the handle again, but the door wouldn't budge.

"Whah da fuck is dis shit, a Stephen King movie," he yelled. "Black people hate horror movies so Sammy and his friends started to freak the fuck out.

And then the driving cop came running down the street yelling, "Hey! Hey, stop right there!"

He pulled out his gun and Sammy and his friends took off running. Driving cop came jogging his fat-ass up to the car. I thought he was way outta shape and his huge gut only reaffirmed that suspicion. Officer Jessup stepped in front of him, but driving cop walked right through him like he wasn't even there. My lips lost all muscle-control and a little thinga drool even dripped outta my mouth. I thought I was going insane.

Driving cop unlocked the door and got back in.

"Trying to escape, *huh*? You know those fucking niggers," he asked me.

"No, sir," I said. "I hate black people."

"Well who doesn't? That's the smartest thing you've said all night," and he started the car and tore off down the street.

I turned and looked out the rear window saw Officer Jessup standing there, his body getting smaller and smaller as we drove away. I turned back around and I thought I felt something snap inside my brain, like, a click, or something, like, the sound of an eggshell breaking. It made me think of that "Don't do drugs" commercial that was always on TV, the one where they show a hot frying pan and an egg.

"This is your brain on drugs . . . Any questions?"

I started stressing out big-time, and I could feel my armpits getting all sweaty with worry and grief over possibly losing my mind.

"Hey buddy," I said to the driving cop.

He planned on ignoring me until he looked into the rearview mirror and saw my face. His eyes widened and he said, "Yeah, what's the matter? Did you eat something?"

"I think that I need to see a doctor."

"We're gonna get a nurse to clean up that cut in your mouth when we get to the station, ok?"

That reminded me of the gaping wound in my mouth and I swallowed the rest of the blood that was collecting under my tongue.

"No, I mean, like, I think, like, I need something kinda, like, a head doctor. You know? Like, somebody to talk to. I'm, like," I rubbed my cheek on my shoulder to wipe off some sweat, "I'm, like, seeing things, and hearing things."

"Uh huh," he nodded. "We'll be there soon. You really stink man. You're armpit smell could steamclean a diesel engine. You need a shower."

The cop turned on the radio. I mean the radio that plays music and that song by Wheezer, *The Sweater Song,* was playing. A car went by us heading in the other direction and the kid at the wheel was singing the words to the same song and tapping his steering wheel. I thought it was, like, a coincidental funny-type of thing and I started laughing out loud. Everything was funny to me all of the sudden. I was laughing so fast it was getting hard to breathe.

"Just hold on now," the cop said to me. "We'll be there soon, ok?"

30

Jail. I was surprised I hadn't spent a night behind bars yet. And even though things were as they were, I didn't really think that now would be the time to break that streak. It was mainly because I had been down this road quite a few times before as a juvenile. I had been arrested plenty of times already, but never for offenses like I had managed to rack up that night at Erin's house. I had been pinched for the usual kid stuff, like, underage drinking, vandalism, curfew violations, and other petty stuff. Each time I had been cuffed, stuffed into the back of a car, harassed by cops, threatened with jail, and then released to one of my parents or some other adult that knew me well enough to pick me up at some police station in some narrow-minded Regionrat town in the middle of any given night. Usually things even happened in that order, but there was one minor detail I wasn't counting on that was working against me this time—I wasn't a juvenile anymore. I had turned eighteen the last September.

Besides, believe it or not, my freedom was the last thing on my mind as I rode to the Granite Police Station in the back of a squad car. I was a hundred percent sure I was going crazy, what with my constant struggle with depression, drug abuse, sudden violence syndrome, and my new hallucinations of Bible quoting cops. It was scary to me, and I halfway wanted them to lock me up for a while, just so I could finally straighten my life up. I knew in order for me to straighten out I'd have to remove myself, somehow, from my negative environment, which was The Region.

Since I had confessed my insanity to the driving cop the two of us didn't communicate at all until we arrived at the police station. He probably didn't talk to me because no one enjoys talking to mentally ill people, and I never feel like talking when I know the listener thinks I'm stupid.

He took me inside through a side door and stressed, "Stand next to the wall please, and wait until I get back."

I stood by the wall and asked him, "When are you coming back?"

"Just wait!"

I knew what he was doing. They teach psychological warfare in the police academy. When you're arrested they apply waiting torture. Every time they quickly take you into a new room, you have to wait anywhere from fifteen minutes to over an hour, or longer, depending on how much they feel like messing with your head. It's just like Hollywood.

Another reason cops want you to wait as long as possible is because it gives you lotsa time to think about what you've done, and it causes you to try to predict your fate or try to guess how the situation will turn out. And usually a person will imagine greater consequences than will actually take place for the crime. Basically, the longer you stand around waiting for something to happen, the worse you determine things to be. I still figured they would eventually let me go that night. I just thought it would be a long wait this time. I wouldn't have been surprised if the sun was coming up by the time I walked outta the front door.

Oh, and there's no clocks to look at anywhere in a police station so you never know what time it is and crappiest of all you can't tell how long you've been there, which is the worst torture. Wearing a watch won't help either because they take it from you when they book you.

I felt like I was standing against that cold brick wall forever. I was standing there so long I started to fall asleep a few times. I had an itch on the bottom of my foot that was driving me crazy and I couldn't get to it through my boots. I wasn't allowed to sit down either. Whenever I tried to some cop would come in and tell me to stand up. That's another thing they do. They let you see them every now and then while you're waiting, just to get your hopes up. You see a cop and you think something's about to happen, but they usually just tell you to stand up and then they disappear again, which is exactly how Hollywood works.

So I waited. And I waited. I'm not sure, but it was a long time I was standing there. I started to doze off and slump down on the floor when the driving cop came back into the room and yelled at me.

"Wake up!"

I opened my eyes in a glaze, because I hadn't realized I had fallen asleep.

"Follow me," he ordered and he opened a door that led down a long dark hallway.

I didn't dig it at all, but I followed his orders, because I had no choice. I scuffed my feet along the floor in pursuit of him. All I wanted to do was wipe the sleep gunk from my dried and sleep-crusted eyes. I cursed myself for taking basic bodily functions for granted before. Just being able to scratch a body part seemed a luxury to me now.

He led me into an office with a desk and file cabinets and crap like that. There was nobody else in the office. I just figured it was driving cop's office. I was wrong.

"Wait here," he said as he uncuffed me and had me sit in a chair.

I was so relieved he was taking the cuffs off of me. It was a great sign of the possibility of a quick release, but my dreams of freedom where squashed when he took my left arm and cuffed it to a steel bar that was attached to the wall. I was still trapped, but at least my right arm was free, just like Hollywood.

"Sergeant Barone will be here to see you shortly."

As soon as driving cop left the room I took my right arm and scratched and rubbed and tickled every part of my body I could reach. And then I waited. And waited. There was no clock in the office.

"What kinda office has no clock," I mumbled to myself. "This is so fucked up."

I tried to lean back and rest, but there wasn't any slack with the cuffs so every time I leaned back my arm pulled itself to the maximum length just inches before the back support. I tried to dangle myself from the wall, but the cuffs were digging into my wrist and it hurt like hell every time I tried. I couldn't scoot the chair closer either because it was bolted to the floor.

And then I waited some more.

I thought about what I was gonna tell the cop when he came in to see me.

What's the truth, I asked myself. *Did I do something wrong, other than hiding out on somebody else's property? Jeremy hit me first. Anything I did after that was self-defense.*

It was my word against his. I wished I knew what the cops already knew. I wondered what Erin must have told them after I called her a bitch and socked her boyfriend in the face. She probably stuck it to me. Driving cop kept talking to me like I had randomly attacked Jeremy. I wondered if that's what everyone told the cops, that I just walked up to Jeremy Otsap and jumped him. That seemed like a fairy tale considering I was half his size. Who in the hell would believe something like that?

So I waited.

I spent the time thinking this crap over. It was all a horrible misunderstanding. I closed my eyes and tried to imagine a story to entertain myself. It was a story about me. I was the star and I was a professional baseball player and everybody loved me. I was a local hero, but I was humble so I shrugged off the attention as much as possible, but I always loved going back to the old playground and hamming it up with the kids. I did interviews with magazines about my long struggle from the bowels of jail to professional athlete stardom. I was the man.

Then a man clearing his throat startled me awake. There was a fat old cop sitting at the desk and I wiped drool on my shirt collar.

"This is not a motel, Mr. Kozlowski."

"*Um*," I stuttered. "I, I, *ah*, *um*, I, d, didn't think that, I didn't think, you know, that it was, *um*, a motel."

"Very well," he said. "My name is Officer Phil Barone. I'm here to conduct an investigation into the facts of what occurred tonight."

"Ok," I said as I sat up straight in my chair. "Do you know what time it is by any chance?"

"Don't worry about that," he said. "Now, it seems there was some sorta fight in which you were directly involved in at," he stopped to read the packet of paper he had stapled together lying in front of him on his desk. He started chewing on the end of his pen and continued, "at, *uh*, 287 North Elm Street. Is this correct?"

"Yeah, but it wasn't like—"

"Just answer the question please."

"Yes, sir. I was involved."

"Ok. Then it seems a fight erupted between you and Mr.—" He stopped to look at his paper again.

"Otsap," I did him the favor.

"Yes, thank you. Mr. Otsap and you became involved in a fight and the result is he's having emergency surgery at Saint Catherine's Hospital and you're being detained."

"Jesus," I said surprised. "He's having surgery?"

"Yes. He is. He's been hurt pretty badly and apparently he's lost quite a bit of blood. Now, according to the *law*," he said the word 'law' like I had never heard of it before. "You'll be detained with us until Mr. Otsap is feeling fit enough to appear at a hearing that will ultimately determine if you can be charged or not."

"You're kidding, right," I asked. "I thought you had to charge me within twenty-four hours."

"Who told you that," he laughed. "No, we don't. And I'm not kidding. I'm actually being very serious and I think you should be just as serious. This is a very serious matter you've become involved in. You're in a lotta trouble here, son."

"But you can't keep me in *jail*. Christ, he's the one who hit—"

"Mr. Kozlowski," he cut me off raising his voice. "I can, and will keep you in jail until we sort out all the facts. As to how long that takes is hard to tell, but I'll tell you one thing: the longer you sit here and dick around with me, the longer you'll be our guest. Now, do you wanna be honest with me and tell me the truth about what happened?"

"I'm trying to tell you the truth. I've really got nothing to hide."

"Good, then you can start by telling me every thing that happened from the time you arrived at the party until our officers found you hiding out in Mrs. Petrovic's yard."

"Ok," I said.

He reacted by taking out his Dictaphone and placing it on the desk. He pressed record.

"What's that thing for," I asked.

"Well, *umghh*..." He cleared his throat. "I need to record a statement from you."

"What do you mean?"

"You need to give me your side of the story about what happened tonight, but before you do, you should know this tape will be admissible at your hearing so it's important you tell the absolute truth. And be careful not to leave anything outta your statement. Tell me exactly what you remember."

"So," I said. "Ok. I think I understand, but don't you think I should, like, have, like, some kinda lawyer present for this?"

"Do you have an attorney?"

"Well—"

"Look," he said leaning forward and resting his elbows on the desk. He pressed stop on the Dictaphone. "If you don't have an attorney we can appoint a public defender to handle your case. Now, if you say you've done nothing wrong, and you're telling the truth, I don't see why you'd need to take all of these precautions about attorneys. Even if you had one sitting next to you, you'd still have to record a statement for our records. I'm just trying to be honest with you, Raymond. And remember, the more truth you tell the shorter amount of time you'll be spending behind bars. So, I assume you understand, and if you're ready then so am I."

He pressed record again softly so I wouldn't be able to tell.

But I could tell.

"I've been recording all this time so you know I'm not hiding anything from you or giving you any advice that wouldn't benefit your, *uh*, unique situation."

"Oh ... kay ..."

He smiled widely. He had yellow teeth. They were perfectly sized teeth and they looked wooden from the yellow stains. I wondered if they were dentures.

"Ok, well," I started to explain. "I was just hanging out at home watching TV. I didn't plan on going anywhere. A friend of mine stopped by a little before midnight—"

"What's your friend's name? Does he have a name?"

"Well, yeah. He has a name, but is it really important?"

"It's important to me. What's his name?"

"Gabe is his name. *Gabe Reynolds*," I answered like I wasn't sure what to say.

"Ok. Go on," he said.

"*Um*, where was I?"

"Hanging out, doing nothing."

"Right, I was hanging out and Gabe came over and extended an invitation to me to go to this girl's house. It's a girl I kinda like and she was having some friends over, you know, playing cards and listening to music and all that—"

"What's her name?"

"Jesus, you're after everybody?"

"I'm not after anyone, Raymond. I'm just trying to sort out the facts."

"*Uh*, Erin Watkins is her name. She's the girl whose house the fight happened at. She's the girl I like. She's prettier than hell, but she lies her ass off, crazy bitc—" I caught myself and rephrased. "Girl. She's a crazy girl. So we drive over there, Gabe and I, and we're hanging out for a while. Then me and Erin and some other kids went into the garage to have a cigarette and watch some MTV."

"Who went to the garage with you?"

"Jeez, *uh*, well, it was me, Erin, a dude named Bobby Cluck. And this girl named Jolene, don't know her last name."

"Were you kids smoking any marijuana in the garage?"

"*Huh*," I gulped. "What? No."

"You know what I mean, kid. Were you smoking marijuana in the garage?"

"No. No, sir. I don't smoke that stuff. I'm being serious."

"Well, we took this Bobby Cluck into custody for possession of marijuana. He had some joints on his person. He said you all were smoking marijuana in the garage and the drugs belonged to you, Raymond. He said you told him to hold onto it while you fought outside. Is this true?"

"That little shit!"

"Is it true," he asked.

He was fucking with me and making the whole thing up, but I couldn't tell at the time. I actually thought cops had to tell the truth while conducting an interrogation. I didn't realize back then that coercing a confession with lies was not only legal, but was also common. Bobby never said shit about me. They were just trying to fool me.

"Hell no! It ain't true at all. I swear to God!"

"Ok. Go on please."

"Shit, *um*, well, these guys showed up—"

"Who? What *guys*?"

"Shit. I don't know, some assholes. I only knew the kid who got hit by me."

"So you hit him first?"

"*Nooo*," I dragged it out. "As a matter of fact, he socked me first because he's this girl Erin's boyfriend and he's all jealous at me for being around her and all. Look inside my mouth if you don't believe me. I gotta gash about ten miles wide in here." I pulled down my bottom lip to show him. "He plays football, man. He's about fifty times bigger than I am. I'm swallowing blood as we speak."

"Ok. Go on."

"Well, they showed up and I went outside, because it was kinda obvious they were there to kick my ass. There's been talk about it for a while. So I go out there and he drops me with a right, or something, and then kicks me in the ribs a coupla times."

"So he hit you first?"

"*Exactly*!"

"Go on."

"Well, then his girl Erin gets in the way. And the guy Jeremy Otsap slaps the shit outta her for sticking up for me. I mean he decked this poor girl. So I get up, right? And I work him over while he's not looking. I get in some lucky shots and the guy goes down. And then I ran and hid in that lady's yard. And that's when you guys picked me up. I only hid because I was scared Jeremy Otsap was gonna find me and kill me; otherwise I wouldn't have run away. And that's everything I know."

I picked up the Dictaphone and put it up to my mouth and said, "That's the whole truth, and nothing but the truth. So help me God."

And I put it back on the desk.

Sergeant Barone didn't think this was amusing.

31

Much, much later, the cops finally put me into a prowler and drove me to the Lake County Jail. Lake County Jail was in a rural area and it sat on about a hundred acres of land. The land didn't have any trees or bushes or anything, but the grass was well trimmed and the rest of the land was just flat. If you were to escape from this jail, after getting under, or over, three sets of ten foot barbed-wire fences, you'd have to run for about five minutes in any direction just to get off the property. If you made it that far you'd come up against a twenty foot fence complete with watch-towers where armed snipers would be waiting for you.

The building itself was four stories of stacked shithouse red bricks with slits for windows, all of them too small to fit a body through. From the outside, the jail had the appearance of an old Victorian hospital, a huge red brick structure. It was built around the turn of the century back when Hilljacks ran the place. Back then the Hilljacks were ninety percent of the population. That was before Blacks, Latinos and the "Civilized" Eastern Europeans came over. Back then the Hilljacks ruled, but now they were all crammed into the dried up piss puddle that was known to us as modern day Black Oak. *"The city with insufficient sewage"* is their slogan, and the dandelion their flower. And if they aren't kicking it in Black Oak then they're inmates at Lake County Jail.

Lake County Jail was really a prehistoric mutilating, torturing and discriminating facility. The Region's leaders pawned it off on the other Hilljacks as some sorta political Christian rehab place for sinners.

The sun was coming up when we got there, but I couldn't see it because it was hidden behind the jail. They did that on purpose too. Cops can even hide the sun. Most crooks are booked and admitted in the early morning after waiting all night. And they, no doubt, built the building so when you approached you couldn't see the sun. It was missed opportunity number one for the prisoner.

The first thing they do after checking you in is they make you take a shower. It's not a hot comforting shower either. They find the fattest, sleaziest cop to escort you to the shower room, and when we got to the shower place the fat guy made me strip all my clothes until I was butt-naked. Then he made me stick my tongue out so he could check to see that I wasn't hiding anything in my mouth. He looked under my armpits and even in my ass-crack, the Brown Star. Then he left the room and made me wait in the hallway, butt-naked!

I waited there a long time, and some female prisoners were even escorted by me while I was hanging out (so to speak). Then after awhile that fat cop came back and led me into the shower room. It was a ceramic tiled room with one rusty showerhead. There was no sink, mirror, or toilet, and no bench or privacy whatsoever. The soap they give you is nothing more than ultra-medicated dog shampoo. It smelled so strong you could get high off of it if you wanted to. It was supposed to kill any type of bugs that may have been living on your body like crabs, lice, chiggers, cooties, and other Regionrat unmentionables.

The cop turned on the icy-cold water and made me get under it with the dog shampoo. It was cold as hell and the sleazy cop made me scrub every little part and crack of my body as he watched and smiled.

"Go'head, boy," he'd say. "Git it all over. Thas right, even up in there."

Then he shut off the water and left the room. He didn't give me a towel or anything. He just left me standing there shivering to death. He was gone so long my hair was almost completely dry by the time somebody came back. A big black lady guard came back in his place and she brought me my prison clothes, which were pink tightie-whitey underwear and a pair of pink sweatpants and a white T-shirt. She also had a pair of black dress socks and pink slippers for me to put on.

After I got dressed the lady led me back into the hallway where

I first stood naked and she made me wait there, but before she left me she handcuffed me to the wall. Except this time I didn't have to wait alone. There were two dudes there who looked about my age and they were naked like I had just been. They were still in the pre-shower stage. They told me they got busted for stealing a car in Colorado and driving it out here. They were on their way to New York City and they kept insisting to me that they were innocent, as if I was a judge or something. They seemed to have no shame in being naked and I could totally tell they had been locked up before.

You're gonna think I'm pulling your leg when I tell you this, but one of the dudes got a boner while he was waiting. I swear if we weren't all handcuffed to the wall I would've kicked his teeth in. His friend was giving him a hard time about the boner—no pun intended. And homey who was sporting the hardwood kept swearing up and down that it always did that when it got cold. We called him on that excuse easily, because everybody knows a guy's dick shrivels up when it gets cold. I think he was some kinda pervert or something. They asked me what I was in there for and I told them that I mugged a guy and hit him in the head with a shovel about fifty times.

"No shit," the one without the boner asked me. "What're they chargin ya for?"

"Tempted *moider*," I said trying to sound like a Hilljack.

I saw on a movie once where the inmates had to exaggerate about the crime they committed when they got to prison because if the other guys think you're a sissy it's all over. So that's what I told them.

They asked me if the guy was dead and I told them, "If he was dead I wouldn't be getting charged with attempted murder, but more like murder in the first degree."

The guy with the boner looked away when I said this.

The black lady came back awhile later and led me into this waiting room outside an office. Before they put you in a cage, they let you talk to this person that gives you legal advice about your particular situation. Once I got into the office I noticed a clock on the wall. It was the first time I got to see one since I was at Erin's house the night before. It was 9:14 in the morning.

"Have a seat right there, son," the guy said to me.

He wasn't wearing a police uniform and I didn't think he was even a cop. It was a relief to see a civilian and I had an inkling of hope that he was actually there to help me. I almost felt that he could be trusted by his lack of a badge alone.

"You've been arrested and charged with assault with a deadly weapon. And it says in my report the individual assaulted by you has been taken to the hospital where he is undergoing emergency surgery to repair his jaw, which was shattered. He's there as we speak. Now, by law you have to remain behind bars until Mr. Otsap has recovered enough from his injuries to attend your hearing on this matter. Do you understand where I'm coming from?"

"Yeah," I said. "But how long is that gonna take, for him to get better I mean?"

"Well," he cleared his throat. "It really depends on the severity of the injury, which, according to this report seems pretty bad. *Uh*, it says here," he pointed. "His jaw has been shattered, *um*, he's missing some teeth, and he had to be stitched up considerably on the inside of his mouth. Not to mention he has three cracked ribs from the assault. I gotta ask," he laughed. "It says here this guy is six-one and two-hundred and twenty-five pounds. And from looking at you, I can't imagine you being much of at threat to a guy like that. He must have pissed you off pretty bad. What did you hit him with?"

"I hit him with my fist."

"It says here that there was a weapon used."

"Just my fist," I said. "I bet they didn't find a weapon because I didn't use one."

"Do you know any type of martial art, because that can be counted as a weapon."

"No."

"Well, then what caused you to lash out at him like that?"

"Desperation. That's it. He hit me in the mouth and kicked me in the ribs when I was down, so I got back up and went after him. My guess is he's embarrassed by what happened and is making all this up to save his image."

"I see. Well, there does seem to be quite a few conflicting stories about what happened and one girl in particular, the one who resides at the home where this occurred even gave a story similar to the one you just described to me. Now, even if what you're saying is true, it doesn't change the fact that you need to remain here at the jail until you and Mr. Otsap are able to both attend a hearing to determine if you can be fully detained. I'm guessing he'll be recovering from surgery for a day or two, maybe three, and then he'll be sent home, but most likely he'll need to rest for another day or two. I think we can get away with scheduling a hearing a week from Monday, but I'll have to call his doctor to make sure. You can be released if you post bond, which is five-thousand dollars."

"That sucks," I said.

"Tell me about it," he said. "Now, do you have a family attorney that would normally represent you in a situation such as this?"

"No, not one that I can think of."

"In that case one will be appointed to you by the Public Defender's Office. Now, you'll be getting one phone call, which you'll be able to use in a few minutes. As for your stay here, visiting hours are between 10:00 in the morning and 2:00 in the afternoon, and that's on every day except Sunday. On Sunday you get the entire day from 7:00 in the morning until 8:00 at night. Since I can see obvious bruises on your face and blood around your mouth, it's standard that you're taken to the hospital to see a doctor before you officially begin your stay here at Lake County Jail. So after you've made your one phone call, I'll make arrangements to have you taken to Methodist Hospital. Do you have any questions so far?"

"Yeah, *um*, So somebody has to pay five-grand to get me out?"

"No. You only need to pay five-hundred of that."

"Ok, I understand everything."

"Good. I'll call the guard and have them take you to use the telephone, and then they'll transport you to see a doctor."

"Oh, one more thing," I said. "What're the chances of me being convicted based on the evidence?"

"Well, based on evidence alone, I'd say slim to none, since there isn't any. The stories don't match up and there never was a weapon recovered, so it'll come down to your word against his in the long run, but I'm not a judge so what I'm saying is totally off the record."

"And what is the average sentence for something like this?"

"Two years maximum sentence, but that can be a suspended sentence."

"Great," I shrugged.

I ended up just calling my mom and leaving a message on her machine because she was at work. I knew she couldn't bail me out or anything, but she should at least know. I would have called my dad too, but I wasn't entirely sure he would be home today, and I didn't wanna leave a message like this that might go unchecked for awhile. I almost thought about not calling anyone, but my family is the type that wouldn't come looking for me for weeks. I could rot to death in jail before anyone even noticed I was missing.

One thing was for certain—I wasn't gonna graduate now. I'd drop out and get my GED before I'd ever return to Granite to repeat my senior year. It was then that I thought maybe I'd become a biker and ride a Harley Davidson all over the country for the rest of my life. It's not really important what you do, but how you do it. Everyone has to become something, and there's certainly no shame in riding a Harley.

I was one of two white guys in the entire wing that they assigned me to. They stuck me in a cell with the other Caucasian, who was an older man they fittingly called Whitey. The black guys gave me a nickname also as the guards were walking me to the cell.

They kept shouting, "Lil' Cute Crakah!" So that became my jail name from then on. They called me "Saltine Crakah" or just "Lil' Crakah" for short.

Whitey was about sixty years old and that's just a guess. He was a big old man, but he seemed real nice. He wasn't a genuine nice guy, but more like a stupid nice. I pegged him for a sixty I.Q., maybe less. He would only talk about the same things over and over. And I'm not talking about the same topic. He'd say the same sentence over and over.

Here, I'll show you:

"Hey, kid. You gotta job?"

"I'm a cook at a restaurant," I said and I sat on the chair. I was lying.

"Oh yeah," he was interested. "I was a cook once at a place called Salty's over in Hammond. You ever heard of Salty's?"

"Nope."

"I'm a painter by trade, but the painting business was slow. A friend of mine was the assistant manager at Salty's so I worked there as a broiler cook. That was a busy place," he laughed. "On a Friday, um—no it was Saturdays. On Sundays that place would do, like, ten grand! That's a lotta fucking sailors, because only sailors would come and eat there. Ten grand! That's a lotta money and that was in, um, 1979. That was a lotta money back then!"

"Yep."

"So ten grand in 1980. Jesus. I told you I was the broiler cook right?"

"Yep."

"You ever heard of Salty's?"

"Nope."

"Like I said, I was the broiler cook. Broiler cooks are supposed to get chef's pay, but they paid me pantry money. I'll tell ya, from 12:00 to 2:00 on Saturdays I'd go through four-hundred French Dips. That's a lotta fucking French Dips, ain't it?"

"Yep."

"Two-hundred French Dips! Sometimes that place was so busy I'd have sixty, seventy steaks going on the broiler all at once! How are you supposed to keep track of eighty steaks when this one is medium rare and this one is well done? All different kindsa steaks going all at once! Did I tell you at Salty's I'd have to make two-hundred French Dips in two hours?"

"I think so."

"That's a lotta French dips, ain't it? There was this guy who trained me, he was a little Filipino guy, Flip was his name. He quit to go drive a garbage truck for the city. This guy would have ninety steaks going and he'd come over and help me with sandwiches while he was doing it! Unbelievable! How do you keep track of that many steaks?"

"I don't know."

"I'll tell ya, we had this special where we had a five pound steak. And if you could eat it, you got it for free. Only one guy ate the whole thing in two years while I was working there. You got the steak and you had to eat a baked potato, *um*, and a salad—no wait, a salad and fries, and the steak and you got it for free. That's a big fucking steak," he laughed. "It'd take you, like, three days just to digest it. The guy who ate it was this little guy too. He was a fisherman or a sailor. They called him Shake, I think. That place was so busy, sometimes they'd do ten grand. Ten grand! Did I tell ya, from 10:00 to 12:00 we'd do, like, three-hundred French Dips! That's a lotta French Dips! That five pound steak was the special and if you could eat it, a baked potato, fries and a salad, you got it for free. Who would like to eat a steak like that?"

"I wouldn't."

"That steak was so big it looked like a roast!"

"*Whoa*," I'd say.

"One time we made a Prime Rib and this new kid took it outta the oven an put it right into the walk-in while we were closing. The next morning it was ruined! The manager was hysterical! He said 'I'm not gonna fire you this time, but next time you're gone.' He was hysterical. On Mondays and Tuesdays at Salty's we'd go through five-hundred French Dips in an hour. That's a lotta French Dips!"

Whitey just went on and on. Around noon he'd go get some lunch in the cafeteria or go do whatever he had to do, and when we'd run into each other again he'd start in with the whole French Dip story, and I'd have to sit through it all over again. It was all he ever talked about. I think he was in jail for annoying somebody to death.

So I was curious and I asked him, "What the hell are you in here for?"

"I'm in here for six counts of indecent exposure."

The day after there was a fight in the cafeteria during lunch, so they brought us something to eat while we sat in our cells. I had a cold hotdog, some fruit salad and a little pint of milk. Old Whitey had the same thing and I imagine everybody on our cellblock had the same thing to eat also.

"Last summer I went to Vegas with my friend Louie Cardigan. You ever been to Vegas," Whitey asked me while he inhaled the hotdog.

"Nope."

"Ah, you have to go. I only go for the hookers. It gets hotter than hell there in the summer, like a hundred and ten degrees," he laughed.

He had this nasal laugh that actually seemed to come outta his nose as he clinched his teeth together. It was a sinister laugh if I had ever heard one.

"Yep, it gets a hundred and twenty, but everything in Vegas is air-conditioned, especially the brothels. You never even go outside the whole time you're there. The restaurant at the Hotel I stayed at had a special. On Fridays you get steak and shrimp." He paused and scratched his head. "No prawns! You get steak and prawns and a salad bar for five-ninety-five, and on Tuesdays you get a cheeseburger for two-twenty five or two tacos for a dollar," he laughed. "You can't do no better than two tacos for a dollar."

"That's crazy."

"Yeah, and you could spend a week in Vegas and not see the whole strip. The strip is like ten miles long. Or is it a mile? You should go to Reno sometime. It's like Vegas, except you can walk to just about every place. It's a lot smaller, but it's still a good time, ya know?"

"Yep."

I fucking *hate* talking to crazy people.

"The hotel we stayed at had these maids who clean your room in the middle of the night while you're out gambling. They knock and if you don't answer they'll come in and change your sheets and vacuum, empty the trash and replace all the soaps and coffee. If you don't want them to clean your room, or you're sleeping, you're supposed to put a 'Do Not Disturb' sign on the door. If they find one they leave you a note that says, ya know, 'We were here, but you were sleeping.' I mean, you don't need your sheets changed every damn day. Did I ever tell you about that restaurant I worked at where I had to make a hundred French Dips in an hour?"

And so on.

On Monday I had this little crackerjack hearing that I didn't understand. I didn't get why I was in court and Jeremy was not there like they had said he needed to be. Apparently I didn't need an attorney because there wasn't one there for me. The judge just kinda reviewed the charges and set a court date for me in three months, which meant I'd be rotting in jail unless I got bailed out.

32

Jail is pretty much the scariest place I've ever been to in my entire life. I'm not a big guy at all. I'm coordinated and I'm able to defend myself to a certain degree, but there's a very pathetic mismatch between your everyday regular prisoner and me.

In the civilian life, being tuff is defined in a very different way than it is in jail. Outside of prison, talk goes a long way. I could be in a bar, or at school, or around my friends, or even at work or any-place, and I could talk a great deal about how I could kick this guy's ass or that guy's ass. A lotta times talking alone is enough to convince people not to push you around. A suburban white guy could go his whole life without having to back up his mouth.

In jail there's never any talk like that. That is, unless you're willing to back it up one-hundred percent of the time. If you're in jail and a big criminal says he's gonna kick your teeth in, then he's gonna do it. If he says he's gonna take a spoon shank and drive it into your belly during breakfast, then he's gonna do it. And if he says he's gonna make you suck his dick and then he's gonna lay into your ass when the lights go out, then he's not messing around. The problem with being in jail is you don't get the luxury of a warning like you would if you're a surburban white guy in a tavern. In fact, more often than not, a jailhouse thug will just do to you whatever he wants to you and not even say a word about it before it happens. You could be minding your own business, reading, watching TV, playing cards, writing a letter to your girl, whatever, and *wham!* He could be on you in a matter of a second. I speak from experience because while I was in jail, I experienced nightmarish things and I never even saw them coming.

I was in the yard at times during the first week I was locked up and one time I was just sitting off by myself and I was reading *The Silence of the Lambs* by Thomas Harris when five black dudes surrounded me. They were each so big the entire sun was blocked out. I thought there was a solar eclipse going on. The leader grabbed my book and tore it in half at the binding and then tossed it over his shoulder. All these separated pages with murderous psycho-babble on them fluttered around like exploded pillow-feathers.

"What do you want," I asked the brother directly in front of me, my voice shaking.

He didn't answer. As if choreographed, they all grabbed me and I was thrown onto the ground. Someone kicked me in the eye and the pain spun me around until I was lying on my back. They were all standing around me, and I watched them stomp me about the head and face. One of them grabbed me by my hair and hurled me about five feet. A fist full of my hair was actually ripped clean from my scalp and blood ran down my face.

One of them started yelling, "Git his draws down! Git his fuckin draws down!"

They yanked my pants down around my ankles and then they picked me up and slumped me over a picnic table. They were about to screw me. I heard whistles blowing and I turned and saw guards running over holding cans of mace. They started spraying and my attackers fled into the crowd where they were rounded up by other guards and taken away. Two other guards drug me away by my legs and threw me into an ambulance and they took me to the emergency room where I was treated for a laceration above my eye, a fractured finger, and they had to re-stitch the inside of my mouth.

On the way back to the big house it really started to set in on me that I just almost got raped and murdered on a prison playground by a few oversized black fellows. Not many people ever get to have a realization like that and it ended up breaking my brain a little more.

As we were driving down the highway I was staring outta the window and pretending my hand was cutting through all the old farmhouses and the trees and telephone poles on the side of the road. It was like my arm was a lightning fast chainsaw that sliced everything in two. When I got bored with pretending about a chainsaw, I imagined my hand was a dirt bike and it was jumping every obstruction and obstacle it came across.

They ended up putting me in an isolation cell that night. I think it was Tuesday night, but I'm not sure. They put me there simply so no one would kill me. It wasn't that they were particularly concerned with whether I lived or died, they just didn't wanna clean up any messes, and the death of an inmate is a big one to step in if you're the warden of a prison.

My cell was just like you see in the movies, as far as isolation cells go. The walls were padded and white. There was a stainless steel toilet, sink, and even a stainless steel bed. There was no window. The floors were covered with gray granite tile. I had to stay in there all the time, even for meals. They only lemme out for an hour each day for exercise. And the only thing they gave me besides cold food was a Bible.

This is the type of place where you can find yourself doing things you never expected or imagined you would ever do for entertainment. And the difference between finding something to occupy your time and just doing nothing is, like, choosing to remain sane or to go completely mad.

I'd put my finger on the floor and I'd trace the cracks and pretend it was a racecar weaving it's way along a street. I'd lay on my back and find excitement in finding a fly had buzzed into my room. I watched the aimless fly with the eye of a scientist. I studied its flight patterns, its habits, and I would really sit and wonder, I'd dwell about what the fly was really thinking. Does it think? Does it even have thoughts?

Sometimes I'd try to read the lines in my palm. I didn't know anything about palm reading, but I thought if I looked at my hand long enough I might start understanding. I could never figure it out so for a twist I'd flip my hand over and examine the pores on the back. Or I'd scan the hair on my arms. I wondered if I was ugly or not. Did my hair look stupid? Should I cut it? What about my feet? Did I have ugly feet? I'd take my shoes and socks off and look at them for hours. In fact, I'd do just about anything to avoid reading The Bible.

A coupla days later I was still asleep when I woke up to the sound of a key unlocking the door to my cell. A guard walked in and tossed me a brown paper bag. It bounced off my legs and landed on the floor, spilling its contents like an overturned dumptruck on the highway.

"These are your personal belongings. Get dressed. You've made bail."

"You're kidding," I said. "Who—"

"Nevermind that," the guard said. "Just get dressed before I change my mind."

33

I walked through the front doors of Lake County Jail and I smiled.

The wind blew across my face and I smelled the breeze. It was a foul breeze, but I smelled it anyway. It was the smell of freedom. I felt just like a bad motherfucker.

"Hey," somebody shouted.

I looked around to see where it was coming from. I wasn't even sure if they were talking to me. And then I saw them: Patrick, Ricky, and Matt Morris. They were leaning up against Ricky's Honda Accord like Ferris Bueller picking up Sloan at school.

"Let's go," Patrick shouted.

I jogged down the steps and walked the last ten with my arms out. I wanted to hug them for getting me outta there.

Matt Morris goes, "Ray! You're outta there!"

"Did you guys bail me out," I asked. "Jesus. Five-hundred bucks. I thought I was gonna die in that place."

"You look like Ricky after a cracked-out Tuesday night," Patrick laughed. "Did you hurt your finger when some big nigger made you shove it up his ass? That's funny to me."

"It was sorta like that," I laughed. "I haven't even taken a shower since I first got in the place. All I could do was wash up in a sink."

"Well," Patrick lectured me. "It cost us five-hundred bucks to bust you out. We had to pull three mall missions to come up with that kinda cash. Plus Ricky had to suck his old piano teacher's dick for the last fifty bucks, but he said it was totally worth it."

"Fuck off, Patrick," Ricky defended himself.

"Look," I said. "I'll pay you guys back just as soon—"

"Forget that paying back action, Ray," Ricky said. "We don't need your Polish ass to pay us back, but we do need your help today with a mission."

"Can I take a shower first," I asked.

Matt tossed his smoked cigarette onto the hood of a squad car and he explained what was about to go down.

"We're gonna go to my house so you can shower up and change your clothes."

"Yeah," Patrick said. "You can take a shower. Just don't jack off in there. It's been a long time since you've gotten some pussy. We don't got all day. Then we need your help with the *Ultimate Mission*. We're busting into the clubhouse at Shorewood. Inside there's a safe that might have four grand inside of it."

"How do you know," I asked nervously.

"We have an informant," he said.

"We're just gonna break into the clubhouse in *broad daylight*," I asked.

"That's the best time," Matt laughed. "Let's get the hell outta here."

Matt Morris lived in a modest house in an extremely wealthy neighborhood. Both of his parents were doctors and they had six kids, one adopted because the first five came out as boys so they went out and gotta little girl.

Even though the house was modest, there were lotsa renovations done to it. The basement was completely done over where they added two bedrooms, a livingroom and a full bathroom. On the main floor they actually added an extension that ran the length of the house. The new part was made up of two rooms, a living room and a dining room. There was also a bedroom on the main floor, the original living room, a huge kitchen, a screened in porch, a laundry room and two bathrooms. Upstairs there was another bathroom and four more bedrooms. On paper here, it sounds anything but modest, but I guess what I mean is it was modest only in comparison to some of the other houses that kids from Andrean lived in, like Ricky's for instance, which is a borderline mansion.

At Matt's house I took a shower and dried off with somebody else's towel, combed my hair with somebody else's comb, brushed my teeth with somebody else's toothbrush, and shaved with somebody else's razor. I had this euphoric feeling from being freed and while I was in the shower I did the sign of the cross and said a few Hail Marys and a coupla Our Fathers. I also borrowed some athletic tape from Matt and I re-taped my cracked finger, which made me seethe with pain, and checked the bruises on my face. The guys had gotten me an outfit to wear from Matt's closet. They got me a pair of cream-colored cargo pants and a thin gray sweater from Eddie Bauer. After I slicked my hair into place I was ready to go. I looked preppy and proper except for the bruises and cuts on my face.

"Yo, Ray," Ricky commented when I came out of the bathroom. "You look like you just shoved your finger up some black dude's ass and paid the price for it."

"Yeah," I said. "You look like you gotta black dude's ass."

"What's that," Ricky asked me. "Another nigga crack? Is that all you guys can think of to harass me with? You poke fun at the color of my skin?"

"Would you rather I poke fun at your size," I asked him. "I mean I'm a small dude, but you, you could substitute for a credit card to pick a lock you're so fucking skinny."

"Yeah," Patrick said. "Plus don't forget, Ricky. Don't forget you're a little nigger who smokes rock and sucks dicks."

We all laughed at that one.

"All right," Ricky said all pissed-off. "I'll just leave you stupid bastards here and I'll go collect the four grand myself. I'm the one who found out about it in the first place. How's that sound to you turds?"

"So," Patrick said. "You're gonna drive there, keep watch, pick the lock to the office with your skinny-ass body no less, and carry the heavy safe, all by yourself? And to top it off, you're gonna do it all in broad daylight? Don't be a fucking idiot, Ricky."

Matt shouted, "Ricky! NOH! You're losing your cool!"

"Well, you know what, dudes. I'm totally tired of these fucking nigga jokes."

"Dude," I said to him in a serious way. "We didn't mean anything by it. I swear to fucking God we didn't. We just do it to be funny and all."

"Ricky," Matt Morris said as he put his hand on Ricky's shoulder. "You can't sit here and tell me the shit we say to you ain't funny. You can't."

"Yeah. Well, are you honkey-ass crackerjack-fucks ready to go do this or what?"

"Yeah. I'm ready," Patrick said to him all sympathetic. "But first, Ricky, you gotta do something about that fucking nigger cologne that you're wearing."

We all laughed again. Even Ricky did a little. It was funny to us.

"I mean what is that shit," Patrick asked him. "Is that the secret weapon, Drakar Noir?"

Drakar was the "Secret Weapon" back in the day when everybody was listening to butt-rock and Madonna's pop songs. These days only the brothers seemed to be sporting it. When that shit first came out when I was, like, a sixth grader, the stuff was going for, like, a hundred bucks a bottle. It was pricey shit. Now it was like ten bucks for the same bottle. Around the time things were actually happening in this book, we were into colognes like Claiborne for Men, Obsession, and Eternity (this was the Big Time shit), and if you wanted to be different you sported something like Polo or CK One. But never, I mean never never ever never, would I be caught dead wearing the "Secret Weapon," at least not in that decade.

34

Later that afternoon the gray clouds hung heavy and low and it seemed the only reason they moved at all was because they were being tickled by the tops of hundred year old oak trees and poplars. I was sitting in the back seat and nodding off from not getting proper rest behind bars. When you're locked up in jail there's usually one thing you would almost die for if you were released, and for me, it was my bed. I missed sleeping in my bed more than anything, even more than smoking reefer.

Matt Morris rolled a ridiculously huge joint while Ricky pushed the Accord down Old Lincoln Highway at nervous speeds. It's a pretty scary experience to be the passenger in a car with Ricky at the wheel. He drives really fast, like, all the time. Patrick drives fast all the time too, but with him behind the wheel you can at least tell he's in control of the machine. He's a fast and highly skilled driving techni-cian, while Ricky is nothing more than a careless borderline junkie with a heavy foot. Half the time he's not even looking at the road and he's got the driving record to prove it: it's littered with one car traffic accidents, reckless driving tickets, non-moving infractions, and he's even got a charge of almost killing somebody because of his negligence behind the wheel.

This joint that Morris rolled was just plain idiotic. He used three papers - *THE LONG WAY* - to get the job done. He must've tossed in a whole eighth. Sure. The joint had good form, but it was hard to smoke because the pull was covering too much distance from cherry to mouth. I'm a straight-up power-hitter. If I have a hard time pulling fire through a joint then something ain't right with the roll. There are times when I've really gotta work to get a joint going, and this was definitely one of those times. I took the first few puffs and got it fired up enough to pass around.

It's usually about a solid thirty-minute drive from Matt Morris' house to the Shorewood Clubhouse. Ricky got us there in just under twenty minutes, but not without us being shown three seperate middle fingers and getting honked at six or seven times.

On paper it was a pretty simple mission. We had a copied key that was supposed to fit right into the back-door. We walk in. We grab the safe. We walk out. The only reason we needed four dudes was one person needed to be a lookout/driver and the other three were for lifting. We didn't know how big or small the safe was. Better "safe" than sorry.

I was the lookout/driver, the easiest job, but a very important one. We had a coupla walkie-talkies too. Ricky had one and I had one. I was just supposed to sit on the bench and start pressing the Morse code button S.O.S.-style the moment I spotted trouble. Since Matt Morris had managed to scam a copied key to the back-door of the clubhouse I wasn't worried about this job at all. Because we had the key, it wasn't even really, like, breaking and entering. It was basically just entering. We knew the key fit the back door because Matt had already tested it the day before, and it was highly possible that the same key might work for the office-door.

Worst case scenario had the guys walking in through the back-door, prying open the office-door, and carrying the safe right outta there. Matt had some inside information that the safe was a medium-sized one and it wasn't bolted to the ground.

Matt's informant, who used to clean the community pool for a summer job said the safe was, "Lighter than fuck, and could easily be tossed into the trunk of the car."

He didn't actually come out and specifically tell Matt. He said this just while bullshitting with other kids at a party. Matt overheard the conversation and ripped off his keyring, copied the key, then planted the keyring back in the kid's car so the clubhouse management wouldn't flip out and change the locks.

I took my place on the bench and I was reading a People Magazine with the walkie-talkie chilling right on my lap. Just in case.

The guys took outta basketball from the car and were dribbling it up the sidewalk and talking bullshit to each other like they were just gonna shoot some hoops at the little park behind the clubhouse. When they got to the back-door they looked at me and I gave them a peace sign to signal to them that the coast was clear.

Matt took the key and unlocked the back-door and they went

inside and closed the door quietly behind them.

I was thinking it would be a three to five minute job. Tops. But three to five minutes is a long time to wait for the cops to show up. I looked at my watch.

They were two minutes into the operation and still inside. Everything was cool with me though—there was no one snooping around—but then it started to rain suddenly, and hard. The rain really blew my cover. Only a freak would be sitting in a downpour reading a People Magazine on a park bench.

I tried to radio them real quick.

"Dudes? Over?"

I got nothing but static.

"Guys ... it's raining really hard. I might have to abandon my post. Over? Can you guys hear me? I might have to bail."

Still nothing but fuzz. For some reason they weren't copying. So I figured I'd just go sit in the car and keep watch from there. It didn't really matter because they couldn't hear me anyway, rendering my job totally useless.

Back in the car I didn't have the panoramic view like I had from the bench, but it would suit me fine if I just kept shifting my head around. The only problem was when I got into the car there was the other walkie-talkie sitting unattended on the front seat. Stupid dumbass fucking Ricky forgot to bring it in. My job in this whole operation was suddenly completely useless.

I looked at my watch and they had been in there for over three minutes already and I was starting to get really impatient.

I was looking through the rearview mirror when I saw a local cop's prowler coming up over the hill. I thought I was gonna swallow my own tongue from some good old-fashioned THC panic. It would be pretty stupid of me to get thrown back into the slammer just hours after I got released on bail. I'm sure it's been done before though, I at least tried to play it cool. I picked up the People Magazine and tried to look like I was just reading and minding my own business. I glanced at my watch. We were building on four minutes here. The cop passed me real slow and I saw him staring at me hard as he drove by. I looked like an idiot sitting in a parked car in the rain reading a magazine. I never thought that a little rain could totally fuck my cover into crumbs. When he got to the stop sign he waited for about thirty seconds and then he did a U-turn and pulled up right behind the Accord with his lights flashing.

"Fuck!"

I quickly scanned my situation. I had to come up with a good enough lie so this cop would leave me alone. I knew for a fact the car was registered to Ricky's mom Carmen. She bought it and because of Ricky's driving record and insurance bills being outrageous if at all possible nothing was ever in his name.

The cop got outta the car and approached me from the driver's side where I was now sitting. I rolled down the window as he walked up. When he leaned down to conduct his investigation his back was to the clubhouse, so he wouldn't be able to see the guys if they happened to come bolting outta there.

"License and registration please," he requested. "Can I ask what your business is here this afternoon?"

"Oh, well," I thought as I reached into the glovebox and pulled out a folder with all of the car stuff inside of it.

Ricky gets pulled over all the time so I had gotten a chance before to see where he kept all the papers.

"I was just waiting for my girlfriend to get back, sir."

I handed him the registration and my driver's license.

"Where is your girlfriend?"

"She's out running."

"In a thunderstorm?"

"It started to rain suddenly. Besides, she hates running when it's sunny. She thinks it's too hot outside to breath when it's sunny. So when it rains she likes to drive over here and jog around the park. This is her car, sir. I don't even have the keys, because I'm just waiting."

"I haven't seen anyone jogging around the park, son."

"It's a big park," I said.

"Thank you, but I don't need a geography lesson, ok?"

He scanned down at the registration and smiled at me.

"So how old is your girlfriend? Just curious."

"Actually she's almost fifty."

"Fifty?"

"Yeah, but she looks thirty or thirty-five."

"And you are ... how old," he asked scanning the birth date on my license.

"I'm eighteen," I said. "We're totally legal."

"*Uh hmm,*" he grunted as he looked over the registration.

Just then the guys came sneaking outta the clubhouse carrying the safe. When they saw the cop talking to me they froze and then they took off running around the back of the clubhouse and they disappeared.

"So when do you expect your girlfriend to be back?"

"Probably a little while longer still. She's into marathons."

"I'll be back in a second," the cop told me. He took my ID back to his car so he could run my info through his computer and see if I'm wanted for anything. He had my fake ID. Franco Peters.

The guys and I had developed different hand signals for our mall missions and specifically for situations like this. I saw Patrick peek around the corner and look at me so I fake-sneezed into my palms. That meant, "Shit is not cool." Then I yawned and this meant, "Stay put." He put his pinky up in the air telling me that he understood and he ducked outta sight again.

The cop came back to the car.

"Step outside of the vehicle," he told me, which is almost always a bad thing, especially when it's raining.

I got out and he gave me the old pat down and luckily for me, since I had just gotten outta jail I had nothing incriminating on my person.

"Do you have any drugs or weapons in the vehicle," he asked me.

"No, sir," I said. "You can go ahead and look if you like."

Usually we keep the cars clean from drugs when we go on missions like this, and I remember seeing Matt put the rest of the weed in his pocket, so I was counting on the car being empty of anything that I could get arrested for. The problem with this situation is it's Ricky's car we're talking about, so there was always the chance of a some cocaine residue on a small mirror, or maybe a crack pipe wedged underneath the seat. All I could do was take my chances.

Just then some back-up cop rolled up and the first cop casually stepped towards me and placed me in handcuffs.

"Am I being arrested for something," I asked.

"Not at the moment. This is just for everyone's safety as we search your vehicle. If we find nothing I'll take the cuffs off and you can be on your way."

"Oh. Good," I said. "And yes you can search my vehicle. Thanks for asking."

They didn't know what to make of my comment, but I said it to chill them out and to let them know I really believed I was clean.

"Is there anything in the car I should know about before we search, like, weapons or drugs?"

"No. I don't do drugs, sir. And I don't need weapons."

The two cops started picking apart the car very slowly. They took out the walkie-talkies and placed them on the hood of the car as if they were suspicious. In fact, they were suspicious.

The one cop was like, "Walkie-talkies?"

They were just looking for anything they could mess me up with. They found a pair of binoculars and placed them next to the walkie-talkies. Then -I couldn't believe it- they found an envelope with some pictures of some passed-out naked girl!

And then the cop was like, "Pictures of passed-out naked girls?"

"What are the walkie-talkies for," the backup cop asked me.

"Communication I guess. I don't know really. They belong to the son of my girlfriend. He's older than I am," I said laughing a little.

"*Uh huh*," the one cop said to me. Then he asked, "What's with the amature porn? Who's the girl in the picture?"

"Oh," I said quickly. "Jennifer Bentley. That's my buddy's girl-friend. She's twenty years old, guys. She can do whatever she wants."

The cops weren't wearing any raingear and one of them started complaining that all his gadgets were getting soaked and that he was getting cold. I gotta clean face. I seemed like I was being honest.

The cop who first approached me started to unlock the cuffs. "You're lucky you weren't lying to us. You're free to go."

"Oh. Good. Don't worry about me. I'll just use the towel in the back seat to dry off, and I'm not just saying that to be a smart-ass. I understand you guys are just doing your jobs, even in the rain."

"Just get outta here," the one cop said to me. "We don't wanna see this car still parked here when we make our rounds again, because next time things won't go so easily."

"Yes, sir," I obliged. "I'll get my ass outta here just as soon as my girl gets back to the car. Don't forget, she's got the keys."

Just as soon as the cop cars had turned the corner and were outta sight I got back into the passenger's side of car and immediately hit the button that pops open the trunk. A few seconds the guys came running from the bushes with the safe. They were soaking wet and they threw the hunk of metal into the trun. Ricky's informant was right. It could be easily tossed into the trunk of a car. Ricky slammed it shut, jumped into the driver's seat, and we tore outta Shorewood like drug-dealers escaping a raid. Those were two of the most clueless cops I had ever come across. What if that naked girl was, like, a missing person or something?

35

We decided to head out to my apartment in Granite because it was the furthest place away from the crime scene. When we walked in the front door my dad and his best friend Topper were sitting at the kitchen table and they were wasted from drinking screwdrivers. My older bother Terry was on the couch watching Sportscenter.

"Hey look at these little assholes," Topper yelled to my dad as we walked into the apartment one by one, with Matt and Patrick carrying the safe.

"Hey, Topper," I said. "Don't worry. None of us are cops."

"Hey, guys," my dad said. "What's with the safe?"

I told Patrick and Matt to go ahead down the hall and put the safe on the floor of my room. Ricky followed them down the hall and so did my older brother Terry because he was curious. A mysterious safe was the most intriguing thing to come through the door since my brother found fifteen pounds of weed stashed behind a grocery store one time, and he just carried it back home in a garbage bag and laid it all out on our kitchen counter.

My dad wanted to know where the safe came from.

"We found it on the side of the road, dad," I tried to be honest. "Has anyone called for me? I just got outta jail. Did you know that?"

"Hey," Topper yelled. "Finders keepers, losers weepers, *eh*, ya little asshole?"

"Some girl keeps calling. She won't leave her name," my dad said. "What the *hell* were you in jail for? Why didn't you call me? We thought you were at mom's all this time."

"I got in a fight the other night."

Topper asked me, "What the hell is jail like these days?"

"Oh. Good. Jail is just like going to daycare."

"Your school called me. What's with you skipping school? What the *hell* is going on? They say I have to meet with the principal before you go back."

"I've missed too many days because I've been in jail, dad. What do you want me to do? I can't go to class when I'm locked in a cage."

"Don't make too much noise with that safe!"

"I won't," I said as I went into my room and closed the door. The guys had the thing on my bed and they were all studying it.

"How are we gonna get it open," I asked.

"Yeah," Terry said. "That's what I wanna know."

"I gotta fucking key," Patrick said. "I think. No wait. Do I?"

He had a ring of stolen keys all gathered together on one keyring, but all from many different stolen key missions just like this one.

"You mean you didn't try it while you were there?"

"Fuck no," Patrick said, "It took too long for Ricky to smash the glass-door to the office. Besides, I was laughing too hard." Patrick took the keys outta his pocket and said, "It's fucking jackpot time, fellas."

He put the key in and it wouldn't turn. The key didn't work!

"Shit," Patrick said. "This key is bogus! This ain't funny to me."

"Can't you just pick the lock, guy," Ricky asked.

"Fuck no," Patrick said. "If I could get into a safe like this I'd be knocking around banks for a living. You would need a master lock-picker to get into this fucker.

Matt scratched his head, "Either that or a blow torch."

"Let's call Karl Miles," I suggested.

Karl Miles is that X-Games guy I told you about before, the one who grew up with Patrick and then started hanging around me. He's the lanky kid with superhuman strength. Karl is a master lock-picker. He's got high tech tools and everything. He started getting into it when we were, like, fourteen or some shit. He used to order all these gadgets and gizmos from spy magazines and after a while he landed a lock-picking set and it's been a hobby of his ever since. Karl is not an opportunist though, so he just does it for fun.

"That's not a bad idea, Ray," Matt Morris agreed.

I picked up the cordless and called Karl.

"Who's there," Karl greeted in his weird whispery voice.

"Dude. It's Ray. What are you doing, masturbating?"

"What's up, Ray? Look I'm kinda busy right now. Can I call you back?"

"No. No. No. I need to talk to you. Patrick and I are over here with Ricky and Terry. We're at my apartment. We need your help picking a lock."

"What kind? Hold on a sec," he said and he cleared his throat and then covered up the phone and I could hear his muffled speak as he talked back and forth with what sounded like a girl's voice. Then I heard all these cracks and scrapes like the Karl's phone was being tossed all about.

"Sorry," he said. He was short on breath. The way he was talking to me was like carrying on a conversation with somebody on a treadmill. "I was just putting Julie into position." Then he said to this girl, "Say hi to my friend Ray, Julie. He's nice."

He held the phone out and all I heard was her moaning and

grunting as if Karl and her were actually having sex while he was on the phone with me.

"What kinda lock is it," Karl asked me all casually.

"I dunno. It's a safe. What are you doing?"

"A safe? I'm not sure if I can do it. What kinda safe is it?"

"It's just one of them Sentry ones you get at K-Mart."

"Are you positive it's just a Sentry?"

"Yeah."

"I mean, does it say it's a fucking Sentry?"

"Yeah."

"I guess I can do it. What's in it for me, Ray? Did you guys bother discussing that before you decided to call?" Then Karl told me to, "Hold on again real quick," and he put his phone down and I started hearing all these strange noises again like slapping skin and moaning and grunting.

"This guy is a trip," I told Patrick, Ricky, Terry and Matt. And then I rolled my eyes, "I think he's having sex with somebody named Julie. Plus he wants to know what's in it for him if he comes over and unlocks this shit."

"Tell that stupid nigger I'll give him some money to buy some more modeling glue for his race-cars," Patrick said.

"*Seriously*," I said. "Should we cut him some of the loot or what?"

"Tell him we'll give him at least a hundred," Patrick budged.

I got back on the phone and he was waiting for me and asking for me.

I told him, "How's a hundred bucks sound, at the least?"

"For a hundred I'll be there in an hour. For two-hundred I can be there in ten minutes."

"Bring all your tools," I said. "I'll see you in an hour."

"No kidding," he said sarcastically. "Are you sure? You think I should bring some tools?"

"Later," I said and I hung up the phone.

"He'll be here in an hour," I said. "With his tools."

Terry got bored with waiting for Karl so he went over to his buddy's house to take bong rips and watch the Bulls game. Patrick started to rifle through my CD collection and he pulled out a Jim

Carroll Band album and played that song called *People Who Died*. Ricky and Matt Morris turned on my little TV and started messing around with Madden 95 on the Sega.

That's when the phone rang. It was The Brain, and I hadn't talked to him since right before I got pinched on that Friday night with the Jeremy Otsap fight and all.

"Hey. What's new," I said to The Brain through static on the cordless.

I pulled the antenna up farther and the sound got clearer.

"How was the slammer, hoss? I talked to Matt yesterday and he said they were gonna bail you out."

"It wasn't too cool, man. I'm glad to be free. I don't plan on ever going back to that place. I'd flee to Mexico before I'd ever face doing time again. I swear to God. Jail is no place to raise humans."

"I hear you," he said. "Look. I couldn't get a hold of that jacket."

"Fuck. Are you serious?"

"I'm dead serial," he said. "I couldn't get my hands on it. Sorry, but that bitch Erin wouldn't lemme have it."

"What do you mean she wouldn't *let* you?"

"She accused me of trying to *steal* the fucking thing."

"Get the fuck outta here!"

"I ain't lying."

"So where is it, do you know?"

"Yeah. It's still at her fucking house as far as I know."

"So she's holding it hostage? That's fucking great," I sarcastically said.

"She's says, 'If he wants it, he's gotta come and get it.' If that's not fucked up then I don't know what is."

"That's *really* fucked up all right. What the fuck. Is that a threat or a flirt? Did she sound pissed? I mean, when she said I had to come and get it? Because I don't want it to be some kinda trap, like I get there to pick it up and there's dudes there waiting for me, you picking up what I'm throwing down?"

"Totally. I don't' think that's the case though," The Brain said. "She actually sounded concerned the next day when I told her I saw you being hauled away by the cops. Besides, Jeremy Otsap had to go back to college with his mouth wired shut and he's eating chicken soup through a straw. I heard he declined to press charges. And without him I don't think anybody gives two shits about you, not even the cops."

"No charges? When did you hear this?"

"Just this morning. Tim Miller told me."

"That's a little reassuring, I guess. What happened to Jeremy anyway, like, after I socked him? The pigs told me he had to go to the hospital or some crap."

"Fuck yeah he went to the hospital," The Brain got loud. "Dude had to have emergency surgery and shit. They had to wire his fucking jaw shut because you shattered it."

"*Jesus*," I said. Then I covered the phone and said to the guys, "I *shattered* that kids jaw the other night! How ya like me *now*!"

The Brain went on.

"Yeah. You fucked him up real good. Everywhere I go, everybody is talking about it."

"That's nuts."

"Yeah. So I wouldn't worry about any Jocks trying to stick it to you after what you did to Jeremy's face," The Brain laughed like the villains do in old black and white monster movies.

"Even still, I don't really wanna take my chances. So what's up for tonight, what is it, Thursday or Friday?"

"It's Friday dude. You've been holed up in the slammer for a whole week."

"God. It seems like a fucking month."

"I can imagine."

"Look. I might feel like getting together tonight. Maybe we can pull a mission and go get my jacket if it's cool with Erin, but I don't know if I can muster up the courage to call her after everything that went down. My dad says some girl has been calling but—"

"Didn't he take a message, hoss?"

"The girl wouldn't leave her name, which leads me to believe it could have been Erin, but it's too hard to tell. Then again it could've been Kim or Milada anyone for that matter. It's just a hunch. I might have to call Gabe and have him do the talking for me."

"Fuck Gabe, he does a lotta talking all right, for *himself* I like that crackhead like yesterday's turds. He's notorious for going after every other dude's chick. He plays that friend bullshit with the girls and then pulls out his gay-ass moves when the boyfriend is away."

"*Hmm*," I sighed. "Look, can I call you back? I've got some buddies over and we're in the middle of trying to fix something."

"Sure, man."

"Ok. I'll give you a call in a coupla hours. I might feel like celebrating here pretty soon so keep me in mind if anything good comes up or if you feel like helping me get my jacket back."

"Actually, I plan on hooking up with some **Acid** tonight. You down?"

"Yeah. Yeah. Yeah. I'm down. Just lemme know if it works out."

"Sure."

"Peace out," I said and I hung up.

36

There was a knock at my bedroom door about an hour and a half after I got off the phone with The Brain. It was Karl and he was carrying a brown leather duffel bag with all of his lock picking works.

"What's up, Karl," I said and we shook hands brother-style. "Thanks for coming by."

"No problem, Ray. For another hundred I would've been here fifty minutes ago," Karl said as he walked in and greeted everybody. "Hey fucks," he said. "Patrick, what's with no return phone calls anymore?"

"Karl," Patrick said. "I didn't think we had to talk on the phone everyday to stimulate the friendship."

"Yeah, yeah, yeah," Karl said. "Hey there, Matt. Ricky, how's that niggerish stuff going for you?"

"Fuck that, Karl," Ricky shouted. "You gonna bust open this safe or what?"

"Chill out, guys. I got my tools right here. Who's got my hundred, Malcolm X," Karl said to Ricky.

We all laughed. It was yet another black joke for Ricky.

"I'm not playin when I tell you this, guy. Chill with the nigger jokes! Jesus. I'm fuckin South American! I ain't from fuckin Africa."

"So where's the Sentry," Karl asked.

"It's right here on the bed," I said and I put my hand on top of it.

"*That?*" Karl laughed. "That thing is pathetic. I call that a lock box. You guys just wasted a hundred bucks. Any old boyscout could break into this."

"It's fucking locked, Karl," Matt Morris said. "We can't open it for shit."

"Do you guys care if I damage it while I'm cracking it open?"

Karl had a wild look in his eyes like he planned on tearing the safe to shreds.

We all looked at each other and we all said, "No, we don't mind a bit."

Karl unzipped his bag and took out a little box with all these long poker-like gadgets on it. Then he took out a crowbar.

"*Hmm*," Karl thought to himself as he picked up the safe and looked at it. "Do you have a hammer, Ray? I forgot mine at the house."

"Hold on," I said and I went down the hall to get a hammer.

I found one in the hall closet. I took the hammer back to my room and I shut my door, locked it, and then I handed the hammer to Karl.

"Thanks," he said. "This should only take a minute."

He took out his little poker tools and inserted each one into the lock and wiggled them around. When he looked like he wasn't satisfied with the way they wiggled he would try a different one.

"So what are we looking for in this thing," Karl asked us.

"*Cash*," Patrick said. "It's not a fucking piggybank, Karl. We're not in the business of going broke, dude."

"Actually," Karl began with a frown like he couldn't find the right poker tool. "I didn't know you guys had any business."

Then Karl grunted a solid little "Fuck it" and picked up the crowbar and put the claw of it into the crack of the door to the safe. Then he took the hammer and tapped on the end of the crowbar until it was stuck in the crack. He actually let go of the crowbar and it stuck there in the crack of the door, suspended in midair.

"I'm gonna put it on the floor. I need a coupla you fags to step on it so it don't move while I pry it open."

He took it down off the bed and put it onto the floor and Patrick stood on it since he was the heaviest. Matt Morris and I got down and held it in place.

"Ok," Karl briefed us.

Karl tried to pry it open with all his strength, but it didn't open.

"Let's turn it on the side," Karl suggested, almost exhausted. "This isn't working."

He turned it onto its side so the crowbar was sticking out parallel with the floor.

"I'm gonna jump on it so hold it still."

Karl got on my bed an jumped down onto the crowbar and when he hit we heard a loud snapping sound like you hear when somebody's arm gets busted. Karl fell outta control and landed on me. We all gathered ourselves and looked at the safe. The door was wide open.

Patrick picked up the broken box and set it back onto the bed. Inside were four leather bank bags with zippers and inside each one was a bank deposit that would never make it to the teller. We undid all the bags and laid the cash out onto the bed, putting the ones in a stack, then the fives, then the tens, then the twenties, fifties, hundreds, and so on. Patrick counted the loot and it came out to four-thousand-seven-hundred and fifty-four dollars and some change. It was a bigger score than we expected and this was good. It came out to be one-thousand and eighty-eight dollars divided by four of us. So we gave Karl the one-hundred and eighty-eight and we each kept a grand. It was a glorious score.

37

After everybody had insane cash in their pockets suddenly they all wanted to leave. Ricky said he was going over to Jon's house in Valparaiso. Jon was everybody's dope dealer. Ricky sold weed a little bit just because he thought it was fun. And whenever Ricky had cash he'd always book over to see Jon so he could grab a few ounces.

Patrick and Matt and Karl said they were gonna go pick up a few cases of beer and call some bitches. They asked me if I wanted to come along, but I declined mainly because I was still really tired from bein in Jail.

I just wanted to stay home so I could rest and maybe decide what to do with my money. I didn't rack my brain on how to spend it, but rather how to hide it. I was pretty sure what I was gonna use the cash for. And I knew it would be a while before I could actually apply it to what I wanted. Keeping all that money in a safe place for the time being was my biggest problem right then.

Right after I smoked a little bitta weed some paranoia slithered about from that cop investigating me in front of the clubhouse. The Cop had gotten the license plate and I figured it was only a matter of time before the crime was reported and the cops started sniffing around Ricky's house asking questions.

Would he crack under the pressure?

I didn't think so, Ricky was a lotta things, but a narc wasn't one of them. Despite what most teenagers think, the police aren't stupid, and even without a confession from Ricky there was an off chance they could still nail him and then go onto nail Matt Morris and Patrick and me. I didn't wanna take the chance of the cops getting to me and finding a whole shitload of evidence at my place. I decided I would hope for the best and prepare for the worst.

So here's what I did: I enlisted my little brother Magic-Mike to help me hide my share of the money until things blew over. He was living with my mom in Michigan City so I called him and told him I was putting the money in the mailbox, and when he got it I carefully instructed him to hide it in a really safe place until I got there to claim it. Magic-Mike was trustworthy. He's six years younger than I am, which would have made him about twelve or thirteen at the time, but he was down enough to have a good nickname. He wasn't the type to ask too many questions or steal my money. Plus it was common knowledge that I'd kick his ass if he tried any funny business with my cash.

The next morning I sent him a letter with eight-hundred dollars cash in it and I kept a hundred in my wallet that would go towards fast food, beer and weed. I stashed another hundred under my mattress. It's pretty stupid to mail that much cash, but I'm a guy who has a lotta faith in the US Postal System. I've never, ever had a letter or a package misplaced in my lifetime. And I've mailed all kinds of things from rare coins to ounces of weed to cash. The old courier always comes through.

I took the safe and threw it into the trunk of The Poop. Then I drove to McDonald's and tossed it into the dumpster. It was only then that I felt cleansed of guilt. Now if the coppers came to my door asking questions they wouldn't find a safe or any cash and at the very least I could play dumb.

When I got back home my dad and Topper were gone. I figured they went down to Dante's or to The Back Door for Bloody Mary's. So I was home alone.

I called The Brain.

"What up," I said when he answered the phone.

"Nothing. What're you doing," he asked.

"Nothing."

"Did you get that thing with your friends worked out?"

"Yes, and it went very well. I can't wait to tell you about it. Like, when we're not on the phone, if you catch my drift. What's up for tonight?"

"I'm just playing my guitar and smoking weed with Jacob Drake. We don't know what we're gonna do later. Maybe trip out."

"He's there?"

"Yep."

"Tell him hey."

"Ray says hey," The Brain muffed the phone and said to Jacob.

"*Wassup*," I heard Jacob growl over The Brain's strumming notes from his guitar. "When we gonna play hockey again, *biatch*!"

"Tell him next time we play I'm gonna give him an ass-pounding," I laughed. "So what's up with those dosages?"

"Gabe just went to go pick'em up. He should be back soon. Are you down with tripping out or what?"

"Fuck yeah. Who's all dropping tonight?"

"Me. You. Jacob the nigger to my right. Gabe. Erin. Maybe some other dudes. Some random bitches. I don't know. It really depends on how much we have to go around."

"Sounds like the biggest sausage fest of the year."

"Settle down, Ray. There's gonna be bitches there. Believe that. They just ain't tripping if we can't get enough."

"Like who?"

"Well, like Milada—"

"*Bunk!*"

"Tell me about it. Jolene is coming. Gisela's gook-ass too."

"Fuck off," Jacob yelled. "She ain't a gook. She's Oriental!"

"I'll tell you what. I'm just gonna chill at home, so give me a ring when Gabe gets back. I just got outta the cage so I think I'm gonna try to take a little nap in the meantime. How's that shit sound?"

"Sounds fine to me," The Brain agreed. "I just learned how to play *Betterman*."

"What's that," I asked.

"It's fucking Pearl Jam! Jesus."

"Right," I said. "I knew that."

"I'll play it for you tonight. It sounds tight."

"Sure thing," I said and I hung up the phone.

I just stared at the floor and thought about nothing at all. It was a habit I picked up in jail. It was almost 10:00 already and I thought maybe I'd try to attempt that nap. So I took a shower and then I crashed on the couch and smoked a phat joint. I turned on *60 Minutes* and by the time it was over I was asleep.

38

It turns out I wasn't asleep for long. The Brain called me back within the hour. *60 Minutes* was rolling its ending credits when the cordless rang out from on top of my chest where I had left it. I looked around the room and tried to regain my senses.

I picked up the phone and hit the **TALK** button with my index finger and said, "Hello?" in a husky voice.

"Wake up, sally," The Brain excitedly shouted. "It's on!"

"*Huh*," I asked.

I was confused. I sat up on the couch and ran my fingers through my hair to see just how messed up it was from sleeping.

"What's on, the dose thing?"

"The dose thing," The Brain agreed. "It's fucking on! He even got double from what he said he was gonna get. I knew this dick was good for something."

"Whatever," Gabe called from the background.

"He's there already," I asked The Brain. "What time is it?"

"Eleven. Yep. Gabe's right here."

"Ask him how much a piece the squares are selling for."

The Brain took his mouth away from the receiver and called to Gabe, "Dude wants to know how much for one."

"Seven," Gabe said very quickly like he'd been asked a hundred times already.

"Seven? Damn that's expensive. It must be good shit."

"It is. It's supposed to be the best in a while."

"Tell Gabe I'm buying all of them for everybody who's tripping tonight. I came across a little cash and I wanna blow it on something."

"Are you *serious*," The Brain was surprised.

"Yeah. I'm *dead serious*."

"Hey," The Brain called to Gabe. "Ray's buying for everybody tonight. That cool with you guys," he sarcastically laughed.

"Fine—"

"Oh! I'm feeling that shit," Jacob sang out, cutting off Gabe's words. "Where's Ray gettin that kinda money?"

I said to The Brain, "I bet he looks like an idiot with that afro bouncing all over the place."

"I hear ya," The Brain said. "It's probably—"

"What'dee say," Jacob shouted in his loud-mouth style.

"He says to cut that fucking shitty Afro off your head."

"Fuck you guys!"

"He says fuck you," The Brain told me.

"Yeah," I laughed. "I heard his ass over the phone ... Listen. Can you dudes pick me up? I don't wanna trip out and have to drive."

"Yeah. No sweat," The Brain said. "We can scoop you up in Gabe's shitty car. Erin's is where it's at tonight."

"Where's mom and dad?"

"Don't know. Don't care. We just know they ain't gonna be around tonight."

"I guess you're right. So, I'll see you guys ... when?"

"Aboutta half hour, maybe an hour. Tops. It depends on when these assholes get their shit together."

"Sound's fair," I confirmed. "See ya then."

And I hung up.

39

Acid. The stuff was everywhere while I was in high school and it was highly, highly, illegal. Word around town was each hit of **Acid** carried a year in jail. All through high school I would hear these horror stories about **Acid**. A sheet of **Acid** holds a hundred hits on it and if you got caught with one of those you could pretty much kiss the rest of your life away.

Let's review: A hit comes from a sheet, and a sheet was once part of a book. Dudes who carry around books of **Acid** looking to do deals are Public Enemy Number One. They are like the crazed hyper-active assholes looking for trouble, or action, whichever comes first.

Just like any business, there's a lotta marketing that goes into selling **Acid**. It's not like weed or cocaine. You can't tell how good it is by seeing it or tasting it. It's pretty much a gamble. Most people rely on word of mouth about which hits are good and which are bunk. Bunk means it's not laced with anything. It's dead. It's just paper with a pinhead of speed dropped onto it and you got dicked over on a deal. It's a bummer, but can best be described as bunk. Then how can you tell if you get good stuff or bad stuff? Network marketing, advertising, and instinct. Most sheets of **Acid** are printed with pictures on them. Not a huge picture, but tiny individual pictures on each square hit. Some might have a sunfish, or a picture of Jesus, maybe an evergreen tree, or even a picture of Fred Flintstone. It could be a picture of anything; it doesn't matter, because all the picture is used for is to set it apart from the competition.

Here's how it works: Let's say a book of **Acid** with pictures of tiny half moons on them is smuggled into The Region by a Hippie on a Greyhound bus. Another book with little roses printed on them is snuck in by a Preppie Frat Boy fresh outta college. Then a Mexican driving a old Ford LTD delivers to the ghetto a sheet of doses with pictures of little flames on them. Let's say for the sake of the **Acid** coming from the ghetto that the flame hits are bunk. The half moons are pretty good. The roses are outta this world. They all hit the streets and begin to circulate.

Johnny buys six half moons and shares them with two of his buddies. They take two each. They trip outta little, get a good body buzz, and then after four to six hours they're sober again, but completely awake, because the doses were laced heavy with speed. The half moons were pretty decent, but nothing to write home to mom about, if that's what you're into. They did have a good time though, and when their friends ask how the half moons tasted Johnny and his buddies say, "They're ok. They'll get you off if you take enough of them."

The word's gone out.

Rachel and her cousin Christine meet some Mexican at the mall and he sells them four hits with the little flames on them. The girls shell out twenty bucks for a potential good time. Let's say Rachel has never taken **Acid,** but old Christine is a pro—let's say she's tripped dozens and dozens of times. After the sun sets they drive to the beach and they each drop two hits and they wait ... and they wait. Two hours go by and Christine doesn't feel anything, but Rachel is acting goofy because she's getting off on the anticipation of tripping. To her, it's the classic placebo effect. The flames were bunk as bunk can be though.

The next day Christine is asked how the **Acid** tasted and she says, "Fucking flames, don't by'em. They're way phony. I should've known better then to cop off a spicxican."

Christine is bummed out from getting ripped off and she's determined to spread the word about the bogus little flame hits. Rachel is asked the same question at a different time and a different place.

She says, "Well, I think it was good, but I'm not sure. I didn't really feel all that much, but I heard it doesn't work on people taking it the first time."

That's complete bullshit of course. A hit of **Acid** will work on most people the same, no matter how many times a person has taken it. Rachel is just relieved that she didn't end up tripping out, because she was scared of what might have happened. She only wanted to take it to get it over with, so she could say that she'd done it. The word goes out. The little flames are weak.

Here's a scenario that actually happened: Gabe calls up his buddy Billy Pozzo. Pozzo's got some extra hits of **Acid** for sale. It seems he picked up three different kinds from three different dudes at the Grateful Dead concert. He gotta real good deal on all of them so he bought them in bulk hoping to unload them and turn a little profit back in The Region. Billy Pozzo mentions to Gabe during Spanish class that he's holding because Gabe is always good for a few buys. They agree go hook up later that night, the same night I threw the safe into the McDonald's dumpster.

When Gabe gets to Pozzo's house he soon discovers that Pozzo has a little variety action going on with his selection of psychedelics. Pozzo greets Gabe at the front door and invites him into his room.

"Com'n into my office," Pozzo says.

His mother Maude Pozzo is on the couch and she's reading the new issue of People Magazine: The Year's Best and Worst Dressed Celebrities. "Hi, Gabe," she says without looking up from the article about who's hot and who's not in Hollywood. "Just a god awful dress," she mutters and shakes her head. Then turns the page. She's reading the magazine back to front.

"Hey, Mrs. P," Gabe says as Billy Pozzo and him sneak off down the hall unsuspected.

Once inside the bedroom Billy Pozzo locks the door.

"I've got some serious shit," he says as Gabe tosses some unfolded laundry from his bed and sits down. "Wait till you see it, Gabe."

"I'm waiting," Gabe says as he watches Billy unlock his little safe and pull out a three different sheets of aluminum foil, each one folded into some kinda envelope or pocket.

"There's a little pair of scissors and some tweezers on the nightstand next to you," Pozzo tells him. "Can you grab'em for me?"

Gabe hands him the tools and Pozzo sits next to him on the bed and prepares to operate.

TIMEOUT.

Why the aluminum foil, the scissors, and the tweezers? The only stupid questions are the ones not asked, right? Hits of **Acid** have to be kept in something resistant to being soaked, some kinda non-absorbent material, because the drop of **Acid** that was placed on each square to begin with will just leak into whatever it touches, thus thinning out the high and eventually ruining it. So obviously paper storage is outta the question. Even a plastic baggy isn't always the best thing to use. Foil is the best method for keeping your hits of **Acid** and it's the most common method. As for the scissors and the tweezers, you can't handle the **Acid** with your bare hands for the same reasons, because it will absorb into your skin and then you end up tripping out without planning on it, which normally isn't too cool. A sheet of **Acid** is usually a piece of perforated, thick-cut paper and the little squares are all ready to be pulled apart, so you need to use the scissors and the tweezers to remove each square. Pozzo unfolds each piece of foil and lays them side by side on the bed with the hits exposed.

"Ok," he begins to explain. "I've got, roughly, thirty of each kind. You can get as much, or as little, as you want to. These," he pointed to the flames. "These are three dollars a square and they come with a money back guarantee because I've heard that they might be a little weak."

"Yeah, I've heard about those," Gabe says. "All the Mexicans are running around with those. Get them outta my face, please."

"Sure. I've heard the same shit. And these," he pointed to the half moons. "They're four bucks a piece. They're pretty good and I've tried these myself. I took three and got off pretty good. I ended up going to the woods with some friends and freaking out on the trees and all the sounds ... pretty good time, mostly body buzz though, very little visual anything."

"And what about the little Roses?"

"And these, *the Roses*," Pozzo smiled. "These are seven a piece."

"*Seven*, are you nuts?"

"No, I'm not crazy. These are killer doses. All you need is one and you're flying. Gabe, trust me. I'm not a porch-monkey from Gary. There's hardly any speed at all in the Roses, mostly pure **Acid**. Really clean shit. If I were you, I'd get the Roses. You can't beat'em. They're a total knock-out."

"I need at least ten, and all I have is fifty bucks, but what I could do is, I could sell the other twenty worth and just kick it down to you tomorrow or the day after if that's cool. You know I'm good for it. I got them all sold already. I just need to collect the cash."

"That works," Pozzo said. "I trust you. So ten Roses it is," and he began to cut out ten squares.

"Here's the fifty," Gabe said and he took a wad of cash outta his pocket and laid it onto the nightstand.

"Trust me," Pozzo promised. "You won't be sorry, dude."

"If these are bogus hits I'm gonna come back here and slaughter the whole Pozzo family with the rusted tail pipe that fell off of my car this afternoon," Gabe said as an ill attempt at some humor. Billy Pozzo wasn't sure if he saw it the same way because Gabe was anything but predictable, and you could never be sure if he was joking or not. He stopped the cutting for a second and stared at Gabe, trying to look him in the eyes to see the real truth.

"What," Gabe looked surprised. "I'm fucking kidding!"

40

The Brain and Gabe and Jacob arrived at my apartment a little bit later. I didn't hear them pull up because they were driving in Jacob's car, which was a Crown Victoria, a white one, and old. The Brain had told me they would be driving Gabe's car.

"What's up kids," I shouted over the blasting music as I got into the car. *Runnin' Down a Dream* by Tom Petty and the Heartbreakers was playing on the radio and Jacob and Gabe were in the middle of a heated argument about whether or not Babe Ruth was the greatest baseball player of all time.

"Oh yeah," Jacob shouted over his shoulder to Gabe, who was sitting next to me in the back. "I figured you'd say Ruth, because you both is some fat slobs."

"Fuck. You're a tool," Gabe called him. "I say Ruth because he was the only guy ever to play who was a great pitcher as well as a powerful hitter. Mays, Mantle, Gehrig. All those guys were great, but they were two-dimensional. I mean they were hitters and fielders. Ruth was a hitter, a fielder, and a pitcher. In fact, he could play every single position on the diamond."

Gabe wiped the sweat from his forehead with his sleeve.

Then Jacob goes, "Ty Cobb's is the greatest *mothuh fuguh* ever to play the game." Jacob drove outta my parking lot and headed up the LaSalle street. "Cobb hit over four-hundred for five seasons in a row. And I might have to educate you a lil'bit, Gabe, but Cobb transformed the game. Before his ass came along it was a leisurely game, like golf. He turned baseball into war. *Whazzup* up back there, Ray! What about you, dip-shit? Who do you think was the greatest baller ever to play?"

"That's a good question," I answered all cool as I pulled outta joint from my shirt pocket. "Anybody gotta fire for this?"

The Brain whipped outta Zippo and blazed a flame in front of my face as I puffed on the weed stick and lit it, and then I passed it to Gabe and continued to explain my opinion on the subject of Hall of Famers.

"There's a good argument to be made about Ruth because he was so much better than the other players of his time, and he was a showman. Some people say he had the heart the size of a watermelon—"

"You mean he had the gut the size of a watermelon," The Brain said as he took the joint hand off from Gabe and put it to his lips.

We all laughed. That was funny to us.

"Good point," I said. "That's Ty Cobb's way of looking at it. You also have to consider they started using a new kinda baseball when Ruth was a young guy, maybe his second year in the big leagues. Before that the yarn wasn't wound as tightly and they only went through a few balls per game. It was common that the balls would become lopsided and shit and they'd travel through the air funny. Plus the pitchers would do everything they could to fuck up the ball. Spit. Tar. Scuff. Scratch. They'd put mud on the ball. It would get to the point where the ball would actually be all brownish looking by the third or fourth inning, so it was really hard for the hitters to see. And for the record: the only reason Cobb didn't hit that many homers is because he didn't wanna."

"What do you mean he didn't wanna hit homers," Gabe confronted me as I took a drag and handed off to him. "That's horseshit, Ray. Who wouldn't wanna hit homers?"

"Cobb was a baseball fundamentalist. He just wanted to put the ball into play so he could run the bases, which is where he was the greatest ever to play. As a baserunner he was the best ever, without question. He used to sharpen the spikes on his shoes just so he could plant them into the guts of the infielders. He was such a mean fucker, and a *racist*. Everybody hated him."

"Why did they change the balls," The Brain asked me. "It was because a guy got killed when he got hit by a pitch he couldn't see because the ball was all brown. I can't remember his name, but he got clobbered with a high fastball that shattered his skull and he died the next day. Everyone thought it was because the ball was too hard to see. So they started winding them tighter and they used a new ball every time the old one got dirty and all, so hitters could see it well enough to duck outta the way when it came rocketing at their heads from the mound."

"Yeah, yeah, yeah. So who's the greatest, Ray," Jacob asked me. "You never answered the question."

"Jackie Robinson was the best ever," I said. "In fact, I could rattle off ten other black guys who were better than Cobb and Ruth, guys who played in the Negro League."

"Fucking ... *niggers*," The Brain shouted in surprise as we pulled into Erin's driveway. "Don't be a nigger-lover."

"Hey. Watch your language, man," I scolded. "You're gonna offend Jacob. He's got an afro. Here we are. I don't know about you guys, but I'm ready to trip my balls off tonight. By the way, I thought you dicks were gonna be taking Gabe's car. What happened?"

"My tail pipe got rusted and fell off," Gabe said as he rolled up his window and opened his door. "It's too loud. I'm afraid of getting pulled over for it."

We all got outta the Crown Victoria and walked up to the front door. There were no outside lights on and it was so dark that I could hardly tell where I was going.

Gabe had a hyper-attack and he climbed up into an apple tree and started throwing little unripe baby apples at us, the little green ones are harder than working on a Toyota engine.

"What the fuck is your problem, Gabe," The Brain hissed as he got nailed with an apple. "Stupid mother fucker!"

"Really," I disciplined Gabe. "Come down from there! If you start overheating while people are dosing someone's liable to kill themselves tonight."

"Or liable to kill your dumb-ass, Gabe," Jacob warned him as he shook his afro all about and rang the doorbell.

"I was just fucking around," Gabe explained.

He jumped down from his lofty branch and dusted off his jeans and re-did the tightroll job around his ankles.

"If I were you," I suggested to Gabe. "I'd leave the jeans the way they were."

"What do you mean, Ray? You don't dig it? That's why you ain't cool like me."

Erin answered the door.

"Dudes," Erin greeted us. "I've been waiting for hours. It's almost fucking midnight already. I'm glad you finally showed. We were beginning to worry. It's The Brain! Hey! Jacob, hi! I dig the afro. It gets more puffy every time I see it, dude."

"Thanks, blondie," Jacob said as he patted his afro.

"Ray," she said as she hugged me. "You look great. Did you just get outta jail or what?"

"This morning," I said. "Is everything cool around here," I made sure as I peeked around the corner to see who was in the livingroom.

"Oh," Erin waved as if my concerns where ridiculous. "Nothing to worry about, dude. I promise. You've got superstar protection tonight. Just the girls and you guys are here—strictly a private function."

Erin followed us when we got into the house.

"Make yourselves comfortable, dudes! Ray, come with me upstairs and I can give you your little lucky jacket. It's in the hall closet, but first lemme show you something in my room."

"Sure thing," I said.

The other guys started gasping and cracking sex jokes when she invited me upstairs.

"Where a rubber up there, hoss," The Brain chuckled as Erin and I walked up the steps. "She'll give you the clap. And then somebody will show up to beat you down."

"Shut the hell up," she hissed at The Brain.

"Hey, bitch! Maybe you don't remember, but Ray got his ass kicked last time he was here! I'm just trying to do him a fucking favor."

"Dude," I calmed down The Brain. "It's cool. I'll be ok."

When the guys disappeared into the livingroom Erin and I looked at each other and smiled.

"He's very protective," I explained. "He's always talking too much shit to everybody."

"Oh, he doesn't bother me. The Brain's been coming here for a thousand years," she said. "And we're totally good friends."

She turned and walked upstairs and I followed in rearview. It made me think of my Bob Marley shirt.

Where the fuck is that shirt?

She led me down the hall and into her room. The lights were off and she wasn't reaching for any switch as she closed the door behind me. She grabbed me and pulled me into her and we kissed. At first I was frozen, because I wasn't expecting it, but then I warmed up to her and relaxed. It wasn't a sexy kiss—I mean it was sexy, but it was way more of a romantic kiss. My chest heated up and I got nervous. She started unzipping my jeans and I reached up under her shirt and unsnapped her bra in the front and her tits popped out and I grabbed them and pushed her onto the bed as she tugged my jeans down around my ankles. I unzipped her jeans and started peeling them from her sloped ass and I had to take them completely off so I could tug down her panties and politely spread her legs. We started having sex and then she pushed me away and shoved me onto my back and started riding me for a while. She got hot and took her shirt completely off so I could see her tits. Her nipples were erect. I felt them with my fingertips. And then she got off me and got down on the bed on all fours and said, "Do me doggie."

So I did.

Wouldn't you?

And then soon after I came inside of her.

"Wow," was all I could say. "You're on the pill right?"

"Sure. Yeah. I mean, I think so."

"Oh. Good."

We laid on the bed and held each other for a few more minutes.

"I'm so sorry about the way things happened last time, Raymond."

I smiled, trying not to laugh, "And this is how you make it up to me?"

"No, dude. I had sex with you because I'm falling in love."

"Come again?"

"I Love you," she said to me. "I really do. What about you? How do you feel about me?"

"*Uh*, well, Erin. Love is a word that gets tossed around a lot. I mean, I've really been into you for a long time now, ever since we first met, but it wouldn't be fair for me to be telling you I loved you at this point. I hardly even know you, or what you're all about."

"So you may love me, but even if you did you wouldn't tell me?"

"Take it any way you like," I said. "But I guess you could say that. Frankly, I'm just really scared of loving someone like you. I feel like it's forbidden, or that everything is working against us ever being together."

"I feel the same way, Raymond, but I want things to change."

"What about *him*?"

"God, you say *him* like it's a four letter word."

"It's a three letter word."

"Com'n. Things are over with Jeremy and me. They have been over for a long time now. He's even seeing somebody else. It's just taking some getting used to for both of us."

"I've got stitches in my mouth that prove you and him are both uncomfortable with the situation."

When I said that she acted sad and seemed, like, she was now choosing her words more carefully.

"Well, Raymond. We should be getting back downstairs. Look. I've got your jacket in the hall closet. You can grab it whenever you feel like it."

"Yeah, I will. Are you gonna trip out tonight?"

"Yeah," she said softly. "And you?"

"I'm buying for everybody here."

"That's so cool of you, dude."

"It's not a big deal."

"Yeah," she said softly.

I could tell just by looking at her eyes that she was still hiding things from me. We both kinda got up off the bed and started getting dressed.

"Where's your parents?"

"They're in Ohio visiting my older brother for the weekend. Where's my underwear?"

"Cool, cool," I said. "They're on the pillow."

"Yeah, dude. Very cool," she teased.

"Look, I'll see you downstairs," I said. "I've gotta use the bathroom. It's around the corner here, right?"

"Yeah, second door over. I'll see you downstairs." I started to make a break for it and she stopped me and called, "Ray," like she forgot to say something.

I didn't say anything. I just turned and made eye contact with her.

"I love you. I want us both to have a really good time tonight."

"So do I," I smiled. "So do I, Erin."

"Ray?"

"Yeah?"

"Your fly's down."

41

It was mathematically right that night with four girls and four guys, it was definitely not a Sausage Festival. Don't get me wrong, it wasn't good because of any kinda sexual symmetry. It was good because it's important for a girl, or a guy, while dosing on **Acid**, to have someone to relate to if needed. In fact, for this reason alone it might have been better to have only girls or only guys.

Picture this: you're on **Acid** and you're the only guy with six girls. Scary thought isn't it?

Or the other way around: you're a girl with a bunch of teenage boys—probably even more frightening, *huh?*

If you've never taken **Acid** then more power to you, because if I could go back in time I never would've dropped fifty-some times or however many times I did it. I've suffered a little permanent psychological damage, which you might have suspected from me writing a book like this.

After I took a piss Erin was waiting for me in the hallway and we walked downstairs together and Gabe was at the diningroom table opening up the foil of **Acid** and everybody seemed excited. The energy in the room was buzzing and cracking.

Jolene was there, Leslie Hipp, and Milada too. Jolene, Erin, and Leslie had dropped **Acid** before. I could tell just by looking at them. Milada was messing things up right from the start. She was a rookie **Acid**-taker and everybody knew it. She just wasn't being cool.

She was saying things like, "Oh my God, *that's* what it looks like? I thought it was supposed to be *sugar* cubes!"

I said, "What up," to Jolene and Leslie.

I didn't even wanna talk to Milada because she was trouble, what with Kimber telling me Milada's spreading rumors about her and I just to piss her ex-boyfriend off. But of course, just when I felt that I had successfully ignored her, she did what's to be expected of psycho women. She confronted me and basically forced me to have a conversation with her. It was a traumatic experience and, man, you should've seen the look on Erin's face when she saw Milada showing so much interest in me. I did *not* want these two chicks taking **Acid** around each other, but unfortunately it was inevitable. If things began to be twisted with those two girls I knew right then that I'd be pulling a Wizard of Oz and telling myself there was no place like home. And to top everything off, the song that started playing on the stereo was *Cruel Summer* by Bananarama. Strictly bunk. If that doesn't foreshadow a tragedy I don't know what does.

It was time to pass around the squares. Gabe wanted everyone to line up as he took a pair of tweezers and, one at a time, gently placed a dose on everyone's tongue. Everyone knew what to expect except for Milada.

"Oh no," she waved him off like he had a shit stain on his finger and he was trying to touch her with it. "You're not putting *that* on my tongue!"

"*Com'n*," Gabe reasoned. "Don't be gay!"

He barged passed her defense and put the square right on the center of her tongue.

"Oh my God. It tastes like pennies," she confessed.

"Just keep it on your tongue until it dissolves," I said. "It'll be all right, Milada. I promise."

I wanted to tell her there was something about her personality that was really scaring me, some type of communication break-down between us, but I knew it would spoil everybody's mood if I did, so I kept quiet.

Gabe put a dose into my mouth Communion-style and I thought of where the tweezers must have come from. I pictured Gabe picking at his toes with them and I almost wanted to uncork my eyes from their sockets.

We all dropped our tabs and went about our business, which is what was supposed to happen. You just do your thing and keep your eyes off the clock and then— **WHAM!** It hits you pretty much all at once. If you don't know, it takes anywhere between a half-hour to an hour for it to kick in, sometimes it can take longer. And when it does kick in it's like bunches of laughter and excitement and raw adrenaline rushing over you, like, as if in the form of warm water being dumped all over your body, over and over again.

We were all still in the livingroom just kicking it and after *Cruel Summer* ended then *One More Night* by Phil Collins started playing. It was only a minute or two after we all dropped and Milada already started asking questions.

"I don't feel it! Leslie, is it working for you?"

I rolled my eyes and Jacob shouted at her, "Goddammit, *Biatch!*" He had heard enough. "It takes a while, Milada!"

"*Sorry*," Milada was embarassed.

"You don't have to be sorry," I told her. "He yells at everybody. He's crazy."

"Yeah. He's crazy all right," Gabe cut in. "Once he tortured and killed four cats in the alley behind school."

"Gabe," The Brain yelled. "Shut the fuck up! I just dropped **Acid** and if you fuck my trip up with you're creepy talk you know I'll be choking you to death! I'll cut off your fucking air supply!"

"I love that band," Leslie let us know.

"Whachew talkin bout, Gabe," Jacob asked. "I didn't kill no cats!"

"He's not talking about anything even remotely true, Milada," I told her. "Are you, Gabe? Tell her, dickhead!"

"Goddamn. I'm just fucking around. You fellas don't have to get all pissed."

"Gabe," Jolene cut in. "It's over. Just take it back."

"All right. I take it back."

Meanwhile Milada was just plain speechless from what Gabe said and from the anxiety and anticipation of an unfamiliar psychedelic experience. I almost felt sorry for her. But then again, I almost didn't.

A half-hour had gone by and we were all outside smoking cigarettes. Even those of us who didn't normally smoke were smoking, just because during this important hour we all wanted to stick together with everything we did. None of us were tripping yet, but the new-found sense of togetherness that didn't exist before we dropped told us all the shit was kicking in big time. We had mysteriously become a tribe. It was only a matter of time now. In fact, from the way I was beginning to feel, I could tell without a doubt it was only a matter of minutes before the circus came to town. We were all so wrapped up in our conversation, yet no could pay attention to anybody else. Nobody could listen. We were all just telling long-winded stories all at the same time. There was no taking turns like you'd expect in a normal conversation. And nobody could finish a point or a story or even a sentence or a thought. Things were left hanging.

"So, Ray," Jacob put me on the spot. "Tell us about Seattle."

"Seattle," I questioned at first, and then began to explain. "Seattle's a pretty cool place. You dudes would love kicking it there."

"Why," Erin was genuinely curious.

"Why? Because Seattle has everything you could ever want— opportunity, nature, a nightlife, low crime and peace and quiet. Oh,

and the air is so *unpolluted* that you can tell. I mean it's really fresh air, and there are mountains, volcanoes, and even waterfalls—fucking waterfalls! There are cougars and coyotes in the fucking woods! And get this, everybody in Seattle pronounces their words correctly when they talk. All the white people do at least."

"What do you mean," The Brain kept it going.

"For example: listen to Jacob talk—"

"What the fuck is you talkin about, *Biatch*!"

"Just hear me out, Jacob. You guys hear that? People here gotta accent."

The thought of me comparing them with Jacob Drake caused everyone to laugh. It was funny to them.

"Ok, ok, ok. Maybe he's an extreme example. Anyway, we talk funny compared to other people in the country. We use a lotta slang and cuss words and it's so normal that we don't even notice. In Seattle people talk so soft and perfectly I can't even understand the motherfuckers, so not only can I not understand them, but I can't hear them either. Half the fucking time I'm just nodding my head and saying the word *hella*, which is the code word in Seattle."

"That's heavy shit," The Brain agreed. "But we talk funny and they look funny, ain't it?"

"Well," I smiled at Leslie. "If you wanna get technical, and I'm not referring to any person in this group, but comparatively people around here look funny."

"What! Now he's burning everyone in the hood. Everyone's at risk," Jacob started wigging out. "*Whoa*!"

"Hey now," I tried to slow shit down.

Gabe sang out, "*Hey now. Hey now. Don't dream it's over!*"

I lauged at Gabe and tried to continue, "Hear me out for a second and I'll give you a very reasonable explanation."

"This better be good," Leslie Hipp warned me.

I almost laughed it off because, next to Jacob and his afro, she was the funniest looking person there. At least Jacob is actually a handsome dude. It's just that the afro looks whack.

"Ok," I said. "Here's three solid reasons, and they're, like, cause and effect, ok? For starters, the Ozone Layer here is all chewed away by all of the pollution, which causes the sun to beat down on us all summer, which in turn causes our skin to age a lot quicker."

"I call bullshit," Gabe shouted quickly. "What are you a fucking scientist?"

"What do you mean you call *bullshit*," I demanded.

"Bullshit!"

"Yeah," Leslie tried to prove me wrong. "The sun makes your skin like leather, and that preserves you—doesn't it everybody?"

"Did you learn that from watching Baywatch," I asked. "Hello, in the real world too much exposure to the sun is extremely damaging to the skin. Everybody knows that. How do I know? Well, other than within intelligent cultures it's common knowledge, I read books!"

"I call bullshit too," The Brain shouted at me. "He only reads the USA Today Sports Section."

"Fuck you guys!"

"Ok, ok, ok," Jolene calmed everyone down. "I actually agree with Ray, but let's hear the other two reasons why people in The Region look so funny. Give him a chance to bail himself outta this one."

"Yeah, let's hear it," Leslie prodded.

"I don't think I look very funny at all," Milada defended herself. "Do I look funny to you, Ray?"

"Ask me next time we're in a really dark movie theater together," I said like a dick. "I'm not scared. I'll explain."

"Oh, what a dick," Erin labled me.

"Hey!"

"Look. Look. Look and listen. I'm fucking kidding. Chill the fuck out, everybody. Ok now, here's the two other scientifically proven reasons why people in The Region look funny as hell. Here goes. One—"

"This is number two," Leslie corrected me.

"Two," I yelled. "A very poor diet!"

"What," Gabe questioned. "How the hell do you know what people eat?"

"What nothing," I stopped him cold. "What did you have for lunch today? You had a fucking greasy-ass Polish sausage and a large

French fries, and you washed it down with a super colossal Coca–*fucking*–Cola!"

"I had chicken tacos," Milada let everyone know.

"*Crap!*"

"It's not crap! Tacos are good for you."

"Not fucking chicken tacos from Taco Bell," I said. "Look. Most people in Seattle are vegetarians. What's a vegetarian," I asked everyone.

"*Uh*, someone who doesn't eat meat," Erin slurred like a smart–ass.

"Right. Someone who doesn't eat fatty, greasy, bad-for-you meat from Taco Bell!"

"You eat McDonalds three times a week," Jacob busted me.

"So what!"

"Yeah," Milada added. "And what's with you getting hot-wings at KFC the other week? I saw him there. 20-piece hot-wings and a large Coca–*fucking*–Cola!"

"But I'm not a hypocrite!"

"You're totally being a hypocrite, hoss," The Brain yelled at me. "You're criticizing people who eat the same shit you do, and by the way I had a fucking chef salad for lunch today and none of you cock-suckers can tell me that's bad for you!"

"I'm not criticizing. I'm proving a point. I would expect *you* to know the difference!"

"I know the difference when I smell some bullshit!"

Everybody laughed at me and it became clear they were starting to gang up on me. It was a seven on one debate.

"What's the third reason, hotshot," Gabe set me up for more abuse.

"I don't know if you guys can handle the third reason."

"That's cause there ain't a third reason," Jacob called me out. "You got nothing, Ray! Nothing!"

"Watch it, Jacob," I warned. "You, outta everyone, should fear the third reason. Look. You guys are obviously taking offense to my purely diplomatic and semi-politically correct point of view."

"Nobody's taking offense," Jolene told me. "We're just giving you a hard time."

"Tell us," Leslie prompted me.

"Tell us the third reason," Milada insisted. "I'm interested."

"Ok," I smiled. "The third reason is this ... *inbreeding!*"

"Oh my God! I can't believe you just said that," Leslie shouted at me. She was laughing so hard she almost fell outta her lawnchair.

"I'm serious. What's Granite populated with? Second generation hillbillies that's what. What's a hillbilly? A farmer who lives out in the boonies. What happens when farmers live in the boonies? They fuck their first cousins and sisters out of necessity! Inbreeding!"

"I call *bullshit*," Jacob slammed me.

"You should talk," I told him.

"Whatever. You're a Pollack!"

"I bet any money there's somebody in this yard who has parents or grandparents who are first cousins."

"Nobody here has that problem," Leslie assured me.

"Well," I continued. "Nobody's gonna admit it. Too much sunburns and greasy Polish sausages and inbreeding equals X-Files-type characters equals somebody in this room and a majority of the population in this second generation hillbilly town."

"I call *such* bullshit," Erin said and we all started laughing. It was funny to all of us. "I think you're the one who is inbred, Raymond!"

"*Uh*, excuse me," I explained. "I was born in a big city. I was born in Chicago, ok? Not only are my parents not cousins, but they are so unalike they hate each other's guts and they're as divorced as you can possibly get."

I was really starting to feel body-buzzed. I looked at my watch and saw it was forty minutes later from when we all dropped.

"Let's play Truth or Dare," Gabe insisted.

"No way," I stopped him. "Don't even start that dumb shit."

"Why not," Jolene asked me. "Something to hide? Some gross family secret?"

They all laughed at me.

"Absolutely not," I flat-out insisted. "Every time I play this game somebody ends up being publicly humiliated and I don't know about you guys, but that ain't what I wanna see while I'm taking **Acid**."

"He's gotta point," The Brain agreed. "I don't feel like seeing that shit either."

"Ok, ok, ok," Leslie bargained. "How about a modified version of Truth or Dare?"

"What do you mean," Erin asked her.

"I mean no humiliating dares. We all judge whether it's too humiliating or not. Basically, if you wouldn't be caught dead doing it, then it's too much. But if not, then it's perfectly legal."

"Would you be caught dead making out with Milada," I asked Leslie.

"*Gross*," Milada yelled.

"Gross for her," I flipped the coin.

"That's not *too* gross," Leslie actually admitted.

"*Hah*! Lesbian," I called her. "I can't wait for your turn. Let's fucking do it! But wait a second. Is everybody feeling what I'm feeling? I'm about to peak. I'm fucking buzzing—"

"Me too," Jacob yelled.

"I'm well on my way," The Brain let everybody know.

"I'm not sure," Milada was confused. "But I feel totally weird. Is that what it is? Feeling totally weird?"

"I'm about to zoom outta here," Jolene laughed.

"So am I," Erin was freaking and peaking.

"I'm bonkers," Gabe added. "But that ain't nothing new."

"Oh," Leslie screeched. "We're all tripping! What are we waiting for, Ray?"

"Hold on. I'm gonna do a fun little experiment."

I walked inside and turned off the radio.

"What are you gonna do, Raymond," Erin followed me inside.

"I know what he's doing," Gabe got excited. "Let's all go in. He always does this when we dose. It's awesome!"

"Ok," I tried to calm everybody down. "Erin, I need your help. And we have to hurry before everybody's too far gone. Help me turn all the lights off, but leave this one above the table on for right now. Everybody sit at the table for a sec. Chill out. Gabe, just act like you're gonna chill out."

Erin and I turned all the other lights off and we all sat at the table.

"Ok," I cautioned. "I'm gonna flip this last switch in a second and it's gonna be totally dark, but here's the rules of the game. No one can talk. I just want you to look, ok, and listen. Look and listen," I repeated. "Everybody got that?"

They all agreed.

Then Leslie excitedly chirped, "Just do it already!"

"Ok, ok, ok. Here goes," I said. "You guys are gonna love this. I swear! Ready?"

"Com'n!"

"Do it!"

I flipped off the last light above that table. Everybody followed orders perfectly as pitch black blanketed the room. It was a glorious moment as the spirit shapes that only live in darkness danced in front of our eyes and we listened to sounds we'd never listened to before, the sounds that only blind people can usually hear. The clock ticked repeatedly, and the tick-tock of it echoed like eight millimeter filmed Nazi troops marching, only more pleasant. Cars whizzed by outside. The house creaked and then settled in the wind, and we listened to each other breathe. An owl hooted outside and everybody freaked and started tripping over each other in a panic so I turned the light back on, which only sent our peak into full-speed as we all celebrated everything that ever existed all at once. I put on a Janis Joplin CD and hit the **NEXT** button on the stereo until it played *Summertime*. We were having the time of our lives; we were outta our minds.

An **Acid** trip is something like a dream. It's about as real and concrete as our normal unconscious dreams. You remember the trips in absolute detail the next morning. As the next day ends you only remember about half of the trip. And as more time piles on top of your memory the trip almost completely fades into an abyss and is eventually forgotten. Then nothing is left but flashes of images that may or may not be true.

I remember the television was showing some old black and white movie about a robot that wanted to be human. The moral of the story was the robot wanted to be a good robot, but it wasn't always that easy on a count that he wasn't human and couldn't properly understand how to act out the right feelings. Sometimes he was a bad robot and he'd hide in the bushes at the park and try to pounce on little children and women. Other times he was kind. Compassionate. I thought the robot was gonna turn real if I kept watching so I turned it off and I decided to run around the back yard for a little while. I thought maybe I'd even climb a tree. Gabe was outside and I asked him if he wanted to climb a tree with me. He was scared though, and he didn't wanna go climbing with me, and I suddenly wanted to include everyone into some kinda experience. I figured we should all play a game. And I wanted to bring this idea up to Gabe with an **Acid**ic exaggeration of enthusiasm, only I wasn't sure what kinda game we should play.

"I got it," Gabe yelled and then he was afraid he was being too loud so he grabbed me and whispered into my ear, "Let's play kick the can."

He smiled at me and I could see the pores on his face breathing and the little wiry hairs of his eyebrows seemed to dance to the music coming from inside the house, which was *Betterman* by Pearl Jam. The Brain was inside dancing around, but how did Gabe know that I wanted to play a game? I hadn't even told him yet.

"Gabe," I whispered back. "Kick the can is the best idea I've ever heard and I gotta tell you: I've never heard a whisper like that before. It was, like, mysterious and blunt and creepy. You catch my drift?"

He grabbed my shoulders and probably shook me violently although I was too buzzed to notice and he yelled into my face, "All we need is ... a can!"

"You're exactly right! I bet there's a can outside here in the yard somewhere. All we have to do is find it. You look in the bushes and I'll look up in this tree here—"

"Ok, ok, ok, ok, ok, ok, ok, ok, but I have to ask you. Your hair, it's sticking out all over the place. And why aren't your lips moving when you talk? I think we're communicating with, like, telepathy."

"Yeah, Ray. Your lips are moving right now and you're not even talking so what do you call that?"

"Yo," a deep voice called to us.

Gabe and I turned and looked at the person. His eyes were like little flashlights shining into our faces. Gabe and I froze.

"It's me ya assholes. It's Jacob!"

"Jesus," I said. "Jacob. Your fucking eyes are, like, flashlights!"

"I know it," he said. "I was just reading the Bible I found by the couch. Sombody must've put it there on purpose. I opened it up at random. I threw it against the wall and it fell onto the floor. And I picked it up. It was tuned into Revelations. I tried to read, but the words started skipping all over each other so I had to stop, but I felt the Holy Spirit kinda suck all the badness outta me, like, I think I'm the purest form of man that ever lived."

"That's totally rad," Gabe told him. "That's totally rad. That's totally rad. That's totally rad."

"Jesus, Jacob," I was blown away. "That's incredible! Tell me what your message is."

"My message?"

He paused for a second or two before answering. Gabe wiped the sweat from his face with his sleeve.

"My message is: we gotta candle burning upstairs in Erin's room. We ain't got much time. Everyone who's everyone is there and they wanted me to come and find you two. They sent me on this wild goose-chase, but everywhere's it was dark and I wasn't sure if I could ever find you guys."

"Oh my God, Gabe," I whispered. "Did you hear him? There's a candle. Did you hear that?"

"Can you show us where it is, Jacob," Gabe asked. "Can you? Can you? Can you? Can you? Can you?"

"Shit yeah. Follow me," he instructed us and he led us through the dark house.

In the livingroom someone had turned the television back on and the robot was sitting with a pretty girl by a lake and they were holding hands. There was a line of dialogue I caught as we tiptoed upstairs.

The robot told the girl, "Even machines need love and understanding, Heather."

Gabe's Swatch-Watch was glowing in the dark and as he swung his arms the beam of light created this solid arc of spirit. They were tracers. They were really heavy tracers and it was at that moment that I came to the conclusion that my money to buy all the **Acid** was well spent.

I'd buy **Acid** *like this for a perfect stranger,* I thought. *I'd be doing them a favor.*

We stopped in front of a closed door upstairs.

Jacob briefed us before we went inside.

"So look here. This is Erin's room. There's a candle in there, ok. Are you guys absolutely sure you're ready for this?"

"I've never been more ready than I am now," Gabe said. "I'm ready. I'm ready. I'm ready. I need to pee."

"I'm ready too, Jacob," I let him know. "I don't need to pee."

I took a deep breath as Jacob turned the doorknob. I swore I could hear the rushing of all the oceans with every breath I took. As the door opened the sound of music came creeping out. A candle flickered in the center of the room. My friends were around the flame and music notes danced over their heads. The song was *Never Tear Us Apart* by INXS.

"You guys are the most beautiful angels I've ever seen," I told everyone. "All I feel from this circle, for the first time in my life, is pure joy. I feel joy that dances on with the sounds that float by over our heads."

"I know, Raymond," Erin looked me in the eyes. "That's why we called you two. We wanted to share this with you."

"I'm tripping my fucking balls off," The Brain yelled. "*Whoa!*"

The candle on the floor might as well have been a bonfire because that's the way I saw it. And the girls danced around it like it was some kinda huge inextinguishable oil-drum fire. I don't like to dance, but I was digging what was going on around me. Gabe flipped on a small reading lamp and was scrolling through Erin's CD collection and I took a seat at the desk. I pulled out my weed sack and pinched a big joint's worth and scattered the buds onto the desk as I surgically removed the stems and seeds.

I glanced over at Jacob. He was sitting, like, an orphan around the candle and he was resting his chin on both hands with his arms based firmly in on his knees. He seemed mesmerized and completely confused. The Brain was just chilling the fuck out on the bed, pupils like outer-space black holes and he was drooling over the dancing girls. I wasn't all that impressed by the show, which was why I decided to roll a phatty to try to enhance my mood.

If you've seen one Indiana girl you've seen them all, I thought. *Same old damaged hair. Same old tired eyes. Same old sunburned and peeled and spotted skin.*

At least that's what I saw under the magnifying glass that was my imagination. I pulled out a ZigZag leaf and piled the shake along its crease and I rolled up a sturdy joint. I had plenty to smoke, so I threw my manners out the window and I lit it and did myself the honors of taking the first hit, and then the second, and the third before I passed it on to Jolene as she strutted by with her body twitching to the beat. I had to take three hits because with eight people in the room that thing would most likely be a burnt up shriveled roach by the time it cycled around to me again. I didn't really mind though. I just wanted everyone to get along. I wanted them to just have a good time. I can't relax unless people around me keep chilling. So I would always deputize myself as the stabilizer.

Gabe had started playing some Digital Underground, the *Sex Packets* album. Erin swayed towards me and grabbed my hand, indicating that she wanted me to dance with her, but I wasn't having it. I absolutely hated to dance to the point where it's like a phobia and I kept pulling my hand away, trying to be nice, and praying that she'd leave me be alone. I'd feel more comfortable running around town naked than I would having to dance in front of a bunch of other dudes. The third time she tugged on my arm I became frightened and I jerked my arm back and snapped angrily.

"Fucking let go of me!"

The music was so loud that I didn't even make a scene. I yelled as loud as I could and the only person who even noticed was Erin. She gave me an expected, extremely negative, reaction as she huffed and sighed and shot me her dirtiest look. She wanted to play hardball so she went straight to The Brain and offered him the same dancing arm tugging gesture. The Brain obliged and started laying down his groove with Erin. I wasn't gonna take it sitting down so I got up and asked Milada if she wanted to go and sit outside with me.

"Hey," I spoke loudly in her ear to drown out the music. "What do ya say we go check out the back yard?"

Milada was totally off her rocker. "Ok, daddy," she said to me in a daze.

I didn't know if she was calling me daddy to be cute or if she was just insane and (seriously) I didn't care. She had **Acid** for blood now and I'd bet she would've gone outside with me even if I told her that I wanted her to drink my piss. Milada got up and walked out with me and I even shot Erin a dickish wink as I followed Milada outta the room and closed the door behind me.

"Take that whore," I screamed once we were in the hallway.

"What," Milada asked me. "What's wrong?"

The hallway was real dark. Neither of us wanted to attempt any navigation without finding and turning on the light. We were both feeling the wall up and down looking for a switch, but we didn't have any luck whatsoever.

"This is *sooo* stupid," I grieved in frustration. "I can't see straight. Isn't there supposed to be some kinda universal spot for a light switch. Like, I thought they regulated this shit."

"You mean where to put light switches?"

"Yeah, like, there should be a law to keep people from breaking their necks."

"There's not. You know that. You know you can't just put a switch wherever it's convenient. It all depends on how the house is wired. In an old house like this it could be anywhere."

"How do you know this?"

"You taught me, daddy. You're an electrician."

"No shit," I asked. "I am?"

I reached into my pocket and pulled out the lighter and struck a flame that illuminated the hallway in a soft orange light.

"How's this? Scooby-Doo style."

"That's way better," she said as I followed her down the steps.

She turned on a small lamp near the kitchen.

"It's weird, Milada, how calm and quiet it is down here. Upstairs in that room it's, like, a circus right now."

Both Milada and I were slowly starting to come down. Milada was coming in and out of reality and I was coasting down a smooth slope.

"I know. It's *sooo* annoying isn't it, with everybody jumping around and acting obnoxious?"

"Very."

"Hold on, daddy! I wanna get my jacket before we go outside. It might be cold."

"Holy shit," I blurted. "That reminds me. I'll be right back."

I ran upstairs and darted into the hallway. I flipped on the light and opened the closet door. And there it was just as I had imagined. My black leather jacket, hanging on a wire hanger, undisturbed and giving forth its familiar leather smell. I pulled it outta the closet and slipped it off the hanger and I put it on.

"Delightful," I whispered to myself and I trotted back downstairs and managed to catch the quiet sound of Milada opening the sliding glass door that led into the back yard.

"Hold that door, sweetie," I called to her and I hurried to follow. "Thanks."

"Don't mention it."

Outside I zipped up my jacket, "Jesus, it is pretty cool out here tonight. Spring's taking its damn sweet time getting here."

"Hey, do you think you could walk me home, daddy," Milada asked me.

At first I was confused and thought I had said something that offended her.

"Sure," I said automatically. "Something the matter?"

"Oh no," she insisted. "It's just that I have a curfew. Mom is expecting me. See," she held up her watch. "It's nearly midnight and I have to be home by then. You don't have to, I mean, I only live around the block. It's just that it's kinda scary around here at night, especially with that freak on the loose, the one in the papers."

"Of course I'll walk you home. God, I wouldn't have it any

other way."

"Thanks, daddy," she said sweetly and we started walking around the side of the house towards the street.

It reminded me of when I took a whiz in Sydney's car the other night.

"What are you smiling about," Milada asked me.

"*Me*," I questioned. "Oh. I was just thinking about something a friend of mine did the other day. I'd tell you about it, but I guess you'd have to be there to get it."

"Oh," she said quietly. "It's so nice and peaceful around here at night, isn't it?"

"Yeah, as peaceful as it's gonna get I guess."

We walked for a while and didn't say anything to each other. I was thinking about jail and worrying about going to court. I wondered what would happen to my life if the judge sentenced me to more time.

I'd leave the state if I could, I thought to myself.

"I think it's nice when people don't have to talk to each other all the time," she said.

"*Huh?*"

"Well, I was thinking how when people don't really know each other, like us, they're always trying to out chat the other, each person playing off the last thing the other said, always trying to top it with something a little more interesting. You know, one person talks about their grandmother's bad hips and then the other person has to tell about their grandmother's amputated limbs, and then it just gets totally stupid after that."

I laughed and said, "Or when somebody tells you about a near death experience and you cut in with a story about how you actually were dead for thirty seconds and then came back to life. You think that one would be hard to top and then the other joker starts telling about how his cousin actually is dead and comes back every now and then to haunt the family on holidays."

I smiled knowing that I was just playing on her theory. It was true though. She was right. People seemed to do that shit all the time.

"See, you're doing it right now."

"I know, but I'm doing it on purpose, for amusement purposes. Strictly for entertainment."

"I see," she sighed.

"You know, when I was a kid, about five or six or something, I used to hide in my house and wonder how long it would take for my parents to notice I was missing."

"*Really*," she asked, like I had said something strange.

"Really," I insisted. "Sometimes I'd wait in a closet or under a table for hours. After a while I'd start crying and just give up."

"Oh my God. That's *sooo* sad, daddy."

"Stop calling me that, Milada. My name is Ray. I ain't your daddy."

"Sorry, I didn't realize. What am I calling you?"

"You keep thinking I'm your dad."

"No I don't. You're Ray. I know that."

"*Well.*"

"No really. It's sad, but that's nothing. When I was a kid I'd just run away into the woods for days—"

"Shut the hell up," I joked. "You're doing it right now. I knew you would so I was just setting you up."

After a about thirty seconds of silence Milada said, "So is it true?"

"What?"

"Did you hide just to see if people noticed you were gone or not?"

"Oh, yeah. It's true."

"That's really sad."

Milada started walking into a yard and I noticed it was her house. A white flashing memory washed over me and temporarily blinded me from the dark reality that night. For a brief moment I was reliving the first time I had seen Milada that day when Erin had picked her up for school. That was the day when all of my troubles started.

"You can come into my yard. It's ok," she said like I was strange.

"Oh. Jesus Christ. I'm sorry. This **Acid** is making me space out a little," I admitted as I walked towards her. "Are you still feeling anything?"

"I'm not sure, but it's hard to say. Everything feels normal except it doesn't feel like it's really happening. It's kinda like a dream where everything actually makes sense for a change," Milada blew her breath into the wind and watched it turn into a white cloud in the chill. "It's getting cold again."

"I know."

"What about you, Raymond? Are you still feeling it or..."

"I'm feeling it. Most definitely. I'm just not completely messed up anymore. I like how you described it, about the dream. Even though **Acid** is really messed up to take for your body, I love doing it sometimes because there's this part of the experience, like, right now where I actually have self-confidence. I actually feel, like, I've got the entire world figured out. I guess if it's true that people never really know the truth about why this universe exists until you die, well this is as close as it gets to true wisdom—for me at least. The problem is I always forget all the profound secrets I figured out by the next day. I'm sure by tomorrow everything will be just a fuzzy kinda recollection. You know what song is in my head right now?"

"What," Milada asked as a little cloud of mist escaped from her lips.

"*Time After Time*, by Cyndi Lauper."

"That's a good song."

"Sometimes it is," I murmured. "Sometimes."

"So what are you gonna do for the rest of the night? Going back to Erin's to hang out?"

I looked off into the trees above. I've always been easily mesmerized by leaves rustling around.

"I don't know."

"Do you feel like hanging outta little more, like on the steps here?"

"Sure, but don't you have to be getting in, it's almost—"

"I'm home. It's ok. I just have to be on the property by a certain time. We can hang out and talk outside if we're quiet."

"Jesus, are we talking too loud?"

I got paranoid at that idea. It's almost impossible to judge the volume of sound while taking **Acid**. Sometimes every sound seems magnified.

"No, I don't thinks so. I was just saying."

I stood and thought about it for a moment or two and then decided maybe not.

"Maybe not, on second thought," I said. "It's just that I better be going also. I've gotta long walk home and I wanna make the journey before the cops come out looking for strays. I could do without any trouble at this point."

"Ok," she understood. "How is your face healing by the way? You don't look like anything even happened to you, except for that black eye."

"I don't bruise very easily, but I've got some stitches inside my mouth."

I brushed my tongue up against them and probed to see if they still hurt. They still did a little bit.

"That sucks. I still can't believe Erin let that happen to you."

"It wasn't her fault really. I mean, I kinda did my part to let things build up to that point, with what happened with that girl Ari. I should know better than to get mixed up in other people's business."

"Yeah, but I think Erin let things get outta hand with the rumors about you and her."

I smiled as if I knew what she was talking about and then when I realized that I didn't I asked, "What rumors are those, about us, like, ... liking each other?"

"*Uh*, it's a little more complex than that," she laughed. "You can't expect me to believe you haven't heard."

"*Um*, but I haven't heard. Tell me. What's supposed to be going on with us?"

"God, Ray. Wake up and smell the coffee. Do you think Jeremy attacked you because he heard you liked Erin? Lot's of guys like Erin because of the way she comes across to most boys, but Jeremy Otsap doesn't go attacking every guy who likes her."

"Ok, this is getting interesting. Seriously, I wanna know. Tell me."

"Oh gosh, I can't. How can you not know? Give me some

guesses because I feel stupid just hinting around about it. Because, what if it's true? It might really gross me out if it was the truth and not just a rumor."

"Ok," I sighed and sat on the lawn and stared back up at the trees. "Now you're going too far. I wanna know. What's the stupid-ass gross rumor about her and me. You *have* to tell me. There's no way of getting outta it now. Tell me, now. Please, I can't take it anymore."

There was a cracking noise like airtight seals busting from some-body coming from the front door. The foreign noise scared the crap outta me and I pretty much leapt to my feat and was ready to run. The door moved and a man, who I guessed was the father of the house, pushed the storm door open and grunted, "Milada, that you?"

"Yes."

"It's late," he said and he took a moment to look me over. "Who's you're friend?"

"This is Raymond. He goes to my school."

"Hello, sir," I said with my pupils as big as outer-space black holes, absorbing all the light around my body until they were re-spectable looking voids. My hair must have gone wild with **Acid** and my skin felt pasty and almost translucent. I felt as if I must look horrible. "Nice to meet you."

He stared me down and said, "Yeah, well," he paused. "It's getting late."

"Ok," she said. "I'll be there in a second."

"Just hurry up. You're keeping your mother up."

"*Ok*," she said again like a snob, dragging the word out with a whining tone.

He closed the door and turned on every outside light. Being around sober adults while I was tripping never seemed to come easy for me. I started backing outta the driveway while I told Milada that I'd see her later.

"Bye, Raymond," she whispered. "Call me, ok?"

"I don't have your number. If you give it to me now you know I'll loose it. I'm a stoner."

"You can find it," she said. "Get it from Erin, maybe."

She was smiling like a cunning hand-drawn cat from an old cartoon. She was practically daring me to call her, thus allowing her manipulative self to shine through like a blinding feminine laser.

Let the games begin, I thought.

Goddamn, I forgot to stay long enough for her to tell me the rumor about me and Erin.

42

The main thing I noticed on my walk home from Milada's house that night was how dark it was outside. It was as if the sun had never existed in the first place. It was a long walk home, at least a coupla miles, and I would've never attempted that sorta trek if I weren't jacked to the gills with the speed laced **Acid** that I took earlier. Every few blocks or so I would jog until I needed a breather. I had to get home as soon as possible. That was my main priority since I had to stay outta jail. It was only a matter of time before the cops started sniffing around for fresh meat caught out past curfew.

I jogged past Erin's backyard and heard my friends as they huddled around in the grass and whispered secrets and profound thoughts to each other, things that would easily be forgotten in twelve hours. They seemed to be in the middle of their post trip huddle where things are muttered that would never be said under normal circumstances. It was a strange night and even their soft secret words seemed to float on forever and never die out. I was kinda tempted to join them in their seclusion just because of the shear danger that awaited me on those loose and lonely streets, but for lack of better judgment I ran on, cutting in and outta the streetlights and diving into the bushes to avoid close calls as cop cars zipped around corners outta nowhere.

Just to kill time, I began to pretend I was some kinda secret agent that was caught behind enemy lines. I moved through the streets as fast and as quietly as possible, never snapping a twig or kicking a pebble. I used stealth as I crept through Main Street Park and past some older kids who where hanging around a few parked cars as they smoked joints and did key-bumps of coke. I actually think one of them noticed me sneaking around and yelled something at me, but I just pretended it never happened. Nobody ever sees a secret agent. Besides, I was halfway home already, halfway to freedom. I was getting cold and I zipped my leather jacket all the way up to my throat and flipped my collar up even though it probably looked Fonzarelli-style gay. The desire I had for playing video games and smoking pot and for some heat was so overwhelming that I bolted into a strenuous running pace for the last mile. I couldn't remember the last time I had so much stamina in my lungs. I ran hard, taking mechanical breaths as I watched each foot outstretch the other in endless repetitions.

A little over five-minutes later I safely trotted into the parking lot of my apartment complex, breathing so heavily I thought I might suffocate from complete exhaustion. I stood hunched over with my palms pressed against my knees and looking up at my place. I cleared my throat and spat a huge glob of smoked by-product mucus onto the pavement. The livingroom light was on. Both my dad's and my brother's cars were parked out front. The only reason I felt bothered by this at all was because I was tripping. I wasn't worried though, because even though my dad was actually home he was most likely in bed and when he slept there was nothing that would wake him up. He usually drank himself to sleep, and on regular occasions he'd cry out words of gibberish in his sleep. My brother Terry was probably up smoking dope and watching TV and I was glad for this because I didn't think I could take being alone after my iron man-style hike home. I thought maybe it'd be cool to take some bong rips and some NHL 95 on the Sega.

The main thing I learned that night from my experience was how stupid the girls I knew were. I saw through them like never before. It was as if they all chose a different character to be, and spent all their time acting out their roles, playing off one another, and leading each other on. Nothing seemed real to me anymore. My life had become such a mess that I swore to myself, in the parking lot that I would change. I'd quit smoking weed—quit doing all drugs in fact. I was gonna get good grades in school and I'd try to get into shape both physically and mentally. I actually got on my knees and begged God for mercy, strength, and courage. I prayed with more heart than I had ever done before.

I hated who I was. Who had I been kidding all this time? For years I thought I had it all figured out. I actually thought my brain was sharp. I had been absolutely positive that all the success in this world was as good as mine, just as soon as I got outta high school, but every time I looked into the eyes of one of the phony kids in my school I saw my reflection, and there on my knees I realized the most profound thing ever: there was no difference between them and me. I was a total loser, but I was gonna change all that. Starting Monday, or maybe Tuesday or Wednesday at the latest.

43

Monday and Tuesday came and went with a flurry of joints. Over the next few weeks I accepted the fact that I was pathetic and I would have to learn to live with the realistic existence of myself. My heart had somehow, somewhere died, and I honestly stopped caring about the person I was becoming. I no longer felt comfortable being alone and I threw myself at whoever would spend the time with me. Sometimes I'd go to The Brain's house after school and I'd pull bong-loads while he talked shit about people and and strummed poorly performed Pearl Jam covers on his guitar. I'd get so stoned that I'd half sit/half lie on his waterbed and pray that the end would come soon. What with that shitty-ass place to live and all the lies and cheating and shitty guitar music I was tired of living. There just wasn't anything to do. I was bored, which is the worst thing ever.

Sometimes I'd show up at Jacob's house unannounced and watched corny love movies with him and Gisela. When they weren't around, I'd show up at Gabe's house and watch sitcoms with his All-American family. During the drive home I'd smoke two joints all by myself and I'd pass out as soon as I would hit my bed. In the morning before school I'd pull down another joint or two, repeat the process at lunch, and start working out some fellows who I could smoke out after school let out. Sometimes after classes I'd get together with some of the boys who had dropped out and we'd all meet at Stan Garcia's house for what we called a "Burn Down Session." We would pass around as many joints as we could afford, like, two or three, while we listened to bands like Alice Cooper, Pantera, Metallica, Danzig, and even Gwar—whatever was metal.

Stan lived in the basement of his grandfather's house and he had concrete floors, makeshift walls that were bed sheets hung from the ceiling, and he slept on two mattresses stacked on top of each other. No sheets were needed. He kept his clothes in unfolded piles and the whole place smelled like stale cat piss. It totally seemed that I was the only one who seemed to notice the stench. It was like they were so used to it they didn't even smell anything.

Because I felt so lonely and insecure, for the first time in my life I had begun to really seek out the love of a girl. I'm talking about True Love, not this Erin or Kim or Milada bullshit. I wanted to be in love like what I saw in movies. I didn't know any girls anymore though. I was desperate. I'd call Erin almost everyday, but she was always (according to her father) at diving practice, and she was supposed to call me back. She never would. For a fall back I called Milada, but she had gotten back together with her ex-boyfriend. He was over there the time I called and it made for an awkward, strange, and embarrassing phone call. I swore I'd never speak to her again.

I even called Kim expecting to restart some kinda relationship, even though I hadn't so much as called her since the last time she told me never to call her again. I expected too much. She politely told me that she was with somebody else now and she actually asked me, again, not to call her anymore. I couldn't believe it! After four years of on again off again relationships with her, after always leaving the door open for future opportunities—now this. I was cut off for life.

44

And then on Thursday night, March 25th, my life changed forever.

I was alone and sinking into a deep funktafied depression. A big weed drought had blown in from Mexico. I had been outta weed for two days and I couldn't find anybody who even had any scraps to smoke with me. The whole town was dry. The Poop wouldn't start anymore and I wasn't about to waste the money I had stashed away to fix it. The Poop was such a piece of shit I couldn't even get a hundred bucks if I tried to sell it.

It was almost 11:00 at night and my brother had gone back to college and my dad was back in Florida visiting his wife. I called a few people, but nobody was home. I kept listening to *Come As You Are* by Nirvana and eventually I passed out on the couch in my boxer shorts.

Suddenly there was a buzz at the door and it startled me into waking up.

There it was again: *buzz, buzz, buzz*.

I got up and pressed the **TALK** button on the intercom.

"Who is it?"

"Is Ray there," a female asked.

"This is. Who's this?"

"Jolene."

"Jolene?"

"Yeah," she was annoyed. "*Remember*? Com'n, don't play like you don't know me. It's cold out here!"

"Oh, ok, ok," I said. "Hold up," and I pressed the security button to let her in.

Even though I was only wearing a pair of boxer shorts I wasn't shy. And it wasn't because I felt hunky or anything, far from it. It was just, for some reason, I wasn't attracted to Jolene at all. It was like, thinking back now, she was probably too smart for me or too real of a person, one or the other. Not that I was a complete idiot, but I would only date stupid girls because it was the only type of girl that would buy my act. I opened the front door and let her in.

She unzipped her jacket and said, "Jesus, Ray. "It's fucking hot in here."

"Sorry," I said and I fumbled with the thermostat on the wall.

"Why the *hell* are you sorry?"

"I don't know."

"You don't *know?* Where's your clothes?"

"I was just sleeping. Sorry. What's up? What brings you around?"

I scratched my head and walked over to my jeans that were wadded up on the floor. I put them on. It's so gay now, but I also had a wife-beater shirt and I put it on. I wasn't muscular enough to really pull it off, but at least I wasn't a fat hairy bastard. So I wore the wife-beater. They're comfortable. They were kinda *in* back then since they were all the rage in California seven years before that night.

"You don't have a bag I can score do you," she asked me right away.

"Fuck no. I don't got nothing. There's a drought."

"Yeah. I know. Any coke or anything else?"

"Hell no, Jolene. What makes you think I sell cocaine anyway?"

"I don't. I was just wondering if you had any you wanted to share."

"No. Unfortunately I'm in the most horrible situation. I've been dry for days. I was actually hoping I'd be able to score something off of you."

"Well fuck," she said. "I don't have anything either. Do you feel like cruising around for something?"

"Like, now," I asked. "Tonight?"

"Sure."

I thought about it for only a second.

"Ok. Lemme get a warmer shirt on and a jacket. I don't feel much like going to school tomorrow anyway," I smiled honestly. "I've missed so many days already I might as well miss the rest of the year."

I went into my room and put on my black shirt with the American flag that said **Try To Burn** *This* **Asshole** on it. And I put on my lucky leather jacket, just in case. I looked at myself in front of the mirror briefly.

"I think I need a tattoo," I yelled as I adjusted the leather collar on my jacket. I went back into the living room and finished my statement. "Whad'ya think, *huh*? A tattoo? You got one don't you?"

"I've got three tattoos."

"No shit, of what," I asked her.

"Around my belly button," she lifted her shirt, "I've got this sun. It's kinda psychedelic and it's so hot. And on my shoulder I've gotta dove. And then I have this tribal design on the back of my calf."

"That's cool. Which is the newest?"

"The sun on my stomach."

"Yeah. What's her name just gotta tattoo also."

"You mean *Erin*," she laughed. "As if you don't remember her name."

Then she slowly walked outta the front door and I followed her.

"Why should I," I asked defensively. "There's a lotta other names I could remember before hers."

"As if you don't like her," Jolene shrugged.

I slammed shut the deadbolt with my key and I dropped them into the inside pocket of my jacket.

"*Whoa*," I said raising my palms to her. "Just because I might have liked her a little, like, *three months ago* doesn't mean I got this permanent fixation with her. She's not exactly Miss America or anything. She might not even be a miss at all for all I know. She might be lying about that too."

"*Whatever.*"

"Whatever. That's all you can say because I'm right."

We went outta the front door of my building and a gust of frosty wind whipped across my face and sent an adrenaline filled chill down my back. It was a huge blast of wind that probably blew over from the windy city to especially hit me. It bowled me over hard and I wobbled a bit.

"As a matter of fact, I gotta girlfriend anyway. And besides, I haven't even spoken to Erin in weeks. She's became, like, analogue to me."

"This way," she pointed to the other end of the parking lot.

"*Analogue*, what's that mean?"

"You never hearda analogue? She's outdated, like an Atari. Meaning only a guy who enjoys collecting old junk can appreciate the value of a girl like that. She's an old pair of sneakers, comfortable to some simple types, revolting to classy people."

"That's rude," she said. "The car's right over there parked along the sidewalk."

It was a Trans-Am or a Camaro or something. It was hard to tell in the dark. Her car looked different from what I remembered. I could have sworn she was driving a Mustang or something. She ran up to the driver's side window and rapped on it a few times and spoke loudly through the glass, "Wake up, asshole!"

This guy shot up into a sitting position. He had apparently been passed out, spreading his juiced body like Jell-O across the front seats.

"*This* ain't your car," I asked Jolene.

"Hell no," she said like this car was a piece of shit.

It looked nice to me.

"Get in," she ordered me as she walked over to the passenger side where I was standing.

I opened the car door and said to the driver, "Hey, dude. How's it going?"

"Great," he said as he turned down the volume of the stereo. *Wooden Ships* by Crosby, Stills, Nash, and Young was playing as I propped the front seat forward and climbed into the back. Jolene got in the front seat and slammed the door shut behind her.

"Shit, Ace! It's fucking *cold* outside," she shivered.

"Jesus! I'll blast the heat."

Ace flipped as many switches as he could until the air started pumping from the vents.

"What's his name," he asked her.

"Oh, sorry," she said. "Ace, this is Ray. Ray, likewise."

"Nice to meet you, man," I gestered to him and I leaned forward and extended my hand for a shake, but as soon as I did Ace punched the car into first gear and peeled out into the street. The sudden acceleration pressed me back into my seat and it pissed me off a little. I really considered working over Ace when the car stopped, but deep down I knew I was just pissed because I was so sober. If I were baked I would never get upset over such a thing.

"So, Ray," he asked me. "I haven't seen you around Granite before. Why not?"

"You just won't catch me at the bowling alley."

"You must be a new radical," he said.

The car began to drift to the side of the road, foot by foot. We got closer and closer to slamming into one of the parked cars. Ace let the car slide so far Jolene had to turn the wheel back herself and straighten out the car.

"Ace! Watch where you're fucking driving," Jolene lashed out.

"*Radical*," I mumbled to myself. "Fucking asshole, *new radical* he says. What's that supposed to mean?" I leaned forward and shouted up to them, "So where are we headed, *Face?*"

"*Ace,*" he yelled at me. "My name is Ace!"

"Ok, Ace. Please chill," Jolene scolded.

"What a stupid name."

She turned to me to answer. "We're gonna go back to Sydney's house. She had a big bash tonight. It's over now, but my car is still there, which we need to pick up, and I left a fresh six-pack of beer in the fridge. I need to grab it before somebody drinks it."

Sydney's house: My memory flashed pictures. First, of her convertible she always drives around. Then I thought of her and her friends tossing trash at me, then of me pissing in her car and slashing the tires. That was the best ever. I smiled and felt like the most evil person I knew, and it made me happy. It was funny to me. I began to imagine a setup and I wondered if Jolene would do that to me or not. I mean, she *seemed* pretty cool, but I hardly knew her at all. I started jumping to all these paranoid conclusions until I decided most likely, nobody knew who trashed Sydney's car. I sat back in my seat and tried to relax.

"Whatever happens, happens," I whispered to myself. "Gracefully."

We pulled up in front of a white house with some tacky-ass fake shudders. Ace left the engine running and didn't appear to be getting out of the vehicle with Jolene and I.

"Thanks, Ace," Jolene said as she opened the door, got out, and released the front seat to go forward so that I could squeeze out.

"Later, fuck-face," I said as I got out.

But he didn't hear me. The guy had actually passed out again and was sleeping against the window.

I stood on the sidewalk and straightened my clothes.

"Yo. Your friend is asleep again," I said to her.

"What," she gasped in surprise. "*Again?*" She leaned down to look inside the car. "Hey," she snapped and clapped her hands together a few times. "Wake up, Ace!"

"What the hell," he yelled as he startled himself into waking up again, perhaps for the last time. "I'm fine, I'm fine, I'm fine. Just leave me be. Lemme get home so I can sleep."

"Ok," Jolene said and closed the door to the car and Ace drove off into the darkness and vanished quickly, because he never did have his headlights on the whole time we were driving.

"He could have killed us," I said.

"He'll be fine," she eased, as if I was concerned about *his* well being. "He just lives down the street a ways."

We went up to the house and went in through the side door. I didn't know Sydney too well, as I've explained—and I didn't care to either. She was revolting to me and that's no exaggeration on my part. I'm not fluffing it up for the sake of drama. She sucked. Big time. She spoke with the shrieked volume of Amtrak train emergency brakes. Her hair was bleached blonde, long and straight, tired, and near her scalp was this dark colored hair tying to press out the blonde parts, like, desert grasses attempting in vain to sprout and shit. Sydney was a broad one. If she were a breakfast item she'd be thick-cut bacon. She had this great big ass, easily as wide as a thirty-inch television screen. And her legs were not long, but short and all one thickness. They were nothing but thighs all the way to the feet. Her gut was round and firm. Her arms were robust also, all biceps. And her shoulders were beefy looking and sloped out at soft angles. The worst thing about her were the stupid things she would say and how she would try to pass them off as intelligent thoughts. As if anybody wants her perspective.

When Jolene and I walked in we stepped into some type of drunken debate with no point whatsoever. Whenever you get a bunch of wasted people in a room who all think they're cool everybody yells to be heard and nobody listens to anybody else.

Here are a few examples:

"A speed trap in Valparaiso is no different from picking up a man for beating his wife in Lake Station. Both need attention." Sydney said this. She also mentioned, "If that little black boy is sitting on the side of the street because his dad hit him with a belt, maybe those black boys in Gary need a little taste of that belt instead of being able to run the streets with guns and knives and drugs, terrorizing that city."

I pretty much just smirked and went, "*Tsss* ..."

The side door led right into the living room, which was actually the kitchen, dining, and livingroom all rolled into one, divided only by the furniture and where the red carpet met the black and white checkered ceramic tile. The walls were painted off white and on them hung prints of famous paintings. Being at least a little bit cultured I recognized them all: *Portrait of a Lady*, by Leonardo Da Vinci, *The Last Judgment*, by Michelangelo, and *Puberty*, by Edward Munch. *Puberty* is a painting you can't help but masturbate to. Just kidding? It's a picture of an twelve or thirteen-year old girl sitting naked on her bed, the sheets white and shadowed in gray, the eyes of the little girl wide, eager, innocent and confused. The budding body of a young woman. Yeah. I guess it's a weird painting, but the art nerds seem to dig it.

From the looks of things, Sydney must have had *some* party that night, but it was late and most of the kids had either passed out or gone home. Inside there was only about a half dozen troopers still alive and drinking. They were listening to country songs on the radio, songs about life, classic cars, birthdays, and love.

I just kept quiet for the most part because I didn't know anyone all that well. Jolene did all the talking anyway. She was like that. This heavy girl who was slushy with beer asked if I wanted a cold one and I said, "No thanks," and she asked Jolene and she didn't want a beer either.

"We just cruised by to grab *my* beer," Jolene let her know. "I left it stashed in the fridge and I wanna take it home and save it for next time."

It was a six-pack of Old Style bottles.

Sydney looked up at me, studying me for signs of suspicion, when I asked her, "So who's the art freak in the house?"

"*Huh?*"

"You heard me, Big Time. The paintings on the wall here," I pointed with my thumb.

A kid on the couch planted a stare on me and I stared him down until he looked away.

"Oh, my mom just bought those ugly things at the thrift store," she said. "They're not even real. They're prints."

"I figured as much," I shrugged. "You know, for a woman who doesn't know much about art to stroll into a thrift store and pick out these three paintings, real or not, is kinda like winning the lottery in a sense. These paintings, even though they're fakes, are priceless even for the opportunity to look at them. Don't you agree, Homer Simpson?"

I leaned down and nudged the kid who had been staring at me.

"Yeah," he cleared his throat. "Sure. I guess."

"Whatever," Sydney said. "Don't try to act like you know what you're talking about."

After a few more minutes of small talk about high school gossip and rumors Jolene and I made an exit back out the side door and that's the first time I laid my eyes on Jolene's car in a clear way. It had an impact on me that rivaled the paintings I had just admired.

The machine, I simply thought.

It was dark red, like maroon, and with black details, and I could tell this because it was parked under the streetlight. It was like a steel predator waiting to kill.

We got in and she started the engine and the fuel-injected sound was beautiful, like a big male cat growling for sex. It was impressive. She pumped the gas and it roared louder and harder out of desperation. She kicked on the heater and we waited for the engine to warm up before we drove away. Jolene asked me if I wanted a beer and again I said no. She didn't want one either, so she took the bottles outta the paper bag and shoved each bottle, one at a time, under the driver's seat. She wanted to hide them just in case, because she was only nineteen and if we got pulled over the cop would wanna glance around the inside of the car.

"What's the use in hiding anything, I mean, really," I grumbled just to make conversation.

"Well, I just don't—"

"Hey," I lifted my hands a little. "I'm just saying, because the cops are so oppressive around here. Shit, if we get pulled over I'll bet a million bucks the assholes tear the whole car apart until they find something, anything that qualifies for an arrest. Then they'll get even more pissed off because you tried to hide the shit from them. I swear to God, Jolene. The best way to weasel out of an arrest is to tell the truth right from the beginning. I'm not saying as soon as you hand the bastard your license to start blurting out how much cocaine you got in the trunk or where you buried the dead body, not like that at all. I'm saying as soon as the cop gets serious, like, he takes off his sunglasses and asks you to step outta the car. I swear, if he starts playing twenty questions then start answering them twenty at a time."

"You wouldn't do that," Jolene laughed at me.

"I *have* done that. Tons of times," I admitted.

"*Really,*" she stared at me.

She turned the heat down a little bit. The car was warm now, but we stayed parked for the moment.

"Really. Like last year for instance," I unbuttoned both sleeves on my jacket so I could glance at my watch every now and then. "Me and Vince Bacon, you know him?"

"No," she admitted. "I've never heard of him."

"That's because he was new last year, like me. I bet you Erin knows him, but he moved back to Illinois. Blue Island."

"He was a fip?"

"*Fip?* Oh yeah, Fuckin Illinois Person. Yeah. He was."

"I hate fips."

"Anyway, me and Vince got pulled over one night. We had just picked up an ounce of weed and were gonna split it. The cop pulled us out and roughed us up a little—"

"Like how," she wanted details.

"Oh, not bad. Just shoved us a little. Nothing major, but we told the cop the truth right away, like, no bullshit, no beating around the bush. As soon as he asked for contraband we told him right were it was. No hassle."

"What happened?"

"His whole attitude changed. He arrested us and took us back to the station. He even took our coats and personal things like we were about to get booked when he started giving us this lecture about disobedience and lack of respect for ourselves, the whole shabang. He took poor Vince into this soft interrogation room and fifteen minutes later they both came out. Then he lets us go free, right? Just like that, uncuffs us and turns us loose, gives our things back and makes us promise not to screw up again. Anyway, to make a short story even shorter, we grab our belongings and get to the car when Vince reaches into his coat pocket for his keys. Guess what he found?"

"I don't know, what?"

"A quarter ounce of fucking kind buds, perfectly weighed out no less!"

"Your lying," she accused.

"No, I swear to God. You can ask the kid Vince next time you see him on the street or something. That is if you ever get to meet him. The cop took most of it, but gave some back to us."

"So what happened to the rest of the pot?"

"Hell, he kept it, held on to it, probably went home and smoked his ass to sleep."

We fell into a moment of silence.

"This is a nice car, Jolene. Is it a Mustang?"

"Yes."

"What year," I asked, even though I didn't know anything about cars. It was just a common question people ask when they discuss a particular vehicle.

"It's an eighty-nine."

"No shit. I wouldn't know and eighty-nine from a fifty-nine."

"No shit," she smiled.

"How long have you had this thing?"

"Not long. About a year. I spent my graduation money on the down payment and I gotta loan and I'm in the process of paying the rest of it off, but I still owe a shit load to the bank. At this rate I should have it paid off in about *four* years. The payments are so high too and I just had to let my insurance cancel and I'm hoping they don't notify the bank and repo my car."

"Damn, that's a long time."

"Yeah. I know, but I just love this car and it's worth it, even if I can't quite afford it. This car's my baby, Ray. Nobody drives this thing but me. I've never let anybody else drive this car."

"Shit, I could never handle a car like this, too fast. I'd be dead in a week if I had this thing to drive."

"Why's that?"

"Because, I'd wanna drive it a hundred miles an hour all the time, and eventually I'd crash and burn."

"Yeah. Well," she exhaled. "It would be a great way to go out," she said. "In your own fast car."

"Yeah. I guess. If you say so."

The car was an automatic and she put it into drive and we drove out into the darkness and took the next right around the corner.

"Let's check out and see if my older brother Shane is home," she suggested. "He might have some weed and if not we can always just drink that beer under the seat back at your place if we strike out."

Some cheesy song by Lenny Kravitz was playing. She just smiled and turned up the stereo really loud. Right after the Kravitz song ended, one more cheese-ball tune by The Beastie Boys came on. I thought it was weird that I hadn't smoked any weed in almost two days.

I thought of Ace real quick. *Who the hell is that guy? Why hadn't I seen him before? And what the hell is a new radical anyway?*

I wanted to ask Jolene about him, but the music was too loud. She wouldn't be able to hear me.

I smoked a lotta weed back then and for me not to get stoned less than five times in a day was strange, let alone two freaking days. I didn't feel bad for a change though. I felt pretty good. Being sober is just like being high when you're whacked out twenty-four hours a day. I was tripping on how good I felt. I didn't even wanna drink or smoke anything.

Maybe I'm growing up, I thought.

I didn't mind.

It's best to just let these things happen, I agreed with myself.

When we got to her brother's house nobody was home and all the lights were off. The whole place was darker than the inside of my older sister's closet with the door shut. Jolene didn't have a key and, somewhat disappointed, we went back to the Mustang and started her back up, but we stood outside in the driveway for a few minutes to have a cigarette since we couldn't smoke in the car. Besides, maybe this Shane guy, her brother, "Would be right back," she suggested.

The driveway was made of gravel and I wrote my initials in the tiny rocks with my shoe.

Jolene looked and asked, "R ... K ...that's your initials, right?"

I nodded yes and blew smoke rings that weren't very good. She smirked and wrote her initials in the driveway also.

J C

We waited about fifteen minutes. Jolene talked mostly about her boyfriend James. They had been fighting lately and she was worried because they had been together for four years and it wasn't normal for them to be fighting so often.

I told her, "Don't worry about trivial stuff and just focus on the good things, like just having someone you love and trust to be with." It was easy for me to say. "But," I continued. "On the other hand, it's not healthy to be with the same guy all through high school."

She asked me about Erin, and it made me depressed so I said there wasn't much to talk about and I changed the subject to Jeremy Otsap, and what an idiot he was.

We were both getting cold and Shane never showed up, so Jolene grabbed some paper outta the car and wrote her brother a quick note and slid it into the crack of the screen door. It would be a note that he most likely would hold on to for the rest of his life.

We got in the car and it was nice and warm because the engine had been running. I figured this was a good time to ask her to give me a lift back to the apartment, maybe I would go to school the next day after all. I was feeling pretty good and school didn't seem so bad for a change. I wasn't really tired yet, so I thought about watching a movie I had rented the day before, *Better Off Dead*, or maybe I'd play some NBA LIVE 94 on Sega, but then again, I felt too good to go home just to sit on my ass, so even though it was almost 1:00 in the morning I was still down for whatever.

"What do you say we just drive around and listen to some music," I suggested.

"Ok."

She put the Mustang in reverse and backed outta the driveway, and at the end of her brother's street we took a left up Main Street.

"So Erin tells me you two aren't seeing each other anymore."

She turned to ask and then put her eyes back on the road. We stopped at a red light.

"I guess you could say that," I shrugged. "Especially since we were never seeing each other in the first place."

"Do you still like her," she asked curiously, as if she hadn't been listening to a single word I was saying.

"I'm not sure I ever did, you know? You have to really *know* someone to, you know, *like* them."

"She really likes you. She told me today."

"Like hell she does," I laughed. "I whipped her boyfriend's ass. That night we tripped out her and I got in a fight. She won't even return my phone calls."

I didn't believe her, the Erin I knew was a liar and a whore. I thought of her kissing Jeremy Otsap, and then of when her and I when we first kissed at Ricky's house, and then of her kissing her boyfriend at one of his college frat parties. And then of me and Erin having sex real quick in her room. This girl was a germ. She was all over the place and I was onto her.

"Erin's a whore," I said rather harshly. "And I don't really care if she likes me or not."

The light turned green and we headed towards Highland in the same direction down Main Street.

"Jesus, Ray. That's my good friend you're talking about."

"Sorry, but I just don't like her, never did really."

"If you never did, then why did you two sleep together, just curious? You don't have to tell me if you don't wanna."

All of the stores were closed and only a few cars were still out this late at night. We passed a liquor store and two black guys were at the counter buying some beer. One of the guys was pointing a pistol at the clerk.

"Let's see," I said. "If I say it's none of your business, would you automatically think we did sleep together, or would you think we didn't?"

"I'd think you did. Besides, I know Erin. She's one of my best friends. If you did, I know about it already."

"Yeah. We covered that detail on trip night last week. Well, I hate to break it to you, but you don't know her as well as you think you do, because I never slept with her, ever. Believe me, I'd tell you if I did. I just kissed her a coupla times."

"I'll take your word for it, Ray," she sighed and smiled at me again in a really nice way.

I knew that she didn't believe me.

Did this girl like me? There was no way that she would, I thought. *Jolene loved James Chapman, and she wasn't a bimbo like her friend Erin.*

Only bimbos liked me. It was a strict law.

I can't imagine her wanting to cheat. She just wouldn't do that. But then again, I thought, *it is the nineties. And how well do I know Jolene?*

Not well at all.

"So what about you," I asked. "What about *your* personal life?"

We passed a cop heading in the opposite direction, but he didn't turn around to follow us, he just kept going. I watched his taillights the whole way in the side mirror until the cop disappeared over the hill. Today looking back, I wish the cop had stopped us.

"My ... *personal* ... *life*," she slurred as if she were reading a headline in the newspaper.

"Your personal life," I said it trying to mimic the way she said it, like a headline.

The radio was tuned in to WCKG, the classic rock station. Back then classic rock was still The Doors, The Grateful Dead, Led Zeppelin, and Jimi Hendrix, that sorta music. Now classic rock is U2, The Police, anything from the eighties. They were broadcasting a show called *Gettin The Led Out* where they played non-stop, back to back hits by Led Zeppelin until 2:00 in the morning. Now it was *When the Levee Breaks.*

"I gotta better idea," she said. "How about let's not."

After some silence: "Yeah, I'm sure it would end up boring me to death anyway," I predicted.

"What makes you say that," she asked. "As if!"

"Well, for one, in case you haven't noticed this is Granite, Indiana."

"Actually we're in Highland now and we're almost in Hammond."

"Ok," I said rephrasing my statement. "This is Northwest Indiana, The *fucking* Region, and there's nothing interesting about this place or any of its inhabitants. The best this place has to offer is litter, road construction and oily rivers."

"Oh, is that right, Raymond?"

"That's right."

"I'm not so sure about that. You could write a book about this place, or a movie. I mean, I know it's a dull place to some people, and believe me because I can't stand it here either, but you'd be surprised at some of the things you might hear about people around here. This place is a lotta things, but boring it ain't."

"Oh like hell," I sighed in disgust. "Nobody in their right mind would write a book about people in Granite," I smiled at my transparent reflection in the window. "Oh yeah, then tell me something about Erin," I dared. "Tell me something ... *personal.*"

"You want me to talk about my friend, like, in a *bad* way?"

"Not exactly. I guess that would be stretching the rules. How about something everybody knows about her except me."

"That's a tuff one, Ray."

"How's that? I've known her for just a few months."

"Ok, lemme think a second."

"Tell me something juicy, something, you know, interesting. Tell me something *book worthy*."

"Ok, here goes," she swallowed and smiled bashfully.

"Now we're rolling, baby," I said.

"This is something everybody knows and she wouldn't deny."

"Lemme have it. And don't con me," I cautioned. "We both know there's nothing she wouldn't deny."

"She slept with Jeremy who's her ex-boyfriend now, right?"

"Are you asking me or telling me?"

"Telling. While Derrick, who was her boyfriend at the time, was in the next room passed out drunk."

"That's kinda juicy," I agreed. "And not at all surprising I might add."

"There's more."

"Oh yeah! Now you're talking."

"Well, next day she called Derrick and dumped him."

She scratched her nose and glanced at it in the rearview mirror, probably checking for a make-up smudge, or just digging because she was jonesing to get high. "Told him something, like, she couldn't trust him, that was the reason."

"*Get out*," I scoffed. "She's telling people about trust?"

"Truth," Jolene laughed. "She told him he was too *untrustworthy*."

"That fiend! That's funny to me."

"Twelve hours later she was officially with Jeremy, saying stuff to him, like, how she was gonna love him for the rest of his life. You should have seen her blushing whenever he called, even getting tears in her eyes when she read his letters in front of us. She's such an actress sometimes I can't stand it—like, if you love somebody then you don't make such a strange public theatrical production outta their love letters to you."

"Good point."

"Thanks. And she had everyone believing it, *especially* Jeremy. He totally changed when he got together with her. I mean, he used to be so easy going and calm. Never had a care in the world."

"That doesn't sound like the Jeremy I've met," I said as I stroked my chin, faking a touch of pain and trying to add a dash of charm and wit.

"Oh, Ray, you wouldn't believe it. He turned into such a possessive freak over her. Watching her, following her—oh, the questioning he'd do to anyone who was ever even around her when he wasn't there. It was worrisome, I mean really. He's huge and was acting like a borderline psycho. That should make anyone nervous, but not Erin. She loved every minute of it, the late night drive-bys, the early morning phone calls, the threats, the shakes—"

"The shakes?"

"Yeah, *the shakes.* You know, grabbing a girl's arms and squeezing and shaking her, like, in a violent way."

"You're kidding me. What an asshole! I don't get it. Some people act like Jeremy is like this with everybody and then other people say he's only like that because of me. Don't get me wrong though. I've wanted to slap the shit out of a bitch plenty of times, but it doesn't mean I ever went and did it. Only a coward lays a hand on a woman."

"It almost makes you wanna feel sorry for Erin, doesn't it?"

"I wouldn't go that far," I laughed backwards through my nose.

"That's what she wants. It fuels her ... like desire fuels an underdog."

"She still is, right," I asked.

"Still is *what?*"

"Like *that.* Manipulative and shit."

"I don't know. You tell me," Jolene smiled.

"Most definitely."

"It gets worse. Then a few months later after she dumped Derrick, Jeremy left to go to college up in Wisconsin. He left her his car because she told him she didn't feel safe using hers and he didn't need it up at school anyway. He was planning on just leaving it parked, but he let her have the keys and drive it around, a Ford Thunderbird."

"That same one I saw him drive before?"

"Yeah, and the first night the guy is gone Erin makes plans with Derrick, told him how much she missed him and how he didn't understand how much she loved him, and that she made a huge mistake. Blah, blah, blah. They made plans. Erin hopped in the Thunderbird and picked him up."

"Where'd they go?"

"They drove to Merrillville and got a motel room and they stayed overnight. Derrick shelled out, like, seventy dollars for a room at the Red Lion."

"Such a whore."

"She's bipolar."

"That *is* interesting. I stand corrected."

"See," she smiled. "There is stuff to think about in Granite."

"Yeah right. Erin's a cheap thrill. I'll never give her a second thought. The only place a person would write about her is in a comic strip. She's not book worthy."

"I thought you two kinda *liked* each other," Jolene mentioned. "Why so harsh?"

"Shit. I thought *you* two liked each other also."

"Yeah. Well, if you think she doesn't talk behind people's backs you're crazy."

"Is that it? Is that the end of Erin's scandals?"

"Pretty much, until you came into the picture. You're the sequel. Jeremy: Psycho Jealous Boyfriend from Hell. Part 2."

"Did you hear she slept with Ricky," I asked. "Did she ever tell you that?"

"*Ricky*, your friend? That little black boy at the party a while ago?"

"He's South American. Yeah. I heard he slept with her last week."

"I never heard that, and I doubt it happened. Erin likes a lotta different guys, but I don't think she'd like Ricky. He's practically a little boy, Ray."

"He's the same age as her."

"Where did you hear that, about the sex I mean?"

"My friend Patrick told me. She called him and wanted Ricky to take her out on his boat. The rest is history. I mean, what more do you need to do for a girl like that?"

"Ray, she really likes you. At least that's what she says. She says it's different with you. You're different. I don't think the story about

Ricky is true."

"The only thing she likes about me is that it pisses Jeremy off."

"As a matter of fact, she said she was head over heels *in love* with you, just the other day."

"She said that?"

"Ray, I'm her best friend. I read the letters before she gives them to you."

"What letters," I asked trying to play stupid.

"The *love* letters."

"Oh. Oh. Oh. Those *love* letters. Now I remember."

We drove over some abandoned railroad tracks and there was a big forest-green sign that said: **WELCOME TO ILLINOIS**. The letters were made of reflective white tape and the message of our new territory flashed a blinding warning/welcome to us as we zipped by. We kept driving. Neither one of us seemed to care where we were going.

"So what else do you know about us," I nervously asked her.

"I know you weren't telling me the truth when I asked if you two slept together or not. And you said no."

"She'd be lying if she told you that," I said.

Deny until you die. That's the only way to get through it.

"Yeah. Right, Ray."

"I swear to God we didn't sleep together."

"I don't think so."

"Well, we didn't, for the record."

"Ray, why would I care if you did? Lot's of guys like Erin. Believe me, you're not the first."

"So I've heard."

"She told me everything, Ray. You had sex with her in her room the other week. It was the night we all dropped **Acid**."

"Look, Jolene," I fake-laughed. "Sometimes everything isn't shit. Whatever she told you is fine by me, because nobody ever knows the truth about anything anyway. So who gives a shit if I slept with the damn girl or not? People will believe whatever they wanna, including you. What really matters is what I believe. All these rumors in this town should be chapping my hide by now, but they never bother me, because I don't give a shit about rumors. I don't care what people say. It's funny, because now I know what Milada was talking about when she told me about the gross rumors going around about me and Erin."

"I've told you the truth about things tonight, Ray. Nothing has been said that's a rumor."

"Then why the hell you telling me?"

"Shit. I don't know. Because I feel like I can trust you. There's something different about you, Ray. It's, like, you have this seductive web for confessions, like, you're a black hole where secrets go to vanish."

"Maybe so," I whispered. "At least you better hope I am."

Over the next hour or so Jolene and I drove the deserted middle America streets past closed gas stations, stray dogs looking for garbage cans to tip, and past police cars prowling for crooks. We talked and talked. It was one of those conversations, a good one, where we both fought to be the next one to say something interesting. We were getting to know each other. I told her about my childhood, about my parents, about my brothers and sisters, about my favorite things and my least favorite things. I told her why I moved to Seattle and why I decided to come home. I explained what happened with Erin and me. I really liked Erin and I thought she liked me. Jolene said she already knew that. I told her everything, I was exposed and I hardly even knew this girl. I didn't even know her last name, just the initial, the letter C.

Jolene told me about her childhood too, and about how Granite has never changed much in her nineteen years. Just more blacks. I wasn't surprised. She told me about how her and James Chapman met and how she could never love anyone as much as she loved that boy. She told me about how someone had molested her when she was little, a secret she made me swear on my life that I wouldn't ever tell anyone. It's a secret I've kept until now. Of course, I know much more than just the statement. And I feel awful about it, but as a writer some things are necessary to tell, especially when people's lives are at stake. She told me how she wanted to be a doctor and about the college she was gonna go to and about the receptionist job she worked full-time to pay for the Mustang. I heard all about her family as well, and all about James Chapman.

"Do you mind if I smoke one of your cigarettes," I asked looking at the clock. It was just after 3:00 in the morning.

"Actually, I'd prefer if you didn't. It's the only rule I have about this car. That, and no one is allowed to drive it but me. I don't have any insurance anymore, can't afford it. I need to fnd a cheaper policy before the bank repos my car for not having coverage."

"It's cool," I said. "I don't light up very much anyway, not habitually I mean."

I put the cigarette back in the pack.

"Do you like The Dead," she asked.

"The Grateful Dead? I hate'em. They suck. There I said it. I'd be grateful if Jerry Garcia was dead. I heard one time, in this book that I read, that every new corpse in this world is like an improvement."

"I just wanna put this damn tape in. Do you mind if we listen to it?"

"No," I said. "Why should I care? Play what ever you wanna. It's your damn car."

I hated The Grateful Dead enough to where when I heard them I would get aggressively angry. I'd wanna kick the shit outta Jerry and any hippie in sight. I think what bugged me is their music sounded basically pretty bad, and their songs were no better written than Kenny Rogers' songs, yet what they had that Kenny didn't even come close to having was a huge loyal drugged-out uneducated following, a big-time bandwagon. The Grateful Dead had perhaps the greatest dipshit flock of posers in rock-n-roll history. I couldn't tell all of that to Jolene though, especially after she confessed everything to me from the beginning to the end.

"Jesus, how the hell did we get this deep into Illinois," I yawned. "It's past 3:00 in the goddamn morning ... Frankfort," I whispered.

I read the sign on a one-level brick building:

FRANKFORT DRY CLEANERS

"I don't even know where the hell we are. I'm completely lost,"

I admitted. "If you were to drop me off right here and you made me try to find my way home without asking for any directions, I'd never make it."

A few more seconds of silence crept silver-fish style.

She said nothing.

"It's funny when you think about it," I spoke up. "If you were to close my eyes, spin me around about a hundred fucking times and place me in the pitch black darkness anywhere in The Region I'd know right where I was. I could tell you instantly where's north, south, east or west. And Illinois is, like, what ... ten miles away? The border you wouldn't even notice if the signs weren't there. Do the same thing to me and stick me anywhere on this side of the stateline and I'm totally lost. It's like the street signs don't make any sense to me over here. They might as well be spelled backwards ... and in Arabic. All these towns over here, Blackhawk Village, Homewood, Blue Island, Calumet City ... I don't have the foggiest idea where these towns are in relation to each other. My buddy sometimes takes me to Blackhawk Village to cop weed and when I go, I feel like if I weren't with him I wouldn't be able to find my way there or back. Like, this place. This Illinois is some kinda other planet to me, some kinda forbidden place."

"I know where we are," she assured me. "My mom used to work in Frankfort."

I noticed I didn't have my seatbelt on and I always wore my seatbelt. I buckled it and then after a few seconds, I unbuckled it again not knowing why, and I left it off.

We were driving nice and slow, about fifty-five on the highway, and headed towards I-80/94 East so we could make it back to Indiana. Suddenly the Grateful Dead stopped playing and the cassette deck coughed up the tape. It was ejected.

"What the—," I laughed.

"Oh it always does that for some reason. It freaks out when the tape gets too hot."

"What, eats your tapes? I bet it only happens when you play The Dead."

"You don't think my tape-deck likes Jerry?"

It took about thirty seconds for the radio to kick on and when it did it played *Tom Sawyer* by Rush. I felt weird, like, I was missing or forgetting something. I needed a cigarette.

This day was just too sober for me.

For the first time in nearly three hours since Jolene picked me up at the apartment, nobody said anything for at least three minutes. There was only a song by Rush. I liked the song, but I've never admitted it until now, because I was afraid if I openly admitted to liking one of their songs I might be a closet Rush fan—and I'm not even. I'd rather be thrown to the prison rapists than live with that label.

I thought of Jolene as a little girl being molested. I had to shut my eyes and grind my teeth before the vision faded. I wondered if it really happened, if she was lying or dreaming. I wondered why in the hell she told me. It's sick to think that people do that to kids. Just when I thought people couldn't be more evil and pathetic than they already are I hear some crazy shit like that. Did she still talk to the guy? Did her mother or her father know? I didn't wanna ask and I figured I'd just try to forget she ever told me. It was disgusting.

I felt stupid for letting Jolene bait me into telling her everything about Erin and me. I shouldn't have said anything. I wished I had never come home from Seattle because here I was ditching school again, using drugs, getting into trouble with the cops, failing all of my classes, getting involved with the wrong girls, getting hunted by angry boyfriends—it was getting to be a serious drag.

"You know the what biggest difference between Seattle and Chicago is?"

"Nope," she admitted. "I've never thought about it."

"In Seattle, when the light turns green and the walk light starts to flash at street corners, the people have the right a way. Like, the cars actually wait for all these people to cross the street before they turn or go straight or whatever. It sucks because you could wait at an intersection, like, for five light changes before you get to turn be-cause all the cars are waiting for these slow ass people to cross the street. The pedestrians in Seattle have no fear. They stand right on the edge of the curb as cars go zipping by, not even giving it a second thought that a car could come racing by and clip them, but in Chicago, as you know, the cars have the right a way. This is God's city, where machines dominate and threaten man. You don't dare cross the street whenever you damn well please in Chicago, no matter what the light says. When I was in Seattle, I swear, I came close to killing at least four people a day for the first few weeks I was there."

"I bet there's a lotta differences, *huh?*"

I sighed as if there was too many to even mention, "Oh shit yeah," I breathed. "Everything. I mean, from the mountains to the trees and right down to the way the people look, act, and talk. I don't know if I ever told you this, but for the first month I was out there, people talked so quietly and calm, and they pronounced every word, clearly, but in some kinda one-dimensional mono-toned rhythm. I couldn't understand a single fucking word people were saying. I was so used to people around here shouting cuss words, slang, and basically shredding the English language. People using any prepositional phrase they choose, whether it's correct or not."

"What's a prepositional phrase?"

"I don't know," I admitted.

Jolene yawned, but tried to hide it by seizing control of her face muscles, "Shit. Can you imagine how hard it would be for someone in Seattle to come to Chicago and try to understand what people are saying? It would be brutal."

"Well," I thought about it. "It might not be as hard as you think, because everybody around here uses body language and hand gestures while they talk. They use their hands to mimic actions, especially the black people. I bet this would be heaven for a deaf person."

I cocked my head and looked up at the stars through the sunroof. I wanted to find The Big Dipper and I was wondering if it was really up there, but I wasn't very good at spotting star patterns and I didn't see it.

I breathed in.

I breathed out.

I blinked and rubbed my eyes as I felt sleep creeping in like the moment you realize that you've gotten way too drunk. It's useless to fight it. My eyelids forced themselves closed against my will once a minute, then every forty-five seconds or so, then thirty. I was glad we were finally headed home and I pictured myself crashing on my bed as soon as I got in the door. I thought about how good it would feel to be resting on my soft mattress with the covers pulled up and my head resting on two pillows. I'd be just lying there, breathing in, breathing out, thinking, letting dreams and fantasies entertain, and falling asleep.

I couldn't wait for that moment.

Then for some reason I thought about her.

Where was Erin? What was she doing?

We still went about fifty-five or sixty miles per hour. *Tom Sawyer* still played and was almost over. There was this small white Toyota Tercel that whizzed by us peacefully at about seventy miles an hour. It minded its own business and switched to our lane once it went by us.

Probably some guy on his way home from the night shift, I imagined and watched my eyelids press closed.

I saw a red fuzzy light and I forced them open again. I watched the white car slowly increase its distance ahead of us.

Maybe it was just someone on a road trip trying to make up for lost time. It was a just a small, white Toyota Tercel.

"That guy thinks he's going so fast," she said, temporarily snapping me out of my doze.

"*Huh,* I guess. If you say so."

"You know something about that car," she asked as if she were letting me in on something.

"What about it," I tossed back, confused.

I was glad I didn't have to drive. I'd have fallen asleep at the wheel.

"That ain't fast."

"It ain't?"

"Hell no."

"No kidding, what's fast then?"

"I'll show you," she said and pressed on the gas pedal.

We switched into the fast lane, the passing lane. I didn't say anything. I wasn't a backseat driver. I grabbed the door handle, not the handle to open the door, but the one you use to pull it shut from the inside, and the one you hold onto when you were freaked out and slamming on the imaginary brake—the panic handle.

We closed in on the white car within seconds. Jolene gave it more gas and we crept up along side the car and then matched speeds. The engine growled loudly.

Jolene laughed a little and then leaned over me and gave the driver of the white car the bird, pressing her finger against the glass near the side of my head, her sweater hanging down and brushing across the back of my hands. I inhaled her perfume and the smell of her shampoo.

I couldn't get myself to look the driver of the white car in the eyes, because I was embarrassed and I didn't want whoever it was to kick my ass. It was almost is if I actually thought the person would think I wasn't noticing Jolene delivering the obscene gesture. It would be my ass that gets kicked, not hers. Girls never understand that because most of them don't know how it feels to get their asses stomped.

For all I knew it could've been some old lady, but I didn't wanna take my chances. Jolene was having fun. She was proving something to me, and to herself, and to the driver of the white car—she was having a coming of age as they say, when a person realizes for a few brief moments that they can be larger than life. She was acting crazy and rowdy. And it was a side of Jolene that I'd seen a few glimpses of before, but never so bold.

She was leaning over me and giving the driver of the small white car the finger, the middle one. I got more embarrassed and didn't look. Instead I watched her left hand as it still gripped the wheel, driving. She leaned further across me, pressing the bird all the way against the glass, and her left hand moved with her, still gripping the wheel. The sudden change of direction caused by the turning of the wheel made Jolene lose her equilibrium for a moment and she jumped back into her seat and rushed the wheel straight again, but it went too far and we lost control.

The rear of the Mustang started to slide as Jolene struggled. We could've easily been going about seventy-five miles per hour, but I can't remember exactly, all I know is it was fast. Everything was moving by and passing rapidly. She frantically cussed and pulled at the wheel, and then pushed, and turned it back in the other direction, then another way. The Mustang violently jolted back to the right and it still slid with its tires screeching and laying dead rubber on the pavement. She was panicking. I was confident in the fact that there wasn't any other traffic. It was an empty highway and the small white car kept going.

The Mustang slid 180-degrees and I put one hand on the dash and one on the back of my seat, trying to brace myself. We were flying outta control, going backwards, and still really fast. I watched her hands acting in emergency, trying to grapple the spastic wheel and to steady the car and finally it went straight-backwards. The transmission popped and a sound like a bullet rattled us as the engine threw a rod.

"It's cool, just hold it steady," I shouted.

Seconds later we hit the median, which was a dugout grassy embankment used to handle drainage. The back of the car stuck into the bottom of the ditch and the front end lifted up and Jolene and I smacked foreheads. Hard. So hard I saw stars and I blacked out—

The next thing I remember seems only seconds later, but I think it may have been minutes or even longer. I didn't even know if I had been knocked out cold or not. I was just standing there in the ditch and facing a direction where nothing was in front of me but a two lane highway.

It was dark and silent.

The interstate was empty and there was nothing. No little white car. No Mustang. Nothing. All I could see were two lanes on each side of the ditch stretching out into nowhere. We were in the country and there were no streetlights or houses or gas stations. I was alone in the middle of nowhere.

But I'm not really alone, I thought.

Technically Jolene was with me, but I didn't know where she was. I couldn't even see the car. It was probably too damaged to drive. How would we even get home? There were no telephones anywhere. There was nothing but cornfields, pavement, and Jolene and I.

I looked up in the sky searching for answers and there it was, The Big Dipper hanging loose, just chilling in the sky, as plainly seen as anything I had ever witnessed.

"Well, goddamn," I whispered to the constilation. "There you are. It's about time you showed up."

It really started to set in that I was in a car accident and I started to remember the car flipping. I frantically checked my body for breaks while I stood there in the middle of the two highways, in the ditch. I didn't feel any pain anywhere and I was standing and I guessed that was a good thing. I pressed on my arms, my legs, and my head. I wiggled my fingers and toes and everything was still there.

I looked up into the sky again and noticed I wasn't alone after all. There was the moon and the stars. I saw The Big Dipper again, then The Little Dipper, a plane flying over with little red lights flashing in unison at the tips of its wings, and I even heard a barn-owl hooting off in a field. It was the most beautiful and glorious thing I had ever felt.

I felt my lucky leather coat on the left sleeve. It was sticky and it didn't look like black leather under the moonlight. It seemed brown, or dark red, like mud or clay. I touched my face and looked at my fingertips, they were stained red.

It was blood.

I was covered in blood!

Jolene!

I was scared and hushed in a panic.

I wondered what I had just been thinking about.

Was I talking out loud?

"And where the hell is Jolene and the car?"

I was convinced I had been standing and staring down a dark lonesome highway for what seemed like ten minutes and I hadn't even turned around to see what was behind me. I was afraid of what I might see.

I turned around slowly, like I was watching a butterfly floating in the wind. I first saw papers scattered and little pieces of torn plastic and shattered red fiberglass littered all over the road, then I saw the car. It was upside-down and the roof was caved in and it lay across the inside lane on the other side of the highway. All around it were little scraps of metal and pulverized glass and shreds of paper. The front door by the driver's side was gone and I walked towards the wreck, my feet crunching on broken glass.

I was losing my cool, going mad, and I welcomed it. The madness soothed me. In fact, I had never felt more normal and in tune with the Earth in my entire life (except for dropping **Acid**). I was touching enlightenment. I felt more than just ok. I actually started to feel fantastic. We had survived this horrible wreck!

"I know she's ok too," I whispered to myself. "She's not here. Must have ... got up and went for help."

I walked around to the other side of the car, inspecting the damage—and that's when I saw her. I saw her lying on the pavement, on her side. She looked asleep, just resting or still knocked out. Her long blonde hair covered her head and shoulders and I couldn't see a bit of her face. She looked so comfortable like she was relaxing on a waterbed. And the seatbelt still on her, the belt and anchors ripped from the frame and twisted around and attached to a piece of driver's seat—a piece of cushion and what was left of the bucketseat.

I stood there a few feet away from her, at first not wanting to disturb her sleep. I felt it would be rude and I wouldn't want her to wake me outta such a peaceful sleep. And then I scanned the car up close. It was completely totaled. It was hardly recognizable. It looked like something outta the mangiest, dirtiest junkyard in the world. I knew she would be heartbroken when she woke up and saw, with her own eyes, what had become of her baby, her most prized possession.

I stepped to her and knelt down to talk to her.

"Jolene are you awake," I timidly asked.

She didn't move.

She said nothing.

"Jolene wake up ... please. It's me."

There was nothing. Her body was motionless, lying on her side with her back to me with her head closest to my feet.

"Jolene, stop clowning. Are you ok or what ... your car is totally fucked up ... I think we need to find a phone or something. I don't think we can drive outta here. It's upside-down, Jolene. The car is really messed up. Maybe your not ok after all, *huh?*"

I was getting worried. I scooted closer to her body and I reached out and touched her shoulder and shook her a little.

"*Jolene,*" I called out a little louder as I pulled on her shoulder and turned her over so she was lying on her back and all of her blonde hair still covered her face. She seemed heavy, like, she was lifeless.

I grabbed some of her hair and put it off to the side so I could see her. It was like nothing I had ever imagined. It wasn't her! It couldn't be. There was no way. This face, it didn't look human. The head was lopsided and huge. The features weren't aligned anymore. The mouth hung open and it wasn't round. It had no particular shape at all. The nose was smashed and her eyes bulged outta their sockets and they weren't next to each other. One was up by what looked like the forehead and the other was down near the nose and the cheek.

I was startled and I jumped back a few feet and just stood and stared. I was mesmerized and shocked. I couldn't take my eyes off of her.

She's dead, I thought. *She's dead. Jolene is dead.*

"Jolene you're dead. Oh my God. It's really death!"

Her eyes were bright blues like a summerish sky. They were beautiful, the most solid eyes I had ever seen. And I never noticed them before. I wondered if anyone ever had. I stepped back another step and almost tripped over a beer bottle. It scared me and I kicked it outta the way with a *ping*. And then I asked myself the most obvious question I couldn't possibly have answered.

"What now? What do I do now?"

My first instinct was to pull her away from the car, because I watched a lotta episodes of *The Fall Guy* and I was afraid it would blow up. But I didn't try to move her anywhere, because she was very dead, and so was the car, just as much as she was, if not more.

I looked both ways, up and down the highway. I didn't even know where I was. I was lost. I saw nothing still, so I just ran, and ran, as fast as I could. And then a few hundred feet away I stopped and realized I couldn't just run away from an accident like this, so I turned and jogged back to Jolene's body and the car.

I could just wait for help, I thought. *Even if it takes until morning.*

It's the only thing I could do. It was the *right* thing to do. As I slowed to a walk I started to sing a little song to myself. It was an oldies song called *Last Kiss*.

"Oh where, oh where can my baby be," I sang.

"The lord took her away from me!"

"She's gone to heaven so I got to be good."

"So I can see by baby when I leave this world!"

I was like fruit loops, sugary and insanely good, whacky, bad for you.

45

"Hey!"

It was like a gunshot. The sound of another voice was a bullet ripping through my skull and spreading my brains all over the place. It scrambled me, a frightening and squalid sound that wasn't natural. It was a shout I wasn't even sure if I had really heard or not, and if I had it must have been my imagination, like when songs I hear on the radio spontaneously play in my mind when I daydream. At any rate, another human screaming, imaginary or not, was something that didn't mix well with what I had experienced so far that night, vodka and milk. I went from walking and singing to a trot and I swallowed my harmony and instead gasped for an extra breath. I exhaled a cold puffy white cloud that faded away in seconds. I shivered.

"Hey! Kid!"

A siren screeched and raped my equilibrium. I almost fell down.

Outta fear I turned around and looked behind me. A white truck with red stripes and letters dominated my real motion picture. The spinning red lights practically screwed the last of my sanity straight into the dirt.

"It's a fucking ambulance," I said to myself with dry, scratchy, and nervous words. I hyperventilated, *"Thank God."*

"Hey, kid! Stop right there," the man held out his wave to me. He had straight brown hair and the wind was blowing it in every direction like pool balls breaking.

"Oh hey, dude," I was calling back out to him in the wind and I imagined myself to be Laura from *Little House on the Prairie* calling to her stupid little bitch-ass mutt who inspired me to watch the show every week as a kid because I was hoping to see the little yapper get stomped by a cow.

Good God! Was I really like that Little House on the Prairie girl?

He walked up to me looking unshaven and callus.

"All right," he asked me, but he didn't want an answer.

He began taking control of the situation at once.

"Go sit down right there, please," he pointed to a patch of grass a few feet from the emergency lane.

His partner, the other medic, ran by quickly and held a leather medical-looking bag. He tore around the end of the wreck, whether it was the front or the back of the car was impossible to tell at that point. I watched him catch a first glimpse of Jolene. Although I couldn't physically see her, I could tell just right where she was lying just by the look in that medic's eyes. It was the look of absolute poverty and shame that's usually only seen in the eyes of the terminally ill. From his look I could tell that I forgot to turn her back over. The first thing he saw was her face. He fell to his knees like a wrestling referee dropping for a three count when one of the wrestlers gets pinned. I felt happy, like, I had just cheated death, like, I was the luckiest son of a bitch on the planet. And I felt ten times smarter and ten times stronger than ever before.

"Hey," the medic in front of me said as he clapped his palms together to assist in getting my full attention. "I asked you a question, kid."

"Wha—"

"Are ya hurt anywhere?"

"Kid," I repeated in a mumble. Then I smiled and said, "*Ah hell no!*"

He quickly finished snapping on his rubber gloves, "Where's this blood coming from?"

"I," I hesitated. "I don't know."

He had a cloth rag and he began to wipe the blood, which was beginning to stick, from my face. I could hear the other sirens in the distance. They called out to us. The cops showed up first, then the crash scene investigators, then the firetruck. By the time I was able to focus on my surroundings again I was sitting in the back doorway of the ambulance. There was an officer in front of me. He wondered if I was capable of answering questions.

"Were you involved in the accident," he asked, even though he knew the answer already. Maybe it was procedure.

"Yes'ir."

"There's blood on your face and clothes."

I rolled my eyes, "I know, sir."

"Do you know where you're hurt?"

"They tell me it's my head," I felt the new bandages wrapped around my head. "Guess I got a Band-Aid now. I don't think I can feel anything. I'm confused."

"You can't feel anything," the cop frowned down at me. "You mean you can't feel *anything* at all?"

"I don't feel any pain, really, not that much anymore," I said. "And I don't think I can feel any negativity anymore."

I was smiling. I was just saying stupid stuff to entertain myself. To the cop I must have sounded like a crazed freak. To me it was a startling revelation, the secret answer.

"Yeah. Well, *whatever.* I'll see if I can get somebody to look at you in a second."

The one medic still knelt at Jolene's side, waiting for something. He touched her on the shoulder and he looked away and he started dry heaving. The other civil servants began to comfort him as they led him away. A fireman laid a gray fire resistant blanket over her body.

Another medic walked over to us and nodded to me. I couldn't remember if he was the guy I had seen at first or not. A Crash Scene Investigator placed little tiny cones all over the road, another Crash Scene Investigator measured parts of the wreckage. Everyone had brown hair it seemed, everyone flashed a badge and some kinda gold platted name pin.

The cop turned to a medic who had just walked up and explained, "The kid's pretty out of it."

"I don't blame him. It's pretty horrible."

"I don't think we'll be needing to interview him. From talking to the CSI guys, it's pretty obvious," he said.

It was obvious to me that they freely talked as if I wasn't even near them.

"The CSI guys already determined this kid isn't the driver. I mean," he hushed to a whisper. "The girl's still kinda attached to the driver's seat, part of it anyway. The anchor ripped completely from the frame and wound around her. I've never seen that before."

"Jesus," the medic whispered back. "I hadn't even noticed."

"Yeah," he said covering his mouth. "She's still caught up on the damn seat by the broken seatbelt. It's like some fishing-line tangled around a dead turtle. We just need to give him a Breathalyzer. Do you think he's with it enough?"

"I'll see," the medic said and he put his hand on my shoulder. "Son, the officer needs you to blow into this instrument."

The cop confronted me.

"Have you been drinking or doing drugs, or anything at all tonight that might cause you to become disoriented?"

"No, sir." I shivered. "I'm just cold."

"I'll get you a blanket," the medic said and he ran off.

The cop held the Breathalyzer up to my lips.

"I need you to blow, and keep blowing until I say it's ok to stop. It should be real simple, ok?"

"Fine."

He placed the device on my lips and when he said, "Ok," and nodded at me.

I started to blow through the little tube and it got all fogged up inside. I blew in a steady wave of breath until he told me when to stop. He took the device and read some sorta digital meter that was hooked up to it.

He sighed, "*Hmm*, nothing. You're clean."

"I better be," I said. "I haven't had anything to drink in days. I'm probably the most sober person on this highway right now."

"Well," the cop shrugged. "I highly doubt it. There's all sortsa drunks out tonight."

The medic came back with the same kinda gray blanket that they covered Jolene's body with and hung it over my drooping shoulders.

"There," he said. "Now I need you to lay down on the cot so we can strap you in and give you a lift to the hospital."

46

As the ambulance pulled away from the scene a different cop got into the back with the medic and I. He introduced himself as Officer Mike Conroy. The driver flipped on the siren and it began to wail and moan as the roar of the engine provided noise support and we hauled ass down the highway towards the hospital.

Officer Mike Conroy leaned a little closer and I could smell leather. It was his jacket. He was a motorcycle cop.

"Look. I ain't gonna lie to you. The Crash Scene Investigators are conducting a thorough examination of the wreckage as we speak, so it would be easiest if you answer all of my questions truthfully, because believe me, kid, they'll find out the truth anyway."

He was threatening me—or at least I took it as a threat. They could find out whatever they wanted to in regards to what caused the accident, but I knew that I was his only hope in finding out what really happened in the moments leading up to the crash. And to him, I was a possible suspect, even though I knew that I was merely a victim. Officer Mike Conroy was thinking about vehicular homicide. I could tell this man was one of those cops who believes everyone is always guilty of something.

"So lemme get this straight," he began and paused.

He took outta notebook and a pen and tried to write in the date at the top of the page, but the motion of the ambulance swerving and turning made his writing difficult.

"The name is Raymond, right? Raymond what?"

"Yeah. *Um* ... Kozlowski. Raymond Kozlowski."

"And your friend's name? First and last."

"I don't know her last name."

"Stop bullshitting. Name. First and last. Don't make me ask you again."

"Her first name is Jolene. I swear to God I don't know her last name."

"Let's talk about the what led up to the crash. So you and the girl were out for a little *joyride?* How fast were you driving?"

"*She* was driving. And it wasn't a *joyride.*"

"Where do you two kids live?"

"Granite, over in Indiana."

"What brings you two all the way out here if you came from Granite? It's practically 4:00 in the morning."

"We were just driving and talking. We just lost track of time. That's all."

"Were either of you drinking or using drugs?"

"No."

"And what caused the accident if neither of you had been drinking or on drugs?"

"Well," I started to explain. "We were driving towards I-80/94 because we wanted to head back to Indiana."

"Go ahead, continue. I'm listening."

"So we were just driving and—"

"How fast," Officer Mike Conroy cut me off.

"About sixty. Maybe faster. Could've been a little faster."

"That's it, sixty? The CSI guys will check the speedometer," he cautioned as if Jolene had to have been going a lot faster than that.

"At first sixty, then we were going faster when we crashed."

"And then what happened?"

"Well, this little white car came by and it passed us and it was probably going about seventy or seventy-five."

We hit a bump in the road and my bed shook. The shocks underneath us squeaked and then settled again.

"I'm not really sure, but it passed us pretty quickly. I hardly noticed it at first, because it wasn't, like, the car cut us off or anything. It was just minding its own business. I think I was dozing off, because I missed something. Something made her mad. Jolene got pissed and she stepped on the gas and caught up to the car and we were driving alongside of it. So maybe the car did cut us off. If it did, like I said, I didn't see it." I swallowed my spit and then licked my dry lips and continued, "The other car switched into the slow lane and we were in the fast lane."

"What did the driver of the white car look like," the cop asked.

"Don't know. I didn't look over."

"Was it a male or female? At least you could tell me that."

"Like I said, I didn't look over. I don't know. I didn't look over," I repeated again. "Jolene leaned over me and gave the other car the finger, and when she did we lost control and started sliding and spinning out. Then we crashed and the next thing I knew," I breathed in. "I was standing in the grass and everything was quiet. The white car was gone. And that's all I remember."

"Ok," the officer said as we rolled over speedbumps in the hospital parking lot. "Well, I'll be keeping in touch with you as the investigation progresses. If you remember anything else you think we should know, I strongly suggest you give me a call."

The ambulance parked in front of the emergency room and Officer Mike Conroy gave me his card. I put it in my pocket.

I remembered a lot more as it was, but I'd be damned if I was gonna tell Mike Conroy the *cop*. As if

I was gonna tell him that, "Yeah, Jolene was out partying all night at Sydney's house. And then we were driving around and hoping to score some coke."

That would've made a great headline for the Hammond Times. I can see it now.

**Granite Teens in Search of Drugs
Involved in Early AM Crash; Girl Dies.**

"I will," I said. "I'll call if I remember anything else at all."

The medics tore open the back door and slid my cot out and they carried me into the emergency room.

47

"That pig thinks that I was driving the car," I hissed to myself as huge gushing tears welled up into my eyes. It hurt to realize that somebody would actually think I was responsible for all of the tragic carnage of that twisted burning wreck and for Jolene being dead.

"God, how can she be dead," I moaned, still talking to myself.

They were rushing me down some hallway and nurses would appear outta nowhere and latch onto my cot, which was rolling on wheels now, like clingy parasite fish on the belly of a whale.

Where did they take Jolene? Where was she?

I was starting to miss her already and I thought about whether or not I should ask if she was really dead or not. Maybe she was still alive and only looked dead. What if that was true? I mean, no one had actually told me that she had actually died yet. Surely they would tell me so right away if it were true.

I missed her.

It's funny, because I sure as hell didn't miss her while she was alive. I didn't even know her last name. And now in the wake of her death I was mourning her loss. I wasn't the only one. I'd come to find that out in a big way at the wake and the funeral in the week that followed.

"Is the girl all right," I asked a nurse.

"I don't know what her status is, honey. She was taken away by another ambulance. She was transported to another hospital."

"Which hospital are we at?"

"Olympia Fields Hospital."

"Where the *hell* is that?"

"It's in Hazel Crest, Illinois."

"Oh."

We fell silent again. I didn't know where Hazel Crest was and I felt stupid for not knowing, so I didn't ask any more questions.

Maybe I did know, like, before the crash, and now I don't know.

I had no clue. I could remember just about everything: my full name, my birthday, my address, the names of everyone in my family, and even my locker combination. But then again, how can a guy tell if he's not forgetting anything if he can't remember anything about what he might have forgotten?

This was a very fucked up situation I was wrapped up in here. Me being rushed to the hospital, a dead girl, a totaled sports car, an ongoing police investigation, my dad was on vacation in Florida, my brother was probably back at college, and so were my two older sisters, my little brother was living with my mom some two hours away from where I was and I couldn't remember anybody's phone number. I could've sworn I knew some phone numbers before. It could take days for anybody to even find out I was missing. I was filled with so many uncertainties. Who I was, who would I become? I just wanted to go home and smoke a joint and play some Sega.

I should've never left the apartment.

They cut my clothes off at the emergency room, starting with the cuff of my blue jeans, up the left leg, and all the way up my shirt. A nurse had taken off my lucky leather jacket and I had no idea what she had done with it. It was gone. A few other nurses and a coupla doctor-type people were fussing over me. Two big orderly dudes picked me up off the cot and put me onto another one, a nicer one, I guessed. It was more like a bed. I only had my boxer shorts on and they were cut down the side and were kinda falling off. Soon, if they weren't careful, I'd be exposing myself against my will. That was the last kinda bullshit I needed.

They wheeled me down a hallway and then down another. And we got to this big room, some kinda section for critically injured people. It was a busy room and there were people hurt and crying everywhere and I only saw a few other doctors around. The ones I saw looked really busy. Along the walls were these little rooms that were sectioned off with only curtains, so there wasn't much privacy as far as noise went. The nurse lady pushed me into an empty parking spot and locked me in place in the center of the little room next to a big medical machine.

The nurse lady left right after telling me that someone would be over to see me shortly and that they had to deal with the most seriously injured patients first. I told her that I understood and that I was glad I wasn't being seen first.

Next to me, on the other side of the curtain, an old man groaned in pain and he kept pleading for help, but no one came to shut him up, so I had to just listen to him whine.

I couldn't believe what was happening. Four hours before I was hanging out with Gabe and The Brain and we were trying to score some weed, but we never did, so we just smoked a few cigarettes and dicked around my dad's apartment until it got dark, and then they both split. Man, would they be surprised to find out that I was lying in a room for critically injured people all the way in Illinois. And I was only wearing my cut up boxer shorts, and Jolene was dead. They *really* wouldn't believe that. The Brain didn't even know that Jolene and I knew each other well enough that we'd be cruising around together in the middle of the night. It was all just mind boggling as I tried to make a bit of sense of it all.

My left eye was hurting and my vision was getting blurry and it was starting to worry me. I was cold and I wanted a blanket. I was thirsty and I wanted some water. I was lonely and I wanted to see my mother.

After awhile this nurse, an old black lady, came over and I was glad to see somebody. The old man next to me was still going at it.

"Is that guy all right," I asked her.

"Oh, don't you worry about him, sugar," she said. "He's gonna be just fine. We need to get you into this hospital gown."

She reached down and started to remove the rags that used to be my boxers and I was shy and embarrassed.

"Oh, come on now. Don't be fussy in front of me. I got six boys at home and you ain't got nothing I ain't seen before."

The nurse looked familiar.

"Do you work at a jail sometimes too?"

"No, sugar. I just work here."

She got me into the gown, did some things with the machine, and then sat me up and made me take a pill.

"What is it," I asked her.

"Oh, it's just a little something for the pain. That eye of yours is probably hurting pretty good by now isn't it?"

"Yeah. It is. So that's all I get is some pills? I just flew through a windshield," I laughed quietly.

She helped me wash the pill down with a cup of water, put a blanket over me, and then she left.

Then I fell asleep for a while.

Then I woke up.

When was somebody gonna tell me if she was dead or alive?

About ten minutes after I woke up they tried to tell me. In walked my mother, a doctor, and a priest. It was the perfect beginning of some untold joke. That's right: a priest. He was an old unhealthy looking man and he was bald with a few silver whiskers on his chin. He had round wire glasses. Under his arm was The Bible. He looked exhausted. He looked like he need to drink more tomato juice.

I was really feeling sleepy and I didn't get up or even have the strength any more to move when they approached me. I was buzzed off that pain pill the black lady nurse gave to me. I just lay there and stared at the ceiling. The three of them gathered around me and looked down at me like I was the play they were designing during a flag football game. Maybe the priest was calling a *Hail Mary*.

"What is this," I whispered hoarsely. "The anointing of the sick or something?"

The priest started saying prayers over me as he guided his hand over my body in the Sign of the Cross. He did this over and over again as he prayed, in *Latin*.

"Wow," I hoarsely whispered. "Holy crap, mom. You went and got me a real one didn't you? That's funny to me."

A tear ran down her cheek and fell coldly onto the back of my hand. I looked down and watched it run down my skin and drop onto the sheet.

"Just kidding, mom. Hello, Father," I said to the priest and I smiled and laughed to myself. It was funny to me to call him *Father*. *As if*, I thought.

My mom was sniffling back her tears and I knew she was upset. I mean *really* upset. In the almost twenty years that I remember anything about the woman I swear I've seen her cry under five times, and this was one of those times.

After the priest finished his routine she put her hand on my forehead and pushed back my hair, being careful not to hurt my face.

"How do you feel, Raymond," she asked, trying to act strong.

She didn't want me to see her cry so she tried to hide it. In my family crying is a sign of weakness. If you had a crying problem then it was assumed you were having a nervous breakdown. My two older sisters used to have nervous breakdowns all the time, but my mom hardly ever did. So it was pretty much outta character for her to cry.

"I'm feeling pretty cool, mom."

"That's good," she smiled. "Father Brandon would like to tell you something, honey."

"Oh," I groaned. "Let it rip, buddy."

My mother wasn't much of a religious person. As far as I knew she never believed in God. She used to take the whole family to church every Sunday when we were all kids, but I think it was just because my dad was a big time Roman Catholic. He was all up into it. We even had to go to Catholic schools, which coincidentally is where I met the biggest crooks.

Father Brandon leaned in towards me and did the Sign of the Cross over me with his whole arm. And then he started saying a few Catholic prayers over me, this time in English. There was one that I recognized as The Anointing of the Sick, which they usually only say when someone in the church is deathly ill or is on the verge of death. It's kinda creepy to hear, especially when the priest is saying it for you.

When Father Brandon was finished he said to me, "My son, I'm afraid that we have some," he hesitated and chose his words carefully. "Some rather disappointing news to tell you."

They all looked at each other hoping that somebody else would give me the bad news.

"What? What is it," I asked, even though I knew what he was gonna say to me. It was the death speech.

My mother squeezed my hand.

"Raymond, your girlfriend is dead. She didn't make it."

"We're all very sorry, Raymond," Father Brandon said as he took out a handkerchief and wiped the sweat from his cheeks. He was relieved that my mom took the fall for him.

"I know she's dead," I told them. "You didn't have to make such a big deal about it."

"Oh dear," Father Brandon mumbled.

"She wasn't my girlfriend."

"Then your friend," my mom corrected herself.

"It's ok for telling me though, I mean, I appreciate you guys finally, like, officially told me. So now at least it's for real."

Everybody started to leave except for my mom and on his way out Father Brandon said, "Now that wasn't so bad, was it," to one of the nurses.

Twenty or thirty more minutes went by and then two different doctors came in with a pretty nurse. They asked my mom if she could please wait in the waiting room while they did whatever it was they were planning to do, because they had some forms for her to fill out. She told me that she loved me and I told her that I loved her also. I had never told her that before. She left.

One doctor had a clipboard and a pen for writing. They greeted me with a friendly and collective, "Hello," and I didn't say anything back because I was feeling high and woozy. The nurse put an IV into my hand and she hooked these wires up to my chest and turned the machine on and I watched my heart beat on the screen. The doctor mentioned something about getting me into a permanent room. Then they left and I stared at the ceiling and thought about life and I listened to the old man cry to his wife. I tried to figure out what was wrong with the poor old bastard. From what I could gather from their conversation, he had some respiratory pain thing going on, but I couldn't tell for sure.

Finally I was just sick of listening to him cry and I griped, "Shut the fuck up already!"

He immediately fell silent. And I didn't hear a peep out of him for some time. I was getting really sleepy and my eyelids were getting so heavy that I couldn't keep them open any longer. I let them close and I shut out the world and started dreaming. I fell asleep.

Later ...

I was starting to wake up, but I hadn't opened my eyes yet. There was still this marvelous darkness and I had a slight headache. I didn't wanna go to school yet, and I wished that when I opened my eyes and read the alarm clock it would still be the middle of the night and I could go back to sleep. The alarm hadn't gone off yet and that was a good sign. I remembered having these crazy dreams about car accidents and rap concerts and girls and somebody was rolling joints, but I couldn't recall much more than that.

I opened one eye and I was shocked so much by what I saw that I almost jumped right outta my skin. I wasn't in my bedroom as I thought. I was in a hospital room with a tube up my nose. And then it all came gushing back to me. I remembered everything. The clock said 5:45 in the morning. I had slept for only an hour or so. My mom was asleep next to me in a chair that looked impossible to sleep in, but she was doing it. I decided to wake her up.

"*Mom*," I whispered loudly. "Are you awake?"

"*Hmm* ... yeah, I am now." She straightened up in her chair and said, "How are you feeling?"

"Never been better," I said sarcastically as reality came rushing back to me like bad habits. "Do you know if they're gonna let me outta this place anytime soon?" I moaned, "I can't stand being confined to this bed."

"Well, hopefully not any time soon. Your skull is fractured in three places. Can't you feel it?"

"No. I can't," and I felt above my left eye and it was like feeling a big plump tomato, and it was totally numb. "Did they do something to it?"

"They want to you to have surgery, but they can't do anything until the swelling goes down, and that could take a week or so. I don't know," she shook her head sadly. "It doesn't look too good though."

"Then what's it look like?"

"Well," mom began to describe it like we were at the Art Museum examining a piece of work by somebody like Gustave Dore. Like a picture with so many intriguing details that you just don't know where to begin. Instead she decided to be blunt and frank, like her personality. "It looks like you got hit with a giant sledge hammer. The doctor's said you're gonna have reconstructive surgery to fix it, but there not sure when, because the swelling is still too thick."

Mom had this way to her at that moment. It was something I had never seen before, as if she were a girl now and no longer an old lady, as I saw her. She was fifty-two years old. For once I didn't see a woman made up of anguish, stress, and wrinkles in her face. She was more like a pretty lady, one with curiosity, and optimism, and grace, as she smiled and carried on the conversation as if we were old friends from way back, instead of mom and kid.

"You're gonna be fine, just fine," she continued and then paused to think for just a second. "All I got was a phone call. They asked me if you were my son." She started to have a nervous breakdown as I noticed a tear gush in the tiniest way down her cheek. It was choking me up and I felt like breaking down with her, because I could only imagine the hopeless despair that she must have felt. She must have thought the worst. Like they were calling to tell her that I was presumed dead. "I thought they were gonna ask me if I could come and identify your body," she nervously laughed.

I closed my right eye because I wanted to see if I was blind in my left eye or not. There was just a stick of light coming into my head from the squint of my swollen and pressed together eyelids, which felt more like orange peels than skin. The little bit that I saw was blurry and mashed together.

"And then the man on the telephone," she continued. "An officer named Conrad . . . *somethingorother*. Conally? Conner? I can't remember. He told me you were involved in an accident. And I just knew you were dead," she laughed again at the thought. "And I swear my heart stopped beating and I couldn't breathe anymore. The thought of something terrible happening to you was killing me. I would've wanted to die if I hadn't told myself that I had to be strong for your brothers and sisters. And then he said you were still alive and it was the most tremendous mood swing I had ever felt. I was so grateful that I didn't lose you."

Her breakdown was getting more apparent with every word she said. She had resorted to pulling out a tissue from her pocket. It looked as if it had already been spent on past bouts with snot. Those snotty wads of tissue always grossed me out. For some reason, women are always tossing them on the floor. It takes a close second behind gum in the ashtray as being the grossest thing on Earth.

"But then he said you were badly injured," she sniffled and wiped her eyes. "And that I needed to come to the hospital so I could be involved in the decision-making. It was horrible and that's all he said he could tell me. The whole three hours it took to drive here were, like, absolutely hellishly long. I kept thinking the worst, like, of you being confined to a wheelchair for the rest of your life. Not knowing, that was the worst part of it all. Not knowing."

48

I woke up again at the hospital some time later and my mom wasn't in the chair any longer. It was the next day and the sunlight was covering me and slowly baking me under the blankets. They had been pulled all the way up to my chin.

Someone must have thought I was cold last night, I thought.

My one eye was shut completely and it wouldn't open at all no matter how hard I tried and my head was pounding and every time it throbbed a sharp pain would run down the middle of my brain.

It was only a matter of time before my friends from school were gonna come and see how I was doing. I had slept in until eleven and I was sure the rumor ripple had spread through school some time ago. The other kids had probably heard by now that Jolene was dead and I was still laid up in the hospital. I figured some kids would leave school early to mourn Jolene's death. She was really popular. It was only a matter of time until The Brain, Gabe, and Jacob showed up to see how I was doing. Erin would probably be with them too, and maybe Milada. The nurse came in and served me some breakfast. I wasn't hungry so I just drank the grape juice. It was in a little can that you had to pull off a tiny tab to drink. I asked for a straw and the lady told me I couldn't have one, doctors orders.

"Your sinus cavities are shattered," she reminded me. "No drinking from a straw. No sucking."

"That's funny to me."

Then she left saying that the doctor would be in soon to check on me. I really didn't know if Erin would come and see me or not. At first I was just speculating. I thought not, because we weren't really seeing each other anymore. I broke it off on the count that she basically wouldn't speak to me anymore. I couldn't trust her. Besides, Jolene was her best friend, and I was sure that Erin had to be too frantic to worry about paying me a visit in a random hospital in some strip-malled town in Northeast Illinois that was so far away. At least I was alive.

A short time later my Patrick came into the room. He had drove down from Chicago as soon as my brother Terry had called him and told him what happened.

"Jesus fucking Christ. I had one hell of a time trying to find this place," he said first thing as he plopped down on the chair where my mom had slept. "You clean up good, dude. You look pretty hot."

"Hey, Patrick," I rasped. "I didn't expect to see you. I thought you were at outta town, man."

"Fuck that. I was close by in Chicago, seeing some friends. No big deal. Your brother called me and told me what happened. He wanted me to pick you up and bring you back home. Said your mom might have to work and shit. He said they were letting you go this morning. It's almost noon. When are they gonna spring you outta this joint?"

"Beats the hell outta me," I admitted. "They haven't told me jackshit."

"That's funny to me," Patrick said as he dug carefully through his shirt pocket. "I hope you catch AIDS from drinking that grape juice. You look like the Elephant Man."

He found what he was looking for, pinched it, and the presented it to me. It was a fat joint. "Anyway, *uh*, I heard from a reliable source they were gonna turn you loose on society this morning. Thought we could burn this baby on the way home. It's a long drive," he enticed. "A very long drive." Then he paused as if he was about to put on an act. "You do drugs don't you? Marijuana?"

"Shit, Patrick," I laughed as much as I could. Any kinda facial expressions were beginning to hurt, which made spontaneous mood changes a bit of an obstacle. "Since when do you smoke weed?"

"I don't, man. After hearing about what you just went though it made me think that life is pretty fucking fragile and if it'll make you feel better to get high then I'll get high too."

"I don't even think I've seen a doctor yet. Just a bunch of fucking fat-ass nurses."

Patrick put the joint back in his pocket and got up and walked towards the TV that was mounted on the wall.

"Guess we'll be here a little while then. I can wait. How do you turn this piece of shit on? *Hardcopy* is about to start. Tupac verses Biggie Smalls. It's the best."

"I'm not really sure how to turn it on. I haven't even watched it at all yet."

"I got it," he said as he turned the power on and watched the screen light up.

Patrick studied the picture that slowly appeared and started cycling through the channels until he came across *Harcopy*. He sat back in his chair and became engrossed in the celebrity gossip on the television. I tried to watch also. I thought it would do me some good to take my mind off of things. I tried to watch, but I just got sleepy until I eventually stopped fighting it and I closed my eyes. As I drifted off to sleep I noticed I was thankful that Patrick wasn't talking about what had happened to me, instead he stuck to his guns and pretended like nothing had happened. I appreciated that. It's a nice feeling when you can be around someone during a rough time and know that you don't have to explain anything to them if you don't feel like it.

49

I woke up to some doctors and nurses who had surrounded me and were poking at my face. Patrick was gone and my mother had taken his place. She had my little brother Magic Mike with her and he slouched in the chair and otherwise looked pretty bored. The television was off.

"He'll be just fine after the surgery," the doctor said to the others in the room. "We just need to get another X-ray done to determine exactly where the breaks are." He turned to my mother and said, "We're gonna try to schedule surgery next Friday or Saturday, Mrs. Kozlowski. We have to wait for the swelling to go down, sure, but we also don't wanna wait too long and run the risk of more damage occurring." Then he noticed that I was awake and he addressed me directly. "Raymond, how are you feeling today?"

"Ok, I guess."

"Raymond, it's my opinion that you have a fractured cheek and there was some damage done to your sinus cavities.

"Is that an opinion or is it a fact," I asked.

"A fact. I bet you've been experiencing some difficulty breathing."

"I have," I said as I scooted my body up into a sitting position. "My nose is all stuffed up. I can't breathe for shit."

"That's to be expected. It will probably be difficult to breathe until we are able to perform the surgery. In the meantime I need to give you some basic instructions so we can prevent any further damage from being done."

"Ok," I said.

"First of all, we believe your sinus cavities have, believe it or not, been shattered by the trauma to your head. Therefore, it's very important that you avoid all exercise, as well as doing really common things like drinking from a straw, or blowing your nose with some tissue. You need to stay clear of any kind of sucking or blowing out through your nose. Also, we suspect the break in your cheekbone is significant enough that we might be planning on reinforcing the bone with two steel plates. One, which we would place above the eye, and the other just over the cheekbone. If this is needed then it's important that you do your best to avoid any kinda further injuries to the area. Don't do things like playing tackle football without some kinda protective head gear, any kinda games or activities that run a risk of physical contact are the ones you need to be careful of. And especially you can't be punched or kicked in the area around your eyes. No violence. It's very important that, at least for the next few years, you do your best to avoid any kinda confrontations."

That part really got to me in a bad way. That meant I couldn't even fight anybody. How could a guy go through life in The Region without fighting?

It was physical impossibility, I thought.

It made me feel like a useless gimp and it made me sad. My eyes began to water and I had to fight myself to keep from crying.

"Ok," I said with my voice shaking. "I'll try."

"*Ahhm*," he nodded and agreed with his progress. "Very well then, Raymond. Someone will be in soon to escort you to the imaging area to have your X-rays taken again. After that we'll start drawing up your paperwork so you can be released." He stepped closer to me and rested his left hand on my shoulder. His wedding ring was a huge diamond studded expensive beauty. "You've been through a lotta grief. I'm sure you could use some quality time with friends and loved ones. We'll try to get you outta here as soon as we can, ok?"

"Ok."

"Very well then," he said as he motioned for the group to exit the room. "Ms. Kozlowski," he nodded to my mother. "It's been a pleasure. You've gotta fine son here."

"Thank you, doctor," she said.

50

My mother took her seat next to the door, resting her chin in the cup of her palm.

"Well," she said, trying her best to be encouraging. "Guess it'll be pretty soon that you get outta here. I might have to leave for work soon, but Patrick gave me his pager number and he said he'd come get you when you're ready."

It was a statement that needed no response, something obvious to both of us that my mother had just brought up to slice the silence. The air was so thick and full of despair in my room.

I felt my face. It was swollen so much that I touched skin long before I expected to. I felt worthless and fragile. A physical life can end so quickly and easily. One minute you're here and full of hope and power, and the next you could be hanging halfway outta car as it skips down the highway like a flipped coin that gets dropped.

The smell of the hospital and all the strange voices that called out in the night only made things seem worse. A guy couldn't get away with living in The Region without being able to defend himself. Without being able to fight it just wasn't possible to get by.

They wanted to put steel plates in my face. I couldn't believe it. No getting hit in the face.

"No violence," the doctor specifically instructed.

I was as good as handicapped. I was hurt bad, both physically and mentally. None of my friends had come to see me. I wondered if they thought I was dead. I wished that I were dead. I'd rather be dead than be vulnerable for the rest of my life.

I should have asked more questions, I thought.

Like, what would happen if I *did* get hit in the face? All he said was for it not to happen. Would I go blind? Would my face cave in entirely? Would my skull always be weak, or was it just until the bone had time to heal completely? My eyes began to water uncontrollably. Tears began to form and quiver in a pool in my eyes. They wanted to drip. I tried not to blink in hopes the tears would just evaporate as fast as they formed. I didn't wanna have a nervous breakdown in front of my mom. The snot began to run from my nose and my breathing started to fall outta its rhythm. I felt like I was choking. I didn't wanna have to tell anyone that Jolene was dead. I prayed that everyone knew what had happened already and I wouldn't have to explain myself or describe what had happened that night. I wanted to get off easy.

My mom looked at me, took a deep breath, and said, "I know you must feel terrible, Raymond."

I lost it right there and began to sob and sniffle. I began to heave and wail.

"I'm scared," I managed to say between cries. "I'm so fucking scared."

She got up and sat on my bed next to me. She put her arms around me and held me close, rocking me as if I was still a baby and not a drug addicted young man. I felt powerless. Instead of holding her also, all I could do was let my arms fall limp.

"Why did she," I sniffled "Have to die," I asked, yelling and sobbing. "Why did she have to fucking die on me? I can't fucking handle this by myself! I need some help."

"I know," she answered. "I know. I'll get you some help. I'll get you some."

For a long time I just sat there and let my mom hold me. My face was buried in her sweater and resting on her chest. I let my eyes close on thier own and my breathing went back to normal. I had so many questions about what had happened. Why had I lived and not died like Jolene? Was there some sorta purpose in my life that she didn't have? I found that hard to believe. I saw no real reason why my life would have more of a destiny than hers. If anything, I was the one who should've been killed. At least she was a good person. At least she had goals and a work ethic. I hated working. All I wanted to do was play video games, get high, and try to pick up girls. I didn't see what good it was doing to society by me living instead of her.

Then I began to wonder if there were greater powers at work here. Like some kinda God-type thing, Jesus or otherwise, that played with human lives like a little girl playing dolls in her dollhouse. I began to suspect that maybe God was an organizer, and every bit of every person's life was mapped out and pre-planned. I thought that probably people had their times to be born and their times to die, and no matter what you are doing or where you are at your time to die it's gonna happen. Or maybe still there was some sorta reason that I had lived. Maybe I had some sorta unfinished business left to take care of in my life. Or maybe it was just plain luck, like, a roll of the dice. Life is like craps perhaps, and I had rolled a seven and had lived and Jolene had rolled a three and died. Tragedy had struck and, for whatever reason, I was still alive. I felt really lucky and fortunate and everything else. I really wanted to use this as a positive turning point in my life. And above all obstacles, I wanted to overcome my problems and faults and I wanted to do something with my life. I wanted success and I wanted to earn it.

The only thing was that after nearly being killed, I felt that my opinion of what success was starting to change. Maybe success wasn't about money or power. Maybe it was simply about achieving happiness and contentment. Is a garbage man successful if he has a wife and family that he loves and is proud of? Maybe so. And then again, maybe not. What if success was only about respect? Earning the respect of the people around you, whether happy or sad, rich or poor, maybe that is where it's at. Whatever success really was, however it's described, I wanted it in my life.

I was practically asleep again when I felt my mother gently lay me down on my pillow, being careful not to wake me. I was exhausted, and in a heartbeat I was deep into a slumber that comes once in a lifetime. I wouldn't be awake again twelve hours.

51

It was pretty late when I regained consciousness. Apparently they had forgotten to let me go home. Visiting hours had ended already and I sat up in my bed and tried to ignore the fact that I was alone. Friends and family and hospital officials should know better than to leave a person alone after they had just seen somebody else die.

Pretty careless, I thought. *What if I was suicidal?*

An intense pain plunged in suddenly. My bladder was about to burst and I felt like if I didn't take a piss within the next thirty seconds or so that I'd have to pee myself. I flung the blanket away from my legs and I swung my feet over the edge of the bed and crept down into a feeble walk. The blood rushed to the wound on my head and it began to throb in a blunt Jazz rhythm.

It took me a second or two to remember how to walk and then it came to me suddenly, one foot in front of the other. I shoved open the bathroom door and felt the side of the wall for the lightswitch. I flipped on the light. There was a shower and a toilet. Both were equipped with handicapped handles on the walls for support. I hurried and put up the lid of the toilet and not even a second later I let the urine flow as it hit the toilet water in a steady and forceful stream. When I was finished I shook out the last few drops and tied my hospital gown back into place. I moved to the sink and began to wash my hands. I grew interested in the way the water flowed over my skin and ran down the drain. I bent forward and drank huge gulps from the faucet and felt the water flow down into my stomach.

I couldn't believe all of the wonderful things in the world that I had taken for granted before. Things like water, dirt, trees, flowers, love, friends, and dreams. These were all things that I held in no special regard before, treating them much like I would treat a disposable razor or a toothbrush. I would use them until I felt like I was ready for the next one and I'd toss out the old for the new. I couldn't believe how stupid I used to be.

I turned off the water and looked at my face in the mirror. It didn't look like me. Part of my old face was there, like the chin and most of the right side of my face, but most of the left side was swelled, enormously bruised and cut. There were still red streaks and stains of dried blood on my skin. Even parts of my hair were clustered dreads full of dried blood. I probed my scalp with my fingertips, searching for wounds, and only found one good-sized gash on the top of my head near the part line. I fingered the abrasion, which had formed into a mounded scab. When I touched it the pain was very sharp and some blood coated my fingertips. I felt the cut more closely and noticed some kinda foreign object embedded into my skin. At first I thought maybe it was a rock. I pinched the object and gently pulled it from my scalp. I held it to my good eye and recognized it as shrapnel from the windshield, a piece of thick glass. I dropped it into the sink and it dinged and bounced and swirled around the porcelain until it fell down the drain and vanished. I turned the water back on and tried to wash the blood away, but it had started to stain too quickly and I had to take the tip of my finger and rub out the redness like I do now when I drip toothpaste into the sink.

I hobbled back to my bed and got under the covers. I felt cold and my whole body began to shake. I curled my legs up and hugged them close to my chest and I shut my good eye tight. I started to think about the kinds of music and songs I liked. I figured maybe if I imagined one of my favorite songs playing it would provide some make-shift typea entertainment. I needed something, anything, that would take my mind off the accident. I shuffled through a few familiar songs and settled on one that I liked. It was *Betterman* by Pearl Jam.

52

I woke up very early the next morning. It was just after 5:00. I was pretty sure it was Saturday morning, but for some reason I was confused about if that was true or not. Maybe it was Sunday. I was pretty much positive that it wasn't Friday. For about sixty seconds I had forgotten that Jolene had died and it made me depressed when I remembered. I took a deep breath, did the sign of the cross and folded my hands together and I prayed. "Dear, God," I whispered. "Please give me the strength I need to get through this. Please don't let my injuries be as severe as the doctors say. And please, God, please protect Jolene. Make sure she gets into Heaven. She was a great person. Amen."

I paused for a few seconds because I had run outta words already. I felt, like, I should say more and be more articulate when speaking with God. I had to say something though, so I said the Our Father even though I couldn't really remember how the words went.

"Our Father who art in Heaven," I rehearsed. "Hallowed be thy name. Thy kingdom come, thy will be done. On Earth as it is in Heaven. Give us this day our daily bread and forgive us our trespasses as we forgive those who have trespassed against us. And lead us not into temptation, but deliver us from evil." I thought for a second trying to figure out which part of the prayer that I had forgotten. I couldn't remember so I ended it with a chilled out, "Amen."

I was very hungry and I couldn't think of the last time I had eaten. I wondered what was for breakfast around there. I felt a little bit better after praying. It's a pretty big relief when you can put everything into God's hands and not have to rely totally on yourself. Who knows if you can really do that or not, but for a few minutes it works.

"I wonder what time room service starts," I said to myself.

I picked up my little gadget with the button on it to call the nurse. I pressed it and waited for a response.

About forty-five seconds later a woman's voice said, "Yes, can I help you?"

"Can I get some room service," I asked loudly.

"I'll have them bring some breakfast just as soon as they can. Would you like a drink of water in the meantime," the voice asked through the tiny speaker.

"No," I said plainly.

She didn't respond. I wondered how long it would take them to fix up some breakfast and I was puzzled as to why she hadn't asked me what I wanted to eat or given me a menu or something. I kinda expected them to give me some kinda choice. After all, this was a hospital and not a prison.

"You would think a joint like this would have it all worked out," I said to myself. "Fuck, 5:30 in the morning. What are you supposed to do?"

I turned on the television and for lack of anything better to watch I turned on the news. It was either that, a juicer infomercial, or an aerobics show with a homo hosting. During the news I almost expected to see a story about the car accident. To me it seemed newsworthy: terrible car wreck; hometown girl dies, but they didn't mention it at all. All they seemed to talk about was the politics and the price of steel and construction and the weather. When the news ended I shut the TV off and tried to get some more rest, but it was useless. I had slept too long and I had plenty of energy.

"Goddamn," I whispered to myself. "If I only could smoke a big fat bowl right now. I feel like the result of some kinda sick Polish joke."

I leaned my head back, stared at the florescent lights on the ceiling, and I laughed at the thought of it. I didn't even have a book. I hadn't been that bored since I was in jail with nothing but the Bible to read. I wished I had a copy of that book again. I would have read just about anything at a time like that, but to have to sit and stare at the ceiling was really bad. It didn't take long for the haunting thoughts to start creeping into my mind. A picture of Jolene's face would flash into my imagination. First of her regular everyday face and then quickly of what it looked like after the accident. It made me cringe and I grabbed a tuft of my hair and pulled it in frustration. I pictured her car flipping down the highway with her torso hanging out and smacking the pavement like a human weedwacker. I starting grinding my teeth and praying that the thoughts would go away. I thought about big thick wooden castle doors and I closed them and locked them with deadbolts over and over, but I couldn't keep out my crazy thoughts. I remembered smelling her perfume and feeling the fuzziness of her sweater as she leaned over me to give that car the finger.

Flashing quickly back in time I was again standing in the middle of the highway right after the crash. I remembered touching my hand to my face and feeling the slick, yet sticky, blood that had bled so much that it coated my leather jacket like caramel on an apple. It was my lucky leather jacket and I had just realized I had no idea what had happened to it. I couldn't remember. They probably put all of my personal belongings into some box or locker or something. They would probably give the stuff back to me when they released me. They would take good care of it.

It's not like this is prison, I thought.

"This might be worse than prison," I whispered to myself.

My good eye widened and got shifty. It scanned the room and examined every foot of space. I began thinking of horrible things, like, of people I cared about being terribly and brutally murdered over and over again. I pictured Erin being burned and tortured by a Satanic cult and Kim being beaten on the head with a crowbar by a burgler/rapist. I saw every detail. Even the blood splattering on the wall after each time the steel club pulverized her skull. I shook my head to try to erase the thoughts, but they were still there. This girl from my school entered the picture. I didn't even know her name, but I had seen her every day. She lived in a little red house. There was a man at her front door. She knew him and invited him in. He made me nervous and I tried to warn her but no sound would come out when I screamed. She shut the front door behind them and locked it. Something happened. Something was said that pissed the man off and he attacked her there in the livingroom. After beating her he dragged her body down the hall to the bedroom.

"No," I cried quietly. "Stop," I whispered.

He started raping her. She screamed for mercy, but he didn't care. He found a curling iron and plugged it in and taunted her while he waited for it to heat up. The rod turned into a glowing red like a fiery coal. He took the curling iron and began to insert it into her and I could hear the skin begin to sizzle and crack with blisters. I could even smell it cooking. I started screaming from far away. It was a deep scream from a dark place in my body. As I screamed the feeling rushed up from my gut and shot out through my face as I jumped and sat up. I was still screaming as I sat there awake and breathing heavily. I was sweating and I started to realize it was just a nightmare. I had been sleeping.

"Jesus Christ," I panted. "Jesus *fucking* Christ!" I panted like a dog and tried to catch my breath. "Water," I called out. "Water," I said louder, hoping somebody would hear me.

There was a soft knock at the door and it was being pushed open. It was a man pulling a cart into my room.

"Good morning," the old black man said. "Got you some breakfast here. Do you want me to just set it aside here or would you like me to set you up in bed?"

"*Please*," I begged like a junky. "Set me up right here, man. I'm starving to death."

"You ok," he asked me casually as he pulled the cart next to me.

"Fine," I answered quickly. "I'm ok. I'm good."

"I heard the scream," he said.

He flipped open the bed tray and adjusted it a few inches above my thighs. After he had set me up he politely said goodbye and left.

There was some fruit: grapes, orange slices and such, some oatmeal, and some whole-wheat toast with strawberry jelly. Under normal comings and goings I won't eat fruit and I generally hate strawberry jelly, but under those extenuating circumstances I devoured every bit of food in just less than three minutes.

After I finished eating I thought it would be good of me to get outta that bed and stretch my legs so I got up and walked over to the window and drew the blinds open. I was about three floors up and since the Earth is so flat around there I felt like I could see for miles. There was a two-lane road that began at the edge of the hospital property and ran out as far as I could see. The sun was not quite up yet, but night had obviously gone away as the sky was plainly orange and getting lighter and lighter by the minute.

I watched the early morning commuters in their cars as they all stopped obediently at the stop sign and then made the decision to turn or go straight. I watched each car and wondered who the people were who were driving them. I wondered how many of those people were living every day like it could be their last.

Which of those people were villains, I wondered. *And which were heroes?* I put my face to the glass and let my breath fog up a big circle and then I drew an ✗ with my fingertip.

What does X really mean, I pondered.

Different phrases popped into my head like X-Ray and X-Generation. X-ceptional. X-it. I had almost made mine the other night. Jolene was an X now. The place in this world that she used to occupy, where she would eat, drink, and breathe, was now an empty hole. The symbol on the window was an ✗ on the surface where you could stick your fist through and grab and hold onto nothing but a memory that seemed to fade more and more by the second.

What am I supposed to be now, I wondered.

Was I an X where some new life would grow?

53

Around 8:00 or 9:00 in the morning the doctor came in and made his rounds. I was sitting in a chair and flipping a nickel I had found under the radiator. I was trying to guess, with consistency, whether it would end up heads or tails.

"Flipping a coin for fun," the doctor asked. "You must be really bored."

"Heads I win. Tails you lose," I tried to smile.

"I'm not so sure those odds are very agreeable to me."

"Yeah," I explained.

He looked me over and nodded to himself.

"Well, I just wanna have one more CAT–Scan done before we turn you loose. I wanna make sure we aren't overlooking any swelling. Are you experiencing any dizziness or memory loss are you?"

"No."

"Feeling warm?"

He felt my forehead to see if I was running hot.

"No," I said. "What was your first question again?"

"*Uh*," he sighed. "You don't remember?"

"I'm just kidding."

"Very well," he said. "A joke. Good one. Look. I'll pencil you in for an appointment down in radiology in a few minutes. After I examine the results I'll be able to determine, without a doubt, whether or not we can let you go today. Does that sound fair?"

"Sure."

"Very well," he nodded and then stiffly walked outta my room and shut the door behind him.

"*Freak*," I slurred. "I must make a phone call immediately."

I went to the phone and picked up the receiver and pressed nine to dial out and for a second I listened to the dial tone, not sure who to call. It depended on if it was Friday or Saturday morning. I had forgotten again. The process of elimination caused me to dial the only phone number I could remember. I called Ricky.

The phone rang about six times before the answering machine picked up. It was my voice on the tape while I did a Ricky impression. I immediately hung up and hit redial and let the phone ring a few more times. Somebody picked up the phone. There was lots of banging and clicking and scraping sounds as he woke up from a deep sleep and dragged the receiver to his ear.

"What," he was tired. "*Fuck*—"

"Ricky," I cut in. "It's Ray. Are you still sleeping?"

"Yeah, guy. What the fuck do you think I'm doing at eight in the fucking morning! Me and Matt and that bitch Patrick went and saw Cypress Hill last night. I got totally fucked up, we left Patrick in Chicago and Matt went to jail. I didn't get home until five this morning. What the fuck do you want, guy?"

"Nothing," I said calmly. "I'm at the hospital."

"*Huh*," he said as I heard him switch ears with the phone. "What the fuck do you mean you're at the *hospital*? What hospital?"

"Olympia Fields, in Illinois. Didn't Patrick tell you?"

"*Illinois*. Whoa, guy. Spit it out. What's goin on, who's dead and shit? Patrick didn't say anything. He didn't tell us shit."

"He didn't tell you?"

"Tell me what?"

"Funny you should ask," I said. "I got in a car wreck the other day, night before last I think. I was with that Jolene girl from Granite, remember her?"

"Yeah. Yeah, yeah, yeah. That's Erin's friend. What happened?"

"She's dead. She's worm feed and my face is broken. I might have to have surgery and shit."

"Get the fuck outta here! Are you totally being serious?"

"I'm serious."

"You're lying!"

"Nope."

"Whoa. Damn. What the fuck happened?"

"We were riding around in her car and she lost control of the wheel, we started flipping, and the next thing I knew she was dead and I was bleeding to death on the side of the road."

"You've gotta be fucking kidding me, guy."

"Nope."

"That's completely insane, Kozlowski!"

"Tell me about it."

"That's totally wild!"

"I know."

"And she's dead," he asked again. "Jolene from the party the other week? The girl who was at my house?"

"She's as dead as New Kids On The Block."

"Wow. I don't know what to say, guy. I'm sorry. Are you doing ok? I mean, is your brain fucked up, depressed and shit? Are you feeling a little trippy?"

"Not really. I'm just cooped up in this hospital room. They might let me out soon I think. What's up for tonight? I feel like living it up."

"You're a fucking crazy bastard. If I find out you're fucking lying to me I'm gonna destroy you," he warned me. "What's up, what's up. I'll tell you what's up. The Singh's are having a party tonight. Their parents are in Bombay or something. Fuck," he gasped.

"You just blew my fucking mind, guy. I can't talk anymore. Call me when you get home and I'll come and pick you up."

"That's cool. It'll probably be around 3:00 or 4:00 or something."

"Hey. Hey. Hey. Hey, guy. You know what?"

"What?"

"Now that I think about it, Patrick did say something about a car accident. I've just been so fucked up lately, guy. He might've told me. You'd think I'd remember some shit like that."

"You'd think. Yeah. Look. Can I call you back?"

"If I'm not here, then beep me."

"I will. Thanks for listening."

"Sure thing, guy."

"Peace," I said and I hung up.

I crawled back into my factory issued patient bed and pulled the covers over my head and looked around inside.

"I can't believe she's dead," I said to myself. "Crazy stuff."

The door of my room opened slowly. I could hear the door hinges creaking as the wooden slab swung open. I stayed hidden as the hollow clicking of dress shoes against the tile floor beat outta rhythm.

"*Hello*," a woman's voice. She was a fat Mexican lady. I could tell just by listening to her. "You under there?"

I waited a few seconds to think about the right thing to say.

"Yes," I called out and I slowly pulled the covers away from my head. "Are you here to take me to the CAT-Scan?"

"Yes. I am here to take you."

She was pushing a wheelchair and she parked it as close to my bed as possible and asked me to step down and have a seat. I got down and sat in the chair. She flipped open the foot ledges so I wouldn't drag my feet on the ground.

"Wow, curbside service," I complimented.

"You know it," she said as she pushed me out into the hall and headed toward the elevators.

We were rolling.

Once we got into the elevators we went down a few floors and got off near the entrance to the cafeteria. The nurse pushed me down the hall in my chair. She knew where she was going and I could follow along by reading all the signs posted on the walls.

Cafeteria this way.

Surgery that way.

Intensive care turn right.

X-ray turn left.

We hung a left around the corner and traveled through about four sets of double doors until we stopped in front of a door towards the end of a long narrow hallway.

"I'm gonna park you right here so you're outta the way of things. There's somebody still using the machines in there so I'm gonna fill out some of your paperwork and then I'll be right back to get you, ok?"

"Sure, whatever," I said softly.

She walked off, turned a corner, and disappeared. For the first few minutes I was there I just sorta waited because I expected her to be right back to get me like she promised. A few more minutes went by and I figured she was just being held up by something minor. There was no clock in the hallway so I couldn't tell what time it really was. It reminded me of being in jail and it made me smile as I thought again of all the similarities between being in the hospital and being locked up in jail.

The only difference is hope, I thought.

In the hospital you have hope and you feel like they're gonna let you go soon, in just another day or another hour or so. In jail there's no hope. You feel like they'll never let you go.

I started watching the people as they walked by. I stared at them all, but few actually took the time to even look in my direction. Even if they did they quickly looked away. I must have looked terrible sitting in that chair with my face smashed in. People just walked back and forth by the dozens, most of them in a hurry to get somewhere. I felt like a beggar. I started watching the people who were so far away that I couldn't see their faces clearly. I focused on one lady nurse after another, expecting one of them to materialize as the lady who was supposed to take me to get my X-rays. None of them turned out to be her. They were all just strangers.

I started to think about Jolene. I sighed and told myself that she was dead, as if I needed reassuring. I imagined what it must be like at her house right about then. I pictured her mother and her brothers and sisters, cousins, aunts, uncles, grandparents, nieces and nephews. I saw all of them there all huddled around each other, grieving and holding one another. They were sobbing and crying out to God for answers. They seemed desperate. I couldn't even begin to relate to the way that they must have been feeling. People always say they "know how you feel," but they almost never do.

My eyes started to water a bit. I wiped the uninjured one, but the other one hurt to the touch so I had to just let it drip down my cheek. I felt so sad, so alone. I pictured a revolver with the chrome barrel pressed against my temple and having the trigger pulled over and over again, each time with a loud bang and each time bringing sudden death, over and over again.

Somebody approached me from behind and I didn't see them coming. A man put his hand on my shoulder and clutched and squeezed me as if I were his son. I was startled and turned and looked up at him. It was another one of those priest guys that seemed to be on patrol at the hospital.

"Oh. Hello, Father," I said like the good Catholic boy that I was. "I didn't see you there."

"You don't have to call me Father. There is only one Father in heaven."

"Ok. Then what's your name?"

"Chris," he said and extended his arm and clutched my shoulder as if he was proud of me. When he called himself Chris it made me notice he didn't look all that much older than me. He looked like he was in his mid-twenties at the oldest.

"Chris what? You gotta last name?

"It's Farag. Chris Farag."

"If you don't mind, I'd rather call you Father, just outta habit since you're wearing that white collar and all.

"That's fine. You can call me Father. How are you doing, man?"

"All right I guess."

"You don't look *all right* to me."

"Well, my face is pretty messed up, but I'm sure you could tell that already, *huh?*"

"Well. Yes, but I wasn't referring to your injuries. You looked upset sitting here in this wheelchair. Where's your nurse?"

"I don't know."

I felt like I was telling on her. I almost wanted to make an excuse for her but I didn't. I didn't have the strength to.

"She went off somewhere."

"Isn't it a shame that we need hospitals," he said kindly. "The world can be such a terrible place."

"It ain't so bad here, Father."

"You're right, man. You're exactly right. There are worse places aren't there? Hell, this is a place where lotsa people enter Heaven at least, isn't that right?

"What?"

"Huh?"

"You said 'Hell. This is the place where people get into Heavan' and shit. It don't make sense."

"You know what I mean."

"Yeah."

"People who die in hospitals always go to heaven no matter what. Have you ever heard that?"

"I guess."

"How did you come to be here? What happened to your face? Did somebody hit you? Were you attacked? That is, if you don't mind me asking."

"I don't give sh—"

I almost said *shit* in front of him.

I laughed a little and said, "I don't care if you ask me questions. *Um*, I got in a car accident the other night, flew through a windshield and stuff. You've probably seen it a million times in a place like this."

"Yes. I bet I have, but the sight of such injuries, such pain, never becomes routine for me. Were you driving or where you just a passenger?"

"I was a passenger."

"And what of the driver, what happened to them," he asked.

I drew a pause and then answered, "She's dead, Father. She was killed."

I tried to say it matter-of-factly, but it made me tear up a little and I began to get choked up.

"I see," he said. "I'm sorry I asked, but then again I'm not. If you ever intend to be able to cope it's gonna have to become something you're comfortable discussing with other people, even strangers like me. This isn't something you can keep bottled up forever. It would tear you apart inside."

"I think it already has, Father. I feel terrible right away."

"You know, when I when my dad was in Vietnam he saw many of his friends get killed in horrible, sometimes unspeakable, ways. Many of them were just boys like us. They all had dreams and hopes for the future. I think that was the worst part for my dad, was the fact they wouldn't ever get the chance to make those dreams materialize. He could never understand why the Lord God would take the lives of such fine boys, such brave souls."

"Yeah," I said as I looked down at my bare feet. "That's what I don't get. I mean why her, you know? Why not me for instance? What do I have going for me that she didn't? I mean, she at least worked and went to school. All I ever do is chase girls and mess around with my friends. I never do anything important."

"I think you're missing the point, man. It may seem like something terrible has happened to her, but in reality, something terrible has happened to you and her friends and family. You all have lost a loved one, but for her this is something wonderful beyond description. She's in Heaven now."

He smiled as if he was letting me in on the greatest secret ever told.

"I guess that you're right, Father."

"I am."

"Hopefully in the future I'll see things your way, but right now I just feel," I paused. "I don't know, like, Jesus, I don't know."

"You feel like total shit."

"Yeah," I smiled. "Just like total shit."

"Well, even though I'm still young, I'm a man who has seen many things in his days and, let's face it, you're still just a teenager. I didn't come to understand these things overnight when I turned eighteen. Insight and wisdom are both virtues you have to grow into."

"I guess that you're right."

"There you are," a woman called out to me.

It was my nurse.

"I'm so sorry I kept you."

She noticed the priest standing there and she began to explain herself.

"Wouldn't you know it? I went to get the patient's file and I walked right into a sudden heart attack. It was terrible luck. I got back here as soon as I could. Gosh, I hope neither of you were inconvenienced too much."

"It's fine," I said to her.

"*Uh,*" the priest spoke up. "He and I were just discussing the comings and goings of the special opportunities that the Lord brings to us each day."

"Oh," my nurse humored him. "I know what you mean, Father. I do. I'm a Presbyterian myself. Go to church every Sunday."

"That's wonderful," the priest said dryly. "Very nice."

The nurse said goodbye and started to push me into the imaging lab when the priest put his hand on my shoulder and stopped us suddenly.

He looked directly at me and said softly and steadily, "Ray," he nodded and smiled. "This is your big break, dude. Don't lemme down."

I shook it off and pretended that what he had just said was just meaningless gibberish instead of a stern warning from a spiritual, insightful, and wise young man.

"Yeah," I smiled in a shallow way but tried to mask it with sincerity. "Yeah. Yeah. Yeah, Father. You're right. My big break."

The nurse continued to push me into the room and I looked over my shoulder. I had only taken my eyes off of him for an instant when the wheelchair started moving again. I leaned over to tell him thanks, but he was gone already.

I said, "Thanks," to the thin air.

At first the word was loud and firm and when I noticed that he was gone the word flattened in tone and ended in nothing but a breathless mumble as I tried to play it off as if I had never said anything at all.

54

I'm not really sure how my X-rays turned out that day. I imagine they were quite satisfactory since my doctor eventually wrote me a prescription for some sorta antibiotic, advised me not to drink outta straws and then he turned me loose, letting me gather my things and leave with Patrick.

As we drove back to my apartment from the hospital, part of me still expected people from Granite to be worried about me. The way things were turning just didn't make sense. To me it was a simple theory that, until that moment, I thought was a fact. Common Knowledge. These things I knew for sure: Jolene was dead and I had almost died, but through the grace of God I lived. People were supposed to be rallying around me to offer support.

Where were my flowers, my get-well cards?

Where were my friends when I needed them the most?

Not a single person from Granite had come to see me so far. No one person from Granite had called to see how I was doing. Maybe if I was stuck in there another night or two, but up to that point I hadn't heard shit from anybody. I felt the Granite kids had no excuses for not coming to see me, or at the very least picking up the phone to say hi. Granite was only twenty to thirty minutes down the highway from my hospital, an easy drive for such a situation. It was really strange. I thought I had friends in Granite. What about Gabe or The Brain? Erin, for *chrissakes*! Where was she?

Patrick and I didn't talked much. He understood the things going through my head were beyond discussion. Few things are as mentally grappling as dealing with the reasons for a person's death, and even worse, dealing with the effects of a death. Even if he would have asked probing questions I wasn't sure if I even knew the right way to talk about them. Jolene's death was stunning and sad, but my overwhelming feeling was one of thanks. I was just glad to be alive and I had a new found appreciation for all things that I had taken for granted in the past. Things like the smell of the bouquets of flowers from the gift shop in the hospital, the innocence of a child, the sound of running water, and the value of a human life. I know it sounds like a fucking cliché, but it's true. You really realize these things when something like this happens.

When we pulled into the parking lot at my apartment we sat in the car for a few seconds. I could tell that he wanted to say something. He shut the engine off and he reached into his pocket and pulled outta wad of cash.

"There's eight-hundred dollars here," Patrick said and tossed the money into my lap. "Give or take a few, I don't know for sure. I stopped at Popeye's on the way this morning and I didn't have any cash on me. Magic Mike gave it to me this morning."

"My brother."

"He came by the hospital to see you. You were sleeping. Says that you sent it to him in the mail to hold onto. Is this part of the cash we scammed from the clubhouse?"

"Oh right, the money from the safe. Thanks."

"Don't thank me. It's your money."

"Right."

We both got outta the car and walked across the lot towards the front door of the building.

"Your dad's still in Florida," he said, and twirled his car keys around his pointer finger. "I'm not sure if he knows what happened yet."

I unlocked the front door and we went inside and said nothing to each other until we were inside the apartment. The place was spotless.

"Your brother Terry thought maybe you'd like a clean place right now so he said he straightened things outta bit."

"Shit. He didn't have to clean up. I don't fucking care."

"Yeah. Well, he just figured."

"Word."

I was completely exhausted, both mentally and physically. In fact, I was bloody fucking tired. I fell into the couch and leaned my head back against the cushion. I watched my Patrick as he pretended to be busy. He nervously moved things around, like, pens and spare change and clutter, convincing himself he was moving them to a better spot. I let him go about his business without confronting him about his obsessive-compulsive behavior.

I got up and put in a L.L. Cool J disc and scrolled through the songs so that I could play *I'm Going Back To Cali.*

"Don't let it bring you down," Patrick said to me. He knelt down and turned on the TV and the Sega. He wanted to play EA Sports NHL 95. He handed me the Number One control, which every guy knows is a cordial sign of appreciation or respect. The Number One is believed by all video game players to be the lucky one. I held the Number One in my hand as the intro to game played.

The voice for the intro proclaimed, "*E . . . A . . . Sports. It's in the game!*"

"Thanks for the number one, Patrick," I said like I meant it.

And I did mean it.

"Wanna smoke some of your weed before face-off," he asked.

"I can't, man."

"Why not," he looked puzzled. "You can't or you just don't wanna? Did you finally figure out you're a piece of shit pothead?."

"No. I wanna smoke bad, but I can't. My fucking sinus cavities are shattered or something. I can't suck anything."

"Oh. Such a fag."

"I'm serious. I can't take in anything that's like sucking through a straw. More specifically, I can't handle pulling on a joint or smoking a pipe."

"Suit yourself," he said and he reached under the couch and pulled out a steamroller with a freshly packed bowl pressed into it. It was a nice glass shaft about a foot long. A good size for nice solid hits.

I asked him, "Since when the fuck do you smoke pot?"

Patrick hardly ever smoked pot and it was just strange to me to see him as if he had a casual habit. I wondered if he was just trying to make me feel comfortable. I watched him as he lit the corner of the bowl just quickly enough to get it burning and then he killed the flame and let his smoke intake keep it burning. And it burned nice and glowed red as the smoke slowly filled the inside of the glass chamber. When it was filled so much that it turned white like a dense cloud, he uncovered his palm from the end of the steamroller and let the smoke rush into his lungs until all the smoke had exited. He held in the smoke for a few seconds and then released it in a big exhausted gush of spent wind.

The smell of the bud took me by surprise. One reason I was surprised was because I could hardly smell anything with my sinuses being messed up. And also when you smoke as much as I did you never really noticed if it smelled one way or another, but since it had been few days since I had even been around it I was taken back by how much it reeked. The scent may have been strong, but it smelled good. The aroma of the fired weed filled my nose and it brought all of my cravings forward making getting high a sudden priority.

Patrick took another hit and placed the steamroller lightly onto the table indicating that he had had enough. I watched the glass piece as it rested nice and still, a faint wisp of smoke floating lightly from the chamber.

I wanted it.

With every second that ticked off of the clock I wanted to smoke more and more and in return I worried about the condition of the insides of my face less and less.

"Maybe I'll just take a little toke," I suggested.

I gingerly picked up the glass pipe and placed it to my lips. I covered the end with my palm and pressed the pipe firmly against my face. I struck a flame with the lighter and barely touched it to the bud. I inhaled slowly and easily much like I would by breathing until I tasted the smoke as it rolled across my tongue, tumbled down my throat, and began to fill my lungs. About halfway through the inhalation process I released my palm from the end and I collected the smoke that remained in a gentle gulp. I held it in briefly and then let it out just as easily. I could feel my stress creeping away already so I put the steamroller back onto the table and pressed start on the number one. Patrick toggled through the options and soon the game began. I chose the Blackhawks and he played with the Redwings.

"How did it feel," he asked.

"Felt ok. I just don't get why you're smoking pot all of the sudden."

"Why is it a big deal?"

"It's not."

"Then shut the fuck up and play."

I watched my players skate around the ice and I did my best to manipulate them, but something just didn't seem right. I couldn't focus. Patrick scored his first goal during the first few minutes into the game, and then scored again as soon as we put the puck into play again.

"Do you know if anybody called while I was gone? Did my brother tell you any messages?"

"Just Gabe."

"Just Gabe," I repeated.

"Oh, and The Brain called the hospital this morning, wanted to know how you were doing."

"What did you tell him," I asked, knowing that he wasn't really paying attention to me.

His eyes were fixed on the screen and his players seemed always to be a step ahead of mine as they countered every offensive opportunity that I tried to capitalize on.

"Told him you were cool."

When the game was over the score was ugly. I lost eight to nothing. He had forty shots on goal and I had something like sixteen.

"Pretty lopsided victory," Patrick said. "You're Sega skills blow. Feel like playing again?"

"*Nah*," I sighed. "I can't seem to concentrate."

"Fine by me," Patrick commented plainly. "Well," he continued. "I don't know about you, but I think I'm gonna smoke another bowl, then I'm off to get some ribtips and roll back to my place.

I'm fucking starving."

"Yeah," I sighed as I looked out the sliding glass door, remembering my first day back at school when Gabe and Erin had picked me up that morning, and how we got high. That was when I first met Milada too.

Funny, I thought. *It was only a little less than three months ago, but it seemed like years.*

So much had happened to me since then that I felt years older than eighteen.

"I ain't really hungry," I mentioned.

"Fine. Fine. Fine," he said again and he stood up and felt his front pocket to see if his keys were still there.

"Yeah," I said.

I shrugged and waved off the idea that something might be bothering me. I didn't wanna seem weak.

"Ok, take it easy then and call me later," he said and he walked out.

"Alone again," I whispered to myself and again I fixed my gazed on the outside.

I focused on the tree by the deck and I watched the leafless twigs bounce in the chilly breezes that blew all the way in from Lake Michigan in waves.

"Dance," I said softly. "Dance."

55

Monday morning was on me Andre the Giant-style before I was ready for it. I never ended up going out with Patrick or Ricky the night after I got outta the hospital—instead I opted to stay home and sulk, and I refused any company. On Monday I woke up way earlier than usual, around 5:30. It was still dark outside and I was alone. My brother hadn't come home the last night and my dad was still in Florida. He had called and planned on coming home on Wednesday so he could take me to see the doctor about my face, which was looking pretty fugly (that ain't a typo; f + ugly = fugly). The whole left side of my face had swelled and mutated into something that looked like a big and rotten lumpy red bellpepper, and all black and blue. I had been wearing sunglasses all day and night to try to cover it up, but the damage to the flesh was just too widespread. Even my neck was turning yellow.

Monday was the morning I had to go back to school. I hadn't talked to anybody from Granite since before the accident happened and I wasn't really sure what to expect. All I could do was prepare for the worst and hope for the best. I just felt like something terrible was going on behind my back. Some feelings of mine might have just been paranoia since I had been smoking reefer about once every hour just so I could cope with the constant nightmare of the car accident. I just knew something was up. It was strange that none of my Granite friends had tried to get a hold of me to see if I was still alive. Contrary to the week before, no people were stopping by at random hours and my phone had pretty much stopped ringing altogether. I thought for a second that perhaps none of the other kids had heard about what had happened with Jolene and I, that maybe there was some logical explanation for my alienation, but I couldn't think of anything reasonable and nothing seemed possible.

I sat around until about 7:45 waiting for Gabe to show up. He had been picking me up for school everyday for the last month or so. Every morning he had showed up without fail. I would hear his muffler coughing and I would run out to his car and we'd drive around for ten or fifteen minutes and smoke bowls before school started. At 7:50 I had lost all patience and I called his house, but nobody answered so I put on a sweater and I started walking to school, one foot in front of the other with my head down.

I walked onto campus with my sunglasses wrapped too tightly around my swelled skull, my hair pulled back and covered with a black bandana, and a totally stoned face. At Granite High School things appeared to be business as usual. I was about five minutes late and the parking lot was filled with cars and most of the kids had already taken their places in their first period classes. As I walked down the hallway, past all the lockers, I felt dead like a zombie, like,

I was only watching things happen and not actually living and experiencing them. I couldn't even tell if I was really breathing or not.

When I got to my first period Art Appreciation class the door was closed. I wrapped my cold hand around the handle and froze for a second. I tried to mentally round up whatever pride I had left so I could face these strange kids, some of which I thought were my friends. Nobody who I ever really hung around with was in that class so I told myself that whatever happened when I opened the door wouldn't be that bad. So reluctantly I turned the steel handle and pulled open the door and I stepped inside. Instantly a hush fell over the room as I walked slowly to my desk in the back of the room. I listened to my heels clicking softly on the tile floor and through my shades I could plainly see that everyone in the room was staring at me like I was a ghost. I slouched down in my chair and folded my hands neatly on my desk. Since I was way in the back most of the kids had no choice but to turn their backs on me.

The teacher cleared his throat and straightened his eyeglasses and attempted to great me.

"Mr. Kozlowski, good morning," he said as he tried to mask the indifference in his voice.

I knew then that everyone knew. I had no books or pens or anything that you needed for class. Somehow I had forgotten I needed anything for school so I just sat there quietly as I peered through my glasses at my teacher as he tried to continue with the lesson. I wanted to fit in, but I was too afraid to ask for a piece of paper and too embarrassed to borrow a pen from someone. I had never taken notes before so there was no point in starting then. It was obvious to me that I was a distraction to the entire room.

When the bell rang all the kids filed out of the room as quickly as possible, I followed them just like one of the sheep. In the hallway it was very crowded as kids hurried past. I walked steadily towards my General Math class and up ahead I could see that I was approaching Erin's locker. I could see her standing there with her friends, Leslie Hipp and Sydney. Erin was wearing the exact same outfit she wore that morning a few months before when she secretly handed me a note on my first day back at school. Things had come full-circle. She was still very pretty, but now she appeared drained and empty. She looked like she hadn't slept in a while.

I cleared my throat and took a deep breath and I walked up to them and said, "Hello."

It seemed to echo in my head over and over.

The girls turned to me, looking me over as they did. They didn't say anything at all with their voices, but their blood-shot eyes said a million words. They seemed scared of me. They looked right through me, like, I was some kinda big frightening crackhead begger from Chicago. They were hoping that I'd just walk away.

So I did.

As quietly as I had approached I just walked away, and I had started to realize that something very terrible had gone wrong. I knew somehow, someway, they felt that I was responsible for what happened to their best friend. From their viewpoint I was a killer, as if Jolene's death was entirely my fault. Now I understood why they had been staying away. I knew why nobody had even bothered to call to see if I was ok, because they didn't really care, other than them hoping I would actually die too.

Things had gotten too weird for me to handle and as I walked towards my General Math class I started to cry a little. I was glad I was wearing shades so nobody could see it. As I walked along I could hear the other kids talking about me. As I walked past huddles I could catch bits and pieces of the things they were saying about me.

I actually heard one girl say to her friend, "Do you really think he killed her?"

And another guy blatantly told me I was, "Good as dead in this town."

He said it right to my face in the same tone of voice his hillbilly grandfather probably told to niggers years before. It was pure hatred. Things had gotten serious so I walked right past my General Math class and I went straight outta the exit doors of the school and I walked quickly back to my apartment, to the only place that seemed safe for me.

When I walked into the apartment my brother Terry was sitting on the couch watching Sportscenter. When I sat down he asked me why I wasn't at school. And when he did I just completely lost control. I started crying and sobbing so much I couldn't even answer his question. It was a nervous breakdown. He picked up the remote control and turned off the television and he looked about as concerned as you would expect him to look. He wanted to hug me and hold me, but we had never had that kinda relationship so he just sat there and waited for me to catch my breath and calm down. As he waited he tried to offer bits of advice.

"Look. It's gonna be fine, Ray. I mean, sure the girl is dead ... but you gotta move on, man."

"It's not *that*," I screamed. "It's not *that!*" I cried and carried on some more. "Oh my God," I cupped my hands together and buried my face into them.

"What is it then," he asked.

I was making him nervous. There was a cashed bowl on the table and I had probably caught him just as he had finished getting high.

"The other people," I heaved, forcing the words to roll off my tongue. "The other fucking people! They think I fucking killed her! They think I was fucking driving the fucking car!"

"Holy shit," he said and he looked down at the ground and shook his head and tried to think of something to say. "Are you serious? That's terrible."

"Goddamn right it's fucking terrible," I yelled at him. "What the fuck am I supposed to do now!"

It wasn't really a question I was asking him, but more like an insane order from someone that had gone berserk and had totally lost control. I was demanding answers.

"I've gotta go back to that fucking school until June and everybody thinks I killed her!"

I was screaming at him now so loudly that my vocal cords were getting sore.

He stood up suddenly and yelled back at me, "Well *did* you?"

He stopped me in my tracks and I froze.

"*Huh*," I mumbled.

"Did you?"

"Did I what, *kill* her? Is that what you're asking me," I swallowed some blood that had started seep from some part inside my mouth. "No, all right! I didn't fucking kill her. Is that what you wanna hear!"

"*Yes*," he said forcefully. "That's exactly what I wanna hear. And you know something ... I believe you, because I know you're telling the truth. Those cops at the accident know you're telling the truth. If you don't believe me ask mom. We talked to all of those Crash Scene Investigators! Who do you think had to fucking talk to them at the hospital? It wasn't the old man. He's in fucking Florida still. If you think I don't know what's going on you're kidding yourself, but you know what?"

"*What.*" I whimpered.

"It doesn't matter what anybody thinks. That fucking dead girl knows, wherever she is. She fucking *knows* you're telling the truth, and *that* should be all that matters. You need to stop worrying about what all those pussies at your school are saying about you because they don't know what the truth is. You know something, and I hate to say this, Ray, but you need to stop acting, like, helpless and start being a fucking man. This week ain't gonna be too pretty for you. It's not gonna get any better any time soon. You've gotta wake and a funeral to go to."

"*Ah*, fuck that," I screamed at him. "How can I go to the fucking funeral, man?"

I was almost laughing at the thought of me actually showing up to the thing. It wasn't a funny laugh, because after what I had just gone through I didn't find much humor in anything. It was more like an "I'm about to crack" laugh.

"Well, if you don't go you'll regret it for the rest of your life." He stared me down after he said it, forcing me to make eye contact. "Think about it."

"I gotta make a phone call," I told him.

And I went into my room. When I went inside I closed my door behind me and I pulled out the wad of cash Patrick had given to me and I stared at it.

"This just might be my ticket outta here," I whispered to the money and then I locked it up in my safe.

I picked up the cordless from the charger and I dialed Gabe's phone number. My heart pounded harder than the bass from *8 Ball* by Eazy-E. I was so nervous I had to force myself not get so scared that I would hang up. Gabe was the one who answered.

"Hello," he said, sounding like his regular self, except for the fact that he seemed calm, almost subdued.

"Hey," I sighed. "It's me, man. Can you talk right now?"

"Yeah, Ray. Hold on a second. Lemme switch phones."

After he put me on hold he came back on the phone about thirty seconds later and he told me, "Look, Ray. If you don't mind I'm gonna speak frankly. We've been friends for a while and I mean this, I think that you're one of my best friends and nothing really can change that."

"Ok."

"And," he paused to think. "I don't know what happened with you and Jolene. Only you and her know, but I've been hearing a lotta shit about it."

I swallowed outta fear, "Like what?"

"Nevermind that. None of it really matters, because there's no way of telling what's true and what's not. Like I said before, we're friends, so I just have one question to ask you and I want you to tell me the fucking truth, because whatever you tell me I'm sticking by you no matter what."

"Ok."

"Where you driving that fucking car? Did you kill her?"

"No, Gabe. I swear to fucking *God* I didn't. I wasn't driving and that's the *truth*."

He paused again and said, "Ok, then. I believe you."

"Thanks, Gabe. That means a lot to me."

"I know it does, Ray. Look. There's a lot I need to tell you about, like, what's going on with everybody. Can I cruise by?"

"Yeah. Like when? Wait, why aren't you in school?"

"I didn't feel like going. I'll be by soon. I need to pick up The

Brain on the way over. He's with us too."

"Ok, thanks again."

"You bet, buddy," he said sincerely. "See ya in a bit."

And he hung up.

56

Things were getting pretty heavy. I felt like a fugitive giant who was looking for a place to hide. It stressed me out and I was dealing with the fact that hiding out just wasn't gonna happen for me. I was gonna have to face all of this stuff head-on like the Japs at Pearl Harbor. I got out my bong and packed a big fat bowl and I sat on my bed and smoked it as I waited for Gabe and The Brain to get there. I thanked God that they were sticking by me, because I really didn't think they would. I was actually surprised.

Even though Gabe and The Brain showed up about twenty minutes later it seemed like forever because the whole time I was trying to size up the entire situation in front of me. I didn't know exactly what everybody was saying, or thinking, about what had happened with me and Jolene. I didn't know who was with me, aside from Gabe and The Brain, and who exactly was against me. Where was the truth in all of this? My homecoming from Seattle just wasn't turning out how I pictured it at all. I really thought that, after this accident, at the very worst I'd be a symbol of admiration for surviving and being the last person to see Jolene alive. I never thought in my wildest dreams they'd blame me for killing her. I couldn't think of a more harsh accusation.

So we sat in my room and passed the bong around a few times. The Brain was sad and quiet. He was kinda close to Jolene and he seemed to be in shock a little bit. Gabe, as usual, did all the talking. He began to lay it all out in front of me and didn't hold any of the ugly stuff back. He gave me the straight dope.

"The other night," he began. "The night after Jolene died, a bunch of us got together at Sydney's house. Tons of people were there. Everybody you know, Ray, and even some people you don't know. The Brain and I were there. We saw the whole thing. Everybody was sitting around and acting bummed, some people were crying. And then Leslie Hipp, during a time when it was really quiet, asks everyone 'How do we know what really happened?' Everybody got quiet. And then Erin says all of the sudden that she knows what happened. Everybody was shocked as hell. I mean, nobody knew how in the hell she would know anything, but we were all ready to listen. You know how people are, Ray. 'He killed her,' she said—just like that. Like it was a fucking fact or something."

"How would she know," I asked defensively.

"She told everybody she saw you guys driving around, said she saw you drive by when she was parked at a redlight. She says you were driving Jolene's car and you guys were headed east towards Illinois."

"What," I stood up and almost kicked over the bong. "That fucking whore! Why in the fuck would she say that?"

"We don't know," The Brain admitted to me.

"Yeah," Gabe said. "She just said it outta nowhere and of course everybody believes the bitch."

"It gets worse," The Brain warned.

"It can't get any worse, dude," I told him. I put my head down and sighed, "How much worse?"

"A bunch of dudes were talking about killing you afterwards," Gabe explained to me. "I'm not sure how serious they were, but they were saying it."

"Killing me? What is this, *The Outsiders*? Fuck! Motherfucker," I cursed. "*Who*? What fucking guys?"

"Who do you think," The Brain said as if it was obvious. "Jeremy Otsap and his boys. Tim Miller too. That's who."

"Lemme guess," I said. "Jeremy Otsap got back together with Erin didn't he?"

They both nodded yes.

"It's all starting to make sense," Gabe suggested to me.

"Yeah it is." I sat there quietly for a second and then I started to get pissed. "I'm not scared of those fuckers. I'm getting a pistol first thing in the morning. If any of those bastards so much as lay a finger on me I'm gonna blow'em away."

"You don't wanna do that, Ray," The Brain said.

"Look," I was frustrated. I felt like giving up. I was tired of thinking about it. "I know this is gonna be hard, but I don't wanna talk about this shit anymore. Can we just go play NHL 95 or something?"

The Brain and Gabe looked at each other briefly.

"Sure thing, Ray," Gabe said.

We got up and played video games for the rest of the night. We didn't talk about Jolene or Erin or any of that crap for a few hours, which was a nice relief for me. I needed a break.

57

On Thursday morning I reported to the hospital for surgery. My dad drove me all the way back to Illinois at 6:00 in the morning. The swelling hadn't gone down very much on my face, but my doctor, afraid that the swelling was on the verge of causing me permanent damage, scheduled my operation first thing that morning. Stripped to my hospital gown, I laid on my bed in a large room with other patients who I assumed were scheduled for surgery also. The nurses kept doing shit to my eye that they said was supposed to make the swelling go down faster. I had my CD player and headphones plugged into my ears and I played *I Won't Do What You Tell Me* by Rage Against the Machine, over and over and over and over.

Soon my doctor had arrived with his team. I turned off my music and he briefly advised me again on what they were gonna do to me.

"Good morning, Raymond," he said. "How are we feeling?"

"Moderate."

"I suppose that's good enough. This is Mr. Grekorvich," he motioned to the man standing next to him. "He's our anesthesiologist and as soon as we're finished discussing today's order of business he'll begin to prepare you for the procedure. We're gonna be placing two small metal plates under your skin, one covering your left high cheekbone, and the other just above your eyesocket underneath the eyebrow. This is so we can provide additional support for your skull as it tries to heal its fractures. They are not necessarily meant to be permanent, but they can be in as long as they don't cause any future discomfort. We're planning on making just two small incisions. One here," he touched my face with his middlefinger. "Just below the eyebrow, and the other we will make inside your mouth so there will be no noticeable scarring. That's part one. Now, for the second part of your surgery we are gonna repair your sinus cavities, which were badly damaged. This part is a little more difficult because we need to inflate a small balloon in each cavity so we can piece the shattered cavity back together."

"Like Humpty Dumpty," I commented.

"Kinda," the doctor smirked. "Each balloon we inflate will be connected to a small tube. Each tube will exit through your nasal passages and ultimately out through your nostrils. This shouldn't be painful for you, but it will obviously cause difficulty breathing through your nose. Do you have any questions before we begin, Raymond?"

"*Um*, how long do I have to wear those tubes and balloons and stuff in my face?"

"The tubes and balloons will stay until the cavities have sufficiently healed, probably about a month or so, and when that happens we will simply cut the tubes with some scissors, deflate the balloons and pull the discarded rubber outta your cavities through your nose."

"Trippy," I said. "Ok, no more questions. I think I'm ready."

"Very well then," the doctor said. He turned to the anesthesiologist. "Mr. Grekorvich, if you will."

Mr. Grekorvich stepped to the side of my bed and placed what looked like an oxygen mask over my nose and mouth. He flipped a switch on a machine and then he began giving me instructions.

"In a moment," he advised. "You will fall asleep. If you could just do me a favor and simply count to ten out-loud."

"*Now,*" I asked.

"Yes. Please."

"Ok," I said, doubtful that the gas would work on me. "One, two, three, four, five, six—"

And that's when I passed out.

58

When I woke up after surgery I felt exactly like I had just smoked a bunch of crack all night long and I was crashing hard. My eyes were blurry and my neck was sore and stiff. My limbs felt almost too heavy to lift them, but I managed anyway to reach up and gently touch the bandages around my eye. And I ran my finger across the two rubber hoses jutting from my nostrils. The hoses hung down as casually as possible over my mouth and past my chin.

They had me resting up in some sorta ward, which was a huge room or a hall with about a hundred other sorry asses just like myself. We were all trying to recover. It was like a scene in a makeshift hospital during one of those old black and white war movies.

It was a short stay at the hospital this time and it was the last time I was ever admitted as a patient. After I regained my vision and had become alert again, my dad drove me back home and dropped me off. He went out to have a few drinks with some friends.

Since I was home alone I cut to the chase and went straight for the bathroom so I could have a good look at the new me, or the temporarily new me. I had taken another step closer to resembling the Elephant Man. The whole left side of my face was swollen and disfigured. Now the skin was one big black, blue, and yellow bruise. A large bandage covered the whole left side of my forehead. And the entire left side of my face was completely numb to the touch, like a dentist had given me ten shots to the cheek. At some point somebody (my dad) had given my doctor the information that I had been occasionally using drugs, and so the doctor opted to pinch the nerves in my face to control the pain instead of prescribing medication. My dad was from the old school. To him there was no difference between marijuana and cocaine or **Acid**. They were all the same to him. He always believed me smoking pot would cause me to become some kinda illiterate circus freak one day.

The tubes dangled from my nose and every time I tried to smile or talk my lips would brush up against them and it tickled. The first adjustment I made was I taped the ends of the tubes to my forehead, curling them up and around the outsides of my eyes. I taped them securely with white athletic tape, but that looked just as stupid as before, so I wound a blue bandana into a wide headband and I tied it around my head, covering the taping job that I had done. I still looked funny though, with the tubes hanging out of the sides of the bandana and diving up my nose. So I grabbed my sunglasses and put them on and they did the trick. You had to look twice at me to tell that there was something wrong at all.

Feeling satisfied, I dug my camera outta my desk drawer and I loaded it with film and thought I'd take some pictures of the new me. I stood the camera on the coffee table and I knelt down so I was looking at the lens. I used a ruler to reach over and snap a coupla pictures of myself. After that I packed a bowl and smoked the hell out of it. And then on a whim I grabbed the keys to The Poop, which I hadn't driven in days, and I scooped the camera up and headed out the door. I got it in my head that I'd go out to the crash site and take some pictures. It was really far away so I packed another bowl for the road, not even sure if I would ever even find the exact spot, but I felt it was at least worth a shot. It was weird, but I actually thought maybe, just maybe, Jolene might still be alive. I felt it was perhaps possible that she was still there at the crash site somewhere. If so I wanted to find her.

I traveled the exact route that Jolene and I had taken a few nights before and I played *Ghetto Jam* by Domino about ten times in a row in my tape player. After about an hour or so I was traveling up the same stretch of highway where we had lost control and crashed and suddenly I began to catch glimpses of black skidmarks so I quickly turned on my blinker and pulled over to the right.

I grabbed my camera and stood by The Poop and waited for the cars to pass. When they did I trotted across three lanes and reached the grassy median. There were still little pieces of broken glass and red plastic scattered on the ground. And in the muddy grass were two huge muddy tire-treads that looked like a big spoon had scooped them out. I quickly snapped a few pictures and saw that most of everything else had been taken away. So I just walked around and carefully scanned the ground looking for anything of importance that might have been left behind, like, a ring or a watch or anything personal that I would have wanted to keep—but all I could see was broken glass and litter. I started to feel stupid in thinking that there was any chance of finding Jolene alive. She was definitely dead.

I lumped my way back to The Poop and started the engine and merged into traffic. On my way back home I smoked the other bowl and then I cried. After I cried for a minute or two I calmed down a bit and I was feeling a little better, like, I was carrying less baggage. I started talking to God like I'm sure a lotta people do after they cry.

"God," I huffed aloud. "What the fuck is the matter with me, crying and shit all the time?"

I turned on my blinker and pulled onto the exit back to Indiana.

"Jesus," I muttered to myself between sniffles. "What the hell am I supposed to do now? Funeral is on fucking Saturday. I can't go to that thing. All those people are gonna be there, waiting to kick my ass and shit."

I found an old napkin from a past value meal at McDonald's and I wiped my nose into it and then dropped the dirty thing outta the window. I watched in the rearview mirror as it blew away in a corkscrew and then it disappeared underneath the car behind me.

I turned on the radio and on every station was a loud and annoying commercial so I turned it off.

"Quiet. That's what I want. Maybe I'll take my cash and get outta town for a while."

I looked at myself in the mirror and there was a strange man there wearing a blue bandana and sunglasses, and he was looking right at me.

"Who the fuck is that guy," I smiled at myself.

I got home about forty-five minutes later. I wasn't hungry and, come to think of it, I hadn't really eaten much of anything in a few days. Right away I went to the stereo and shuffled through my CDs, looking for something I hadn't listened to in a while. I found an MC Lite disc. I couldn't even remember where it came from. *Probably from a stupid ex-girlfriend*, I thought and smiled.

I put the disc in and played *I Rock the Party*. I went to the caller ID and saw that Patrick had called so I paged the cordless, found it right in front of me on the counter, and dialed his number. He picked up almost right away.

"Hello," he said. His voice was just as tired and scruffy as always. No matter what time of the day it was he always sounded like he had just woken up.

"What up," I said.

"Hey, Ray. What's going on, man?"

"You know what's up?"

"*What?*"

"Jackshit. That's what," I laughed.

"How did the operation go?"

"It went accordingly. They put the steel plates in my face and I've got these tubes coming outta my nose."

He laughed and said, "That's the worst action ever."

"Tell me about it."

"What's that fucking *crap* that you're listening to?"

"Oh, that. It's MC Lite."

"So *gay.*"

"I know, it's just on the radio. I didn't play it or anything."

"Fag."

"What's up for tonight," I asked.

"Party at Matt Morris' house. Are you down, you feel like doing anything or what?"

"I'm down. I'll drive over in The Poop. It decided to start running again. I'll cruise by around seven or so."

"Cool. Look. I'll see you there. My buddy Vince and I are about to go kick Ernie Powell's ass. Ernie is supposed to fight Juan Taverez, but Vince and I are gonna jump in and kick him in the head and shit."

"That's nice. You guys are fine young men," I said sarcastically.

"Later, buddy."

"Peace out," I said and I hung up.

59

All things considered, I was feeling pretty decent. I had to park The Poop down the street because there was no place in Matt's driveway to park. The driveway was already full at 7:00 and it was completely dark outside. I strolled up the lawn toward Matt's house and my face was protected pretty much by the night. As some of the other kids that I had known from Andrean said hi to me I was able to scoot by without any questions. Some didn't even recognize me and when they did say hello it was as if they were casually greeting a stranger. For the ones that did know it was me, if any of them had heard about what had happened to me, they didn't indicate in any way that such was the case. My bruises were invisible outside in the dark and the only thing that looked strange about me at first glance was the fact that I was wearing sunglasses, but fortunately in high school anything goes, even wearing sunglasses at night.

I knew the mood would change though, just as soon as I walked into the house and into the light. The kids that made up the contents of the party weren't exactly unfamiliar to me. I had gone to school with all of them for a few years and I knew everyone there in one way or another. From first glance at the party I could tell that nothing much had changed with the Andrean kids since I had gotten kicked out a year and a half before. Most notably, there was still a steady stream of U2 blaring from the stereo. That's standard at Catholic school parties. In particular they were playing *One*, which was followed by *Pride* about a minute after I walked in.

The kids that weren't into drugs always partied upstairs and the dopeheads mostly hung out downstairs at Andrean parties. I tried to sneak past the pure people so I could escape to the downstairs, but with my beaten appearance I was kidding myself. I didn't make it three feet when kids who were obviously curious cut in front of my escape route and stopped me with probing questions.

"What happened to your face, Ray," a dude asked.

Some automatically suggested I had just gotten my ass kicked, but when they looked closely and saw the tubes coming outta my nose they grew confused and demanded an explanation from me.

"I got in a car accident," I said plainly. "Flew through the windshield."

Everyone was around me chattering to each other, and then Mike August spoke to me. Mike August used to party with us when we were freshman and he got messed up enough so that we accepted him and then he cleaned up his act, quit using dope, barley drank at all, and earned straight A's. He raised his hand and asked everyone to be quiet a second. His voice was scratchy as it always was; sounding like he smoked three packs a day when he never really smoked anything at all. He was just born sounding that way.

"Ray, you look terrible," he told me. "When did this happen?"

"Almost a week ago, but I'm fine. It looks a lot worse than I feel. I mean, I just had my face surgically repaired and shit today so that's why it looks so bad."

"Jesus, Ray," he felt sorry for me. "Can I talk to you outside for a minute? Do you mind, man?"

"No, Mike. Let's go. I don't mind," I assured him as I peered at the expressions on people's faces through my tinted lenses.

"Good. Follow me outside through the back door."

As I followed Mike August through the crowded room, most of the girls offered up their one-liners of sympathy to me.

They told me things like, "You poor thing, Ray," and, "How terrible."

Some even invited me to come and chat with them later, but I knew they weren't really concerned with my well being as much as they wanted to hear the gossip and circumstances that led up to my accident and ultimately my crushed face.

Mike August and I walked around the side of the house and sat on a bench next to the fishpond. I instinctively fished out a penny from my pocket and chucked it into the water and heard the *blip* from when it broke the surface tension of the pool and sunk silently to the bottom. I wished that I were dead.

"So what's up," I asked Mike.

"*Hah*," he laughed. "Funny. That's what I was gonna ask you, Ray."

"Yeah. Well, this," I touched my face. "It's a little shocking. I know that. It's a long story, but I'll tell it to you if you wanna hear it."

He shook his head. "Not really," he said, waving off my story. "Ray, me and you—we've known each other for, like, four years, right?"

"Three," I answered.

"Almost four."

"Right, man. Almost four."

"You know I used to get down with you guys back when we were freshman."

"*Get down?*"

"Christ, Ray. You know what the hell I'm talking about. The drugs."

"Sure, I remember. Sure, sure, sure."

"Well, I don't know if I ever told you this before, but the reason I let up was because I could tell it was destroying my life in a lotta ways. Hell, I was practically flunking outta school until I wizened up."

"Look, Mike," I said and I stood up as if I was gonna walk away. "I don't know what you're getting at, but if you plan on lecturing me because you think I have a drug problem you should save your breath. I don't have a drug problem, nor am I in the mood for an evaluation."

"Ray, please. Sit down. I'm not trying to lecture you. I'm just trying to talk to you, man to man. Please, Ray. C'mon. This is important, if you'll just let me finish."

"Ok, dude," I said and I sat back down and folded my arms

together. "I'm sorry. It's just I've been through a bunch of crap already this week. I didn't mean to snap at you or anything."

"No sweat, man. I understand. I heard all about what happened to you from Patrick Matt Morris. I don't know how much of it is true, but if any part of what I heard is accurate then I'm sure it was pretty rough. Was that girl, you know, the one who died, was she a friend of yours?"

"Not sure, I only knew her for a few weeks."

"Oh."

"She was a friend of an ex-girlfriend of mine."

"So if you don't mind, I'll just kinda spit it out."

"I'd prefer it."

"Well, I've been hearing a lotta shit about you lately, man."

"People talk. What'd you hear?"

"Just that you've been fighting, that's nothing new. And you got thrown in the slammer and now this girl dies. And don't get me wrong, I know it wasn't your fault. All this time you've been hanging with those dudes, like, Ricky. All the drugs and shit."

"Ricky's a nice guy."

"I know he's cool," Mike explained. "But you know I used to get down with all you guys."

"I don't mean to be rude, Mike, but what's the exact point in all of this? I mean, you're starting to repeat yourself."

He sighed and explained, "The point is I'm no smarter than you are. I know that. Anything I can do, you can do too. If only you'd quit distracting yourself. I just hate to see you fuck your life up. And I know you may not see your life that way, but when I see you on probation with an injured face, tubes and shit coming outta your nose, girls dying, and now you're here at a party, that's kinda fucked up. When we were freshman you were supposed to be the best basketball player in our class. When we were in 8th Grade your name was all over the sports pages. And then you never even got to play in high school because you were always getting high and flunking your classes. Then you got kicked outta school. Now you're at Granite and somebody's dead."

"I see what you're saying. It's just sometimes things aren't always controllable. It's, like, problems snowball."

"Yeah. Look. Ray. I'm done talking. Just think about what I said. And there's one other thing I wanted to throw out there. Since I got a full ride to Notre Dame next fall for academics, my old man got me my own apartment off campus. There's plenty of room there if you feel like you need to get outta town. It'd do you some good to surround yourself with some smart and sober people for a change. And my only rule is no drugs."

"Thanks, Mike. I'll keep you in mind."

"Great. I'm gonna get back inside. It's getting kinda chilly out here."

"Yeah. Me too."

We both got up and started walking back towards the house when I stopped suddenly and said, "Hey you go on without me. I forgot something in my car."

"Ok," he said and he stood and watched me walk off into the darkness.

It was the last time I ever saw him again.

What a fucking drag he is, I thought.

That was the way Mike August was though, and he couldn't help it. He was always trying to play prophet. And I didn't really forget something in my car, I just used it as an excuse so I could escape, because Mike was right about one thing: I really wasn't in much of a mood for parties. I shouldn't have come, but instead of going home I drove out to Valpo to Jon's house. Even if he wasn't home I knew where the spare key was and I could hide-out until he got home. I hadn't really talked to him much since I played that gun joke on his friend Brenda.

As I burned down Old Lincoln Highway I rolled up a nice little joint in my lap and I smoked it during the dark country part between South Lake Mall and the city limits of Valpo. By the time I rolled up Glendale Avenue not only was I baked, but I was also bordering on complete paranoia. I thought every pair of headlights behind me was a cop and I couldn't decide whether to drive the speed limit or five miles over. I didn't stand a prom queen's chance during a riot at the penitentiary if I were to get pulled over. Any cop would take one look at me in my bandana and sunglasses and bruises and call the paddy wagon.

The last five minutes of driving to Jon's was always the most treacherous, because you passed an average of four speed traps between Glendale and his house. Back then the cops in Valpo were always paying attention for lack of anything better to do.

When I pulled up to Jon's house it was a little past 9:30 and most of the lights were off in the house and there weren't any cars parked in the driveway or in the street. It kinda looked like he wasn't home, but you could never tell for sure until you actually tried knocking. I didn't feel much like knocking so I fished the spare key out from under the fake rock and I let myself in. Jon was the only one there, which was a nice relief, and he was passed out on the couch in front of the television that was tuned into the Weather Channel.

I was tired too so I let Jon sleep and I bolted the front door and I plopped down on the other couch across from him and I laid down and tried to fall asleep myself, finding success about five minutes later.

In the morning I was starting to wake up, but I hadn't opened my eyes yet. I was drifting in and outta sleep, here a dream there a dream, and then finding myself sorta conscious again. I felt my sunglasses slowly sliding off my face and I opened my eyes to find Jon holding my shades and looking down at me as he studied my injuries.

"You look, like, total and complete dogshit, just, like, you fell out of a moving car. I hope you aren't planning on getting laid any time soon."

"Gimmie those back, asshole," I said with a hoarse voice and I snatched the glasses back and put them on and sat up and stretched. "*Ah*, what time is it?"

"11:00," he said as he picked up his bong and filled the bowl with a wad of sticky marijuana. "What the hell happened to you?"

"Didn't I tell you?"

"No, why in the hell do you think I'm asking?"

"I got in a car accident, just had surgery and shit."

"How did that happen?"

"Remember that girl Jolene from Granite?"

"No."

"What about that girl Erin I was seeing?"

"Nope," he said as he pulled a tube and handed it to me.

"I can't hit a bong," I said. "My face."

"Oh," he said and he collected the bong and hit it a few more times.

"Well, I was riding around with this Jolene girl and she got in a car accident. I flew through the windshield and broke my face."

"What happened to her?"

"She got killed," I told him.

"*Serious?*"

"Serious."

"That sucks. What are those things coming outta your nose?"

"Tubes. They blew up a two balloons inside my face because I shattered my sinus cavities."

"You look awful," Jon said again. "I can't get over it. I almost wanted to call the exterminator when I saw you sleeping there."

"Thanks, Jon."

"Seriously though, what the hell are you doing driving around like that, sneaking into people's houses and shit? Shouldn't you be in the hospital or something?"

"I'm fine. It looks a lot worse than it is. Trust me."

"I'll take your word for it, Ray. Guess what?"

"*Huh*," I said.

"I'm moving back out to Washington soon. I've gotta friend in Tacoma with a house and he's got a room for me. It's getting too sketchy around here. I need to be able to deal weed in peace. A bunch of people got busted last weekend. I know the cops know about me by now. I figure in Tacoma I can start up a whole new clientele list. Only this time I can do it the right way from the start. You should come with me."

"I've got some extra cash. How are you getting out there," I asked.

"Greyhound bus. That's how I roll."

"I just might take you up on it. I've gotta go to this funeral though this weekend. After that I suppose I'll make up my mind on what I'm gonna do."

"What day is the funeral on?"

"Saturday."

"That's tomorrow, buddy. That means the wake is probably tonight, right?"

"Shit, I lost track of days. I thought today was Thursday. The wake *is* tonight. I have to go. It starts at 7:00."

"That sounds like a real drag," Jon complained.

"You don't know the half of it."

"Why's that?"

"Oh shit, they all think I was driving."

"You mean they think you *killed* her?"

"Yeah. They think I killed her."

"Did you? I mean, I could care less if you did or didn't. I'm just asking."

"No, man. I didn't. It's just a fucked up rumor."

"Fuck them," Jon said as he quickly picked up a rubberband and shot it at the wall. It smacked against the wall and I heard a fly go buzzing away. "If I were you, I wouldn't go. They're just gonna act like fucks towards you."

"Maybe you're right," I said, and I nervously put my hands in my pockets.

"Of course I'm right," Jon took another bong hit and then offered up the bong to me again just to be polite. "Sure," he asked.

"I'm sure. I can't," I took one hand outta my pocket and pointed with my thumb up at my head. "The face."

"How about a pipe? Can you handle something like that?"

"Sure. A pipe is fine, or a joint. I've been smoking both and I haven't had any problems."

"Good," Jon smiled. "It'll help you think."

"Yep," I said.

He got up and went into the kitchen to roll me a joint.

"You know something?"

"What," he called from the other room.

"I've been waiting for people to start dying. I was wondering when it was gonna start happening."

"What do you mean," he asked as he mainly focused on the task at hand, which was twisting me a fat one.

"Well, you know. You always hear of people dying and getting killed in high school and in college. Like, both my sisters had a few of their friends die in car accidents or what not, and Terry, remember his friend Jo-Jo?"

"I remember."

"Remember how he got arrested and hung himself in jail last summer?"

"I remember. That was really sad. He was cool."

"I knew it was just a matter of time before kids our age started biting the dust. Just a few weeks ago I was walking around school thinking it. Like, is that girl or this guy gonna be dead within the next few years, and if so how? Car accident? Murder?"

"I never really thought about it," Jon admitted. "But I see what you mean. People die all the time. It's not a big deal."

"Yeah. I know," I agreed. "But it's just weird when it happens to somebody you know."

Just then Jon stepped back into the room with an impressive little stick of marijuana that was so perfectly wound that only his hands could sculpt something like it. I shared it with Jon since it was his weed and he rolled it, and even though he took all those bong rips already he wasn't one to quit smoking. He could pull tubes all day.

"Maybe your right," I suggested after we finished burning the roach. "Maybe I should just get the hell outta town. I mean, who would really miss me?"

"Nobody," he said, as if it was obvious.

"Gee, thanks," I laughed.

"Well, it's true. You know what I mean," Jon explained. "People come and go."

"I'm gotta go to the wake tonight though," I told him. It was a fact. I had already made up my mind. "I should probably get going soon so I can get ready."

He looked at me like I was an idiot. Jon thought most people were idiots and the ones that weren't still had it in them to act like one every now and then.

"You go do that, Ray," he patronized me. "You go play the brave hero. And when you're done you know where I'll be. Here packing for our move out west."

"Yeah, I know. I'll think about taking off with you. It's just I've gotta show my face, if not for myself then for Jolene. I think she would have wanted me to come, no matter what."

"She's dead, you dumb-ass," he laughed. "She don't want anything from you."

60

Thank God The Brain had so graciously agreed to accompany me to the wake that night. He was gonna go anyway, of course, just like everybody else in Granite, but it was something special that he decided to actually ride over in the same car with me. To me, it really showed a lotta integrity on his part. It was a gesture that still ranks at the top of my list. I'll always feel like I owe him something because I don't know if I could've stood as tall as I intended to without his support. He even brought over some nice shoes for me to wear with my shirt and tie. My Timberline boots had gotten all scratched and scuffed during the accident and I'd been wearing an old leather pair of black Pumas.

The wake started at 7:00. And at 6:00 I stood in front of the mirror as I finished tying the knot in my tie. My arms felt numb and I felt, like, I had to keep reminding myself to breathe. I had to do away with my bandana so I tried to tie my hair back into a ponytail, but there was a problem. After I had flown through the windshield I had gotten some pieces of glass imbedded into my scalp just above my hairline. The nurse had to cut a lock of my hair off so she could clean the wound and get at it with a pair of tweezers to pluck the glass from my skin. So when I tied my hair back there was this little spike that stuck up and it looked horribly stupid. I had to let my hair just hang down and this disappointed me because I was nervous—

I didn't want anything to make me look like I didn't care. Instead I got out the gel and slicked back my hair as much as possible. Even though I knew as it dried it would fall and flop around my head, but at least it would look as if I made an attempt to keep my mop contained. I still looked horrible though with the tubes hanging down.

I was dressed and ready to go fifteen minutes before The Brain even showed up. My nerves were caving in so I rolled a joint and made myself a whiskey on the rocks from my dad's liquor stash. The Brain buzzed my front door just as I finished off the joint and I was caught halfway through the whiskey so I offered him one and he accepted, drank it quickly, and then he helped himself to another. We had a few minutes to kill so he sat down next to me on the couch.

I wasn't much for conversation. In fact I couldn't get myself to say anything at all. The Brain picked up on my mood and he did his best to talk to me.

"You look pretty nice at least, hoss."

I gave him a serious look. His expression was actually expressionless, like a smoothed beach rock. I couldn't keep serious for long. Being nervous made me start to laugh.

"What kinda faggot-ass thing is that to say," I laughed.

And The Brain started laughing too.

"That's what I like to hear, hoss. God, I'm so tired of all this serious bullshit, aren't you?"

"Jesus. I'm totally over it, Victor."

"Oh shit. I almost forgot," The Brain said as he fumbled through his pockets. "I brang something for you." He pulled outta tape, "It's just a song I recorded for you, something that reminded me of you so I thought you might wanna hear the shit," he said as he got up and slid the tape into the player on the stereo. "You probably heard it before."

The song started playing softly and it was *Betterman* by Pearl Jam. I almost felt honored that The Brain felt such a good song reminded me of him. I sat back quietly and listened to the words of the song and every similarity between the lyrics and my life gave me a little bit of a smile.

"You like it," The Brain asked me searching for approval.

"Hell yeah," I said. "I like it."

"Good," he said. "I knew you would. That's why I fucking recorded it."

When the song ended The Brain got up and stopped the tape from playing, rewound it, then pressed play again and sat back down.

"You know," I pointed out. "In that song it talks about a guy lied to by the person he loves. You think that of me?"

The Brain took a deep breath. "Yeah. It kinda reminded me of what shit went down with you and Erin. You should just get outta town. And I know you're gone, Ray. After all this, I'd be surprised if you didn't leave to go somewhere, just to start over."

"You think I really need to start my life over?"

"Yeah, I think you do. This town is never gonna let up on you. You know that. And besides, I don't wanna see you grow old in a place like this. It's too easy for bad things to happen to a person here."

"I just feel, like, I've got these loose ends to tie up before I go and make a decision on whether or not to leave. Part of me wants to go off and start a new life somewhere, and the other part of me doesn't. I've got good friends here, and I feel, like, I actually belong here in a sick sorta way."

"But you don't, man. You don't belong here. This place," he paused. "This place is for people who are treading water. Most of the people who live here, they can't ever leave because they're too scared to go out into the rest of the world and fail. At least if they stay, they can still at least settle for something less, whatever that might be."

"What about you," I asked.

"What about me? I'll get the hell outta The Region eventually. After I finish my apprenticeship for sheet metal and welding. Then I'll be looking at fifty grand a year to start. Then I'm gonna take my skills and find someplace to go."

"How long is that gonna take?"

"Honestly, I don't know. It depends. But I know it'll take at least five years for that to happen."

"That's a long time to wait."

"Yeah. It is," he agreed. "But you know, I've lived here this long, I figure I can do five more years no problem. They'll probably fly by."

"I hope so, Victor. I'd hate to see you rot away in this place, end up being an alcoholic, being thirty years old and alone, a convicted felon, and start dating high school girls. A total loser who got all fat and shit."

The Brain glanced up at the clock on the wall. He sighed and said, "Looks like it's almost time, hoss."

"I think I'm ready, I mean, I guess it's now or never, right?"

He didn't answer right away. Just then the song was ending and the music began to fade away to silence. He looked at me as if he wanted to say something, but was trying to carefully choose his words.

"Look. Ray," he said as he shook his head. "We don't have to go to this thing if you don't wanna."

"No way," I said trying to act tough. "I wanna go. I have to."

"Ok," he said and stood up.

"Let's paint it black, Victor. Like the Stones."

61

It took a lotta guts for me to show up there, but for The Brain it took more than that. For me, I had to go. I had no choice. But The Brain didn't have to show up with me. He could have easily stepped back into the lynch mob. For The Brain, not only did it take guts to make an entrance with me, but it took a lotta heart and character. It was certainly no secret to me why Gabe was keeping his distance that afternoon, but who could blame him.

The Brain crept his Mercury Cougar over the speed bumps as we entered the long driveway of Burns Funeral Home, the place where they embalmed dead people and painted them in makeup and then put them on display. There were literally hundreds of cars parked there. People had come in the hundreds to pay Jolene their last respects, and I was one of them, at least in my eyes. Some people were still kinda trickling in from the parked cars when we got there.

"Well, hoss. Here we are," The Brain said softly. "Check yourself before you wreck yourself."

I looked at myself in the side mirror, "I come real stealth. I'm bad for your health. I'm still ugly," I said.

"Yeah," The Brain laughed as he steered the Cougar into one of the last empty spots. "But only on the outside right?"

"Yep."

We both got outta the car. The Brain whipped outta cigarette and lit it on fire as we walked side by side towards the entrance. The sun was setting and it was getting a little chilly. I watched the building get closer as I peered through my sunglasses. Under the entrance. There were some friends of Jolene's outside smoking. They were all watching me hard, the guys especially. I had partied with a couple of them before and had met them briefly under different circumstances. The Brain and I walked up to them and tried to join their circle, but they greeted us coldly because I was there. I felt terrible as The Brain smoked with them and tried to make small talk. I just stood there, my expression blank and disguised through my shades. Finally the pressure was too much for me, so I excused myself from the group and from The Brain and went inside the front doors.

Once inside, I kinda stopped so I could decide where to go. Every pair of eyes in the lobby turned toward me and the stares stuck to me like a tongue on a metal pole in the middle of winter. If I hadn't been wearing the shades to cover my swollen eye, I could have never seen it all go down, uninterrupted.

To my left were a group of kids a year younger than me: Jacob and Gisela, Susa, Milada, and some other kids in their class. There was no sign of Erin though. Part of me wanted to see her and part of me didn't. In front of me was the hall or whatever you call it, the place where they put the casket and arrange the flowers and all that crap. People were in a line waiting to pay their last respects to Jolene. Since that's what I came there to do I got in line with them.

My mouth went dry and I knew if I tried to speak my voice would probably be hoarse and silent. It was lucky for me that no one would talk to me. My hands went numb and tingled exactly like they would when an arm or a leg falls asleep from lack of circulation. I always used to get that same feeling in my hands right before somebody was about to kick my ass.

One by one the people in front of me approached her casket to kneel and pray or just to say a few kind words until, before I could come to terms, it was my turn. I had to make myself breathe in and out as I walked to the casket that was closed, not open. It was a shiny dark blue box and the people had laid so many flowers on top of it that some of them were falling off onto the carpet. I didn't know what to say so I just extended my hand and I tried to place it on the coffin, but my hands had tensed up into fists and wouldn't open. I had to catch my fingers on a groove carved in the wood of the coffin so I could pry my hands open and when I did I laid both of my palms on the casket and held on.

I felt, like, I should say something important, like, a speech or a poem or even a prayer. But at that moment I could not speak. I was shaking. I was so scared. My eyes watered and a tear fell down my cheek and landed onto the casket, and another, and another followed that. I was crying. And it took every bit of strength to say the most important word that I've ever said in my life. I leaned down and pressed the word from my lips, "Sorry."

I stepped back from the casket and my fingers balled back into fists and I walked off to the right and I came into a room that had coffee and other refreshments. Jolene's mother was in there being comforted by her sons and other relatives. Feeling almost dead myself I approached the woman. She turned and looked at me and was horrified.

"Sorry," I said hoarsely. "I'm sorry."

I know it came out wrong, especially since the lady thought I had killed her daughter. But what I meant was I was sorry it had happened, not that I was sorry for anything I had done to her or her family.

She huffed and wiped her nose with a tissue and she coldly said to me, "You shouldn't have come."

I was blown away. The words almost knocked me out and I found myself wandering around the funeral parlor until I found a place to sit by Jacob, Gisela, and Milada. I wasn't right next to them, but sorta behind them. A few people who were sitting close to there had gotten up and moved away from me. I was so ashamed and I really had no real reason to be. I started to feel cold inside, like, the killer that everyone said I was. I just closed my eyes and cried.

A short time later I heard the folding chair next to me creek as somebody sat down there. I didn't have the heart to look. A soft hand took mine and clasped it. I turned to look and I saw Milada sitting there looking up at me. She just sat there and held my hand in front of everybody. Everybody was watching us. I was sure of it. She didn't seem to care though, and she took my hand and held it in her lap with both of her hands. I couldn't really tell what to make of everything at that point. For me, going from the object of everybody's disdain to an honestly affectionate and caring display like the one Milada showed to me that moment was just like a whiplash of emotion. It was a fucking jolt.

That was right when James Chapman put his hand on my shoulder and leaned towards my ear to whisper, "I wanna talk to you, ok?"

I turned and looked up at him. He was pale and he seemed just as freaked out as I was, if not more.

"Ok, James," I answered.

"Outside," he told me.

And he turned and walked out the double doors.

I could tell he didn't wanna fight me because none of his friends were following him or waiting outside—besides, this wasn't the place for that kinda stuff. After having his girlfriend get killed, suddenly the whole experience had left him shattered.

"Excuse me," I said to Milada and I got up and followed him outside.

The darkness had set in completely outside and I couldn't find him at first through my sunglasses. He had to whistle at me from his car, which was parked about thirty feet away. When he saw me coming he got into the driver's side and sat down at the wheel. I got in on the other side and sat next to him in the passenger's seat. There was a streetlight shining directly into the car that lit us both up. He was gripping the steering wheel so tight that his knuckles were turning white and he had his bottom lip pinched softly between his teeth.

"Look. James," I said, feeling uncomfortable. "I know you must feel—"

"Stop," he commanded, and he shook his head. "I don't wanna hear any bullshit right now."

I was offended and I snapped back quickly, "Oh, then what the *hell* do you wanna hear then, James?"

He didn't answer so I looked over at him and I saw that he was rubbing tears away from his cheeks.

"Shit, I'm sorry," I said.

"It's fine," he let me know with his voice shaking. "All I want," he paused. "All I want is to hear what happened. I wanna hear it from you since you were the last one to see her alive. I'm hearing all this stuff from people and everybody seems to have a different version of what went on, but nobody was there. Nobody can know for sure, except for you."

"I'll tell you everything, man. Outta everybody, God knows you're the one who deserves to hear it straight. I'll tell you everything on one condition."

"What's that," he asked.

"I just wanna lift home. I can't be here anymore. If you give me a lift, I'll tell you everything along the way."

He sighed, "All right, Ray," and he started the engine, put the car into drive, and he slowly rolled the vehicle out into the street and away.

As hard as it was, I managed to tell him everything. I left nothing out and nothing sugar coated. I told him every detail in frank words from the moment Jolene buzzed my front door all the way to when I turned over her dead body and looked into her beautiful eyes.

By the time we pulled up to my apartment he was crying outta control. I felt terrible for him, but it was nice for me to actually get everything off my chest and tell somebody who actually really cared about knowing the truth.

"Are you ok, man," I asked him as he stopped the car in front of my building.

He stopped sobbing just enough to squeak a string of words out, "Fine," he sniffed. "I'm fine. I'll be fine."

"Why don't you come up for a smoke," I asked.

"Smoke," he looked at me questioningly. "Weed?"

"Yeah. Weed," I confirmed.

"*Nah*," he shook his head. "I can't, man. I've gotta get back to the wake."

"Ok," I said and extended my hand to shake. "Cool?"

He grabbed my hand with his and we shook, "Yeah. Cool."

"I'll see you at the funeral tomorrow," I said.

"All right," he sniffled and then wiped his nose with his sleeve.

"Ok then take it easy, James," I said and I got outta the car and slammed the car door and then I stood there and watched him drive away.

"One down, one to go," I whispered to myself.

62

M y mom called and woke me up the next morning and insisted that she accompany me to the funeral so she could offer me some needed support. I really didn't want her to go. Dudes wanted to kick my ass enough as it was, the last thing I really needed was for any foes of mine to see me being protected by my mommy. Just like a mother she could feel the pain that I was feeling and she knew how terrified I was about going to this funeral. I wasn't guilty. Yet I felt guilty because of all the blame. I couldn't shake the burning in my heart.

Mom knew I was dying inside and so she told me a little piece of wisdom, "I've always felt when someone dies unexpectedly— everyone associated with the deceased—friends and family, they all somehow inherit the pain of the loved one they lost … the exact pain their lost friend or family member carried through life. Right now, Ray," she chokingly explained to me. "You are probably feeling the hurt that this poor girl used to feel every day of her life. And the only way you'll ever feel better is for you to show up at this funeral so the hurt can be buried along with that girl. You have to go, Ray. There's no other choice."

She made me kinda tear up. My mom had never really said anything that meaningful to me and I have to admit it was kinda touching, but it made me nervous to hear her talk this way so at the risk of me having a nervous breakdown over the phone with her I had to somehow say something, no matter how insignificant my words may be.

So I commented to her, "Damn, mom. I didn't know you had feelings."

I agreed to let her come pick me up. I told her the service started at 11:00 and was happening at Saint Christopher's Cathedral in Highland. Afterwards everybody was heading out to Meadow Brook Cemetery for the burial. She promised to be at my place by 10:30 to pick me up, and she ended up being ten minutes early, which was weird because my mom was always late. Always.

We drove over to the church and there were so many people attending the service, rows and rows and rows of carefully parked cars, it seemed that we had to park a mile away. I remember walking up to the church, so far and feeling like I was hiking there with my mom when the wind was blowing in hard from Lake Michigan. She kept on trying to get me to talk about the accident. She wanted to get inside my head, but I just didn't feel like talking about it.

The service took place inside the Cathedral in their big church-type area, which was as big as a football field, or so it seemed, and it was packed pew to pew with kids and parents, most of which I had never seen before, but many that I knew.

I scanned the crowd while the choir was singing the hymns and here and there I could spot ex-friends and brand new enemies. A few rows in front of me Sydney was with her family. At least I assumed they were her family because I had never really met them in person. They were all blondes and empty looking, so I was convinced.

Lisa Diamond was way up in front. The only way I could tell that it her was because I could recognize her body language. She sat down, suddenly slouching, and covered her face with her hands and began to bawl.

I could see Erin about halfway up towards the altar. She was right on the aisle and she looked good, but at that moment I hated the bitch and I hoped right then and there, inside a church of all places, that she'd burn in hell.

Halfway through the service Milada came walking back down the aisle, probably to use the restroom or something, and she smiled at me and secretly waved as she walked by. Mom and I sat in the very last row and we were so far back I couldn't hear anything that was being said from the altar. The mass was nothing but a mumble from where we sat and the Eulogy sounded like such a whisper that what was said is still a secret to me. And that's the part I really wanted to hear. The Eulogy is the only marketable part of a funeral and if you miss it, you've been gypped. While we were inside the church a thunderstorm hit slowly with bottomless rumbles.

When the mass ended everyone drove over in the pouring rain to Meadow Brook in a huge convoy. We were the last car in the train. The group of cars had police escorts and everything. You'd think that Jolene was the president or something. At the graveyard I remember hundreds of people standing around in the downpour, most without umbrellas, and watching them lower Jolene's casket into the Earth. A priest was there quoting scriptures from the Bible, and a dark suited elderly man with a brand new silver spade symbolically threw dirt onto the casket, which was followed by everyone tossing flowers into the hole.

And then little by little, people started to leave, most of them were well on their way to forgetting that day. People have to get on with their lives. I saw Tim Miller and Jeremy Otsap there, but they didn't say anything to me. In fact, nobody except for my mom said a word to me the entire time. The most comforting communication came with Milada's nippy wave on her way to the bathroom.

thats all i can say for now

but everybody knows this aint ove

BiO

Outta nothing at all like Air Supply, Richard Laskowski is the Accidental Writer and the author of REGIONRAT, based on the true story of a tragic death that tore apart the lives of a group of NW Indiana friends and the blame and grief that turned them into lifetime enemies (but only after reading the book).

COMPLETELY OPTIONAL DISCLAIMER

Reading REGIONRAT may cause certain complications. Side effects will manifest in bowel habits such as oily spotting, gas with discharge, the urgent need to go to the bathroom, oily or fatty stools, an oily discharge, an increased number of bowel movements, and possibly the inability to control your bowel movements. Some readers have reported other side effects that include skin rash, itching, hives, difficulty breathing or swallowing, swelling of the face or throat, yellowing of the skin or eyes, dark urine, pale or dark stools, blood in urine, pain, inflammation, or rupture of a tendon, rapid, irregular, or pounding heartbeats. Tell the editors of 6GP if any of these symptoms are severe or do not go away.

WHAT THE LADIES WANNA KNOW

Rich is Entry-Level Hollywood. Some D and F Celebs even know him on a first name basis. He is very handsome and funny.

WHAT RICH BRAGS ABOUT

He is a 2-time Valpo Americans Little League Baseball MVP and a 1-time Roman Catholic Diocese of Gary 7th and 8th Grade Basketball MVP.

MEANINGLESS INFORMATION

Rich is currently finishing up two new Northwest Indiana novels and one about Seattle called MASS HELLA. His work has been seen in The Fifteen Project, The Colony, Deek Magazine, The Muse-Apprentice Guild, Midnight Mind, This Is It Magazine, Fictionline, NeeDLe, The Observer, Apparent Depth, Job Stories, and AARGH! The rest of his work has been rejected by almost every place else. He knows very little of most things, but a lotta stuff about little things.

Richard Laskowski has been spotted with

Christopher Hewett ("Mr. Belvedere"), Saddam Hussein, Tim Miller, Punky Brewster, Rockwell, pretty much all the members of Stryper, Marion Barry, Thomas Ian Nicholas, Fidel Castro, Peter Glowski, George W. Bush, Michael Landon, Chrit!, Kim Jong-il, Mullah Mohammad Omar, Jeremy NeeDLE, Sean Astin, James Chapman, Jonathan Ke Quan, Bob Freville, David Koresh, John Thomas Menesini, Clay Aiken, Che Elias, Mr. Wizard, Jason Lee, Catfish Cooper, D.J. Timbo, Jason America and hundreds of last-nameless pretty women.

1887420

Made in the USA